NOEL GRINSTED.

# THE GOAL

THE GOAL

# THE GOAL

**Beating the Competition**

Eliyahu M. Goldratt
and
Jeff Cox

Gower

Published by
Gower Publishing Company Limited,
Gower House,
Croft Road,
Aldershot,
Hants GU11 3HR,
England

Goldratt, Eliyahu M.
  The goal: beating the competition.
  1. Production management — Case studies
  I. Title II. Cox, Jeff, 1951
  658.5 ' 00722 TS155

ISBN 0-566-02683-X

Printed in Great Britain by
Blackmore Press, Longmead, Shaftesbury, Dorset

# INTRODUCTION

"The Goal" is about the OPT principle of manufacturing. It's about people trying to understand what makes their world tick so that they can make it better. As they think logically and consistently about their problems they are able to determine "cause and effect" relationships between their actions and the results. In the process they deduce some basic principles—the OPT principles—which they use to save their plant and make it successful.

I view science as nothing more than an understanding of the way the world is and *why* it is that way. At any given time our scientific knowledge is simply the current state of the art of our understanding. I do not believe in absolute truths. I fear such beliefs because they block the search for better understanding. Whenever we think we have final answers progress, science, and better understanding ceases. Understanding of our world is not something to be pursued for its own sake, however. Knowledge should be pursued, I believe, to make our world better—to make life more fulfilling.

There are several reasons I chose a novel to explain my understanding of manufacturing—how it works (reality) and why it works that way (the OPT principles). First, I wanted to make the OPT principles more understandable and show how they can bring order to the chaos that so often exists in our plants. Second, I wanted to illustrate the power of this understanding and the benefits it can bring. The results achieved are not fantasy; they have been, and are being, achieved in real plants. The western world does not have to become a second or third rate manufacturing power. If we just understand and apply the correct principles, we can compete with anyone. I also hoped that readers would see the validity and value of these principles in other organizations such as banks, hospitals, insurance companies, and our families. Maybe the same potential for growth and improvement exists in all organizations.

Finally, and most importantly, I wanted to show that we can all be outstanding scientists. The secret of being a good scientist, I believe, lies not in our brain power. We have enough. We simply need to look at reality and think logically and precisely about what we see. The key ingredient is to have the courage to face inconsistencies between what we see and deduce and the way things are done. This challenging of basic assumptions is essential to break-throughs. Almost everyone who has worked in a plant is at least uneasy about the use of cost accounting efficiencies to control our actions. Yet few have challenged this sacred cow directly. Progress in understanding requires that we challenge basic assumptions about how the world is and why it is that way. If we can better understand our world and the principles that govern it, I suspect all our lives will be better.

Good luck in your search for these principles and for your own understanding of "The Goal."

# ABOUT THE AUTHOR

Dr. Eliyahu M. Goldratt is an internationally recognized leader in the development of new production control and business management philosophies and systems. He has become a sought-after consultant by many of the country's largest corporations, including Ford Motor Co., General Motors, General Electric, and Westinghouse, to name a few. He is the originator of the mathematics and philosophy underlying the OPT (Optimized Production Technology) System for planning and scheduling manufacturing operations. His work in this area is beginning to revolutionize how managements perceive and manage their production problems. Furthermore, this work is leading to a new approach in running a manufacturing organization. This approach is called the OPT Management System.

He obtained his Bachelor of Science degree from Tel Aviv University and his Master of Science and Doctorate of Philosophy from Bar-Ilan University. In addition to his pioneering work in materials management, he holds patents in a number of other areas ranging from medical devices, to drop irrigation and temperature sensors. Dr. Goldratt is a frequent contributor to scientific journals and has been a lecturer at major corporations and universities.

He is the co-founder and director of Creative Output, Ltd., the managing director of Creative Output (Netherlands) BV and the chairman of Creative Output, Inc. and Creative Output, U.K.

# THE GOAL

# 1

I come through the gate this morning at 7:30 and I can see it from across the lot: the crimson Mercedes. It's parked beside the plant, next to the offices. And it's in *my* space. Who else would do that except Bill Peach? Never mind that the whole lot is practically empty at that hour. Never mind that there are spaces marked "Visitor". No, Bill's got to park in the space with my title on it. Bill likes to make subtle statements. So, okay, he's the division vice-president, and I'm just a mere plant manager. I guess he can park his damn Mercedes wherever he wants.

I put my Buick next to it (in the space marked "Controller"). A glance at the license as I walk around it assures me it has to be Bill's car because the plate says "NUMBER 1." And, as we all know, that's absolutely correct in terms of who Bill always looks out for. He wants his shot at CEO. But so do I. Too bad that I may never get the chance now.

Anyway, I'm walking up to the office doors. Already the adrenalin is pumping. I'm wondering what the hell Bill is doing here. I've lost any hope of getting any work done this morning. I usually go in early to catch up on all the stuff I'm too busy to do during the day, because I can really get a lot done before the phone rings and the meetings start, before the fires break out. But not today.

"Mr. Rogo!" I hear someone calling.

I stop as four people come bursting out of a door on the side of the plant. I see Dempsey, the shift supervisor; Martinez, the union steward; some hourly guy; and a machining center foreman named Ray. And they're all talking at the same time. Dempsey is telling me we've got a problem. Martinez is shouting about how there is going to be a walkout. The hourly guy is saying something about harassment. Ray is yelling that we can't finish some damn thing because we don't have all the parts. Suddenly I'm in the middle of all this. I'm looking at them; they're looking at me. And I haven't even had a cup of coffee yet.

When I finally get everyone calmed down enough to ask what's going on, I learn that Mr. Peach arrived about an hour before me, walked into my plant, and demanded to be shown the status of Customer Order Number 41427.

Well, as fate would have it, nobody happened to know about Customer Order 41427. So Peach had everybody stepping and fetching to chase down the story on it. And it turns out to be a fairly big order. Also a late one. So what else is new? Everything in this plant is late. Based on observation, I'd say this plant has four ranks of priority for orders: Hot . . . Very Hot . . . Red Hot . . . and Do It NOW! We just can't keep ahead of anything.

As soon as he discovers 41427 is nowhere close to being shipped, Peach starts playing expeditor. He's storming around, yelling orders at Dempsey. Finally it's determined almost all the parts needed are ready and waiting—stacks of them. But they can't be assembled. One part of some sub-assembly is missing; it still has to be run through some other operation yet. If the guys don't have the part, they can't assemble, and if they can't assemble, naturally, they can't ship.

They find out the pieces for the missing subassembly are sitting over by one of the n/c machines, where they're waiting their turn to be run. But when they go to that department, they find the machinists are *not* setting up to run the part in question, but instead some other do-it-now job which somebody imposed upon them for some other product.

Peach doesn't give a damn about the other do-it-now job. All he cares about is getting 41427 out the door. So he tells Dempsey to direct his foreman, Ray, to instruct his master machinist to forget about the other super-hot gizmo and get ready to run the missing part for 41427. Whereupon the master machinist looks from Ray to Dempsey to Peach, throws down his wrench, and tells them they're all crazy. It just took him and his helper an hour and a half to set up for the *other* part that everyone needed so desperately. Now they want to forget about it and set up for something else instead? The hell with it! So Peach, always the diplomat, walks past my supervisor and my foreman, and tells the master machinist that if he doesn't do what he's told, he's fired. More words are exchanged. The machinist threatens to walk off the job. The union steward shows up. Everybody is mad. Nobody is working. And now I've got four upset people greeting me bright and early in front of an idle plant.

"So where is Bill Peach now?" I ask.

"He's in your office," says Dempsey.

"Okay, would you go tell him I'll be in to talk to him in a minute," I ask.

# THE GOAL

Dempsey gratefully hurries toward the office doors. I turn to Martinez and the hourly guy, who I discover is the machinist. I tell them that as far as I'm concerned there aren't going to be any firings or suspensions—that the whole thing is just a misunderstanding. Martinez isn't entirely satisfied with that at first, and the machinist sounds as if he wants an apology from Peach. I'm not about to step into that one. I also happen to know that Martinez can't call a walkout on his own authority. So I say if the union wants to file a grievance, okay; I'll be glad to talk to the local president, Mike O'Donnell, later today, and we'll handle everything in due course. Realizing he can't do anything more before talking to O'Donnell anyway, Martinez finally accepts that, and he and the hourly guy start walking back to the plant.

"So let's get them back to work," I tell Ray.

"Sure, but, uh, what should we be working on?" asks Ray. "The job we're set up to run or the one Peach wants?"

"Do the one Peach wants," I tell him.

"Okay, but we'll be wasting a set-up," says Ray.

"So we waste it!" I tell him. "Ray, I don't even know what the situation is. But for Bill to be here, there must be some kind of emergency. Doesn't that seem logical?"

"Yeah, sure," says Ray. "Hey, I just want to know what to do."

"Okay, I know you were just caught in the middle of all this," I say to try to make him feel better. "Let's just get that setup done as quick as we can and start running that part."

"Right," he says.

Inside, Dempsey passes me on his way back to the plant. He's just come from my office and he looks like he's in a hurry to get out of there. He shakes his head at me.

"Good luck," he says out of the corner of his mouth.

The door to my office is wide open. I walk in, and there he is. Bill Peach is sitting behind my desk. He's a stocky, barrel-chested guy with thick, steely-gray hair and eyes that almost match. As I put my briefcase down, the eyes are locked onto me with a look that says *This is your neck, Rogo.*

"Okay, Bill, what's going on?" I ask.

He says, "We've got things to talk about. Sit down."

I say, "I'd like to, but you're in my seat."

It may have been the wrong thing to say.

3

"You want to know why I'm here?" he says. "I'm here to save your lousy skin."

I tell him, "Judging from the reception I just got, I'd say you're here to ruin my labor relations."

He looks straight at me and says, "If you can't make some things happen around here, you're not going to have any labor to worry about. Because you're not going to have this plant to worry about. In fact, you may not have a job to worry about, Rogo."

"Okay, wait a minute, take it easy," I say. "Let's just talk about it. What's the problem with this order?"

First of all, Bill tells me that he got a phone call last night at home around ten o'clock from good old Bucky Burnside, president of one of UniCo's biggest customers. Seems that Bucky was having a fit over the fact that this order of his (41427) is seven weeks late. He proceeded to rake Peach over the coals for about an hour. Bucky apparently had gone out on a limb to sway the order over to us when everybody was telling him to give the business to one of our competitors. He had just had dinner with several of his customers, and they had dumped all over him because their orders were late—which, as it happens, was because of us. So Bucky was mad (and probably a little drunk). Peach was able to pacify him only by promising to deal with the matter personally and by guaranteeing that the order would be shipped by the end of today, no matter what mountains had to be moved.

I try to tell Bill that, yes, we were clearly wrong to have let this order slide, and I'll give it my personal attention, but did he have to come in here this morning and disrupt my whole plant?

So where was I last night, he asks, when he tried to call me at home? Under the circumstances, I can't tell him I have a personal life. I can't tell him that the first two times the phone rang, I let it ring because I was in the middle of a fight with my wife, which, oddly enough, was about how little attention I've been giving her. And the third time, I didn't answer it because we were making up.

I decide to tell Peach I was just late getting home. He doesn't press the issue. Instead, he asks how come I don't know what's going on inside my own plant. He's sick and tired of hearing complaints about late shipments. Why can't I stay on top of things?

"One thing I do know," I tell him, "is that after the second

4

round of layoffs you forced on us three months ago, along with the order for a twenty percent cutback, we're lucky to get anything out the door on time."

"Al," he says quietly, "just build the damn products. You hear me?"

"Then give me the people I need!" I tell him.

"You've got enough people! Look at your efficiencies, for god's sake! You've got room for improvement, Al," he says. "Don't come crying to me about not enough people until you show me you can effectively use what you've got."

I'm about to say something when Peach holds up his hand for me to shut my mouth. He stands up and goes over to close the door. Oh shit, I'm thinking.

He turns by the door and tells me, "Sit down."

I've been standing all this time. I take a seat in one of the chairs in front of the desk, where a visitor would sit. Peach returns behind the desk.

"Look, Al, it's a waste of time to argue about this. Your last operations report tells the story," says Peach.

I say, "Okay, you're right. The issue is getting Burnside's order shipped—"

Peach explodes. "Dammit, the issue is not Burnside's order! Burnside's order is just a symptom of the problem around here. Do you think I'd come down here just to expedite a late order? Do you think I don't have enough to do? I came down here to light a fire under you and everybody else in this plant. This isn't just a matter of customer service. Your plant is losing money."

He pauses for a moment, as if he had to let that sink in. Then—bam—he pounds his fist on the desk top and points his finger at me.

"And if you can't get the orders out the door," he continues, "then I'll show you how to do it. And if you still can't do it, then I've got no use for you *or* this plant."

"Now wait a minute, Bill—"

"Dammit, I don't have a minute!" he roars. "I don't have time for excuses anymore. And I don't need explanations. I need performance. I need shipments. I need income!"

"Yes, I know that, Bill."

"What you may not know is that this division is facing the worst losses in its history. We're falling into a hole so deep we may never get out, and your plant is the anchor pulling us in."

I feel exhausted already. Tiredly I ask him, "Okay, what

do you want from me? I've been here six months. I admit it's gotten worse instead of better since I've been here. But I'm doing the best I can."

"If you want the bottom line, Al, this is it: You've got three months to turn this plant around," Peach says.

"And suppose it can't be done in that time?" I ask.

"Then I'm going to go to the management committee with a recommendation to close the plant," he says.

I sit there speechless. This is definitely worse than anything I expected to hear this morning. And, yet, it's not really that surprising. I glance out the window. The parking lot is filling with the cars of the people coming to work first shift. When I look back, Peach has stood up and is coming around the desk. He sits down in the chair next to me and leans forward. Now comes the reassurance, the pep talk.

"Al, I know that the situation you inherited here wasn't the best. I gave you this job because I thought you were the one who could change this plant from a loser to . . . well, a small winner at least. And I still think that. But if you want to go places in this company, you've got to deliver results."

"But I need time, Bill."

"Sorry, you've got three months. And if things get much worse, I may not even be able to give you that."

I sit there as Bill glances at his watch and stands up, discussion ended.

He says, "If I leave now, I'll only miss my first meeting."

I stand up. He walks to the door.

Hand on the knob, he turns and says with a grin, "Now that I've helped you kick some ass around here, you won't have any trouble getting Bucky's order shipped for me today, will you?"

"We'll ship it, Bill," I say.

"Good," he says with wink as he opens the door.

A minute later, I watch from the window as he gets into his Mercedes and drives toward the gate.

Three months. That's all I can think about.

I don't remember turning away from the window. I don't know how much time has passed. All of a sudden, I'm aware that I'm sitting at my desk and I'm staring into space. I decide I'd better go see for myself what's happening out in the plant. From the shelf by the door, I get my hard hat and safety glasses and head out. I pass my secretary.

"Fran, I'll be out on the floor for a little while," I tell her as I go by.

Fran looks up from a letter she's typing and smiles.

"Okey-dokey," she says. "By the way, was that Peach's car I saw in your space this morning?"

"Yes, it was."

"Nice car," she says and she laughs. "I thought it might be yours when I first saw it."

Then I laugh. She leans forward across the desk.

"Say, how much would a car like that cost?" she asks.

"I don't know exactly, but I think it's around thirty thousand dollars," I tell her.

Fran catches her breath. "You're kidding me! That much? I had no idea a car could cost that much. Wow. Guess I won't be trading in my Chevette on one of those very soon."

She laughs and turns back to her typing.

Fran is an "okey-dokey" lady. How old is she? Early forties I'd guess, with two teen-aged kids she's trying to support. Her ex-husband is an alcoholic. They got divorced a long time ago . . . since then, she's wanted nothing to do with a man. Well, almost nothing. Fran told me all this herself on my second day at the plant. I like her. I like her work, too. We pay her a good wage . . . at least we do now. Anyway, she's still got three months.

Going into the plant is like entering a place where satans and angels have married to make kind of a gray magic. That's what it always feels like to me. All around are things that are mundane and miraculous. I've always found manufacturing plants to be fascinating places—even on just a visual level. But most people don't see them the way I do.

Past a set of double doors separating the office from the plant, the world changes. Overhead is a grid of lamps suspended from the roof trusses, and everything is cast in the warm, orange hues of sodium-iodine light. There is a huge chain-link cage which has row after row of floor-to-roof racks loaded with bins and cartons filled with parts and materials for everything we make. In a skinny aisle between two racks rides a man in the basket of a forklift crane that runs along a track on the ceiling. Out on the floor, a reel of shiny steel slowly unrolls into the machine that every few seconds says "Ca-chunk."

Machines. The plant is really just one vast room, acres of space, filled with machines. They are organized in blocks and the blocks are separated by aisles. Most of the machines are painted in solid Mardi Gras colors—orange, purple, yellow, blue. From some of the newer machines, ruby numbers shine from digital displays. Robotic arms perform programs of mechanical dance.

Here and there, often almost hidden among the machines, are the people. They look over as I walk by. Some of them wave; I wave back. An electric cart whines past, an enormous fat guy driving it. Women at long tables work with rainbows of wire. A grimy guy in amorphous coveralls adjusts his face mask and ignites a welding torch. Behind glass, a buxom, red-haired woman pecks the keys on a computer terminal with an amber display.

Mixed with the sights is the noise, a din with a continuous underlying chord made by the whirr of fans, motors, the air in the ventilators—it all sounds like an endless breath. At random comes a BOOM of something inexplicable. Behind me ring the alarm bells of an overhead crane rumbling up its track. Relays click. The siren sounds. From the P.A. system, a disembodied voice talks like God, intermittently and incomprehensibly, over everything.

Even with all that noise, I hear the whistle. Turning, I see the unmistakable shape of Bob Donovan walking up the aisle. He's some distance away. Bob is what you might call a mountain of a man, standing as he does at six-foot-four. He weighs in at about 250 pounds, a hefty portion of which is beer gut. He isn't the prettiest guy in the world . . . I think his barber was trained by the Marines. And he doesn't talk real fancy; I suspect it's a point of pride with him. But despite a few rough edges, which he guards closely, Bob is a good guy. He's been production manager here for nine years. If you need something to happen, all you do is talk to Bob and if it can be done, it will be by the next time you mention it.

It takes a minute or so for us to reach each other. As we get closer, I can see he isn't very cheerful. I suppose it's mutual.

"Good morning," says Bob.

"I'm not sure what's good about it," I say. "Did you hear about our visitor?"

"Yeah, it's all over the plant," says Bob.

"So I guess you know about the urgency for shipping a certain order number 41427?" I ask him.

He starts to turn red. "That's what I need to talk to you about."

"Why? What's up?"

"I don't know if word reached you yet, but Tony, that master machinist Peach yelled at, quit this morning," says Bob.

"Aw, shit," I mutter.

"I don't think I have to tell you that guys like that are not a dime a dozen. We're going to have a tough time finding a replacement," says Bob.

"Can we get him back?"

"Well, we may not want him back," says Bob. "Before he quit, he did the set-up that Ray told him to do, and put the machine on automatic to do its run. The thing is, he didn't tighten two of the adjusting nuts. We got little bits of machine tool all over the floor now."

"How many parts do we have to scrap?"

"Well, not that many. It only ran for a little while."

"Will we have enough to fill that order?" I ask him.

"I'll have to check," he says. "But, see, the problem is that the machine itself is down and it may stay down for some time."

"Which one is it?" I ask.

"The NCX-10," he says.

I shut my eyes. It's like a cold hand just reached inside me and grabbed the bottom of my stomach. That machine is the only one of its type in the plant. I ask Bob how bad the damage is. He says, "I don't know. They've got the thing half torn apart out there. We're on the phone with the manufacturer right now."

I start walking fast. I want to see it for myself. God, are we in trouble. I glance over at Bob, who is keeping pace with me.

"Do you think it was sabotage?" I ask.

Bob seems surprised. "Well, I can't say. I think the guy was just so upset he couldn't think straight. So he screwed it up."

I can feel my face getting hot. The cold hand is gone. Now I'm so pissed off at Bill Peach that I'm fantasizing about calling him on the phone and screaming in his ear. It's his fault! And in my head I see him. I see him behind my desk and hear him telling me how he's going to show me how to get the orders out the door. Right, Bill. You really showed me how to do it.

# 2

Isn't it strange to feel your own world is falling apart while those of the people close to you are rock steady? And you can't figure out why they're not affected the way you are. About 6:30, I slip away from the plant to run home and grab some dinner. As I come through the door, Julie looks up from the television.

"Hi," she says. "Like my hair?"

She turns her head. The thick, straight brown hair she used to have is now a mass of frizzed ringlets. And it isn't all the same color anymore. It's lighter in places.

"Yeah, looks great," I say automatically.

"The hairdresser said it sets off my eyes," she says, batting her long lashes at me. She has big, pretty blue eyes; they don't need to be "set off" in my opinion, but what do I know?

"Nice," I say.

"Gee, you're not very enthusiastic," she says.

"Sorry, but I've had a rough day."

"Ah, poor baby," she says. "But I've got a great idea! We'll go out to dinner and you can forget all about it."

I shake my head. "I can't. I've got to eat something fast and get back to the plant."

She stands up and puts her hands on her hips. I notice she's wearing a new outfit.

"Well you're a lot of fun!" she says. "And after I got rid of the kids, too."

"Julie, I've got a crisis on my hands. One of my most expensive machines went down this morning, and I need it to process a part for a rush order. I've got to stay on top of this one," I tell her.

"Okay. Fine. There is nothing to eat, because I thought we were going out," she says. "Last night, you said we were going out."

Then I remember. She's right. It was part of the promises when we were making up after the fight.

"I'm sorry. Look, maybe we can go out for an hour or so," I tell her.

"That's your idea of a night on the town?" she says. "Forget it, Al!"

"Listen to me," I tell her. "Bill Peach showed up unexpectedly this morning. He's talking about closing the plant."

Her face changes. Did it brighten?

"Closing the plant . . . really?" she asks.

"Yeah, it's getting very bad."

"Did you talk to him about where your next job would be?" she asks.

After a second of disbelief, I say, "No, I didn't talk to him about my next job. My job is *here*—in this town, at this plant."

She says, "Well, if the plant is going to close, aren't you interested in where you're going to live next? I am."

"He's only talking about it."

"Oh," she says.

I feel myself glaring at her. I say, "You really want to get out of this town as fast as you can, don't you?"

"It isn't my home town, Al. I don't have the same sentimental feelings for it you do," she says.

"We've only been here six months," I say.

"Is that all? A mere six months?" she says. "Al, I have no friends here. There's nobody except you to talk to, and you're not home most of the time. Your family is very nice, but after an hour with your mother, I go crazy. So it doesn't feel like six months to me."

"What do you want me to do? I didn't ask to come here. The company sent me to do a job. It was the luck of the draw," I say.

"Some luck."

"Julie, I do not have time to get into another fight with you," I tell her.

She's starting to cry.

"Fine! Go ahead and leave! I'll just be here by myself," she crys. "Like every night."

"Aw, Julie."

I finally go put my arms around her. We stand together for a few minutes, both of us quiet. When she stops crying, she steps back and looks up at me.

"I'm sorry," she says. "If you have to go back to the plant, then you'd better go."

"Why don't we go out tomorrow night?" I suggest.

She turns up her hands. "Fine . . . whatever."

I turn, then look back. "Will you be okay?"

"Sure. I'll find something to eat in the freezer," she says.

I've forgotten about dinner by now. I say, "Okay, I'll probably pick up something on my way back to the plant. See you later tonight."

Once I'm in the car, I find I've lost my appetite.

Ever since we moved to Bearington, Julie has been having a hard time. Whenever we talk about the town, she always complains about it, and I always find myself defending it.

It's true I was born and raised in Bearington, so I do feel at home here. I know all the streets. I know the best places to go to buy things, the good bars and the places you stay out of, all that stuff. There is a sense of ownership I have for the town, and more affection for it than for some other burg down the highway. It was home for eighteen years.

But I don't think I have too many illusions about it. Bearington is a factory town. Anyone passing through probably wouldn't see anything special about the place. Driving along, I look around and have much the same reaction. The neighborhood where we live looks like any other American suburb. The houses are fairly new. There are shopping centers nearby, a litter of fast-food restaurants, and over next to the Interstate is a big mall. I can't see much difference here from any of the other suburbs where we've lived.

Go to the center of town and it *is* a little depressing. The streets are lined with old brick buildings that have a sooty, crumbling look to them. A number of store fronts are vacant or covered with plywood. There are plenty of railroad tracks, but not many trains.

On the corner of Main and Lincoln is Bearington's one highrise office building, a lone tower on the skyline. When it was being built some ten years ago, the building was considered to be a very big deal around here, all fourteen stories of it. The fire department used it as an excuse to go buy a brand new fire engine, just so it would have a ladder long enough to reach to the top. (Ever since then, I think they've secretly been waiting for a fire to break out in the penthouse just to use the new ladder.) Local boosters immediately claimed that the new office tower was some kind of symbol of Bearington's vitality, a sign of re-birth in an old industrial town. Then a couple of years ago, the building management erected an enormous sign on the roof which says in red block letters: "Buy Me!" It gives a phone number. From the Interstate, it looks like the whole town is for sale. Which isn't too far from the truth.

On my way to work each day, I pass another plant along the road to ours. It sits behind a rusty chain-link fence with barbed wire running along the top. In front of the plant is a paved parking lot—five acres of concrete with tufts of brown grass poking through the cracks. Years have gone by since any cars have parked there. The paint has faded on the walls and they've got a chalky look to them. High on the long front wall you can still make out the company name; there's darker paint where the letters and logo had once been before they were removed.

The company that owned the plant went south. They built a new plant somewhere in North Carolina. Word has it they were trying to run away from a bad situation with their union. Word also has it that the union probably will catch up with them again in about five years or so. But meanwhile they'll have bought themselves five years of lower wages and maybe fewer hassles from the work force. And five years seem like eternity as far as modern management planning is concerned. So Bearington got another industrial dinosaur carcass on its outskirts and about 2,000 people hit the street.

Six months ago, I had occasion to go inside this plant. At the time, we were just looking for some cheap warehouse space nearby. Not that it was my job, but I went over with some other people just to look the place over. (Dreamer that I was when I first got here, I thought maybe someday we'd need more space to expand. What a laugh that is now.) It was the silence that really got to me. Everything was so quiet. Your footsteps echoed. It was weird. All the machines had been removed. It was just a huge empty place.

Driving by it now, I can't help thinking, that's going to be us in three months. It gives me a sick feeling.

I hate to see this stuff happening. The town has been losing major employers at the rate of about one a year ever since the mid-1970s. They fold completely, or they pull out and go elsewhere. There doesn't seem to be any end to it. And now it may be our turn.

When I came back to manage this plant, the Bearington *Herald* did a story on me. I know, big deal. But I was kind of a minor celebrity for a while. The local boy had made it big. It was sort of a high-school fantasy come true. I hate to think that the next time my name is in the paper, the story might be about the plant closing. I'm starting to feel like a traitor to everybody.

Donovan looks like a nervous gorilla when I get back to the plant. With all the running around he's done today, he must have lost five pounds. As I walk up the aisle toward the NCX-10, I watch him shifting his weight from one leg to the other. Then he paces for a few seconds and stops. Suddenly he darts across the aisle to talk to someone. And then he takes off to check on something. I give him a shrill, two-finger whistle, but he doesn't hear it. I have to follow him through two departments before I can catch up with him—back at the NCX-10. He looks surprised to see me.

"We going to make it?" I ask him.

"We're trying," he says.

"Yeah, but can we do it?"

"We're doing our best," he says.

"Bob, are we going to ship the order tonight or not?"

"Maybe."

I turn away and stand there looking at the NCX-10. Which is a lot to look at. It's a big hunk of equipment, our most expensive n/c machine. And it's painted a glossy, distinctive lavender. (Don't ask me why.) On one side is a control board filled with red, green, and amber lights, shiny toggle switches, a jet black keyboard, tape drives, and a computer display. It's a sexy-looking machine. And the focus of it all is the metal-working being done in the middle of it, where a vise holds a piece of steel. Shavings of metal are being sliced away by a cutting tool. A steady wash of turquoise lubricant splashes over the work and carries away the chips. At least the damn thing is working again.

We were lucky today. The damage wasn't as bad as we had first thought. But the service technician didn't start packing his tools until 4:30. By then, it was already second shift.

We held everybody in assembly on overtime, even though overtime is against current division policy. I don't know where we'll bury the expense, but we've got to get this order shipped tonight. I got four phone calls today just from our marketing manager, Johnny Jons. He too has been getting his ear chewed—from Peach, from his own sales people, and from the customer. We absolutely must ship this order tonight.

So I'm hoping nothing else goes wrong. As soon as each part

is finished, it's individually carried over to where it's fitted into the subassembly. And as soon as that happens, the foreman over there is having each subassembly carted down to final assembly. You want to talk about efficiency? People hand-carrying things one at a time, back and forth . . . our output of parts per employee must be ridiculous. It's crazy. In fact, I'm wondering, where did Bob get all the people?

I take a slow look around. There is hardly anybody working in the departments that don't have something to do with 41427. Donovan has stolen every body he could grab and put them all to work on this order. This is not the way it's supposed to be done.

But the order ships.

I glance at my watch. It's a few minutes past 11:00 P.M. We're on the shipping dock. The doors on the back of the tractor-trailer are being closed. The driver is climbing up into his seat. He revs the engine, releases the brakes, and eases out into the night.

I turn to Donovan. He turns to me.

"Congratulations," I tell him.

"Thanks, but don't ask me how we did it," he says.

"Okay, I won't. What do you say we find ourselves some dinner?"

For the first time all day, Donovan smiles. Way off in the distance, the truck shifts gears.

We take Donovan's car because it's closer. The first two places we try are closed. So then I tell Donovan just to follow my directions. We cross the river at 16th Street and drive down Bessemer into South Flat until we get to the mill. Then I tell Donovan to hang a right and we snake our way through the side streets. The houses back in there are built wall to wall, no yards, no grass, no trees. The streets are narrow and everyone parks in the streets, so it makes for some tedious maneuvering. But finally we pull up in front of Sednikk's Bar and Grill.

Donovan takes a look at the place and says, "You sure this is where we want to be?"

"Yeah, yeah. Come on. They've got the best burgers in town," I tell him.

Inside, we take a booth toward the rear. Maxine recognizes me and comes over to make a fuss. We talk for a minute and then Donovan and I order some burgers and fries and beer.

Donovan looks around and says, "How'd you know about this place?"

I say, "Well, I had my first shot-and-a-beer over there at the bar. I think it was the third stool on the left, but it's been a while."

Donovan asks, "Did you start drinking late in life, or did you grow up in this town?"

"I grew up two blocks from here. My father owned a corner grocery store. My brother runs it today."

"I didn't know you were from Bearington," says Donovan.

"With all the transfers, it's taken me about fifteen years to get back here," I say.

The beers arrive.

Maxine says, "These two are on Joe."

She points to Joe Sednikk who stands behind the bar. Donovan and I wave our thanks to him.

Donovan raises his glass, and says, "Here's to getting 41427 out the door."

"I'll drink to that," I say and clink my glass against his.

After a few swallows, Donovan looks much more relaxed. But I'm still thinking about what went on tonight.

"You know, we paid a hell of a price for that shipment," I say. "We lost a good machinist. There's the repair bill on the NCX-10. Plus the overtime."

"Plus the time we lost on the NCX-10 while it was down," adds Donovan. Then he says, "But you got to admit that once we got rolling, we really moved. I wish we could do that every day."

I laugh. "No thanks. I don't need days like this one."

"I don't mean we need Bill Peach to walk into the plant every day. But we *did* ship the order," says Donovan.

"I'm all for shipping orders, Bob, but not the way we did it tonight," I tell him.

"It went out the door, didn't it?"

"Yes, it did. But it was the way that it happened that we can't allow."

"I just saw what had to be done, put everybody to work on it, and the hell with the rules," he says.

"Bob, do you know what our efficiencies would look like if we ran the plant like that every day?" I ask. "We can't just dedicate the entire plant to one order at a time. The economies of scale would disappear. Our costs would go—well, they'd be even worse than they are now. We can't run the plant just by the seat-of-the-pants."

Donovan becomes quiet. Finally he says, "Maybe I learned too many of the wrong things back when I was an expeditor."

"Listen, you did a hell of a job today. I mean that. But we set policy for a purpose. You should know that. And let me tell you that Bill Peach, for all the trouble he caused to get one order shipped, would be back here pounding on our heads at the end of the month if we didn't manage the plant for efficiency."

He nods slowly, but then he asks, "So what do we do the next time this happens?"

I smile.

"Probably the same damn thing," I tell him. Then I turn and say, "Maxine, give us two more here, please. No, on second thought, we're going to save you a lot of walking. Make it a pitcher."

So we made it through today's crisis. We won. Just barely. And now that Donovan is gone and the effects of the alcohol are wearing off, I can't see what there was to celebrate. We managed to ship one very late order today. Whoopee.

The real issue is I've got a manufacturing plant on the critical list. Peach has given it three months to live before he pulls the plug.

That means I have two, maybe three more monthly reports in which to change his mind. After that, the sequence of events will be that he'll go to corporate management and present the numbers. Everybody around the table will look at Granby. Granby will ask a couple of questions, look at the numbers one more time, and nod his head. And that will be it. Once the executive decision has been made, there will be no changing it.

They'll give us time to finish our backlog. And then 600 people will head for the unemployment lines—where they will join their friends and former co-workers, the *other* 600 people whom we have already laid off.

And so the UniWare Division will drop out of yet another market in which it can't compete. Which means the world will no longer be able to buy any more of the fine products we can't make cheap enough or fast enough or good enough or something enough to beat the Japanese. Or most anybody else out there for that matter. That's what makes us another fine division in the UniCo "family" of businesses (which has a record of earnings growth that looks like Kansas), and that's why we'll be just another fine company in the Who-Knows-What Corporation after the big boys at headquarters put together some merger with some other loser. That seems to be the essence of the company's strategic plan these days.

What's the matter with us?

Every six months it seems like some group from corporate is coming out with some new program that's the latest panacea to all our problems. Some of them seem to work, but none of them does any good. We limp along month after month, and it never gets any better. Mostly it gets worse.

Okay. Enough of the bitching, Rogo. Try to calm down. Try to think about this rationally. There's nobody around. It's late. I am alone finally . . . here in the coveted corner office, throne room of my empire, such as it is. No interruptions. The phone is not ringing. So let's try to analyze the situation. Why can't we consistently get a quality product out the door on time at the cost that can beat the competition?

Something is wrong. I don't know what it is, but something basic is very wrong. I must be missing something.

I'm running what *should* be a good plant. Hell, it is a good plant. We've got the technology. We've got some of the best n/c machines money can buy. We've got robots. We've got a computer system that's supposed to do everything but make coffee.

We've got good people. For the most part we do. Okay, we're short in a couple of areas, but the people we have are good for the most part, even though we sure could use more of them. And I don't have too many problems with the union. They're a pain in the ass sometimes, but the competition has unions too. And, hell, the workers made some concessions last time—not as many as we'd have liked, but we have a livable contract.

I've got the machines. I've got the people. I've got all the materials I need. I know there's a market out there, because the competitors' stuff is selling. So what the hell is it?

It's the damn competition. That's what's killing us. Ever since the Japanese entered our markets, the competition has been incredible. Three years ago, they were beating us on quality and product design. We've just about matched them on those. But now they're beating us on price and deliveries. I wish I knew their secret.

What can I possibly do to be more competitive?

I've done cost reduction. No other manager in this division has cut costs to the degree I have. There is nothing left to trim.

And, despite what Peach says, my efficiencies are pretty damn good. He's got other plants with worse, I know that. But the better ones don't have the competition I do. Maybe I could push efficiencies some more, but . . . I don't know. It's like whipping a horse that's already running as fast as it can.

We've just got to do something about late orders. Nothing in this plant ships until it's expedited. We've got stacks and stacks of inventory out there. We release the materials on schedule, but nothing comes out the far end when it's supposed to.

That's not uncommon. Just about every plant I know of has expeditors. And you walk through just about any plant in America about our size and you'll find work-in-process inventory on the same scale as what we have. I don't know what it is. On the one hand, this plant is no worse than most of the ones I've seen— and, in fact, it's better than many. But we're losing money.

If we could just get our backlog out the door. Sometimes it's like little gremlins out there. Every time we start to get it right, they sneak around between shifts when nobody is looking and they change things just enough so everything gets screwed up. I swear it's got to be gremlins.

Or maybe I just don't know enough. But, hell, I've got an engineering degree. I've got an MBA. Peach wouldn't have named me to the job if he hadn't thought I was qualified. So it can't be me. Can it?

Man, how long has it been since I started out down there in industrial engineering as a smart kid who knew everything— fourteen, fifteen years? How many long days have there been since then?

I used to think if I worked hard I could do anything. Since the day I turned twelve I've worked. I worked after school in my old man's grocery store. I worked through high school. When I was old enough, I spent my summers working in the mills around here. I was always told that if I worked hard enough it would pay off in the end. That's true, isn't it? Look at my brother; he took the easy way out by being the first born. Now he owns a grocery store in a bad neighborhood across town. But look at me. I worked hard. I sweated my way through engineering school. I got a job with a big company. I made myself a stranger to my wife and kids. I took all the crap that UniCo could give me and said, "I can't get enough! Give me more!" Boy, am I glad I did! Here I am, thirty-eight years old, and I'm a crummy plant manager! Isn't that wonderful? I'm really having fun now.

Time to get the hell out of here. I've had enough fun for one day.

# 3

I wake up with Julie on top of me. Unfortunately, Julie is not being amorous; she is reaching for the night table where the digital alarm clock says 6:03 A.M. The alarm buzzer has been droning for three minutes. Julie smashes the button to kill it. With a sigh, she rolls off of me. Moments later, I hear her breathing resume a steady pace; she is asleep again. Welcome to a brand new day.

About forty-five minutes later, I'm backing the Buick out of the garage. It's still dark outside. But a few miles down the road the sky lightens. Halfway to the city, the sun rises. By then, I'm too busy thinking to notice it at first. I glance to the side and it's floating out there beyond the trees. What makes me mad sometimes is that I'm always running so hard that—like most other people, I guess—I don't have time to pay attention to all the daily miracles going on around me. Instead of letting my eyes drink in the dawn, I'm watching the road and worrying about Peach. He's called a meeting at headquarters for all the people who directly report to him—in essence, his plant managers and his staff. The meeting, we are told, is to begin promptly at 8:00 A.M. The funny thing is that Peach is not saying what the meeting is about. It's a big secret—you know: hush-hush, like maybe there's a war on or something. He has instructed us to be there at eight and to bring with us reports and other data that'll let us go through a thorough assessment of all the division's operations.

Of course, all of us have found out what the meeting is about. At least we have a fairly good idea. According to the grapevine, Peach is going to use the meeting to lay some news on us about how badly the division performed in the first quarter. Then he's going to hit us with a mandate for a new productivity drive, with targeted goals for each plant and commitments and all that great stuff. I suppose that's the reason for the commandment to be there at eight o'clock on the button with numbers in hand; Peach must've though it would lend a proper note of discipline and urgency to the proceedings.

The irony is that in order to be there at such an early hour, half the people attending will have had to fly in the night before. Which means hotel bills and extra meals. So in order to announce to us how badly the division is doing, Peach is going to pay out a couple of grand more than he would have had to pay if he'd begun the meeting an hour or two later.

I think that Peach may be starting to lose it. Not that I suspect him of drifting toward a breakdown or anything. It's just that everything seems to be an over-reaction on his part these days. He's like a general who knows he is losing the battle, but forgets his strategy in his desperation to win.

He was different a couple of years ago. He was confident. He wasn't afraid to delegate responsibility. He'd let you run your own show—as long as you brought in a respectable bottom line. He tried to be the "enlightened" manager. He wanted to be open to new ideas. If some consultant came in and said, "Employees have to feel good about their work in order to be productive," Peach would try to listen. But that was when sales were better and budgets were flush.

What does he say now?

"I don't give a damn if they feel good," he says. "If it costs an extra nickel, we're not paying for it."

That was what he said to a manager who was trying to sell Peach on the idea of a physical fitness center where employees could work out, the premise being that everyone would do better work because healthy employees are happy employees, etc. Peach practically threw him out of his office.

And now he's walking into my plant and wreaking havoc in the name of improving customer service. That wasn't even the first fight I've had with Peach. There have been a couple of others, although none as serious as yesterday's. What really bugs me is I used to get along very well with Peach. There was a time when I thought we were friends. Back when I was on his staff, we'd sit in his office at the end of the day sometimes and just talk for hours. Once in a while, we'd go out and get a couple of drinks together. Everybody thought I was brown-nosing the guy. But I think he liked me precisely because I wasn't. I just did good work for him. We hit it off together.

Once upon a time, there was a crazy night in Atlanta at the annual sales meeting, when Peach and I and a bunch of wackos from marketing stole the piano from the hotel bar and had a sing-along in the elevator. Other hotel guests who were waiting for an elevator would see the doors open, and there we'd be, midway through the chorus of some Irish drinking song with Peach sitting there at the keyboard tickling those ivories. (He's a pretty good piano player, too). After an hour, the hotel manager finally caught up with us. By then, the crowd had grown too big for the elevator, and we were up on the roof singing to the entire city. I had to pull Bill out of this fight with the two bouncers whom the manager had enlisted to kill the party. What a night that was. Bill and I ended up toasting each other with orange juice at dawn in some greasy-spoon diner on the wrong end of town.

Peach was the one who let me know that I really had a future with this company. He was the guy who pulled me into the picture when I was just a project engineer, when all I knew was how to try hard. He was the one who picked me to go to headquarters. It was Peach who set it up so I could go back and get my MBA.

Now we're screaming at each other. I can't believe it.

By 7:50, I'm parking my car in the garage under the UniCo building. Peach and his division staff occupy three floors of the building. I get out of the car and get my briefcase from the trunk. It weighs about ten pounds today, because it's full of reports and computer printouts. I'm not expecting to have a nice day. With a frown on my face, I start to walk to the elevator.

"Al!" I hear from behind me.

I turn; it's Nathan Selwin coming toward me. I wait for him.

"How's it going?" he asks.

"Okay. Good to see you again," I tell him. We start walking together. "I saw the memo on your appointment to Peach's staff. Congratulations."

"Thanks," he says. "Of course, I don't know if it's the best place to be right now with everything that's going on."

"How come? Bill keeping you working nights?"

"No, it's not that," he says. Then he pauses and looks at me. "Haven't you heard the news?"

"What about?"

He stops suddenly and looks around. There is nobody else around us.

"About the division," he says in a low voice.

I shrug; I don't know what he's talking about.

"The whole division is going to go on the block," he says. "Everybody on Fifteen is crapping in their pants. Peach got the word from Granby a week ago. He's got till the end of the year to improve performance, or the whole division goes up for sale.

And I don't know if it's true, but I heard Granby specifically said that if the division goes, Peach goes with it.''

"Are you sure?"

Nathan nods and adds, "Apparently it's been in the making for quite a while.''

We start walking again.

My first reaction is that it's no wonder Peach has been acting like a madman lately. Everything he's worked for is in jeopardy. If some other corporation buys the division, Peach won't even have a job. The new owners will want to clean house and they're sure to start at the top.

And what about me; will I have a job? Good question, Rogo. Before hearing this, I was going on the assumption that Peach would probably offer me some kind of position if the plant is shut down. That's usually the way it goes. Of course, it may not be what I want. I know there aren't any UniWare plants out there in need of a manager. But I figured maybe Peach would give me my old staff job back—although I also know it's already been filled and I've heard that Peach is very satisfied with the guy. Come to think of it, he did kind of threaten yesterday with his opening remarks that I might not have a job.

*Shit, I could be on the street in three months!*

"Listen, Al, if anybody asks you, you didn't hear any of this from me," says Nat.

And he's gone. I find myself standing alone in the corridor on the fifteenth floor. I don't even remember having gotten on the elevator, but here I am. I vaguely recall Nat talking to me on the way up, saying something about everybody putting out their resumés.

I look around, feel stupid, wonder where I'm supposed to be now, and then I remember the meeting. I head down the hall where I see some others going into a conference room.

I go in and take a seat. Peach is standing at the far end of the table. A slide projector sits in front of him. He's starting to talk. A clock on the wall indicates it's exactly eight o'clock.

I look around at the others. There are about twenty of them, most of them looking at Peach. One of them, Hilton Smyth, is looking at me. He's a plant manager, too, and he's a guy I've never liked much. For one thing, I resent his style—he's always promoting some new thing he's doing, and most of the time what he's doing isn't any different from the things everyone else is doing. Anyway, he's looking at me as if he's checking me out. Is it because I look a little shaken? I wonder what he knows. I stare back at him until he turns toward Peach.

When I'm finally able to tune into what Peach is saying, I find he's turning the discussion over to the division controller, Ethan Frost, a thin and wrinkled old guy who, with a little make-up, could double for the Grim Reaper.

The news this morning befits the messenger. The first quarter has just ended, and it's been a terrible one everywhere. The division is now in real danger of a shortfall in cash. All belts must be tightened.

When Frost is done, Peach stands and proceeds to deliver some stern talk about how we're going to meet this challenge. I try to listen, but after his first couple of sentences, my mind drops out. All I hear are fragments.

". . . imperative for us to minimize the downside risk . . ." ". . . acceptable to our current marketing posture . . ." ". . . without reducing strategic expense . . ." ". . . required sacrifices . . ." ". . . productivity improvements at all locations. . . ."

Graphs from the slide projector begin to flash on the screen. A relentless exchange of measurements between Peach and the others goes on and on. I make an effort, but I just can't concentrate.

". . . first quarter sales down twenty-two percent compared to a year ago . . ." ". . . total raw materials' costs increased . . ." ". . . direct labor ratios of hours applied to hours paid had a three-week high . . ." ". . . now if you look at numbers of hours applied to production versus standard, we're off by over twelve percent on those efficiencies. . ."

I'm telling myself that I've got to get hold of myself and pay attention. I reach into my jacket to get a pen to take some notes.

"And the answer is clear," Peach is saying. "The future of our business depends upon our ability to increase productivity."

But I can't find a pen. So I reach into my other pocket. And I pull out the cigar. I stare at it. I don't smoke anymore. For a few seconds I'm wondering where the hell this cigar came from.

And then I remember.

# 4

Two weeks ago, I'm wearing the same suit as now. This is back in the good days when I think that everything will work out. I'm traveling, and I'm between planes at O'Hare. I've got some time, so I go to one of the airline lounges. Inside, the place is jammed with business types like me. I'm looking for a seat in this place, gazing over the three-piece pinstripes and the women in conservative blazers and so on, when my eye pauses on the yarmulke worn by the man in the sweater. He's sitting next to a lamp, reading, his book in one hand and his cigar in the other. Next to him there happens to be an empty seat. I make for it. Not until I've almost sat down does it strike me I think I know this guy.

Running into someone you know in the middle of one of the busiest airports in the world carries a shock with it. At first, I'm not sure it's really him. But he looks too much like the physicist I used to know for him to be anyone but Jonah. As I start to sit down, he glances up at me from his book, and I see on his face the same unspoken question: Do I know you?

"Jonah?" I ask him.

"Yes?"

"I'm Alex Rogo. Remember me?"

His face tells me that he doesn't quite.

"I knew you some time ago," I tell him. "I was a student. I got a grant to go and study some of the mathematical models you were working on. Remember? I had a beard back then."

A small flash of recognition finally hits him. "Of course! Yes, I do remember you. 'Alex,' was it?"

"Right."

A waitress asks me if I'd like something to drink. I order a scotch and soda and ask Jonah if he'll join me. He decides he'd better not; he has to leave shortly.

"So how are you these days?" I ask.

"Busy," he says. "Very busy. And you?"

"Same here. I'm on my way to Houston right now," I say. "What about you?"

"New York," says Jonah.

He seems a little bored with this line of chit-chat and looks as if he'd like to finish the conversation. A second of quiet falls between us. But, for better or worse, I have this tendency (which I've never been able to bring under control) of filling silence in a conversation with my own voice.

"Funny, but after all those plans I had back then of going into research, I ended up in business," I say. "I'm a plant manager now for UniCo."

Jonah nods. He seems more interested. He takes a puff on his cigar. I keep talking. It doesn't take much to keep me going.

"In fact, that's why I'm on my way to Houston. We belong to a manufacturers' association, and the association invited UniCo to be on a panel to talk about robotics at the annual conference. I got picked by UniCo, because my plant has the most experience with robots."

"I see," says Jonah. "Is this going to be a technical discussion?"

"More business oriented than technical," I say. Then I remember I have something I can show him. "Wait a second. . . ."

I crack open my briefcase on my lap and pull out the advance copy of the program the association sent me.

"Here we are," I say, and read the listing to him. " 'Robotics: Solution for the Eighties to America's Productivity Crisis . . . a panel of users and experts discusses the coming impact of industrial robots on American manufacturing.' "

But when I look back to him, Jonah doesn't seem very impressed. I figure, well, he's an academic person; he's not going to understand the business world.

"You say your plant uses robots?" he asks.

"In a couple of departments, yes," I say.

"Have they really increased productivity at your plant?"

"Sure they have," I say. "We had—what?" I scan the ceiling for the figure. "I think it was a thirty-six percent improvement in one area."

"Really . . . thirty-six percent?" asks Jonah. "So your company is making thirty-six percent more money from your plant just from installing some robots? Incredible."

I can't hold back a smile.

"Well . . . no," I say. "We all wish it were that easy! But it's a lot more complicated than that. See, it was just in one department that we had a thirty-six percent improvement."

Jonah looks at his cigar, then extinguishes it in the ashtray.

"Then you didn't really increase productivity," he says.

I feel my smile freeze.

"I'm not sure I understand," I say.

Jonah leans forward conspiratorially and says, "Let me ask you something—just between us: Was your plant able to ship even one more product per day as a result of what happened in the department where you installed the robots?"

I mumble, "Well, I'd have to check the numbers . . ."

"Did you fire anybody?" he asks.

I lean back, looking at him. What the hell does he mean by that?

"You mean did we lay anybody off? Because we installed the robots?" I say. "No, we have an understanding with our union that nobody will be laid off because of productivity improvement. We shifted the people to other jobs. Of course, when there's a business downturn, we lay people off."

"But the robots themselves didn't reduce your plant's people expense," he says.

"No," I admit.

"Then, tell me, did your inventories go down?" asks Jonah.

I chuckle.

"Hey, Jonah, what is this?" I say to him.

"Just tell me," he says. "Did inventories go down?"

"Offhand, I have to say I don't think so. But I'd really have to check the numbers."

"Check your numbers if you'd like," says Jonah. "But if your inventories haven't gone down . . . and your employee expense was not reduced . . . and if your company isn't selling more products—which obviously it can't, if you're not shipping more of them—then you can't tell me these robots increased your plant's productivity."

In the pit of my stomach, I'm getting this feeling like you'd probably have if you were in an elevator and the cable snapped.

"Yeah, I see what you're saying, in a way," I tell him. "But my efficiencies went up, my costs went down—"

"Did they?" asks Jonah. He closes his book.

"Sure they did. In fact, those efficiencies are averaging well above ninety percent. And my cost per part went down considerably. Let me tell you, to stay competitive these days, we've got to do everything we can to be more efficient and reduce costs."

My drink arrives; the waitress puts it on the table beside me. I hand her a five and wait for her to give me the change.

"With such high efficiencies, you must be running your robots constantly," says Jonah.

"Absolutely," I tell him. "We have to. Otherwise, we'd lose our savings on our cost per part. And efficiencies would go down. That applies not only to the robots, but to our other production resources as well. We have to keep producing to stay efficient and maintain our cost advantage."

"Really?" he says.

"Sure. Of course, that's not to say we don't have our problems."

"I see," says Jonah. Then he smiles. "Come on! Be honest. Your inventories are going through the roof, are they not?"

I look at him. How does he know?

"If you mean our work-in-process—"

"All of your inventories," he says.

"Well, it depends. Some places, yes, they are high," I say.

"And everything is always late?" asks Jonah. "You can't ship anything on time?"

"One thing I'll admit," I tell him, "is that we have a heck of a problem meeting shipping dates. It's a serious issue with customers lately."

Jonah nods, as if he had predicted it.

"Wait a minute here . . . how come you know about these things?" I ask him.

He smiles again.

"Just a hunch," says Jonah. "Besides, I see those symptoms in a lot of the manufacturing plants. You're not alone."

I say, "But aren't you a physicist?"

"I'm a scientist," he says. "And right now you could say I'm doing work in the science of organizations—manufacturing organizations in particular."

"Didn't know there was such a science."

"There is now," he says.

"Whatever it is you're into, you put your finger on a couple of my biggest problems, I have to give you that," I tell him. "How come—"

I stop because Jonah is exclaiming something in Hebrew. He's reached into a pocket of his trousers to take out an old watch.

"Sorry, Alex, but I see I'm going to miss my plane if I don't hurry," he says.

He stands up and reaches for his coat.

"That's too bad," I say. "I'm kind of intrigued by a couple of things you've said."

Jonah pauses.

"Yes, well, if you could start to think about what we've been discussing, you probably could get your plant out of the trouble it's in."

"Hey, maybe I gave you the wrong impression," I tell him. "We've got a few problems, but I wouldn't say the plant is in *trouble*."

He looks me straight in the eye. He knows what's going on, I'm thinking.

"But tell you what," I hear myself saying, "I've got some time to kill. Why don't I walk you down to your plane? Would you mind?"

"No, not at all," he says. "But we have to hurry."

I get up and grab my coat and briefcase. My drink is sitting there. I take a quick slurp off the top and abandon it. Jonah is already edging his way toward the door. He waits for me to catch up with him. Then the two of us step out into the corridor where people are rushing everywhere. Jonah sets off at a fast pace. It takes an effort to keep up with him.

"I'm curious," I tell Jonah, "what made you suspect something might be wrong with my plant?"

"You told me yourself," Jonah says.

"No, I didn't."

"Alex," he says, "it was clear to me from your own words that you're not running as efficient a plant as you think you are. You are running exactly the opposite. You are running a very *in*efficient plant."

"Not according to the measurements," I tell him. "Are you trying to tell me my people are wrong in what they're reporting . . . that they're lying to me or something?"

"No," he says. "It is very unlikely your people are lying to you. But your measurements definitely are."

"Yeah, okay, sometimes we massage the numbers here and there. But everybody has to play that game."

"You're missing the point," he says. "You *think* you're running an efficient plant . . . but your thinking is wrong."

"What's wrong with my thinking? It's no different from the thinking of most other managers."

"Yes, exactly," says Jonah.

"What's that supposed to mean?" I ask; I'm beginning to feel somewhat insulted by this.

"Alex, if you're like nearly everybody else in this world, you've accepted so many things without question that you're not really thinking at all," says Jonah.

"Jonah, I'm thinking all the time," I tell him. "That's part of my job."

He shakes his head.

"Alex, tell me again why you believe your robots are such a great improvement."

"Because they increased productivity," I say.

"And what is productivity?"

I think for a minute, try to remember.

"According to the way my company is defining it," I tell him, "there's a formula you use, something about the value added per employee equals . . . ."

Jonah is shaking his head again.

"Regardless of how your company defines it, that is not what productivity really is," he says. "Forget for just a minute about the formulas and all that, and just tell me in your own words, from your own experience, what does it mean to be productive?"

We rush around a corner. In front of us, I see, are the metal detectors and the security guards. I had intended to stop and say good-bye to him here, but Jonah doesn't slow down.

"Just tell me, what does it mean to be productive?" he asks again as he walks through the metal detector. From the other side he talks to me. "To *you* personally, what does it mean?"

I put my briefcase on the conveyor and follow him through. I'm wondering, what does he want to hear?

On the far side, I'm telling him, "Well, I guess it means that I'm accomplishing something."

"Exactly!" he says. "But you are accomplishing something in terms of what?"

"In terms of my goals," I say.

"Correct!" says Jonah.

He reaches under his sweater into his shirt pocket and pulls out a cigar. He hands it to me.

# THE GOAL

"My compliments," he says. "When you are productive you are accomplishing something in terms of your goal, right?"

"Right," I say as I retrieve my briefcase.

We're rushing past gate after gate. I'm trying to match Jonah stride for stride.

And he's saying, "Alex, I have come to the conclusion that productivity is the act of bringing a company closer to its goal. Every action that brings a company closer to its goal is productive. Every action that does not bring a company closer to its goal is not productive. Do you follow me?"

"Yeah, but . . . really, Jonah, that's just simple common sense," I say to him.

"It's simple logic is what it is," he says.

We stop. I watch him hand his ticket across the counter.

"But it's too simplified," I tell him. "It doesn't tell me anything. I mean, if I'm moving toward my goal I'm productive and if I'm not, then I'm not productive—so what?"

"What I'm telling you is, productivity is meaningless unless you know what your goal is," he says.

He takes his ticket and starts to walk toward the gate.

"Okay, then," I say. "You can look at it this way. One of my company's goals is to increase efficiencies. Therefore, whenever I increase efficiencies, I'm being productive. It's logical."

Jonah stops dead. He turns to me.

"Do you know what your problem is?" he asks me.

"Sure," I say. "I need better efficiencies."

"No, that is not your problem," he says. "Your problem is you don't know what the goal is. And, by the way, there is only one goal, no matter what the company."

That stumps me for a second. Jonah starts walking toward the gate again. It seems everyone else has now gone on board. Only the two of us are left in the waiting area. I keep after him.

"Wait a minute! What do you mean, I don't know what the goal is? I know what the goal is," I tell him.

By now, we're at the door of the plane. Jonah turns to me. The stewardess inside the cabin is looking at us.

"Really? Then, tell me, what is the goal of your manufacturing organization?" he asks.

"The goal is to produce products as efficiently as we can," I tell him.

"Wrong," says Jonah. "That's not it. What is the real goal?"

I stare at him blankly.

The stewardess leans through the door.

"Are either of you going to board this aircraft?"

Jonah says to her, "Just a second, please." Then he turns to me. "Come on, Alex! Quickly! Tell me the real goal, if you know what it is."

"Power?" I suggest.

He looks surprised. "Well . . . not bad, Alex. But you don't get power just by virtue of manufacturing something."

The stewardess is pissed off. "Sir, if you're not getting on this aircraft, you have to go back to the terminal," she says coldly.

Jonah ignores her. "Alex, you cannot understand the meaning of productivity unless you know what the goal is. Until then, you're just playing a lot of games with numbers and words."

"Okay, then it's market share," I tell him. "That's the goal."

"Is it?" he asks.

He steps into the plane.

"Hey! Can't you tell me?" I call to him.

"Think about it, Alex. You can find the answer with your own mind," he says.

He hands the stewardess his ticket, looks at me and waves good-bye. I raise my hand to wave back and discover I'm still holding the cigar he gave me. I put it in my suit jacket pocket. When I look up again, he's gone. An impatient gate-agent appears and tells me flatly she is going to close the door.

# 5

It's a good cigar.

For a connoisseur of tobacco, it might be a little dry, since it spent several weeks inside my suit jacket. But I smoke it with pleasure during Peach's big meeting, while I remember that other, stranger, meeting with Jonah.

Or was it really more strange than this? Peach is up in front of us tapping the center of a graph with a long wood pointer. Smoke whirls slowly in the beam of the slide projector. Across from me, someone is poking earnestly at a calculator. Everyone except me is listening intently, or jotting notes, or offering comments.

". . . consistent parameters . . . essential to gain . . . matrix of advantage . . . extensive pre-profit recovery . . . operational indices . . . provide tangential proof. . . ."

I have no idea what's going on. Their words sound like a different language to me—not a foreign language exactly, but a language I once knew and only vaguely now recall. The terms seem familiar to me. But now I'm not sure what they really mean. They are just words.

*You're just playing a lot of games with numbers and words.*

For a few minutes there in Chicago's O'Hare, I did try to think about what Jonah had said. He'd made a lot of sense to me somehow; he'd had some good points. But it was like somebody from a different world had talked to me. I had to shrug it off. I had to go to Houston and talk about robots. It was time to catch my own plane.

Now I'm wondering if Jonah might be closer to the truth than I first thought. Because as I glance from face to face, I get this gut hunch that none of us here has anything more than a witch doctor's understanding of the medicine we're practicing. Our tribe is dying and we're dancing in our ceremonial smoke to exorcise the devil that's ailing us.

What is the real goal? Nobody here has even asked anything that basic. Peach is chanting about cost opportunities and "productivity" targets and so on. Hilton Smyth is saying hallelujah to whatever Peach proclaims. Does anyone genuinely understand what we're doing?

At ten o'clock, Peach calls a break. Everyone except me exits for the rest rooms or for coffee. I stay seated until they are out of the room.

What the hell am I doing here? I'm wondering what good it is for me—or any of us—to be sitting here in this room. Is this meeting (which is scheduled to last for most of the day) going to make my plant competitive, save my job, or help anybody do anything of benefit to anyone?

I can't handle it. I don't even know what productivity is. So how can this be anything except a total waste? And with that thought I find myself stuffing my papers back into my briefcase. I snap it closed. And then I quietly get up and walk out.

I'm lucky at first. I make it to the elevator without anyone saying anything to me. But while I'm waiting there, Hilton Smyth comes strolling past.

"You're not bailing out on us, are you Al?" he asks.

For a second, I consider ignoring the question. But then I realize Smyth might deliberately say something to Peach.

"Have to," I say to him. "I've got a situation that needs my attention back at the plant."

"What? An emergency?"

"You can call it that."

The elevator opens its doors. I step in. Smyth is looking at me with a quizzical expression as he walks by. The doors close.

It crosses my mind that there is a risk of Peach firing me for walking out of his meeting. But that, to my current frame of mind as I walk through the garage to my car, would only shorten three months of anxiety leading up to what I suspect might be inevitable.

I don't go back to the plant right away. I drive around for a while. I point the car down one road and follow it until I'm tired of it, then take another road. A couple of hours pass. I don't care where I am; I just want to be out. The freedom is kind of exhilarating until it gets boring.

As I'm driving, I try to keep my mind off business. I try to clear my head. The day has turned out to be nice. The sun is out. It's warm. No clouds. Blue sky. Even though the land still has an early spring austerity, everything yellow-brown, it's a good day to be playing hooky.

I remember looking at my watch just before I reach the plant gates and seeing that it's past 1 P.M. I'm slowing down to make the turn through the gate, when—I don't know how else to say it—it just doesn't feel right. I look at the plant. And I put my foot down on the gas and keep going. I'm hungry; I'm thinking maybe I should get some lunch.

But I guess the real reason is I just don't want to be found yet. I need to think and I'll never be able to do it if I go back to the office now.

Up the road about a mile is a little pizza place. I see they're open, so I stop and go in. I'm conservative; I get a medium pizza with double cheese, pepperoni, sausage, mushrooms, green peppers, hot peppers, black olives and onion, and—mmmmmmmmm— a sprinkling of anchovies. While I'm waiting, I can't resist the munchos on the stand by the cash register, and I tell the Sicilian who runs the place to put me down for a couple of bags of beer nuts, some taco chips, and—for later—some pretzels. Trauma whets my appetite.

But there's one problem. You just can't wash down beer nuts with soda. You need beer. And guess what I see in the cooler. Of course, I don't usually drink during the day . . . but I look at the way the light is hitting those frosty cold cans. . . .

"Screw it."

I pull out a six of Bud.

Fourteen dollars and sixty-two cents and I'm out of there.

Just before the plant, on the opposite side of the highway, there is a gravel road leading up a low hillside. It's an access road to a substation about half a mile away. So on impulse, I turn the wheel sharply. The Buick goes bouncing off the highway onto the gravel and only a fast hand saves my pizza from the floor. We raise some dust getting to the top.

I park the car, unbutton my shirt, take off my tie and coat to save them from the inevitable, and open up my goodies.

Some distance below, down across the highway, is my plant. It sits in a field, a big gray steel box without windows. Inside, I know, there are about 400 people at work on day shift. Their cars are parked in the lot. I watch as a truck backs between two others sitting at the unloading docks. The trucks bring the materials which the machines and people inside will use to make something. On the opposite side, more trucks are being filled with what they have produced. In simplest terms, that's what's happening. I'm supposed to manage what goes on down there.

I pop the top on one of the beers and go to work on the pizza.

The plant has the look of a landmark. It's as if it has always been there, as if it will always be there. I happen to know the plant is only about fifteen years old. And it may not be here as many years from now.

So what is the goal?

What are we supposed to be doing here?

What keeps this place working?

Jonah said there was only one goal. Well, I don't see how that can be. We do a lot of things in the course of daily operations, and they're all important. Most of them anyway . . . or we wouldn't do them. What the hell, they all could be goals.

I mean, for instance, one of the things a manufacturing organization must do is buy raw materials. We need these materials in order to manufacture, and we have to obtain them at the best cost, and so purchasing in a cost-effective manner is very important to us.

The pizza, by the way, is primo. I'm chowing down on my second piece when some tiny voice inside my head asks me, But is this the goal? Is cost-effective purchasing the reason for the plant's existence?

I have to laugh. I almost choke.

Yeah, right. Some of the brilliant idiots in Purchasing sure do act as if that's the goal. They're out there renting warehouses to store all the crap they're buying so cost-effectively. What is it we have now? A thirty-two-month supply of copper wire? A seven-month inventory of stainless steel sheet? All kinds of stuff. They've got millions and millions tied up in what they've bought—and at terrific prices.

No, put it that way, and economical purchasing is definitely not the goal of this plant.

What else do we do? We employ people—by the hundreds here, and by the tens of thousands throughout UniCo. We, the people, are supposed to be UniCo's "most important asset," as some P.R. flack worded it once in the annual report. Brush off the bull and it is true the company couldn't function without good people of various skills and professions.

I personally am glad it provides jobs. There is a lot to be said for a steady paycheck. But supplying jobs to people surely isn't why the plant exists. After all, how many people have we laid off so far?

And anyway, even if UniCo offered lifetime employment like some of the Japanese companies, I still couldn't say the goal is jobs. A lot of people seem to think and act as if that were the goal (empire-building department managers and politicians just to name two), but the plant wasn't built for the purpose of paying wages and giving people something to do.

Okay, so why was the plant built in the first place?

It was built to produce products. Why can't that be the goal? Jonah said it wasn't. But I don't see why it isn't the goal. We're a manufacturing company. That means we have to manufacture something, doesn't it? Isn't that the whole point, to produce products? Why else are we here?

I think about some of the buzzwords I've been hearing lately.

What about quality?

Maybe that's it. If you don't manufacture a quality product all you've got at the end is a bunch of expensive mistakes. You have to meet the customer's requirements with a quality product, or before long you won't have a business. UniCo learned its lesson on that point.

But we've already learned that lesson. We've implemented a major effort to improve quality. Why isn't the plant's future secure? And if quality were truly the goal, then how come a company like Rolls Royce very nearly went bankrupt?

Quality alone cannot be the goal. It's important. But it's not the goal. Why? Because of costs?

If low-cost production is essential, then efficiency would seem to be the answer. Okay . . . maybe it's the two of them together: quality and efficiency. They do tend to go hand-in-hand. The fewer errors made, the less re-work you have to do, which can lead to lower costs and so on. Maybe that's what Jonah meant.

Producing a quality product efficiently: that must be the goal. It sure sounds good. "Quality and efficiency." Those are two nice words. Kind of like "Motherhood and the American Way."

I sit back and pop the top on another beer. The pizza is now just a fond memory. For a few moments I feel satisfied.

But something isn't sitting right. And it's more than just indigestion from lunch. To efficiently produce quality products sounds like a good goal. But can that goal keep the plant working?

I'm bothered by some of the examples that come to mind.

# THE GOAL

If the goal is to produce a quality product efficiently, then how come Volkswagen isn't still making Bugs? That was a quality product that could be produced at low cost. Or, going back a ways, how come Douglas didn't keep making DC-3's? From everything I've heard, the DC-3 was a fine aircraft. I'll bet if they had kept making them, they could turn them out today a lot more efficiently than DC-10's.

It's not enough to turn out a quality product on an efficient basis. The goal has to be something else.

But what?

As I drink my beer, I find myself contemplating the smooth finish of the aluminum beer can I hold in my hand. Mass production technology really is something. To think that this can until recently was a rock in the ground. Then we come along with some know-how and some tools and turn the rock into a lightweight, workable metal that you can use over and over again. It's pretty amazing—

Wait a minute, I'm thinking. That's it!

Technology: that's really what it's all about. We have to stay on the leading edge of technology. It's essential to the the the company. If we don't keep pace with technology, we're finished. So that's the goal.

Well, on second thought . . . that isn't right. If technology is the real goal of a manufacturing organization, then how come the most responsible positions aren't in research and development? How come R&D is always off to the side in every organization chart I've ever seen? And suppose we did have the latest of every kind of machine we could use—would it save us? No, it wouldn't. So technology is important, but it isn't the goal.

Maybe the goal is some combination of efficiency, quality and technology. But then I'm back to saying we have a lot of important goals. And that really isn't saying anything, aside from the fact that it doesn't square with what Jonah told me.

I'm stumped.

I gaze down the hillside. In front of the big steel box of the plant there is a smaller box of glass and concrete which houses the offices. Mine is the office on the front left corner. Squinting at it, I can almost see the stack of phone messages my secretary is bringing in by wheelbarrow.

Oh well. I lift my beer for a good long slug. And as I tilt my head back, I see them.

Out beyond the plant are two other long, narrow buildings.

They're our warehouses. They're filled to the roof with spare parts and unsold merchandise we haven't been able to unload yet. Twenty million dollars in finished-goods inventory: quality products of the most current technology, all produced efficiently, all sitting in their boxes, all sealed in plastic with the warranty cards and a whiff of the original factory air—and all waiting for someone to buy them.

So that's it. UniCo obviously doesn't run this plant just to fill a warehouse. The goal is sales.

But if the goal is sales, why didn't Jonah accept market share as the goal? Market share is even more important as a goal than sales. If you have the highest market share, you've got the best sales in your industry. Capture the market and you've got it made. Don't you?

Maybe not. I remember the old line, "We're losing money, but we're going to make it up with volume." A company will sometimes sell at a loss or at a small amount over cost—as UniCo has been known to do—just to unload inventories. You can have a big share of the market, but if you're not making money, who cares?

Money. Well, of course . . . money is the big thing. Peach is going to shut us down because the plant is costing the company too much money. So I have to find ways to reduce the money that the company is losing. . . .

Wait a minute. Suppose I did some incredibly brilliant thing and stemmed the losses so we broke even. Would that save us? Not in the long run, it wouldn't. The plant wasn't built just so it could break even. UniCo is not in business just so it can break even. The company exists to make money.

I see it now.

The goal of a manufacturing organization is to make money.

Why else did J. Bartholomew Granby start his company back in 1881 and go to market with his improved coal stove? Was it for the love of appliances? Was it a magnanimous public gesture to bring warmth and comfort to millions? Hell, no. Old J. Bart did it to make a bundle. And he succeeded—because the stove was a gem of a product in its day. And then investors gave him more money so they could make a bundle and J. Bart could make an even bigger one.

But is making money the only goal? What are all these other things I've been worrying about?

I reach for my briefcase, take out a yellow legal pad and take a pen from my coat pocket. Then I make a list of all the items people think of as being goals: cost-effective purchasing, employing good people, high technology, producing products, producing quality products, selling quality products, capturing market share. I even add some others like communications and customer satisfaction.

All of those are essential to running the business successfully. What do they all do? They enable the company to make money. But they are not the goals themselves; they're just the means of achieving the goal.

How do I know for sure?

Well, I don't. Not absolutely. But adopting "making money" as the goal of a manufacturing organization looks like a pretty good assumption. Because, for one thing, there isn't one item on that list that's worth a damn if the company isn't making money.

Because what happens if a company doesn't make money? If the company doesn't make money by producing and selling products, or by maintenance contracts, or by selling some of its assets, or by some other means . . . the company is finished. It will cease to function. Money must be the goal. Nothing else works in its place. Anyway, it's the one assumption I have to make.

If the goal is to make money, then (putting it in terms Jonah might have used), an action that moves us toward making money is productive. And an action that takes away from making money is non-productive. For the past year or more, the plant has been moving away from the goal more than toward it. So to save the plant, I have to make it productive; I have to make the plant make money for UniCo. That's a simplified statement of what's happening, but it's accurate. At least it's a logical starting point.

Through the windshield, the world is bright and cold. The sunlight seems to have become much more intense. I look around as if I have just come out of a long trance. Everything is familiar, but seems new to me. I take my last swallow of beer. I suddenly feel I have to get going.

# 6

By my watch, it's about 4:30 when I park the Buick in the plant lot. One thing I've effectively managed today is to evade the office. I reach for my briefcase and get out of the car. The glass box of the office in front of me is silent as death. Like an ambush. I know they're all inside waiting for me, waiting to pounce. I decide to disappoint everyone. I decide to take a detour through the plant. I just want to take a fresh look at things.

I walk down to a door into the plant and go inside. From my briefcase, I get the safety glasses I always carry. There is a rack of hard hats by one of the desks over by the wall. I steal one from there, put it on, and walk inside.

As I round a corner and enter one of the work areas, I happen to surprise three guys sitting on a bench in one of the open bays. They're sharing a newspaper, reading and talking with each other. One of them sees me. He nudges the others. The newspaper is folded away with the grace of a snake disappearing in the grass. All three of them nonchalantly become purposeful and go off in three separate directions.

I might have walked on by another time. But today it makes me mad. Dammit, the hourly people know this plant is in trouble. With the layoffs we've had, they have to know. You'd think they'd all try to work harder to save this place. But here we've got three guys, all of them making probably ten or twelve bucks an hour, sitting on their asses. I go and find their supervisor.

After I tell him that three of his people are sitting around with nothing to do, he gives me some excuse about how they're mostly caught up on their quotas and they're waiting for more parts.

So I tell him, "If you can't keep them working, I'll find a department that can. Now find something for them to do. You use your people, or lose 'em—you got it?"

From down the aisle, I look over my shoulder. The super now has the three guys moving some materials from one side of the aisle to the other. I know it's probably just something to keep them busy, but what the hell; at least those guys are working. If I hadn't said something, who knows how long they'd have sat there?

Then it occurs to me: those three guys are doing something now, but is that going to help us make money? They might be working, but are they productive?

For a moment, I consider going back and telling the supervisor to make those guys actually produce. But, well . . . maybe there really isn't anything for them to work on right now. And even though I could perhaps have those guys shifted to someplace where they could produce, how would I know if that work is helping us make money?

That's a weird thought.

Can I assume that making people work and making money are the same thing? We've tended to do that in the past. The basic rule has been just keep everybody and everything out here working all the time; keep pushing that product out the door. And when there isn't any work to do, make some. And when we can't make work, shift people around. And when you still can't make them work, lay them off.

I look around and most people *are* working. Idle people in here are the exception. Just about everybody is working nearly all the time. And we're not making money.

Some stairs zig-zag up one of the walls, access to one of the overhead cranes. I climb them until I am halfway to the roof and can look out over the plant from one of the landings.

Every moment, lots and lots of things are happening down there. Practically everything I'm seeing is a variable. The complexity in this plant—in *any* manufacturing plant—is mind-boggling if you contemplate it. Situations on the floor are always changing. How can I possibly control what goes on? How the hell am I supposed to know if any action in the plant is productive or non-productive toward making money?

The answer is supposed to be in my briefcase, which is heavy in my hand. It's filled with all those reports and printouts and stuff that Lou gave me for the meeting.

We do have lots of measurements that are supposed to tell us if we're productive. But what they really tell us are things like whether somebody down there "worked" for all the hours we paid him or her to work. They tell us whether the output per hour met our standard for the job. They tell us the "cost of products," they tell us "direct labor variances," all that stuff. But how do I really know if what happens here is making money for us, or whether we're just playing accounting games? There must be a connection, but how do I define it?

I shuffle back down the stairs.

Maybe I should just dash off a blistering memo on the evil of reading newspapers on the job. Think that'll put us back in the black?

By the time I finally set foot inside my office, it is past five o'clock and most of the people who might have been waiting for me are gone. Fran was probably one of the first ones out the door. But she has left me all their messages. I can barely see the phone under them. Half of the messages seem to be from Bill Peach. I guess he caught my disappearing act.

With reluctance, I pick up the phone and dial his number. But God is merciful. It rings for a straight two minutes; no answer. I breathe quietly and hang up.

Sitting back in my chair, looking out at the reddish-gold of late afternoon, I keep thinking about measurements, about all the ways we use to evaluate performance: meeting schedules and due dates, inventory turns, total sales, total expenses. Is there a simplified way to know if we're making money?

There is a soft knock at the door.

I turn. It's Lou.

As I mentioned earlier, Lou is the plant controller. He's a paunchy, older man who is about two years away from retirement. In the best accountants' tradition, he wears horn-rimmed bifocal glasses. Even though he dresses in expensive suits, somehow he always seems to look a little frumpled. He came here from corporate about twenty years ago. His hair is snow white. I think his reason for living is to go to the CPA conventions and bust loose. Most of the time, he's very mild-mannered—until you try to put something over on him. Then he turns into Godzilla.

"Hi," he says from the door.

I roll my hand, motioning him to come in.

"Just wanted to mention to you that Bill Peach called this afternoon," says Lou. "Weren't you supposed to be in a meeting with him today?"

"What did Bill want?" I ask, ignoring the question.

"He needed some updates on some figures," he says. "He seemed kind of miffed that you weren't here."

"Did you get him what he needed?" I ask.

"Yeah, most of it," Lou says. "I sent it to him; he should get it in the morning. Most of it was like the stuff I gave you."

"What about the rest?"

"Just a few things I have to pull together," he says. "I should have it sometime tomorrow."

"Let me see it before it goes, okay?" I say. "Just so I know."

"Oh, sure," says Lou.

"Hey, you got a minute?"

"Yeah, what's up?" he asks, probably expecting me to give him the rundown on what's going on between me and Peach.

"Sit down," I tell him.

Lou pulls up a chair.

I think for a second, trying to phrase this correctly. Lou waits expectantly.

"This is just a simple, fundamental question," I say.

Lou smiles. "Those are the kind I like."

"Would you say the goal of this company is to make money?"

He bursts out laughing.

"Are you kidding?" he asks. "Is this a trick question?"

"No, just tell me."

"Of course it's to make money!" he says.

I repeat it to him: "So the goal of the company is to make money, right?"

"Yeah," he says. "We have to produce products, too."

"Okay, now wait a minute," I tell him. "Producing products is just a means to achieve the goal."

I run through the basic line of reasoning with him. He listens. He's a fairly bright guy, Lou. You don't have to explain every little thing to him. At the end of it all, he agrees with me.

"So what are you driving at?"

"How do we know if we're making money?"

"Well, there are a lot of ways," he says.

For the next few minutes, Lou goes on about total sales, and market share, and profitability, and dividends paid to stock-holders, and so on. Finally, I hold up my hand.

"Let me put it this way," I say. "Suppose you're going to re-write the textbooks. Suppose you don't have all those terms and you have to make them up as you go along. What would be the minimum number of measurements you would need in order to know if we are making money?"

Lou puts a finger alongside his face and squints through his bifocals at his shoe.

"Well, you'd have to have some kind of absolute measurement," he says. "Something to tell you in dollars or yen or whatever just how much money you've made."

"Something like net profit, right?" I ask.

"Yeah, net profit," he says. "But you'd need more than just that. Because an absolute measurement isn't going to tell you much."

"Oh yeah?" I say. "If I know how much money I've made, why do I need to know anything else? You follow me? If I add up what I've made, and I subtract my expenses, and I get my net profit—what else do I need to know? I've made, say, $10 million, or $20 million, or whatever."

For a fraction of a second, Lou gets a glint in his eye like I'm real dumb.

"All right," he says. "Let's say you figure it out and you come up with $10 million net profit . . . an absolute measurement. Offhand, that sounds like a lot of money, like you really raked it in. But how much did you start with?"

He pauses for effect.

"You see? How much did it take to make that $10 million? Was it just a million dollars? Then you made ten times more money than you invested. Ten to one. That's pretty goddamned good. But let's say you invested a billion dollars. And you only made a lousy ten million bucks? That's pretty bad."

"Okay, okay," I say. "I was just asking to be sure."

"So you need a relative measurement, too," Lou continues. "You need something like return on investment . . . ROI, some comparison of the money made relative to the money invested."

"All right, but with those two, we ought to be able to tell how well the company is doing overall, shouldn't we?" I ask.

Lou nearly nods, then he gets a faraway look.

"Well. . . ." he says.

I think about it too.

"You know," he says, "it is possible for a company to show net profit and a good ROI and still go bankrupt."

"You mean if it runs out of cash," I say.

"Exactly," he says. "Bad cash flow is what kills most of the businesses that go under."

"So you have to count cash flow as a third measurement?"

He nods.

"Yeah, but suppose you've got enough cash coming in every

46

month to meet expenses for a year," I tell him. "If you've got enough of it, then cash flow doesn't matter."

"But if you don't, nothing else matters," says Lou. "It's a measure of survival: stay above the line and you're okay; go below and you're dead."

We look each other in the eye.

"It's happening to us, isn't it?" Lou asks.

I nod.

Lou looks away. He's quiet.

Then he says, "I knew it was coming. Just a matter of time."

He pauses. He looks back to me.

"What about us?" he asks. "Did Peach say anything?"

"They're thinking about closing us down."

"Will there be a consolidation?" he asks.

What he's really asking is whether he'll have a job.

"I honestly don't know, Lou," I tell him. "I imagine some people might be transferred to other plants or other divisions, but we didn't get into those kinds of specifics."

Lou takes a cigarette out of the pack in his shirt pocket. I watch him stamp the end of it repeatedly on the arm of his chair.

"Two lousy years to go before retirement," he mutters.

"Hey, Lou," I say, trying to lift him out of despair, "the worst it would probably mean for you would be an early retirement."

"Dammit!" he says. "I don't *want* an early retirement!"

We're both quiet for some time. Lou lights his cigarette. We sit there.

Finally I say, "Look, I haven't given up yet."

"Al, if Peach says we're finished—"

"He didn't say that. We've still got time."

"How much?" he asks.

"Three months," I say.

He all but laughs. "Forget it, Al. We'll never make it."

"I said I'm not giving up. Okay?"

For a minute, he doesn't say anything. I sit there knowing I'm not sure if I'm telling him the truth. All I've been able to do so far is figure out that we have to make the plant make money. Fine, Rogo, now *how* do we do it? I hear Lou blow a heavy breath of smoke.

With resignation in his voice, he says, "Okay, Al. I'll give you all the help I can. But . . . ."

He leaves the sentence unfinished, waves his hand in the air.

"I'm going to need that help, Lou," I tell him. "And the first thing I need from you is to keep all this to yourself for the time being. If the word gets out, we won't be able to get anyone to lift a finger around here."

"Okay, but you know this won't stay a secret for long," he says.

I know he's right.

"So how do you plan on saving this place?" Lou asks.

"The first thing I'm trying to do is get a clear picture of what we have to do to stay in business," I say.

"Oh, so that's what all this stuff with the measurements is about," he says. "Listen, Al, don't waste your time with all that. The system is the system. You want to know what's wrong? I'll tell you what the problem is."

And he does. For about an hour. Most of it I've heard before, it's the kind of thing everybody's heard: It's all the union's fault; if everybody would just work harder; nobody gives a damn about quality; look at the Japanese—they know how to work, we've forgotten how; and so on, and so on. He even tells me what sorts of self-flagellation we should administer in order to chasten ourselves. Mostly Lou is just blowing off steam. That's why I let him talk.

But I sit there wondering. Lou actually is a bright guy. We're all fairly bright; UniCo has lots of bright, well-educated people on the payroll. And I sit here listening to Lou pronounce his opinions, which all sound good as they roll off his tongue, and I wonder why it is that we're slipping minute by minute toward oblivion, if we're really so smart.

Sometime after the sun has set, Lou decides to go home. I stay. After Lou has gone, I sit there at my desk with a pad of paper in front of me. On the paper, I write down the three measurements which Lou and I agreed are central to knowing if the company is making money: net profit, ROI and cash flow.

I try to figure out if there is one of those three measurements which can be favored at the expense of the other two and allow me to pursue the goal. From experience, I happen to know there are a lot of games the people at the top can play. They can make the organization deliver a bigger net profit this year at the expense of net profit in years to come (don't fund any R&D, for instance; that kind of thing). They can make a bunch of no-risk decisions and have any one of those measurements look great while the others stink. Aside from that, the ratios between the three might have to vary according to the needs of the business.

But then I sit back.

If I were J. Bart Granby III sitting high atop my company's corporate tower, and if my control over the company were secure, I wouldn't want to play any of those games. I wouldn't want to see one measurement increase while the other two were ignored. I would want to see increases in net profit *and* return on investment *and* cash flow—all three of them. And I would want to see all three of them increase all the time.

Man, think of it. We'd *really* be making money if we could have all of the measurements go up simultaneously and forever.

So this is the goal:

To make money by increasing net profit, while simultaneously increasing return on investment, and simultaneously increasing cash flow.

I write that down in front of me.

I feel like I'm on a roll now. The pieces seem to be fitting together. I have found one clear-cut goal. I've worked out three related measurements to evaluate progress toward the goal. And I have come to the conclusion that simultaneous increases in all three measurements are what we ought to be trying to achieve. Not bad for a day's work. I think Jonah would be proud of me.

Now then, I ask myself, how do I build a direct connection between the three measurements and what goes on in my plant? If I can find some logical relationship between our daily operations and the overall performance of the company then I'll have a basis for knowing if something is productive or non-productive . . . moving toward the goal or away from it.

I go to the window and stare into the blackness.

Half an hour later, it is as dark in my mind as it is outside the window.

Running through my head are ideas about profit margins and capital investments and direct labor content, and it's all very conventional. It's the same basic line of thinking everyone has been following for a hundred years. If I follow it, I'll come to the same conclusions as everyone else and that means I'll have no truer understanding of what's going on than I do now.

I'm stuck.

I turn away from the window. Behind my desk is a bookcase; I pull out a textbook, flip through it, put it back, pull out another, flip through it, put it back.

Finally, I've had it. It's late.

I check my watch—and I'm shocked. It's past ten o'clock. All of a sudden, I realize I never called Julie to let her know I wasn't going to be home for dinner. She's really going to be pissed off at me; she always is when I don't call.

I pick up the phone and dial. Julie answers.

"Hi," I say. "Guess who had a rotten day."

"Oh? So what else is new?" she says. "It so happens my day wasn't too hot either."

"Okay, then we both had rotten days," I tell her. "Sorry I didn't call before. I got wrapped up in something."

Long pause.

"Well, I couldn't get a babysitter anyway," she says.

Then it dawns on me; our postponed night out was supposed to be tonight.

"I'm sorry, Julie. I really am. It just completely slipped my mind," I tell her.

"I made dinner," she says. "When you hadn't shown up after two hours, we ate without you. Yours is in the microwave if you want it."

"Thanks."

"Remember your daughter? The little girl who's in love with you?" Julie asks.

"You don't have to be sarcastic."

"She waited by the front window for you all evening until I made her go to bed."

I shut my eyes.

"Why?" I ask.

"She's got a surprise to show you," says Julie.

I say, "Listen, I'll be home in about an hour."

"No rush," says Julie.

She hangs up before I can say good-bye.

Indeed, there is no point in rushing home at this stage of the game. I get my hard hat and glasses and take a walk out into the plant to pay a visit to Eddie, my second shift supervisor, and see how everything is going.

When I get there, Eddie is not in his office; he's out dealing with something on the floor. I have him paged. Finally, I see him coming from way down at the other end of the plant. I watch him as he walks down. It's a five-minute wait.

Something about Eddie has always irritated me. He's a competent supervisor. Not outstanding, but he's okay. His work is not what bothers me. It's something else.

I watch Eddie's steady gait. Each step is very regular.

Then it hits me. That's what irritates me about Eddie: it's the way he walks. Well, it's more than that; Eddie's walk is symbolic of the kind of person he is. He walks a little bit pigeon-toed. It's as if he's literally walking a straight and narrow line. His hands cross stiffly in front of him, seeming to point at each foot. And he does all this like he read in a manual someplace that this is how walking is supposed to be done.

As he approaches, I'm thinking that Eddie has probably never done anything improper in his entire life—unless it was expected of him. Call him Mr. Regularity.

We talk about some of the orders going through. As usual, everything is out of control. Eddie, of course, doesn't realize this. To him, everything is normal. And if it's normal, it must be right.

He's telling me—in elaborate detail—about what is running tonight. Just for the hell of it, I feel like asking Eddie to define what he's doing tonight in terms of something like net profit.

I want to ask him, "Say, Eddie, how's our impact on ROI been in the last hour? By the way, what's your shift done to improve cash flow? Are we making money?"

It's not that Eddie hasn't heard of those terms. It's just that those concerns are not part of his world. His world is one measured in terms of parts per hour, man-hours worked, numbers of orders filled. He knows labor standards, he knows scrap factors, he knows run times, he knows shipping dates. Net profit, ROI, cash flow—that's just headquarters talk to Eddie. It's absurd to think I could measure Eddie's world by those three. For Eddie, there is only a vague association between what happens on his shift and how much money the company makes. Even if I could open Eddie's mind to the greater universe, it would still be very difficult to draw a clear connection between the values here on the plant floor and the values on the many floors of UniCo headquarters. They're too different.

In the middle of a sentence, Eddie notices I'm looking at him funny.

"Something wrong?" asks Eddie.

# 7

When I get home, the house is dark except for one light. I try to keep it quiet as I come in. True to her word, Julie has left me some dinner in the microwave. As I open the door to see what delectable treat awaits me (it seems to be some variety of mystery meat) I hear a rustling behind me. I turn around, and there stands my little girl, Sharon, at the edge of the kitchen.

"Well! If it isn't Miz Muffet!" I exclaim. "How is the tuffet these days?"

She smiles. "Oh . . . not bad."

"How come you're up so late?" I ask.

She comes forward holding a manila envelope. I sit down at the kitchen table and put her on my knee. She hands the envelope to me to open.

"It's my report card," she says.

"No kidding?"

"You have to look at it," she tells me.

And I do.

"You got all A's!" I say.

I give her a squeeze and big kiss.

"That's terrific!" I tell her. "That's very good, Sharon. I'm really proud of you. And I'll bet you were the only kid in your class to do this well."

She nods. Then she has to tell me everything. I let her go on, and half an hour later, she's barely able to keep her eyes open. I carry her up to her bed.

But tired as I am, I can't sleep. It's past midnight now. I sit in the kitchen, brooding and picking at dinner. My kid is getting A's in the second grade while I'm flunking out in business.

Maybe I should just give up, use what time I've got to try to land another job. According to what Selwin said, that's what everyone at headquarters is doing. Why should I be different?

For a while, I try to convince myself that a call to a head-hunter is the smart thing to do. But, in the end, I can't. A job with another company would get Julie and me out of town, and maybe fortune would bring me an even better position than I've got now (although I doubt it; my track record as a plant manager hasn't exactly been stellar.) What turns me against the idea of looking for another job is I'd feel I were running away. And I just can't do that.

It's not that I feel I owe my life to the plant or the town or the company, but I do feel some responsibility. And aside from that, I've invested a big chunk of my life in UniCo. I want that investment to pay off. Three months is better than nothing for a last chance.

My decision is, I'm going to do everything I can for the three months.

But that decided, the big question arises: what the hell can I really do? I've already done the best I can with what I know. More of the same is not going to do any good.

Unfortunately, I don't have a year to go back to school and re-study a lot of theory. I don't even have the time to read the magazines, papers, and reports piling up in my office. I don't have the time or the budget to screw around with consultants, making studies and all that crap. And anyway, even if I did have the time and money, I'm not sure any of those would give me a much better insight than what I've got now.

I have the feeling there are some things I'm not taking into account. If I'm ever going to get us out of this hole, I can't take anything for granted; I'm going to have to watch closely and think carefully about what is basically going on . . . take it one step at a time.

I slowly realize that the only tools I have—limited as they may be—are my own eyes and ears, my own hands, my own voice, my own mind. That's about it. I am all I have. And the thought keeps coming to me: I don't know if that's enough.

When I finally crawl into bed, Julie is a lump under the sheets. She is exactly the way I left her twenty-one hours ago. She's sleeping. Lying beside her on the mattress, still unable to sleep, I stare at the dark ceiling.

That's when I decide to try to find Jonah again.

# 8

Two steps after rolling out of bed in the morning, I don't like moving at all. But in the midst of a morning shower, memory of my predicament returns. When you've only got three months to work with, you don't have time to waste feeling tired. I rush past Julie—who doesn't have much to say to me—and the kids, who already seem to sense that something is wrong, and head for the plant.

The whole way there I'm thinking about how to get in touch with Jonah. That's the problem. Before I can ask for his help, I've got to find him.

The first thing I do when I get to the office is have Fran barricade the door against the hordes massing outside for frontal attack. Just as I reach my desk, Fran buzzes me; Bill Peach is on the line.

"Great," I mutter.

I pick up the phone.

"Yes, Bill."

"Don't you *ever* walk out of one of my meetings again," rumbles Peach. "Do you understand me?"

"Yes, Bill."

"Now, because of your untimely absence yesterday, we've got some things to go over," he says.

A few minutes later, I've pulled Lou into the office to help me with the answers. Then Peach has dragged in Ethan Frost and we're having a four-way conversation.

And that's the last chance I have to think about Jonah for the rest of the day. After I'm done with Peach, half a dozen people come into my office for a meeting that has been postponed since last week.

The next thing I know, I look out the window and it's dark outside. The sun has set and I'm still in the middle of my sixth meeting of the day. After everyone has gone, I take care of some paperwork. It's past seven when I hop in the car to go home.

While waiting in traffic for a long light to turn green, I finally have the opportunity to remember how the day began. That's when I get back to thinking about Jonah. Two blocks later, I remember my old address book.

# THE GOAL

I pull over at a gas station and use the pay phone to call Julie.

"Hello," she answers.

"Hi, it's me," I say. "Listen, I've got to go over to my mother's for something. I'm not sure how long I'll be, so why don't you go ahead and eat without me."

"The next time you want dinner—"

"Look, don't give me any grief, Julie; this is important."

There is a second of silence before I hear the click.

It's always a little strange going back to the old neighborhood, because everywhere I look is some kind of memory waiting just out of sight in my mind's eye. I pass the corner where I had the fight with Bruno Krebsky. I drive down the street where we played ball summer after summer. I see the alley where I made out for the first time with Angelina. I go past the utility pole upon which I grazed the fender of my old man's Chevy (and subsequently had to work two months in the store for free to pay for the repair). All that stuff. The closer I get to the house, the more memories come crowding in, and the more I get this feeling that's kind of warm and uncomfortably tense.

Julie hates to come here. When we first moved to town, we used to come down every Sunday to see my mother and Danny and his wife, Nicole. But there got to be too many fights about it, so we don't make the trip much anymore.

I park the Buick by the curb in front of the steps to my mother's house. It's a narrow, brick row house, about the same as any other on the street. Down at the corner is my old man's store, the one my brother owns today. The lights are off down there; Danny closes at six. Getting out of my car, I feel conspicuous in my suit and tie.

My mother opens the door.

"Oh my god," she says. She clutches her hands over her heart. "Who's dead?"

"Nobody died, Mom," I say.

"It's Julie, isn't it," she says. "Did she leave you?"

"Not yet," I say.

"Oh," she says. "Well, let me see . . . it isn't Mothers' Day . . ."

"Mom, I'm just here to look for something."

"Look for something? Look for what?" she asks, turning to let me in. "Come in, come in. You're letting all the cold inside. Boy, you gave me a scare. Here you are in town and you never come to see me anymore. What's the matter? You too important now for your old mother?"

"No, of course not, Mom. I've been very busy at the plant," I say.

"Busy, busy," she says leading the way to the kitchen. "You hungry?"

"No, listen, I don't want to put you to any trouble," I say.

She says, "Oh, it's no trouble. I got some ziti I can heat up. You want a salad too?"

"No, listen, a cup of coffee will be fine. I just need to find my old address book," I tell her. "It's the one I had when I was in college. Do you know where it might be?"

We step into the kitchen.

"Your old address book . . ." she muses as she pours a cup of coffee from the percolator. "How about some cake? Danny brought some day-old over last night from the store."

"No thanks, Mom. I'm fine," I say. "It's probably in with all my old notebooks and stuff from school."

She hands me the cup of coffee. "Notebooks . . ."

"Yeah, you know where they might be?"

Her eyes blink. She's thinking.

"Well . . . no. But I put all that stuff up in the attic," she says.

"Okay, I'll go look there," I say.

Coffee in hand, I head for the stairs leading to the second floor and up into the attic.

"Or it might all be in the basement," she says.

Three hours later—after dusting through the drawings I made in the first grade, my model airplanes, an assortment of musical instruments my brother once attempted to play in his quest to become a rock star, my yearbooks, four steamer trunks filled with receipts from my father's business, old love letters, old snapshots, old newspapers, old you-name-it—the address book is still at large. We give up on the attic. My mother prevails upon me to have some ziti. Then we try the basement.

"Oh, look!" says my mother.

"Did you find it?" I ask.

# THE GOAL

"No, but here's a picture of your Uncle Paul before he was arrested for embezzlement. Did I ever tell you that story?"

After another hour, we've gone through everything, and I've had a refresher course in all there is to know about Uncle Paul. Where the hell could it be?

"Well, I don't know," says my mother. "Unless it could be in your old room."

We go upstairs to the room I used to share with Danny. Over in the corner is the old desk where I used to study when I was a kid. I open the top drawer. And, of course, there it is.

"Mom, I need to use your phone."

My mother's phone is located on the landing of the stairs between the floors of the house. It's the same phone that was installed in 1936 after my father began to make enough money from the store to afford one. I sit down on the steps, a pad of paper on my lap, briefcase at my feet. I pick up the receiver, which is heavy enough to bludgeon a burglar into submission. I dial the number, the first of many.

It's one o'clock by now. But I'm calling Israel, which happens to be on the other side of the world from us. And vice versa. Which roughly means their days are our nights, our nights are their mornings, and consequently, one in the morning is not such a bad time to call.

Before long, I've reached a friend I made at the university, someone who knows what's become of Jonah. He finds me another number to call. By two o'clock, I've got the tablet of paper on my lap covered with numbers I've scribbled down, and I'm talking to some people who work with Jonah. I convince one of them to give me the number where I can reach him. By three o'clock, I've found him. He's in London. After several transfers here and there across some office of some company, I'm told that he will call me when he gets in. I don't really believe that, but I doze by the phone. And forty-five minutes later, it rings.

"Alex?"

It's his voice.

"Yes, Jonah," I say.

"I got a message you had called."

"Right," I say. "You remember our meeting in O'Hare."

"Yes, of course I remember it," he says. "And I presume you have something to tell me now."

I freeze for a moment. Then I realize he's referring to his question, what is the goal?

"Right," I say.

"Well?"

I hesitate. My answer seems so ludicrously simple I am suddenly afraid that it must be wrong, that he will laugh at me. But I blurt it out.

"The goal of a manufacturing organization is to make money," I say to him. "And everything else we do is a means to achieve the goal."

But Jonah doesn't laugh at me.

"Very good, Alex. Very good," he says quietly.

"Thanks," I tell him. "But, see, the reason I called was to ask you a question that's kind of related to the discussion we had at O'Hare."

"What's the problem?" he asks.

"Well, in order to know if my plant is helping the company make money, I have to have some kind of measurements," I say. "Right?"

"That's correct," he says.

"And I know that up in the executive suite at company headquarters, they've got measurements like net profit and return on investment and cash flow, which they apply to the overall organization to check on progress toward the goal."

"Yes, go on," says Jonah.

"But where I am, down at the plant level, those measurements don't mean very much. And the measurements I use inside the plant . . . well, I'm not absolutely sure, but I don't think they're really telling me the whole story," I say.

"Yes, I know exactly what you mean," says Jonah.

"So how can I know whether what's happening in my plant is truly productive or non-productive?" I ask.

For a second, it gets quiet on the other end of the line. Then I hear him say to somebody with him, "Tell him I'll be in as soon as I'm through with this call."

Then he speaks to me.

"Alex, you have hit upon something very important," he says. "I only have time to talk to you for a few minutes, but perhaps I can suggest a few things which might help you. You see, there is more than one way to express the goal. Do you understand? The goal stays the same, but we can state it in different ways, ways which mean the same thing as those two words, 'making money.' ''

"Okay," I answer, "so I can say the goal is to increase net profit, while simultaneously increasing both ROI and cash flow, and that's the equivalent of saying the goal is to make money."

"Exactly," he says. "One expression is the equivalent of the other. But as you have discovered, those conventional measurements you use to express the goal do not lend themselves very well to the daily operations of the manufacturing organization. In fact, that's why I developed a different set of measurements."

"What kind of measurements are those?" I ask.

"They're measurements which express the goal of making money perfectly well, but which also permit you to develop operational rules for running your plant," he says. "There are three of them. Their names are throughput, inventory and operational expense."

"Those all sound familiar," I say.

"Yes, but their definitions are not," says Jonah. "In fact, you will probably want to write them down."

Pen in hand, I flip ahead to a clean sheet of paper on my tablet and tell him to go ahead.

"Throughput," he says, "is the rate at which the system generates money through *sales.*"

I write it down word for word.

Then I ask, "But what about production? Wouldn't it be more correct to say—"

"No," he says. "Through *sales*—not through production. If you produce something, but don't sell it, it's not throughput. Got it?"

"Right. I thought maybe because I'm a plant manager I could substitute—"

Jonah cuts me off.

"Alex, let me tell you something," he says. "These definitions, even though they may sound simple, are worded very precisely. And they should be; a measurement not clearly defined is worse than useless. So I suggest you consider them carefully as a group. And remember that if you want to change one of them, you will have to change at least one of the others as well."

"Okay," I say warily.

"The next measurement is inventory," he says. "Inventory

is all the money that the system has invested in purchasing things which it intends to sell."

I write it down, but I'm wondering about it, because it's very different from the traditional definition of inventory.

"And the last measurement?" I ask.

"Operational expense," he says. "Operational expense is all the money the system spends in order to turn inventory into throughput."

"Okay," I say as I write. "But what about the labor invested in inventory? You make it sound as though labor is operational expense."

"Judge it according to the definitions," he says.

"But the value added to the product by direct labor has to be a part of inventory, doesn't it?"

"It might be, but it doesn't have to be," he says.

"Why do you say that?"

"Very simply, I decided to define it this way because I believe it's better not to take the *value* added into account," he says. "It eliminates the confusion over whether a dollar spent is an investment or an expense. That's why I defined inventory and operational expense the way I just gave you."

"Oh," I say. "Okay. But how do I relate these measurements to my plant?"

"Everything you manage in your plant is covered by those measurements," he says.

"Everything?" I say. I don't quite believe him. "But going back to our original conversation, how do I use these measurements to evaluate productivity?"

"Well, obviously you have to express the goal in terms of the measurements," he says, adding, "Hold on a second, Alex." Then I hear him tell someone, "I'll be there in a minute."

"So how do I express the goal?" I ask, anxious to keep the conversation going.

"Alex, I really have to run. And I know you are smart enough to figure it out on your own; all you have to do is think about it," he says. "Just remember we are always talking about the organization as a whole—not about the manufacturing department, or about one plant, or about one department within the plant. We are not concerned with local optimums."

"Local optimums?" I repeat.

Jonah sighs. "I'll have to explain it to you some other time."

"But, Jonah, this isn't enough," I say. "Even if I can define the goal with these measurements, how do I go about deriving operational rules for running my plant?"

"Give me a phone number where you can be reached," he says.

I give him my office number.

"Okay, Alex, I really do have to go now," he says.

"Right," I say. "Thanks for—"

I hear the click from far away.

"—talking to me."

I sit there on the steps for some time staring at the three definitions. At some point, I close my eyes. When I open them again, I see beams of sunlight below me on the living room rug. I haul myself upstairs to my old room and the bed I had when I was a kid. I sleep the rest of the morning with my torso and limbs painstakingly arranged around the lumps in the mattress.

Five hours later, I wake up feeling like a waffle.

# 9

It's eleven o'clock when I wake up. Startled by what time it is, I fall onto my feet and head for the phone to call Fran, so she can let everyone know I haven't gone AWOL.

"Mr. Rogo's office," Fran answers.

"Hi, it's me," I say.

"Well, hello stranger," she says. "We were just about ready to start checking the hospitals for you. Think you'll make it in today?"

"Uh, yeah, I just had something unexpected come up with my mother, kind of an emergency," I say.

"Oh, well, I hope everything's all right."

"Yeah, it's, ah, taken care of now. More or less. Anything going on that I should know about?"

"Well . . . let's see," she says, checking (I suppose) my message slips. "Two of the testing machines in G-aisle are down, and Bob Donovan wants to know if we can ship without testing."

"Tell him absolutely not," I say.

"Okay," says Fran. "And somebody from marketing is calling about a late shipment."

My eyes roll over.

"And there was a fist fight last night on second shift . . . Lou still needs to talk to you about some numbers for Bill Peach . . . a reporter called this morning asking when the plant was going to close; I told him he'd have to talk to you . . . and a woman from corporate communications called about shooting a video tape here about productivity and robots with Mr. Granby," says Fran.

"With *Granby?*"

"That's what she said," says Fran.

"What's the name and number?"

She reads it to me.

"Okay, thanks. See you later," I tell Fran.

I call the woman at corporate right away. I can hardly believe the chairman of the board is going to come to the plant. There must be some mistake. I mean, by the time Granby's limo pulls up to the gate, the whole plant might be closed.

But the woman confirms it; they want to shoot Granby here sometime in the middle of next month.

"We need a robot as a suitable background for Mr. Granby's remarks," says the woman.

"So why did you pick Bearington?" I ask her.

"The director saw a slide of one of yours and he likes the color. He thinks Mr. Granby will look good standing in front of it," she says.

"Oh, I see," I tell her. "Have you talked to Bill Peach about this?"

"No, I didn't think there was any need for that," she says. "Why? Is there a problem?"

"You might want to run this past Bill in case he has any other suggestions," I tell her. "But it's up to you. Just let me know when you have an exact date so I can notify the union and have the area cleaned up."

"Fine. I'll be in touch," she says.

I hang up and sit there on the steps muttering, "So . . . he likes the color."

"What was that all about on the phone just now?" my mother asks. We're sitting together at the table. She's obliged me to have something to eat before I leave.

I tell her about Granby coming.

"Well that sounds like a feather in your cap, the head man—what's his name again?" asks my mother.

"Granby."

"Here he's coming all the way to your factory to see you," she says. "It must be an honor."

"Yeah, it is in a way," I tell her. "But actually he's just coming to have his picture taken with one of my robots."

My mother's eyes blink.

"Robots? Like from out–of–space?" she asks.

"No, not from outer space. These are industrial robots. They're not like the ones on television."

"Oh." Her eyes blink again. "Do they have faces?"

"No, not yet. They mostly have arms . . . which do things like welding, stacking materials, spray painting, and so on. They're run by computer and you can program them to do different jobs," I explain.

Mom nods, still trying to picture what these robots are.

"So why's this Granby guy want to have his picture taken with a bunch of robots who don't even have faces?" she asks.

"I guess because they're the latest thing, and he wants to tell everybody in the corporation that we ought to be using more of them so that—"

I stop and glance away for a second, and see Jonah sitting there smoking his cigar.

"So that what?" asks my mother.

"Uh . . . so that we can increase productivity," I mumble, waving my hand in the air.

And Jonah says, have they really increased productivity at your plant? Sure they have, I say. We had—what?—a thirty-six percent improvement in one area. Jonah puffs his cigar.

"Is something the matter?" my mother asks.

"I just remembered something, that's all."

"What? Something bad?" she asks.

"No, an earlier conversation I had with the man I talked to last night," I say.

My mother puts her hand on my shoulder.

"Alex, what's wrong?" she's asking. "Come on, you can tell me. I know something's wrong. You show up out of the blue on my doorstep, you're calling people all over the place in the middle of the night. What is it?"

"See, Mom, the plant isn't doing so well . . . and, ah . . . well, we're not making any money."

My mother's brow darkens.

"Your big plant not making any money?" she asks. "But you're telling me about this fancy guy Granby coming, and these robot things, whatever they are. And you're not making any money?"

"That's what I said, Mom."

"Don't these robot things work?"

"Mom—"

"If they don't work, maybe the store will take them back."

"Mom, will you forget about the robots!"

She shrugs. "I was just trying to help."

I reach over and pat her hand.

"Yes, I know you were," I say. "Thanks. Really, thanks for everything. Okay? I've got to get going now. I've really got a lot of work to do."

I stand up and go to get my briefcase. My mother follows.

Did I get enough to eat? Would I like a snack to take with me for later in the day? Finally, she takes my sleeve and holds me in one place.

"Listen to me, Al. Maybe you've got some problems. I know you do, but this running all over the place, staying up all night isn't good for you. You've got to stop worrying. It's not going to help you. Look what worrying did to your father," she says. "It killed him."

"But, Mom, he was run over by a bus."

"So if he hadn't been so busy worrying he would have looked before he crossed the street."

I sigh. "Yeah, well, Mom, you may have a point. But it's more complicated than you think."

"I mean it! No worrying!" she says. "And this Granby fellow, if he's making trouble for you, you let me know. I'll call him and tell him what a worker you are. And who should know better than a mother? You leave him to me. I'll straighten him out."

I smile. I put my arm around her shoulders.

"I bet you would, Mom."

"You know I would."

I tell Mom to call me as soon as her phone bill arrives in the mail, and I'll come over and pay it. I give her a hug and a kiss good-bye, and I'm out of there. I walk out into the daylight and get into the Buick. For a moment, I consider going straight to the office. But a glance at the wrinkles in my suit and a rub of the stubble on my chin convinces me to go home and clean up first.

Once I'm on my way, I keep hearing Jonah's voice saying to me: "So your company is making thirty-six percent more money from your plant just by installing some robots? Incredible." And I remember that I was the one who was smiling. I was the one who thought *he* didn't understand the realities of manufacturing. Now I feel like an idiot.

Yes, the goal is to make money. I know that now. And, yes, Jonah, you're right; productivity did not go up thirty-six percent just because we installed some robots. For that matter, did it go up at all? Are we making *any* more money because of the robots? And the truth is, I don't know. I find myself shaking my head.

But I wonder how Jonah knew? He seemed to know right

away that productivity hadn't increased. There were those questions he asked.

One of them, I remember as I'm driving, was whether we had been able to sell any more products as a result of having the robots. Another one was whether we had reduced the number of people on the payroll. Then he had wanted to know if inventories had gone down. Three basic questions.

When I get home, Julie's car is gone. She's out some place, which is just as well. She's probably furious at me. And I simply do not have time to explain right now.

After I'm inside, I open my briefcase to make a note of those questions, and I see the list of measurements Jonah gave me last night. From the second I glance at those definitions again, it's obvious. The questions match the measurements.

That's how Jonah knew. He was using the measurements in the crude form of simple questions to see if his hunch about the robots was correct: did we sell any more products (i.e., did our throughput go up?); did we lay off anybody (did our operational expense go down?); and the last, exactly what he said: did our inventories go down?

With that observation, it doesn't take me long to see how to express the goal through Jonah's measurements. I'm still a little puzzled by the way he worded the definitions. But aside from that, it's clear that every company would want to have its throughput go up. Every company would also want the other two, inventory and operational expense, to go down, if at all possible. And certainly it's best if they all occur simultaneously— just as with the trio that Lou and I found.

So the way to express the goal is this?

Increase throughput while simultaneously reducing both inventory and operating expense.

That means if the robots have made throughput go up and the other two go down, they've made money for the system. But what's really happened since they started working?

I don't know what effect, if any, they've had on throughput. But off the top of my head, I know inventories have generally increased over the past six or seven months, although I can't say for sure if the robots are to blame. The robots *have* increased our depreciation, because they're new equipment, but they haven't directly taken away any jobs from the plant; we simply shifted people around. Which means the robots had to increase operational expense.

Okay, but efficiencies have gone up because of the robots. So maybe that's been our salvation. When efficiencies go up, the cost–per–part has to come down.

But did the cost really come down? How could the cost–per–part go down if operational expense went up?

By the time I make it to the plant, it's one o'clock, and I still haven't thought of a satisfactory answer. I'm still thinking about it as I walk through the office doors. The first thing I do is stop by Lou's office.

"Have you got a couple minutes?" I ask.

"Are you kidding?" he says. "I've been looking for you all morning."

He reaches for a pile of paper on the corner of his desk. I know it's got to be the report he has to send up to division.

"No, I don't want to talk about that right now," I tell him. "I've got something more important on my mind."

I watch his eyebrows go up.

"More important than this report for Peach?"

"Infinitely more important than that," I tell him.

Lou shakes his head as he leans back in his swivel chair and gestures for me to have a seat.

"What can I do for you?"

"After those robots out on the floor came on line, and we got most of the bugs out and all that," I say, "what happened to our sales?"

Lou's eyebrows come back down again; he's leaning forward and squinting at me over his bifocals.

"What kind of question is that?" he asks.

"A smart one, I hope," I say. "I need to know if the robots had any impact on our sales. And specifically if there was any increase after they came on line."

"Increase? Just about all of our sales have been level or in a downhill slide since last year."

I'm a little irritated.

"Well, would you mind just checking?" I ask.

He holds up his hands in surrender.

"Not at all. Got all the time in the world."

Lou opens his desk drawer, and after flipping through some files, starts pulling out handfuls of reports, charts, and graphs. We both start leafing through. But we find that in every case where a robot came on line, there was no increase in sales for any product for which they made parts, not even the slightest blip in the curve. For the heck of it, we also check the shipments made from the plant, but there was no increase there either. In fact, the only increase is in overdue shipments—they've grown rapidly over the last nine months.

Lou looks up at me from the graphs.

"Al, I don't know what you're trying to prove," he says. "But if you want to broadcast some success story on how the robots are going to save the plant with increased sales, the evidence just doesn't exist. The data practically say the opposite."

"That's exactly what I was afraid of," I say.

"What do you mean?"

"I'll explain it in a minute. Let's look at inventories," I tell him. "I want to find out what happened to our work-in-process on parts produced by the robots."

Lou gives up.

"I can't help you there," he says. "I don't have anything on inventories by part number."

"Okay, let's get Stacey in on this."

Stacey Potazenik manages inventory control for the plant. Lou makes a call and pulls her out of another meeting.

Stacey is a woman in her early 40's. She's tall, thin, and brisk in her manner. Her hair is black with strands of gray and she wears big, round glasses. She is always dressed in jackets and skirts; never have I seen her in a blouse with any kind of lace, ribbon or frill. I know almost nothing about her personal life. She wears a ring, but she's never mentioned a husband. She rarely mentions anything about her life outside the plant. I do know she works hard.

When she comes in to see us, I ask her about work-in-process on those parts passing through the robot areas.

"Do you want exact numbers?" she asks.

"No, we just need to know the trends," I say.

"Well, I can tell you without looking that inventories went up on those parts," Stacey says.

"Recently?"

"No, it's been happening since late last summer, around the end of the third quarter," she says. "And you can't blame me for it—even though everyone always does—because I fought it every step of the way."

"What do you mean?"

"You remember, don't you? Or maybe you weren't here then. But when the reports came in, we found the robots in welding were only running at something like thirty percent efficiency. And the other robots weren't much better. Nobody would stand for that."

I look over at Lou.

"We had to do something," he says. "Frost would have had my head if I hadn't spoken up. Those things were brand new and very expensive. They'd never pay for themselves in the projected time if we kept them at thirty percent."

"Okay, hold on a minute," I tell him. I turn back to Stacey. "What did you do then?"

She says, "What *could* I do? I had to release more materials to the floor in all the areas feeding the robots. Giving the robots more to produce increased their efficiencies. But ever since then, we've been ending each month with a surplus of those parts."

"But the important thing was that efficiencies did go up," says Lou, trying to add a bright note. "Nobody can find fault with us on that."

"I'm not sure of that at all any more," I say. "Stacey, why are we getting that surplus? How come we aren't consuming those parts?"

"Well, in a lot of cases, we don't have any orders to fill at present which would call for those parts," she says. "And in the cases where we do have orders, we just can't seem to get enough of the other parts we need."

"How come?"

"You'd have to ask Bob Donovan about that," Stacey says.

"Lou, let's have Bob paged," I say.

Bob comes into the office with a smear of grease on his white shirt right over the bulge of his beer gut, and he's talking nonstop about what's going on with the breakdown of the automatic testing machines.

"Bob," I tell him, "forget about that for now."

"Something else wrong?" he asks.

"Yes, there is. We've just been talking about our local celebrities, the robots," I say.

Bob glances from side to side, wondering, I suppose, what we've been saying.

"What are you worried about them for?" he asks. "The robots work pretty good now."

"We're not so sure about that," I say. "Stacey tells me we've got an excess of parts built by the robots. But in some instances we can't get enough of certain other parts to assemble and ship our orders."

Bob says, "It isn't that we can't *get* enough parts—it's more that we can't seem to get them when we need them. That's true even with a lot of the robot parts. We'll have a pile of something like, say, a CD-50 sit around for months waiting for control boxes. Then we'll get the control boxes, but we won't have something else. Finally we get the something else, and we build the order and ship it. Next thing you know, you're looking around for a CD-50 and you can't find any. We'll have tons of CD-45's and 80's, but no 50's. So we wait. And by the time we get the 50's again, all the control boxes are gone."

"And so on, and so on, and so on," says Stacey.

"But, Stacey, you said the robots were producing a lot of parts for which we don't have product orders," I say. "That means we're producing parts we don't need."

"Everybody tells me we'll use them eventually," she says. Then she adds, "Look, it's the same game everybody plays. Whenever efficiencies take a drop, everybody draws against the future forecast to keep busy. We build inventory. If the forecast doesn't hold up, there's hell to pay. Well, that's what's happening now. We've been building inventory for the better part of a year, and the market hasn't helped us one damn bit."

"I know, Stacey, I know," I tell her. "And I'm not blaming you or anybody. I'm just trying to figure this out."

Restless, I get up and pace.

I say, "So the bottom line is this: to give the robots more to do, we released more materials."

"Which, in turn, increased inventories," says Stacey.

"Which has increased our costs," I add.

"But the cost of those parts went down," says Lou.

"Did it?" I ask. "What about the added carrying cost of

inventory? That's operational expense. And if that went up, how could the cost of parts go down?"

"Look, it depends on volume," says Lou.

"Exactly," I say. *"Sales* volume . . . that's what matters. And when we've got parts that can't be assembled into a product and sold because we don't have the other components, or because we don't have the orders, then we're increasing our costs."

"Al," says Bob, "are you trying to tell us we got screwed by the robots?"

I sit down again.

"We haven't been managing according to the goal," I mutter.

Lou squints. "The goal? You mean our objectives for the month?"

I look around at them.

"I think I need to explain a few things."

# 10

An hour and a half later, I've gone over it all with them.
We're in the conference room, which I've commandeered because it has a chalkboard. On that chalkboard, I've drawn a diagram of the goal. Just now I've written out the definitions of the
three measurements.

All of them are quiet. Finally, Lou speaks up and says,
"Where the heck did you get these definitions anyway?"

"My old physics teacher gave them to me."

"Who?" asks Bob.

"Your old physics teacher?" asks Lou.

"Yeah," I say defensively. "What about it?"

"So what's his name?" asks Bob.

"Or what's 'her' name," says Stacey.

"His name is Jonah. He's from Israel."

Bob says, "Well, what I want to know is, how come in
throughput he says 'sales'? We're manufacturing. We've got
nothing to do with sales; that's marketing."

I shrug. After all, I asked the same question over the phone.
Jonah said the definitions were precise, but I don't know how
to answer Bob. I turn toward the window. Then I see what I
should have remembered.

"Come here," I say to Bob.

He lumbers over. I put a hand on his shoulder and point out
the window.

"What are those?" I ask him.

"Warehouses," he says.

"For what?"

"Finished goods."

"Would the company stay in business if all it did was manufacture products to fill those warehouses?"

"Okay, okay," Bob says sheepishly, seeing the meaning
now. "So we got to sell the stuff to make money."

Lou is still staring at the board.

"Interesting, isn't it, that each one of those definitions contains the word *money*," he says. "Throughput is the money
coming in. Inventory is the money currently inside the system.
And operational expense is the money we have to pay out to

make throughput happen. One measurement for the incoming money, one for the money still stuck inside, and one for the money going out."

"Well, if you think about all the investment represented by what we've got sitting out there on the floor, you know for sure that inventory is money," says Stacey. "But what bothers me is that I don't see how he's treating value added to materials by direct labor."

"I wondered the same thing, and I can only tell you what he told me," I say.

"Which is?"

"He said he thinks that it's just better if value added isn't taken into account. He said that it gets rid of the 'confusion' about what's an investment and what's an expense," I say.

Stacey and the rest of us think about this for a minute. The room gets quiet again.

Then Stacey says, "Maybe Jonah feels direct labor shouldn't be a part of inventory because the time of the employees isn't what we're really selling. We 'buy' time from our employees, in a sense, but we don't sell that time to a customer—unless we're talking about service."

"Hey, hold it," says Bob. "Now look here: if we're selling the product, aren't we also selling the time invested in that product?"

"Okay, but what about idle time?" I ask.

Lou butts in to settle it, saying, "All this is, if I understand it correctly, is a different way of doing the accounting. All employee time—whether it's direct or indirect, idle time or operating time, or whatever—is *operational expense,* according to Jonah. You're still accounting for it. It's just that his way is simpler, and you don't have to play as many games."

Bob puffs out his chest. "Games? We, in operations, are honest, hard–working folk who do not have time for games."

"Yeah, you're too busy turning idle time into process time with the stroke of a pen," says Lou.

"Or turning process time into more piles of inventory," says Stacey.

They go on bantering about this for a minute. Meanwhile, I'm thinking there might be something more to this besides simplification. Jonah mentioned *confusion* between investment and expense; are we confused enough now to be doing something we shouldn't? Then I hear Stacey talking.

"But how do we know the value of our finished goods?" she asks.

"First of all, the market determines the value of the product," says Lou. "And in order for the corporation to make money, the value of the product—and the price we're charging—has to be greater than the combination of the investment in inventory and the total operational expense per unit of what we sell."

I see by the look on Bob's face that he's very skeptical. I ask him what's bothering him.

"Hey, man, this is crazy," Bob grumbles.

"Why?" asks Lou.

"It won't work!" says Bob. "How can you account for everything in the whole damn system with three lousy measurements?"

"Well," says Lou as he ponders the board. "Name something that won't fit in one of those three."

"Tooling, machines . . ." Bob counts them on with his fingers. "This building, the whole plant!"

"Those are in there," says Lou.

"Where?" asks Bob.

Lou turns to him. "Look, those things are part one and part the other. If you've got a machine, the depreciation on that machine is operational expense. Whatever portion of the investment still remains in the machine, which could be sold, is inventory."

"Inventory? I thought inventory was products, and parts and so on," says Bob. "You know, the stuff we're going to sell."

Lou smiles. "Bob, the whole plant is an investment which can be sold—for the right price and under the right circumstances."

And maybe sooner than we'd like, I think.

Stacey says, "So investment is the same thing as inventory."

"What about lubricating oil for the machines?" asks Bob.

"It's operational expense," I tell him. "We're not going to sell that oil to a customer."

"How about scrap?" he asks.

"That's operational expense, too."

"Yeah? What about what we sell to the scrap dealer?"

"Okay, then it's the same as a machine," says Lou. "Any money we've lost is operational expense; any investment that we can sell is inventory."

"The carrying costs have to be operational expense, don't they?" asks Stacey.

Lou and I both nod.

Then I think about the "soft" things in business, things like knowledge—knowledge from consultants, knowledge gained from our own research and development. I throw it out to them to see how they think those things should be classified.

Money for knowledge has us stumped for a while. Then we decide it depends, quite simply, upon what the knowledge is used for. If it's knowledge, say, which gives us a new manufacturing process, something that helps turn inventory into throughput, then the knowledge is operational expense. If we intend to sell the knowledge, as in the case of a patent or a technology license, then it's inventory. But if the knowledge pertains to a product which UniCo itself will build, it's like a machine—an investment to make money which will depreciate in value as time goes on. And, again, the investment that can be sold is inventory; the depreciation is operational expense.

"I got one for you," says Bob. "Here's one that doesn't fit: Granby's chauffeur."

"What?"

"You know, the old buy in the black suit who drives J. Bart Granby's limo for him," says Bob.

"He's operational expense," says Lou.

"Like hell he is! You tell me now Granby's chauffeur turns inventory into throughput," says Bob, and looks around as if he's really got us on this one. "I bet his chauffeur doesn't even know that inventory and throughput exist."

"Unfortunately, neither do some of our secretaries," says Stacey.

I say, "You don't have to have your hands on the product in order to turn inventory into throughput. Every day, Bob, you're out there helping to turn inventory into throughput. But to the people on the floor, it probably looks like all you do is walk around and make life complicated for everyone."

"Yeah, no appreciation from nobody," Bob pouts, "but you still haven't told me how the chauffeur fits in."

"Well, maybe the chauffeur helps Granby have more time to think and deal with customers, etc., while he's commuting here and there," I suggest.

"Bob, why don't you ask Mr. Granby next time you two have lunch," says Stacey.

"That's not as funny as you think," I say. "I just heard this morning that Granby may be coming here to make a video tape on robots."

"Granby's coming here?" asks Bob.

"And if Granby's coming, you can bet Bill Peach and all the others will be tagging along," says Stacey.

"Just what we need," grumbles Lou.

Stacey turns to Bob. "You see now why Al's asking questions about the robots. We've got to look good for Granby."

"We do look good," says Lou. "The efficiencies there are quite acceptable; Granby will not be embarrassed by appearing with the robots on tape."

But I say, "Dammit, I don't care about Granby and his videotape. In fact, I will lay odds that the tape will never be shot here anyway, but that's beside the point. The problem is that everybody—including me until now—has thought these robots have been a big productivity improvement. And we just learned that they're not productive in terms of the goal. The way we've been using them, they're actually *counter*-productive."

Everyone is silent.

Finally, Stacey has the courage to say, "Okay, so somehow we've got to make the robots productive in terms of the goal."

"We've got to do more than that," I say. I turn to Bob and Stacey. "Listen, I've already told Lou, and I guess this is as good a time as any to tell the both of you. I know you'll hear it eventually anyhow."

"Hear what?" asks Bob.

"We've been given an ultimatum by Peach—three months to turn the plant around or he closes us down for good," I say.

Both of them are stunned for a few moments. Then they're both firing questions at me. I take a few minutes and tell them what I know—avoiding the news about the division; I don't want to send them into panic.

Finally, I say, "I know it doesn't seem like a lot of time. It isn't. But until they kick me out of here, I'm not giving up. What you decide to do is your own business, but if you want out, I suggest you leave now. Because for the next three months, I'm going to need everything you can give me. If we can make this place show any progress, I'm going to go to Peach and do whatever I have to make him give us more time."

"Do you really think we can do it?" asks Lou.

"I honestly don't know," I say. "But at least now we can see some of what we're doing wrong."

"So what can we do that's different?" asks Bob.

"Why don't we stop pushing materials through the robots and try to reduce inventories?" suggests Stacey.

"Hey, I'm all for lower inventories," says Bob. "But if we don't produce, our efficiencies go down. Then we're right back where we started."

"Peach isn't going to give us a second chance if all we give him is lower efficiencies," says Lou. "He wants higher efficiencies, not lower."

I run my fingers through my hair.

Then Stacey says, "Maybe you should try calling this guy, Jonah, again. He seems like he's got a good handle on what's what."

"Yeah, at least we could find out what he has to say," says Lou.

"Well, I talked to him last night. That's when he gave me all this stuff," I say, waving to the definitions on the board. "He was supposed to call me . . ."

I look at their faces.

"Well, okay, I'll try him again," I say and reach for my briefcase to get the London number.

I put through a call from the phone in the conference room with the three of them listening expectantly around the table. But he isn't there anymore. Instead I end up talking to some secretary.

"Ah, yes, Mr. Rogo," she says. "Jonah tried to call you, but your secretary said you were in a meeting. He wanted to talk to you before he left London today, but I'm afraid you've missed him."

"Where is he going to be next?" I ask.

"He was flying by Concorde to New York. Perhaps you can catch him at his hotel," she says.

I take down the name of the hotel and thank her. Then I get the number in New York from directory assistance, and expecting only to be able to leave a message for him, I try it. The switchboard puts me through.

"Hello?" says a sleepy voice.

"Jonah? This is Alex Rogo. Did I wake you?"

77

"As a matter of fact, you did."

"Oh, I'm sorry—I'll try not to keep you long. But I really need to talk to you at greater length about what we were discussing last night," I tell him.

"Last night?" he asks. "Yes, I suppose it was 'last night' your time."

"Maybe we could make arrangements for you to come to my plant and meet with me and my staff," I suggest.

"Well, the problem is I have commitments lined up for the next three weeks, and then I'm going back to Israel," he says.

"But, you see, I can't wait that long," I say. "I've got some major problems I have to solve and not a lot of time. I understand now what you meant about the robots and productivity. But my staff and I don't know what the next step should be and . . . uh, well, maybe if I explained a few things to you—"

"Alex, I would like to help you, but I also need to get some sleep. I'm exhausted," he says. "But I have a suggestion: if your schedule permits, why don't I meet with you here tomorrow morning at seven for breakfast at my hotel."

"Tomorrow?"

"That's right," he says. "We'll have about an hour and we can talk. Otherwise . . ."

I look around at the others, all of them watching me anxiously. I tell Jonah to hold on for a second.

"He wants me to come to New York tomorrow," I tell them. "Can anybody think of a reason why I shouldn't go?"

"Are you kidding?" says Stacey.

"Go for it," says Bob.

"What have you got to lose?" says Lou.

I take my hand off the mouthpiece. "Okay, I'll be there," I say.

"Excellent!" Jonah says with relief. "Until then, good night."

When I get back to my office, Fran looks up with surprise from her work.

"So there you are!" she says and reaches for the message slips. "This man called you twice from London. He wouldn't say whether it was important or not."

I say, "I've got a job for you: find a way to get me to New York tonight."

# 11

But Julie does not understand.

"Thanks for the advance notice," she says.

"If I'd known earlier, I'd have told you," I say.

"Everything is unexpected with you lately," she says.

"Don't I always tell you when I know I've got trips coming up?"

She fidgets next to the bedroom door. I'm packing an overnight bag which lies open on the bed. We're alone; Sharon is down the street at a friend's house, and Davey is at band practice.

"When is this going to end?" she asks.

I stop midway through taking some underwear from a drawer. I'm getting irritated by the questions because we just went over the whole thing five minutes ago. Why is it so hard for her to understand?

"Julie, I just don't know," I say. "I've got a lot of problems to solve."

More fidgeting. She doesn't like it. It occurs to me that maybe she doesn't trust me or something.

"Hey, I'll call you as soon as I get to New York," I tell her. "Okay?"

She turns as if she might walk out of the room.

"Fine. Call," she says, "but I might not be here."

I stop again.

"What do you mean by that?"

"I might be out someplace," she says.

"Oh," I say. "Well, I guess I'll have to take my chances."

"I guess you will," she says, furious now, on her way out the door.

I grab an extra shirt and slam the drawer shut. When I finish packing, I go looking for her. I find her in the living room. She stands by the window, biting the end of her thumb. I take her hand and kiss the thumb. Then I try to hug her.

"Listen, I know I've been undependable lately," I say. "But this is important. It's for the plant—"

She shakes her head, pulls away. I follow her into the kitchen. She stands with her back to me.

"Everything is for your job," she says. "It's all you think

about. I can't even count on you for dinner. And the kids are asking me why you're like this—"

There is a tear forming in the corner of her eye. I reach to wipe it away, but she brushes my hand aside.

"No!" she says. "Just go catch your plane to wherever it is you're going."

"Julie—"

She walks past me.

"Julie, this is not fair!" I yell at her.

She turns to me.

"That's right," she says. "*You* are not being fair. To me or to your children."

She goes upstairs without looking back. And I don't even have time to settle this; I'm already late for my flight. I pick up my bag in the hall, sling it over my shoulder, and grab my briefcase on my way out the door.

At 7:10 the next morning, I'm waiting in the hotel lobby for Jonah. He's a few minutes late, but that's not what's on my mind as I pace the carpeted floor. I'm thinking about Julie. I'm worried about her . . . about us. After I checked into my room last night, I tried to call home. No answer. Not even one of the kids picked up the phone. I walked around the room for half an hour, kicked a few things, and tried calling again. Still no answer. From then until two in the morning, I dialed the number every fifteen minutes. Nobody home. At one point I tried the airlines to see if I could get on a plane back, but nothing was flying in that direction at that hour. I finally fell asleep. My wake-up call got me out of bed at six o'clock. I tried the number twice before I left my room this morning. The second time, I let it ring for five minutes. Still no answer.

"Alex!"

I turn. Jonah is walking toward me. He's wearing a white shirt—no tie, no jacket—and plain trousers.

"Good morning," I say as we shake hands. I notice his eyes are puffy, like those of someone who hasn't had a lot of sleep; I think that mine probably look the same.

"Sorry I'm late," he says. "I had dinner last night with some associates and we got into a discussion which went, I believe, until three o'clock in the morning. Let's get a table for breakfast."

I walk with him into the restaurant and the maitre d' leads us to a table with a white linen cloth.

"How did you do with the measurements I defined for you over the telephone?" he asks after we've sat down.

I switch my mind to business, and tell him how I expressed the goal with his measurements. Jonah seems very pleased.

"Excellent," he says. "You have done very well."

"Well, thanks, but I'm afraid I need more than a goal and some measurements to save my plant."

"To save your plant?" he asks.

I say, "Well . . . yes, that's why I'm here. I mean, I didn't just call you to talk philosophy."

He smiles. "No, I didn't think you tracked me down purely for the love of truth. Okay, Alex, tell me what's going on."

"This is confidential," I say to him. Then I explain the situation with the plant and the three-month deadline before it gets closed. Jonah listens attentively. When I've finished, he sits back.

"What do you expect from me?" he asks.

"I don't know if there is one, but I'd like you to help me find the answer that will let me keep my plant alive and my people working," I say.

Jonah looks away for a moment.

"I'll tell you *my* problem," he says. "I have an unbelievable schedule. That's why we're meeting at this ungodly hour, incidentally. With the commitments I already have, there is no way I can spend the time to do all the things you probably would expect from a consultant."

I sigh, very disappointed. I say, "Okay, if you're too busy—"

"Wait, I'm not finished," he says. "That doesn't mean you can't save your plant. I don't have time to solve your problems for you. But that wouldn't be the best thing for you anyway—"

"What do you mean?" I interrupt.

Jonah holds up his hand. "Let me finish!" he says. "From what I've heard, I think you can solve your own problems. What I will do is give you some basic rules to apply. If you and your people follow them intelligently, I think you will save your plant. Fair enough?"

"But, Jonah, we've only got three months," I say.

He nods impatiently. "I know, I know," he says. "Three months is more than enough time to show improvement . . . if you are diligent, that is. And if you aren't, then nothing I say could save you anyway.''

"Oh, you can count on our diligence, for sure," I say.

"Shall we try it then?" he asks.

"Frankly, I don't know what else to do," I say. Then I smile. "I guess I'd better ask what this is going to cost me. Do you have some kind of standard rate or something?"

"No, I don't," he says. "But I'll make a deal with you. Just pay me the value of what you learn from me."

"How will I know what that is?"

"You should have a reasonable idea after we're finished. If your plant folds, then obviously the value of your learning won't have been much; you won't owe me anything. If, on the other hand, you learn enough from me to make billions, then you should pay me accordingly," he says.

I laugh. What have I got to lose?

"Okay, fair enough," I say finally.

We shake hands across the table.

A waiter interrupts to ask if we're ready to order. Neither of us have opened the menus, but it turns out we both just want coffee. The waiter informs us there's a five-dollar minimum for sitting in the dining room. So Jonah tells him to bring us both our own pots of coffee and a quart of milk. He gives us a dirty look and vanishes.

"Now then," Jonah says. "Where shall we begin . . ."

"I thought maybe first we could focus on the robots," I tell him.

Jonah shakes his head.

"Alex, forget about your robots for now. They're like some new industrial toy everybody's discovered. You've got much more fundamental things to concern yourself with," he says.

"But you're not taking into account how important they are to us," I tell him. "They're some of our most expensive equipment. We absolutely have to keep them productive."

"Productive with respect to what?" he asks with an edge in his voice.

"Okay, right . . . we have to keep them productive in terms of the goal," I say. "But I need high efficiencies to make those things pay for themselves, and I only get the efficiencies if they're making parts."

Jonah is shaking his head again.

"Alex, you told me in our first meeting that your plant has very good efficiencies overall. If your efficiencies are so good, then why is your plant in trouble?"

He takes a cigar out of his shirt pocket and bites the end off of it.

"Okay, look, I have to care about efficiencies if only for the reason that my management cares about them," I tell him.

"What's more important to your management, Alex: efficiencies or money?" he asks.

"Money, of course. But isn't high efficiency essential to making money?" I ask him.

"Most of the time, your struggle for high efficiencies is taking you in the opposite direction of your goal."

"I don't understand," I say. "And even if I did, my management wouldn't."

But Jonah lights his cigar and says between puffs, "Okay, let's see if I can help you understand with some basic questions and answers. First tell me this: when you see one of your workers standing idle with nothing to do, is that good or bad for the company?"

"It's bad, of course," I say.

"Always?"

I feel this is a trick question.

"Well, we have to do maintenance—"

"No, no, no, I'm talking about a production employee who is idle because there is no product to be worked on."

"Yes, that's always bad," I say.

"Why?"

I chuckle. "Isn't it obvious? Because it's a waste of money! What are we supposed to do, pay people to do nothing? We can't afford to have idle time. Our costs are too high to tolerate it. It's inefficiency, it's low productivity—no matter how you measure it."

He leans forward as if he's going to whisper a big secret to me.

"Let me tell you something," he says. "A plant in which everyone is working all the time is very inefficient."

"Pardon me?"

"You heard me."

"But how can you prove that?" I ask.

He says, "You've already proven it in your own plant. It's right in front of your eyes. But you don't see it."

Now I shake my head. I say, "Jonah, I don't think we're communicating. You see, in my plant, I don't have extra people. The only way we can get products out the door is to keep everyone working constantly."

"Tell me, Alex, do you have excess inventories in your plant?" he asks.

"Yes, we do," I say.

"Do you have a lot of excess inventories?"

"Well . . . yes."

"Do you have *a lot* of a lot of excess inventories?"

"Yeah, okay, we do have a lot of a lot of excess, but what's the point?"

"Do you realize that the only way you can create excess inventories is by having excess manpower?" he says.

I think about it. After a minute, I have to conclude he's right; machines don't set up and run themselves. People had to create the excess inventory.

"What are you suggesting I do?" I ask. "Lay off more people? I'm practically down to a skeleton force now."

"No, I'm not suggesting that you lay off more people. But I am suggesting that you question how you are managing the capacity of your plant. And let me tell you, it is not according to the goal."

Between us, the waiter sets down two elegant silver pots with steam coming out of their spouts. He puts out a pitcher of cream and pours the coffee. While he does this, I find myself staring toward the window. After a few seconds, I feel Jonah reach over and touch my sleeve.

"Here's what's happening," he says. "Out there in the world at large, you've got a market demand for so much of whatever it is you're producing. And inside your company, you've got so many resources, each of which has so much capacity, to fill that demand. Now, before I go on, do you know what I mean by a 'balanced plant'?"

"You mean balancing a production line?" I ask.

He says, "A balanced plant is essentially what every manufacturing manager in the whole western world has struggled to achieve. It's a plant where the capacity of each and every resource is balanced exactly with demand from the market. Do you know why managers try to do this?"

I tell him, "Well, because if we don't have enough capacity, we're cheating ourselves out of potential throughput. And if we have more than enough capacity, we're wasting money. We're missing an opportunity to reduce operational expense."

"Yes, that's exactly what everybody thinks," says Jonah. "And the tendency for most managers is to trim capacity wherever they can, so no resource is idle, and everybody has something to work on."

"Yeah, sure, I know what you're talking about," I say. "We do that at our plant. In fact, it's done at every plant I've ever seen."

"Do you run a balanced plant?" he asks.

"Well, it's as balanced as we can make it. Of course, we've got some machines sitting idle, but generally that's just outdated equipment. As for people, we've trimmed our capacity as much as we can," I explain. "But nobody ever runs a perfectly balanced plant."

"Funny, I don't know of any balanced plants either," he says. "Why do you think it is that nobody after all this time and effort has ever succeeded in running a balanced plant?"

"I can give you a lot of reasons. The number one reason is that conditions are always changing on us," I say.

"No, actually that isn't the number one reason," he says.

"Sure it is! Look at the things I have to contend with—my vendors, for example. We'll be in the middle of a hot order and discover that the vendor sent us a bad batch of parts. Or look at all the variables in my work force—absenteeism, people who don't care about quality, employee turnover, you name it. And then there's the market itself. The market is always changing. So it's no wonder we get too much capacity in one area and not enough in another."

"Alex, the real reason you cannot balance your plant is much more basic than all of those factors you mentioned. All of those are relatively minor."

"Minor?"

"The real reason is that the closer you come to a balanced plant, the closer you are to bankruptcy."

"Come on!" I say. "You've got to be kidding me."

"Look at this obsession with trimming capacity in terms of

the goal," he says. "When you lay off people, do you increase sales?"

"No, of course not," I say.

"Do you reduce your inventory?" he asks.

"No, not by cutting people," I say. "What we do by laying off workers is cut our expenses."

"Yes, exactly," Jonah says. "You improve only one measurement, operational expense."

"Isn't that enough?"

"Alex, the goal is not to reduce operational expense by itself. The goal is not to improve one measurement in isolation. The goal is to reduce operational expense and reduce inventory while simultaneously increasing throughput," says Jonah.

"Fine. I agree with that," I say. "But if we reduce expenses, and inventory and throughput stay the same, aren't we better off?"

"Yes, *if* you do not increase inventory and/or reduce throughput," he says.

"Okay, right. But balancing capacity doesn't affect either one," I say.

"Oh? It doesn't? How do you know that?"

"We just said—"

"I didn't say anything of the sort. I asked you. And you *assumed* that if you trim capacity to balance with market demand you won't affect throughput or inventory," he says. "But, in fact, that assumption—which is practically universal in the western business world—is totally wrong."

"How do you know it's wrong?"

"For one thing, there is a mathematical proof which could clearly show that when capacity is trimmed exactly to marketing demands, no more and no less, throughput goes down, while inventory goes through the roof," he says. "And because inventory goes up, the *carrying cost* of inventory—which is operational expense—goes up. So it's questionable whether you can even fulfill the intended reduction in your total operational expense, the one measurement you expected to improve."

"How can that be?"

"Because of the combination of two phenomena which are found in every plant," he says. "One phenomenon is called 'dependent events.' Do you know what I mean by that term? I mean that an event, or a series of events, must take place before another can begin . . . the subsequent event *depends* upon the ones prior to it. You follow?''

"Yeah, sure," I say. "But what's the big deal about that?"

"The big deal occurs when dependent events are in combination with another phenomenon called 'statistical fluctuations,' " he says. "Do you know what those are?"

I shrug. "Fluctuations in statistics, right?"

"Let me put it this way," he says. "You know that some types of information can be determined precisely. For instance, if we need to know the seating capacity in this restaurant, we can determine it precisely by counting the number of chairs at each table."

He points around the room.

"But there are other kinds of information we cannot precisely predict. Like how long it will take the waiter to bring us our check. Or how long it will take the chef to make an omelet. Or how many eggs the kitchen will need today. These types of information vary from one instance to the next. They are subject to *statistical fluctuations.*"

"Yeah, but you can generally get an idea of what all those are going to be based on experience," I say.

"But only within a range. Last time, the waiter brought the check in five minutes and 42 seconds. The time before it only took two minutes. And today? Who knows? Could be three, four hours," he says, looking around. "Where the hell is he?"

"Yeah, but if the chef is doing a banquet and he knows how many people are coming and he knows they're all having omelets, then he knows how many eggs he's going to need," I say.

"Exactly?" asks Jonah. "Suppose he drops one on the floor?"

"Okay, so he has a couple extra."

"Most of the factors critical to running your plant successfully cannot be determined precisely ahead of time," he says.

The arm of the waiter comes between us as he puts the totaled check on the table. I pull it to my side of the table.

"All right, I agree," I say. "But in the case of a worker doing the same job day in, day out, those fluctuations average out over a period of time. Frankly, I can't see what either one of those two phenomena have to do with anything."

Jonah stands up, ready to leave.

"I'm not talking about the one or the other alone," he says, "but about the effect of the two of them together. Which is what I want you to think about, because I have to go."

"You're leaving?" I ask.

"I have to," he says.

"Jonah, you can't just run off like this."

"There are clients waiting for me," he says.

"Jonah, I don't have time for riddles. I need answers," I tell him.

He puts his hand on my arm.

"Alex, if I simply told you what to do, ultimately you would fail. You have to gain the understanding for yourself in order to make the rules work," he says.

He shakes my hand.

"Until next time, Alex. Call me when you can tell me what the combination of the two phenomena mean to your plant."

Then he hurries away. Fuming inside, I flag down the waiter and hand him the check and some money. Without waiting for the change, I follow in the direction of Jonah out to the lobby.

I claim my overnight bag from the bellhop at the desk where I checked it, and sling it over my shoulder. As I turn, I see Jonah, still without jacket or tie, talking to a handsome man in a blue pinstripe suit over by the doors to the street. They go through the doors together, and I trudge along a few steps behind them. The man leads Jonah to a black limousine waiting at the curb. As they approach, a chauffeur hops out to open the rear door for them.

I hear the handsome man in the blue pinstripe saying as he gets into the limo behind Jonah, "After the facilities tour, we're scheduled for a meeting with the chairman and several of the board . . ." Waiting inside for them is a silver-haired man who shakes Jonah's hand. The chauffeur closes the door and returns to the wheel. I can see only the vague silhouettes of their heads behind the dark glass as the big car quietly eases into traffic.

I get into a cab.

The driver asks, "Where to, chief?"

# 12

There is a guy I heard about in UniCo who came home from work one night, walked in, and said, "Hi, honey, I'm home!" And his greeting echoed back to him from the empty rooms of his house. His wife had taken everything: the kids, the dog, the goldfish, the furniture, the carpets, the appliances, the curtains, the pictures on the wall, the toothpaste, everything. Well, just about everything—actually, she left him two things: his clothes (which were in a heap on the floor of the bedroom by the closet; she had even taken the hangers), and a note written in lipstick on the bathroom mirror which said, "Good-bye, you bastard!"

As I drive down the street to my house, that kind of vision is running through my mind, and has been periodically since last night. Before I pull into the driveway, I look at the lawn for the telltale signs of tracks left by the wheels of a moving van, but the lawn is unmarred.

I park the Buick in front of the garage. On my way inside, I peek through the glass. Julie's Accord is parked inside, and I look at the sky and silently say, "Thank You."

She's sitting at the kitchen table, her back to me as I come in. I startle her. She stands up right away and turns around. We stare at each other for a second. I can see that the rims of her eyes are red.

"Hi," I say.

"What are you doing home?" Julie asks.

I laugh—not a nice laugh, an exasperated laugh.

"What am *I* doing home? I'm looking for *you!*" I say.

"Well, here I am. Take a good look," she says, frowning at me.

"Yeah, right, here you are now," I say. "But what I want to know is where you were last night."

"I was out," she says.

"All night?"

She's prepared for the question.

"Gee, I'm surprised you even knew I was gone," she says.

"Come on, Julie, let's cut the crap. I must have called the number here a hundred times last night. I was worried sick about you. I tried it again this morning and nobody answered. So I

*89*

know you were gone all night," I say. "And, by the way, where were the kids?"

"They stayed with friends," she says.

"On a school night?" I ask. "And what about you? Did you stay with a *friend?*"

She puts her hands on her hips.

"Yes, as a matter of fact, I did stay with a friend," she says.

"Man or woman?"

Her eyes get hard on me. She takes a step forward.

"You don't care if I'm home with the kids night after night," she says. "But if I go away for one night, all of a sudden you have to know where I've been, what I've done."

"I just feel you owe me some explanation," I say.

"How many times have you been late, or out of town, or who knows where?" she asks.

"But that's business," I say. "And I always tell you where I've been if you ask. Now I'm asking."

"There's nothing to tell," she says. "All that happened was I went out with Jane."

"Jane?" It takes me a minute to remember her. "You mean your friend from where we used to live? You drove all the way back there?"

"I just had to talk to someone," she says. "By the time we'd finished talking, I'd had too much to drink to drive home. Anyway, I knew the kids were okay until morning. So I just stayed at Jane's."

"Okay, but why? How did this come over you all of a sudden?" I ask her.

"Come over me? All of a sudden? Alex, you go off and leave me night after night. It's no wonder that I'm lonely. Nothing suddenly came over me. Ever since you got into management, your career has come first and everyone else takes whatever is left."

"Julie, I've just tried to make a good living for you and the kids," I tell her.

"Is that all? Then why do you keep taking the promotions?"

"What am I supposed to do, turn them down?"

She doesn't answer.

"Look, I put in the hours because I have to, not because I want to," I tell her.

She still doesn't say anything.

"All right, look: I promise I'll make more time for you and the kids," I say. "Honest, I'll spend more time at home."

"Al, it's not going to work. Even when you're home, you're at the office. Sometimes I've seen the kids tell you something two or three times before you hear them."

"It won't be like that when I get out of the jam I'm in right now," I say.

"Do you hear what you're saying? 'When I get out of the jam I'm in right now.' Do you think it's going to change? You've said all that before, Al. Do you know how many times we've been over this?"

"Okay, you're right. We have been over it a lot of times. But, right now, there's nothing I can do," I say.

She looks up at the sky and says, "Your job has always been on the line. Always. So if you're such a marginal employee, why do they keep giving you promotions and more money?"

I pinch the bridge of my nose.

"How do I make you understand this," I say. "I'm not up for another promotion or pay raise this time. This time it's different. Julie, you have no idea what kind of problems I've got at the plant."

"And you have no idea what it's like here at home," she says.

I say, "Okay, look, I'd like to spend more time at home, but the problem is getting the time."

"I don't need all your time," she says. "But I do need some of it, and so do the kids."

"I know that. But to save this plant, I'm going to have to give it all I've got for the next couple of months."

"Couldn't you at least come home for dinner most of the time?" she asks. "The evenings are when I miss you the most. All of us do. It's empty around here without you, even with the kids for company."

"Nice to know I'm wanted. But sometimes I even need the evenings. I just don't have enough time during the day to get to things like paperwork," I say.

"Why don't you bring the paperwork home," she suggests. "Do it here. If you did that, at least we could see you. And maybe I could even help you with some of it."

I lean back. "I don't know if I'll be able to concentrate, but . . . okay, let's try it."

She smiles. "You mean it?"

"Sure, if it doesn't work, we can talk about it," I say. "Deal?"

"Deal," she says.

I lean toward her and ask, "Want to seal it with a handshake or a kiss?"

She comes around the table and sits on my lap and kisses me.

"You know, I sure missed you last night," I tell her.

"Did you?" she says. "I really missed you too. I had no idea singles bars could be so depressing."

"*Singles bars?*"

"It was Jane's idea," she says. "Honest."

I shake my head. "I don't want to hear about it."

"But Jane showed me some new dance steps," she says. "And maybe this weekend—"

I give her a squeeze. "If you want to do something this weekend, baby, I'm all yours."

"Great," she says and whispers in my ear, "You know, it's Friday, so . . . why don't we start early?"

She kisses me again.

And I say, "Julie, I'd really love to, but . . ."

"But?"

"I really should check in at the plant," I say.

She stands up. "Okay, but promise me you'll hurry home tonight."

"Promise," I tell her. "Really, it's going to be a great weekend."

# 13

I open my eyes Saturday morning to see a drab green blur. The blur turns out to be my son, Dave, dressed in his Boy Scout uniform. He is shaking my arm.

"Davey, what are you doing here?" I ask.

He says, "Dad, it's seven o'clock!"

"Seven o'clock? I'm trying to sleep. Aren't you supposed to be watching television or something?"

"We'll be late," he says.

"*We* will be late? For what?"

"For the overnight hike!" he says. "Remember? You promised me I could volunteer you to go along and help the troopmaster."

I mutter something no Boy Scout should ever hear. But Dave isn't fazed.

"Come on. Just get in the shower," he says, as he pulls me out of bed. "I packed your gear last night. Everything's in the car already. We just have to get there by eight."

I manage a last look at Julie, her eyes still shut, and the warm soft mattress as Davey drags me through the door.

An hour and ten minutes later, my son and I arrive at the edge of some forest. Waiting for us is the troop: fifteen boys outfitted in caps, neckerchiefs, merit badges, the works.

Before I have time to say, "Where's the troopmaster?", the other few parents who happen to be lingering with the boys take off in their cars, all pedals to the metal. Looking around, I see that I am the only adult in sight.

"Our troopmaster couldn't make it," says one of the boys.

"How come?"

"He's sick," says another kid next to him.

"Yeah, his hemorrhoids are acting up," says the first. "So it looks like you're in charge now."

"What are we supposed to do, Mr. Rogo?" asks the other kid.

Well, at first I'm a little mad at having all this foisted upon me. But then the idea of having to supervise a bunch of kids doesn't daunt me—after all, I do that every day at the plant. So I gather everyone around. We look at a map and discuss the objectives for this expedition into the perilous wilderness before us.

The plan, I learn, is for the troop to hike through the forest following a blazed trail to someplace called "Devil's Gulch." There we are to bivouac for the evening. In the morning we are to break camp and make our way back to the point of departure, where Mom and Dad are supposed to be waiting for little Freddy and Johnny and friends to walk out of the woods.

First, we have to get to Devil's Gulch, which happens to be about ten miles away. So I line up the troop. They've all got their rucksacks on their backs. Map in hand, I put myself at the front of the line in order to lead the way, and off we go.

The weather is fantastic. The sun is shining through the trees. The skies are blue. It's breezy and the temperature is a little on the cool side, but once we get into the woods, it's just right for walking.

The trail is easy to follow because there are blazes (splotches of yellow paint) on the tree trunks every 10 yards or so. On either side, the undergrowth is thick. We have to hike in single file.

I suppose I'm walking at about two miles per hour, which is about how fast the average person walks. At this rate, I think to myself, we should cover ten miles in about five hours. My watch tells me it's almost 8:30 now. Allowing an hour and a half for breaks and for lunch, we should arrive at Devil's Gulch by three o'clock, no sweat.

After a few minutes, I turn and look back. The column of scouts has spread out to some degree from the close spacing we started with. Instead of a yard or so between boys, there are now larger gaps, some a little larger than others. I keep walking.

But I look back again after a few hundred yards, and the column is stretched out much farther. And a couple of big gaps have appeared. I can barely see the kid at the end of the line.

I decide it's better if I'm at the end of the line instead of at the front. That way I know I'll be able to keep an eye on the whole column, and make sure nobody gets left behind. So I wait for the first boy to catch up to me, and I ask him his name.

"I'm Ron," he says.

"Ron, I want you to lead the column," I tell him, handing over the map. "Just keep following this trail, and set a moderate pace. Okay?"

"Right, Mr. Rogo."

And he sets off at what seems to be a reasonable pace.
"Everybody stay behind Ron!" I call back to the others.
"Nobody passes Ron, because he's got the map. Understand?"
Everybody nods, waves. Everybody understands.

I wait by the side of the trail as the troop passes. My son,
Davey, goes by talking with a friend who walks close behind
him. Now that he's with his buddies, Dave doesn't want to know
me. He's too cool for that. Five or six more come along, all of
them keeping up without any problems. Then there is a gap, followed by a couple more scouts. After them, another, even larger
gap has occurred. I look down the trail. And I see this fat kid.
He already looks a little winded. Behind him is the rest of the
troop.

"What's your name?" I ask as the fat kid draws closer.

"Herbie," says the fat kid.

"You okay, Herbie?"

"Oh, sure, Mr. Rogo," says Herbie. "Boy, it's hot out, isn't
it?"

Herbie continues up the trail and the others follow. Some
of them look as if they'd like to go faster, but they can't get
around Herbie. I fall in behind the last boy. The line stretches
out in front of me, and most of the time, unless we're going over
a hill or around a sharp bend in the trail, I can see everybody.
The column seems to settle into a comfortable rhythm.

Not that the scenery is boring, but after a while I begin to
think about other things. Like Julie, for instance. I really had
wanted to spend this weekend with her. But I'd forgotten all
about this hiking business with Dave. "Typical of you," I guess
she'd say. I don't know how I'm ever going to get the time I
need to spend with her. The only saving grace about this hike
is that she ought to understand I have to be with Dave.

And then there is the conversation I had with Jonah in New
York. I haven't had any time to think about that. I'm rather curious to know what a physics teacher is doing riding around in
limousines with corporate heavyweights. Nor do I understand
what he was trying to make out of those two items he described.
I mean, "dependent events" . . . "statistical fluctuations"—so
what? They're both quite mundane.

Obviously we have dependent events in manufacturing. All
it means is that one operation has to be done before a second
operation can be performed. Parts are made in a sequence of

steps. Machine A has to finish Step One before Worker B can proceed with Step Two. All the parts have to be finished before we can assemble the product. The product has to be assembled before we can ship it. And so on.

But you find dependent events in any process, and not just those in a factory. Driving a car requires a sequence of dependent events. So does the hike we're taking now. In order to arrive at Devil's Gulch, a trail has to be walked. Up front, Ron has to walk the trail before Davey can walk it. Davey has to walk the trail before Herbie can walk it. In order for me to walk the trail, the boy in front of me has to walk it first. It's a simple case of dependent events.

And statistical fluctuations?

I look up and notice that the boy in front of me is going a little faster than I have been. He's a few feet farther ahead of me than he was a minute ago. So I take some bigger steps to catch up. Then, for a second, I'm too close to him, so I slow down.

There: if I'd been measuring my stride, I would have recorded statistical fluctuations. But, again, what's the big deal?

If I say that I'm walking at the rate of "two miles per hour," I don't mean I'm walking exactly at a constant rate of two miles per hour every instant. Sometimes I'll be going 2.5 miles per hour; sometimes maybe I'll be walking at only 1.2 miles per hour. The rate is going to fluctuate according to the length and speed of each step. But over time and distance, I should be *averaging* about two miles per hour, more or less.

The same thing happens in the plant. How long does it take to solder the wire leads on a transformer? Well, if you get out your stopwatch and time the operation over and over again, you might find that it takes, let's say, 4.3 minutes on the average. But the actual time on any given instance may range between 2.1 minutes up to 6.4 minutes. And nobody in advance can say, "This one will take 2.1 minutes . . . this one will take 5.8 minutes." Nobody can predict that information.

So what's wrong with that? Nothing as far as I can see. Anyway, we don't have any choice. What else are we going to use in place of an "average" or an "estimate"?

I find I'm almost stepping on the boy in front of me. We've slowed down somewhat. It's because we're climbing a long, fairly steep hill. All of us are backed up behind Herbie.

"Come on, Herpes!" says one of the kids.

Herpes?

"Yeah, Herpes, let's move it," says another.

"Okay, enough of that," I say to the persecutors.

Then Herbie reaches the top. He turns around. His face is red from the climb.

"Atta boy, Herbie!" I say to encourage him. "Let's keep it moving!"

Herbie disappears over the crest. The others continue the climb, and I trudge behind them until I get to the top. Pausing there, I look down the trail.

Holy cow! Where's Ron? He must be half a mile ahead of us. I can see a couple of boys in front of Herbie, and everyone else is lost in the distance. I cup my hands over my mouth.

"HEY! LET'S GO UP THERE! LET'S CLOSE RANKS!" I yell. "DOUBLE TIME! DOUBLE TIME!"

Herbie eases into a trot. The kids behind him start to run. I jog after them. Rucksacks and canteens and sleeping bags are bouncing and shaking with every step. And Herbie—I don't know what this kid is carrying, but it sounds like he's got a junkyard on his back with all the clattering and clanking he makes when he runs. After a couple hundred yards, we still haven't caught up. Herbie is slowing down. The kids are yelling at him to hurry up. I'm huffing and puffing along. Finally I can see Ron off in the distance.

"HEY RON!" I shout. "HOLD UP!"

The call is relayed up the trail by the other boys. Ron, who probably heard the call the first time, turns and looks back. Herbie, seeing relief in sight, slows to a fast walk. And so do the rest of us. As we approach, all heads are turned our way.

"Ron, I thought I told you to set a moderate pace," I say.

"But I did!" he protests.

"Well, let's just all try to stay together next time," I tell them.

"Hey, Mr. Rogo, whadd'ya say we take five?" asks Herbie.

"Okay, let's take a break," I tell them.

Herbie falls over beside the trail, his tongue hanging out. Everyone reaches for canteens. I find the most comfortable log in sight and sit down. After a few minutes, Davey comes over and sits down next to me.

"You're doing great, Dad," he says.

"Thanks. How far do you think we've come?"

"About two miles," he says.

"Is that all?" I ask. "It feels like we ought to be there by now. We must have covered more distance than two miles."

"Not according to the map Ron has," he says.

"Oh," I say. "Well, I guess we'd better get a move on." The boys are already lining up.

"All right, let's go," I say.

We start out again. The trail is straight here, so I can see everyone. We haven't gone thirty yards before I notice it starting all over again. The line is spreading out; gaps between the boys are widening. Dammit, we're going to be running and stopping all day long if this keeps up. Half the troop is liable to get lost if we can't stay together.

I've got to put an end to this.

The first one I check is Ron. But Ron, indeed, is setting a steady, "average" pace for the troop—a pace nobody should have any trouble with. I look back down the line, and all of the boys are walking at about the same rate as Ron. And Herbie? He's not the problem anymore. Maybe he felt responsible for the last delay, because now he seems to be making a special effort to keep up. He's right on the ass of the kid in front of him.

If we're all walking at about the same pace, why is the distance between Ron, at the front of the line, and me, at the end of the line, increasing?

Statistical fluctuations?

Nah, couldn't be. The fluctuations should be averaging out. We're all moving at about the same speed, so that should mean the distance between any of us will vary somewhat, but will even out over a period of time. The distance between Ron and me should also expand and contract within a certain range, but should average about the same throughout the hike.

But it isn't. As long as each of us is maintaining a normal, moderate pace like Ron, the length of the column is increasing. The gaps between us are expanding.

Except between Herbie and the kid in front of him.

So how is he doing it? I watch him. Every time Herbie gets a step behind, he runs for an extra step. Which means he's actually expending more energy than Ron or the others at the front of the line in order to maintain the same relative speed. I'm wondering how long he'll be able to keep up his walk-run routine.

# THE GOAL

Yet . . . why can't we all just walk at the same pace as Ron and stay together?

I'm watching the line when something up ahead catches my eye. I see Davey slow down for a few seconds. He's adjusting his packstraps. In front of him, Ron continues onward, oblivious. A gap of ten . . . fifteen . . . twenty feet opens up. Which means the entire line has grown by 20 feet.

That's when I begin to understand what's happening.

Ron is setting the pace. Every time someone moves slower than Ron, the line lengthens. It wouldn't even have to be as obvious as when Dave slowed down. If one of the boys takes a step that's half an inch shorter than the one Ron took, the length of the whole line could be affected.

But what happens when someone moves faster than Ron? Aren't the longer or faster steps supposed to make up for the spreading? Don't the differences average out?

Suppose I walk faster. Can I shorten the length of the line? Well, between me and the kid ahead of me is a gap of about five feet. If he continues walking at the same rate, and if I speed up, I can reduce the gap—and maybe reduce the total length of the column, depending upon what's happening up ahead. But I can only do that until I'm bumping the kid's rucksack (and if I did that he'd sure as hell tell his mother). So I have to slow down to his rate.

Once I've closed the gap between us, I can't go any faster than the rate at which the kid in front of me is going. And he ultimately can't go any faster than the kid in front of him. And so on up the line to Ron. Which means that, except for Ron, each of our speeds depends upon the speeds of those in front of us in the line.

It's starting to make sense. Our hike is a set of dependent events . . . in combination with statistical fluctuations. Each of us is fluctuating in speed, faster and slower. But the ability to go faster than average is restricted. It depends upon all the others ahead of me in the line. So even if I could walk five miles per hour, I couldn't do it if the boy in front of me could only walk two miles per hour. And even if the kid directly in front of me could walk that fast, neither of us could do it unless all the boys in the line were moving at five miles per hour at the same time.

So I've got limits on how fast I can go—both my own (I can only go so fast for so long before I fall over and pant to death) and those of the others on the hike. However, there is no limit on my ability to slow down. Or on anyone else's ability to slow down. Or stop. And if any of us did, the line would extend indefinitely.

What's happening isn't an averaging out of the fluctuations in our various speeds, but an *accumulation* of the fluctuations. And mostly it's an accumulation of slowness—*because dependency limits the opportunities for higher fluctuations*. And that's why the line is spreading. We can make the line shrink only by having everyone in the back of the line move much faster than Ron's average over some distance.

Looking ahead, I can see that how much distance each of us has to make up tends to be a matter of where we are in the line. Davey only has to make up for his own slower than average fluctuations relative to Ron—that twenty feet or so which is the gap in front of him. But for Herbie to keep the length of the line from growing, he would have to make up for his own fluctuations plus those of all the kids in front of him. And here I am at the end of the line. To make the total length of the line contract, I have to move faster than average for a distance equal to all the excess space between all the boys. I have to make up for the accumulation of all their slowness.

Then I start to wonder what this could mean to me on the job. In the plant, we've definitely got both dependent events and statistical fluctuations. And here on the trail we've got both of them. What if I were to say that this troop of boys is analogous to a manufacturing system . . . sort of a model. In fact, the troop does produce a product; we produce "walked trail." Ron begins production by consuming the unwalked trail before him, which is the equivalent of raw materials. So Ron processes the trail first by walking over it, then Davey has to process it next, followed by the boy behind him, and so on back to Herbie and the others and on to me.

Each of us is like an operation which has to be performed to produce a product in the plant; each of us is one of a set of dependent events. Does it matter what order we're in? Well, somebody has to be first and somebody else has to be last. So we have dependent events no matter if we switch the order of the boys.

I'm the last operation. Only after I have walked the trail is the product "sold," so to speak. And that would have to be our throughput—not the rate at which Ron walks the trail, but the rate at which I do.

What about the amount of trail between Ron and me? It has to be inventory. Ron is consuming raw materials, so the trail the rest of us are walking is inventory until it passes behind me.

And what is operational expense? It's whatever lets us turn inventory into throughput, which in our case would be the energy the boys need to walk. I can't really quantify that for the model, except that I know when I'm getting tired.

If the distance between Ron and me is expanding, it can only mean that inventory is increasing. Throughput is my rate of walking. Which is influenced by the fluctuating rates of the others. Hmmm. So as the slower than average fluctuations accumulate, they work their way back to me. Which means I have to slow down. Which means that, relative to the growth of inventory, throughput for the entire system goes down.

And operational expense? I'm not sure. For UniCo, whenever inventory goes up, carrying costs on the inventory go up as well. Carrying costs are a part of operational expense, so that measurement also must be going up. In terms of the hike, operational expense is increasing any time we hurry to catch up, because we expend more energy than we otherwise would.

Inventory is going up. Throughput is going down. And operational expense is probably increasing.

Is that what's happening in my plant?

Yes, I think it is.

Just then, I look up and see that I'm nearly running into the kid in front of me.

Ah ha! Okay! Here's proof I must have overlooked something in the analogy. The line in front of me is contracting rather than expanding. Everything must be averaging out after all. I'm going to lean to the side and see Ron walking his average two-mile-an-hour pace.

But Ron is not walking the average pace. He's standing still at the edge of the trail.

"How come we're stopping?"

He says, "Time for lunch, Mr. Rogo."

# 14

"But we're not supposed to be having lunch here," says one of the kids. "We're not supposed to eat until we're farther down the trail, when we reach the Rampage River."

"According to the schedule the troopmaster gave us, we're supposed to eat lunch at 12:00 noon," says Ron.

"And it is now 12:00 noon," Herbie says, pointing to his watch. "So we have to eat lunch."

"But we're supposed to be at Rampage River by now and we're not."

"Who cares?" says Ron. "This is a great spot for lunch. Look around."

Ron has a point. The trail is taking us through a park, and it so happens that we're passing through a picnic area. There are tables, a water pump, garbage cans, barbecue grills—all the necessities. (This is my kind of wilderness I'll have you know.)

"Okay," I say. "Let's just take a vote to see who wants to eat now. Anyone who's hungry, raise your hand."

Everyone raises his hand; it's unanimous. We stop for lunch.

I sit down at one of the tables and ponder a few thoughts as I eat a sandwich. What's bothering me now is that, first of all, there is no real way I could operate a manufacturing plant without having dependent events and statistical fluctuations. I can't get away from that combination. But there must be a way to overcome the effects. I mean, obviously, we'd all go out of business if inventory was always increasing, and throughput was always decreasing.

What if I had a balanced plant, the kind that Jonah was saying managers are constantly trying to achieve, a plant with every resource exactly equal in capacity to demand from the market? In fact, couldn't that be the answer to the problem? If I could get capacity perfectly balanced with demand, wouldn't my excess inventory go away? Wouldn't my shortages of certain parts disappear? And, anyway, how could Jonah be right and everybody else be wrong? Managers have always trimmed capacity to cut costs and increase profits; that's the game.

I'm beginning to think maybe this hiking model has thrown me off. I mean, sure, it shows me the effect of statistical fluctuations and dependent events in combination. But is it a balanced system? Let's say the demand on us is to walk two miles every hour—no more, no less. Could I adjust the capacity of each kid so he would be able to walk two miles per hour and no faster? If I could, I'd simply keep everyone moving constantly at the pace he should go—by yelling, whip–cracking, money, whatever—and everything would be perfectly balanced.

The problem is how can I realistically trim the capacity of fifteen kids? Maybe I could tie each one's ankles with pieces of rope so that each would only take the same size step. But that's a little kinky. Or maybe I could clone myself fifteen times so I have a troop of Alex Rogos with exactly the same trail-walking capacity. But that isn't practical until we get some advancements in clone technology. Or maybe I could set up some other kind of model, a more controllable one, to let me see beyond any doubt what goes on.

I'm puzzling over how to do this when I notice a kid sitting at one of the other tables, rolling a pair of dice. I guess he's practicing for his next trip to Vegas or something. I don't mind—although I'm sure he won't get any merit badges for shooting craps—but the dice give me an idea. I get up and go over to him.

"Say, mind if I borrow those for a while?" I ask.

The kid shrugs, then hands them over.

I go back to the table again and roll the dice a couple of times. Yes, indeed: statistical fluctuations. Every time I roll the dice, I get a random number that is predictable only within a certain range, specifically numbers one to six on each die. Now what I need next for the model is a set of dependent events.

After scavenging around for a minute or two, I find a box of match sticks (the strike-anywhere kind), and some bowls from the aluminum mess kit. I set the bowls in a line along the length of the table and put the matches at one end. And this gives me a model of a perfectly balanced system.

While I'm setting this up and figuring out how to operate the model, Dave wanders over with a friend of his. They stand by the table and watch me roll the die and move matches around.

"What are you doing?" asks Dave.

"Well, I'm sort of inventing a game," I say.

"A game? Really?" says his friend. "Can we play it, Mr. Rogo?"

Why not?

"Sure you can," I say.

All of a sudden Dave is interested.

"Hey, can I play too?" he asks.

"Yeah, I guess I'll let you in," I tell him. "In fact, why don't you round up a couple more of the guys to help us do this."

While they go get the others, I figure out the details. The system I've set up is intended to "process" matches. It does this by moving a quantity of match sticks out of their box, and through each of the bowls in succession. The dice determine how many matches can be moved from one bowl to the next. The dice represent the capacity of each resource, each bowl; the set of bowls are my dependent events, my stages of production. Each has exactly the same capacity as the others, but its actual yield will fluctuate somewhat.

In order to keep those fluctuations minimal, however, I decide to use only one of the dice. This allows the fluctuations to range from one to six. So from the first bowl, I can move to the next bowls in line any quantity of matches ranging from a minimum of one to a maximum of six.

Throughput in this system is the speed at which matches come out of the last bowl. Inventory consists of the total number of matches in all of the bowls at any time. And I'm going to assume that market demand is exactly equal to the average number of matches that the system can process. Production capacity of each resource and market demand are perfectly in balance. So that means I now have a model of a perfectly balanced manufacturing plant.

Five of the boys decide to play. Besides Dave, there are Andy, Ben, Chuck, and Evan. Each of them sits behind one of the bowls. I find some paper and a pencil to record what happens. Then I explain what they're supposed to do.

"The idea is to move as many matches as you can from your bowl to the bowl on your left. When it's your turn, you roll the die, and the number that comes up is the number of matches you can move. Got it?"

They all nod. "But you can only move as many matches as you've got in your bowl. So if you roll a five and you only have two matches in your bowl, then you can only move two matches. And if it comes to your turn and you don't have any matches, then naturally you can't move any."

They nod again.

"How many matches do you think we can move through the line each time we go through the cycle?" I ask them.

Perplexity descends over their faces.

"Well, if you're able to move a maximum of six and a minimum of one when it's your turn, what's the average number you ought to be moving?" I ask them.

"Three," says Andy.

"No, it won't be three," I tell them. "The mid-point between one and six isn't three."

I draw some numbers on my paper.

"Here, look," I say, and I show them this:

1    2    3    4    5    6

And I explain that 3.5 is really the average of those six numbers.

"So how many matches do you think each of you should have moved on the average after we've gone through the cycle a number of times?" I ask.

"Three and a half per turn," says Andy.

"And after ten cycles?"

"Thirty-five," says Chuck.

"And after twenty cycles?"

"Seventy," says Ben.

"Okay, let's see if we can do it," I say.

Then I hear a long sigh from the end of the table. Evan looks at me.

"Would you mind if I don't play this game, Mr. Rogo?" he asks.

"How come?"

"'Cause I think it's going to be kind of boring," he says.

"Yeah," says Chuck. "Just moving matches around. Like who cares, you know?"

"I think I'd rather go tie some knots," says Evan.

"Tell you what," I say. "Just to make it more interesting, we'll have a reward. Let's say that everybody has a quota of 3.5 matches per turn. Anybody who does better than that, who averages more than 3.5 matches, doesn't have to wash any dishes tonight. But anybody who averages less than 3.5 per turn, has to do extra dishes after dinner."

"Yeah, all right!" says Evan.

"You got it!" says Dave.

They're all excited now. They're practicing rolling the die. Meanwhile, I set up a grid on a sheet of paper. What I plan to do is record the amount that each of them deviates from the average. They all start at zero. If the roll of the die is a 4, 5, or 6 then I'll record—respectively—a gain of .5, 1.5, or 2.5. And if the roll is a 1, 2, or 3 then I'll record a loss of −.5, −1.5, or −2.5 respectively. The deviations, of course, have to be cumulative; if someone is 2.5 above, for example, his starting point on the next turn is 2.5, not zero. That's the way it would happen in the plant.

"Okay, everybody ready?" I ask.

"All set."

I give the die to Andy.

He rolls a two. So he takes two matches from the box and puts them in Ben's bowl. By rolling a two, Andy is down 1.5 from his quota of 3.5 and I note the deviation on the chart.

Ben rolls next and the die comes up as a four.

"Hey, Andy," he says. "I need a couple more matches."

"No, no, no, no," I say. "The game does not work that way. You can only pass the matches that are in your bowl."

"But I've only got two," says Ben.

"Then you can only pass two."

"Oh," says Ben.

And he passes his two matches to Chuck. I record a deviation of −1.5 for him too.

Chuck rolls next. He gets a five. But, again, there are only two matches he can move.

"Hey, this isn't fair!" says chuck.

"Sure it is," I tell him. "The name of the game is to move matches. If both Andy and Ben had rolled five's, you'd have five matches to pass. But they didn't. So you don't."

Chuck gives a dirty look to Andy.

"Next time, roll a bigger number," Chuck says.

"Hey, what could I do?!" says Andy.

"Don't worry," Ben says confidently. "We'll catch up."

Chuck passes his measly two matches down to Dave, and I record a deviation of −1.5 for Chuck as well. We watch as Dave rolls the die. His roll is only a one. So he passes one match down to Evan. Then Evan also rolls a one. He takes the one match out of his bowl and puts it on the end of the table. For both Dave and Evan, I write a deviation of −2.5.

"Okay, let's see if we can do better next time," I say.

Andy shakes the die in his hand for what seems like an hour. Everyone is yelling at him to roll. The die goes spinning onto the table. We all look. It's a six.

"All right!"

"Way to go, Andy!"

He takes six match sticks out of the box and hands them to Ben. I record a gain of +2.5 for him, which puts his score at 1.0 on the grid.

Ben takes the die and he too rolls a six. More cheers. He passes all six matches to Chuck. I record the same score for Ben as for Andy.

But Chuck rolls a three. So after he passes three matches to Dave, he still has three left in his bowl. And I note a loss of −0.5 on the chart.

Now Dave rolls the die; it comes up as a six. But he only has four matches to pass—the three that Chuck just passed to him and one from the last round. So he passes four to Evan. I write down a gain of +0.5 for him.

Evan gets a three on the die. So the lone match on the end of the table is joined by three more. Evan still has one left in his bowl. And I record a loss of −0.5 for Evan.

At the end of two rounds, this is what the chart looks like:

| | ANDY | BEN | CHUCK | DAVE | EVAN |
|---|---|---|---|---|---|
| Turn: | 1234567890 | 1234567890 | 1234567890 | 1234567890 | 1234567890 |
| Roll  − − − − | 26 | 46 | 43 | 16 | 13 |
| # Moved − − | 26 | 26 | 23 | 14 | 13 |
| Inventory: | | 00 | 03 | 10 | 01 |

| Change +/− | ANDY | BEN | CHUCK | DAVE | EVAN |
|---|---|---|---|---|---|
| +2 | | | | | |
| +1.5 | | | | | |
| +1 | * | * | | | |
| +0.5 | | | | | |
| 0 | | | | | |
| −1 | | | | | |
| −1.5 | * | * | * | | |
| −2 | | | * | * | |
| −2.5 | | | | * | * |
| −3 | | | | | * |
| −3.5 | | | | | |

We keep going. The die spins on the table and passes from hand to hand. Matches come out of the box and move from bowl to bowl. Andy's rolls are—what else?—very average, no steady run of high or low numbers. He is able to meet the quota and then some. At the other end of the table, it's a different story.

"Hey, let's keep those matches coming."

"Yeah, we need more down here."

"Keep rolling sixes, Andy."

"It isn't Andy, it's Chuck. Look at him, he's got five."

After four turns, I have to add more numbers—negative numbers—to the bottom of the chart. Not for Andy or for Ben or for Chuck, but for Dave and Evan. For them, it looks like there is no bottom deep enough.

After five rounds, the chart looks like this:

```
                ANDY        BEN        CHUCK       DAVE        EVAN
        Turn:   1234567890  1234567890  1234567890  1234567890  1234567890
        - - - - - - - - - - - - - - - - - - - - - - - - - - - - - - - - -
Roll  - - - -   26425       46152       43225       16351       13641
# Moved  - -    26425       26152       23225       14221       13321
        - - - - - - - - - - - - - - - - - - - - - - - - - - - - - - - - -
Inventory:                  00303       03252       10004       01000
        - - - - - - - - - - - - - - - - - - - - - - - - - - - - - - - - -
Change +/-
 +2.5
 +2
 +1.5                        * *
 +1                          *           *
 +0.5
   0- - - - - - - - *- - - - - - - *- - - - - - - - - - - - - - - - - - -
 -0.5                                    *
 -1
 -1.5           *            * *         *
 -2                                      *           *
 -2.5                                                *           *
 -3                                                              *
 -3.5                                    * *         *
 -4                                                              *
 -4.5
 -5                                      *           *
 -5.5                                                            *
 -6
 -6.5
 -7
 -7.5                                                *
 -8                                                             *
 -8.5
```

"How am I doing, Mr. Rogo?" Evan asks me.

"Well, Evan . . . ever hear the story of the Titanic?"

He looks depressed.

"You've got five rounds left," I tell him. "Maybe you can pull through."

"Yeah, remember the law of averages," says Chuck.

"If I have to wash dishes because you guys didn't give me enough matches . . ." says Evan, letting vague implications of threat hang in the air.

"I'm doing my job up here," says Andy.

"Yeah, what's wrong with you guys down there?" asks Ben.

"Hey, I just now got enough of them to pass," says Dave. "I've hardly had any before."

Indeed, some of the inventory which had been stuck in the first three bowls has finally moved to Dave. But now it gets stuck in Dave's bowl. The couple of higher rolls he had in the first five rounds are averaging out. Now he's getting low rolls just when he has inventory to move.

"C'mon, Dave, gimme some matches," says Evan.

Dave rolls a one.

"Aw, Dave! One match!"

"Andy, you hear what we're having for dinner tonight?" asks Ben.

"I think it's spaghetti," says Andy.

"Ah, man, that'll be a mess to clean up."

"Yeah, glad I won't have to do it," says Andy.

"You just wait," says Evan. "You just wait 'til Dave gets some good numbers for a change."

But it doesn't get any better.

"How are we doing now, Mr. Rogo?" asks Evan.

"I think there's a Brillo pad with your name on it."

"All right! No dishes tonight!" shouts Andy.

After ten rounds, this is how the chart looks . . .

I look at the chart. I still can hardly believe it. It was a balanced system. And yet throughput went down. Inventory went up. And operational expense? If there had been carrying costs on the matches, operational expense would have gone up too.

What if this had been a real plant—with real customers? How many units did we manage to ship? We expected to ship thirty-five. But what was our actual throughput? It was only twenty. About half of what we needed. And it was nowhere near the maximum potential of each station. If this had been an actual plant, half of our orders—or more—would have been late. We'd

| | ANDY | BEN | CHUCK | DAVE | EVAN |
|---|---|---|---|---|---|
| Turn: | 1234567890 | 1234567890 | 1234567890 | 1234567890 | 1234567890 |
| Roll ---- | 2642536452 | 4615254633 | 4322561565 | 1635122132 | 1364145342 |
| # Moved -- | 2642536452 | 2615254633 | 2322561565 | 1422122132 | 1332122132 |
| Inventory: | | 0030313132 | 0325214510 | 1000487### | 0100000000 |

Change +/−

```
                ANDY        BEN         CHUCK       DAVE        EVAN
         Turn:  1234567890  1234567890  1234567890  1234567890  1234567890

  +5.5              *
  +5
  +4.5                                     *
  +4                 **                    *
  +3.5               *                      *
  +3
  +2.5
  +2                                        *          *
  +1.5   **                                 *
  +1     *  *        *
  +0.5                                                 *
     0 ----------*-------------*-------------------------------------------
  -0.5              *
  -1                                     *
  -1.5   *           **           *
  -2                                    *         * *
  -2.5                                             *         *
  -3                                                          *
  -3.5                                 ***          *          *
  -4                                                           *
  -4.5
  -5                                   *            *
  -5.5                                                          *
  -6
  -6.5
  -7
  -7.5                                                *
  -8                                                           *
  -8.5
  -9                                                 *
  -9.5                                                         *
  -10
  -10.5                                               *
  -11
  -11.5                                                        *
  -12
  -12.5
  -13                                                *
  -13.5                                               *          *
  -14                                                            *
  -14.5                                              *
  -15
  -15.5                                                          *
```

\#   Dave's inventory for turns 8, 9, and 10 is in double digits, respectively rising to 11 matches, 14 matches, and 17 matches.

never be able to promise specific delivery dates. And if we did, our credibility with customers would drop through the floor.

All of that sounds familiar, doesn't it?

"Hey, we can't stop now!" Evan is clamoring.

"Yeah, let's keep playing," says Dave.

"Okay," says Andy. "What do you want to bet this time? I'll take you on."

"Let's play for who cooks dinner," says Ben.

"Great," says Dave.

"You're on," says Evan.

They roll the die for another twenty rounds, but I run out of paper at the bottom of the page while tracking Dave and Evan. What was I expecting? My initial chart ranged from $+6$ to $-6$. I guess I was expecting some fairly regular highs and lows, a normal sine curve. But I didn't get that. Instead, the chart looks like I'm tracing a cross-section of the Grand Canyon. Inventory moves through the system not in manageable flow, but in waves. The mound of matches in Dave's bowl passes to Evan's and onto the table finally—only to be replaced by another accumulating wave. And the system gets further and further behind schedule.

"Want to play again?" asks Andy.

"Yeah, only this time I get your seat," says Evan.

"No way!" says Andy.

Chuck is in the middle shaking his head, already resigned to defeat. Anyway, it's time to head on up the trail again.

"Some game that turned out to be," says Evan.

"Right, some game," I mumble.

# 15

For a while, I watch the line ahead of me. As usual, the gaps are widening. I shake my head. If I can't even deal with this in a simple hike, how am I going to deal with it in the plant?

What went wrong back there? Why didn't the balanced model work? For about an hour or so, I keep thinking about what happened. Twice I have to stop the troop to let us catch up. Sometime after the second stop, I've fairly well sorted out what happened.

There was no reserve. When the kids downstream in the balanced model got behind, they had no extra capacity to make up for the loss. And as the negative deviations accumulated, they got deeper and deeper in the hole.

Then a long–lost memory from way back in some math class in school comes to mind. It has to do with something called a covariance, the impact of one variable upon others in the same group. A mathematical principle says that in a linear dependency of two or more variables, the fluctuations of the variables down the line will fluctuate around the maximum deviation established by any preceding variables. That explains what happened in the balanced model.

Fine, but what do I do about it?

On the trail, when I see how far behind we are, I can tell everyone to hurry up. Or I can tell Ron to slow down or stop. And we close ranks. Inside a plant, when the departments get behind and work-in-process inventory starts building up, people are shifted around, they're put on overtime, managers start to crack the whip, product moves out the door, and inventories slowly go down again. Yeah, that's it: we run to catch up. (We always run, never stop; the other option, having some workers idle, is taboo.) So why can't we catch up at my plant? It feels like we're always running. We're running so hard we're out of breath.

I look up the trail. Not only are the gaps still occurring, but they're expanding faster than ever! Then I notice something weird. Nobody in the column is stuck on the heels of anybody else. Except me. I'm stuck behind Herbie.

Herbie? What's he doing back here?

# THE GOAL

I lean to the side so I can see the line better. Ron is no longer leading the troop; he's a third of the way back now. And Davey is ahead of him. I don't know who's leading. I can't see that far. Well, son of a gun. The little bastards changed their marching order on me.

"Herbie, how come you're all the way back here?" I ask.

"Oh, hi, Mr. Rogo," says Herbie as he turns around. "I just thought I'd stay back here with you. This way I won't hold anybody up."

He's walking backwards as he says this.

"Uh-huh, well, that's thoughtful of you. Watch out!"

Herbie trips on a tree root and goes flying onto his backside. I help him up.

"Are you okay?" I ask.

"Yeah, but I guess I'd better walk forwards, huh?" he says. "Kind of hard to talk that way though."

"That's okay, Herbie," I tell him as we start walking again. "You just enjoy the hike. I've got lots to think about."

And that's no lie. Because I think Herbie may have just put me onto something. My guess is that Herbie, unless he's trying very hard, as he was before lunch, is the slowest one in the troop. I mean, he seems like a good kid and everything. He's clearly very conscientious—but he's slower than all the others. (Somebody's got to be, right?) So when Herbie is walking at what I'll loosely call his "optimal" pace—a pace that's comfortable to him—he's going to be moving slower than anybody who happens to be behind him. Like me.

At the moment, Herbie isn't limiting the progress of anyone except me. In fact, all the boys have arranged themselves (deliberately or accidentally, I'm not sure which) in an order that allows every one of them to walk without restriction. As I look up the line, I can't see anybody who is being held back by anybody else. The order in which they've put themselves has placed the fastest kid at the front of the line, and the slowest at the back of the line. In effect, each of them, like Herbie, has found an optimal pace for himself. If this were my plant, it would be as if there were a never-ending supply of work—no idle time.

But look at what's happening: the length of the line is spreading farther and faster than ever before. The gaps between the boys are widening. The closer to the front of the line, the wider the gaps become and the faster they expand.

You can look at it this way, too: Herbie is advancing at his own speed, which happens to be slower than my potential speed. But because of dependency, *my* maximum speed is the rate at which Herbie is walking. My rate is throughput. Herbie's rate governs mine. So Herbie really is determining the maximum throughput.

My head feels as though it's going to take off.

Because, see, it really doesn't matter how fast any *one* of us can go, or does go. Somebody up there, whoever is leading right now, is walking faster than average, say, three miles per hour. So what! Is his speed helping the troop *as a whole* to move faster, to gain more throughput? No way. Each of the other boys down the line is walking a little bit faster than the kid directly behind him. Are any of them helping to move the troop faster? Absolutely not. Herbie is walking at his own slower speed. He is the one who is governing throughput for the troop as a whole.

In fact, whoever is moving the slowest in the troop is the one who will govern throughput. And that person may not always be Herbie. Before lunch, Herbie was walking faster. It really wasn't obvious who was the slowest in the troop. So the role of Herbie—the greatest limit on throughput—was actually floating through the troop; it depended upon who was moving the slowest at a particular time. But overall, Herbie has the least capacity for walking. His rate ultimately determines the troop's rate. Which means—

"Hey, look at this, Mr. Rogo," says Herbie.

He's pointing at a marker made of concrete next to the trail. I take a look. Well, I'll be . . . it's a milestone! A genuine, honest-to–god milestone! How many speeches have I heard where somebody talks about these damn things? And this is the first one I've ever come across. This is what it says:

miles

Hmmm. It must mean there are five miles to walk in both directions. So this must be the mid–point of the hike. Five miles to go.

What time is it?

I check my watch. Gee, it's 2:30 P.M. already. And we left

at 8:30 A.M. So subtracting the hour we took for lunch, that means we've covered five miles . . . in five hours?

We aren't moving at two miles per hour. We are moving at the rate of one mile per hour. So with five hours to go . . .

It's going to be DARK by the time we get there.

And Herbie is standing here next to me delaying the throughput of the entire troop.

"Okay, let's go! Let's go!" I tell him.

"All right! All right!" says Herbie, jumping.

What am I going to do?

Rogo, (I'm telling myself in my head), you loser! You can't even manage a troop of Boy Scouts! Up front, you've got some kid who wants to set a speed record. And here you are stuck behind Fat Herbie, the slowest kid in the woods. After an hour, the kid in front—if he's really moving at three miles per hour— is going to be two miles ahead. Which means you're going to have to run two miles to catch up with him.

If this were my plant, Peach wouldn't even give me three months. I'd already be on the street by now. The demand was for us to cover ten miles in five hours, and we've only done half of that. Inventory is racing out of sight. The carrying costs on that inventory would be rising. We'd be ruining the company.

But there really isn't much I can do about Herbie. Maybe I could put him someplace else in the line, but he's not going to move any faster. So it wouldn't make any difference.

Or would it?

"HEY!" I yell forward. "TELL THE KID AT THE FRONT TO STOP WHERE HE IS!"

The boys relay the call up to the front of the column.

"EVERYBODY STAY IN LINE UNTIL WE CATCH UP!" I yell. "DON'T LOSE YOUR PLACE IN THE LINE!"

Fifteen minutes later, the troop is standing in condensed line. I find that Andy is the one who usurped the role of leader. I remind them all to stay in exactly the same places they had when we were walking.

"Okay," I say. "Everybody join hands."

They all look at each other.

"Come on! Just do it!" I tell them. "And don't let go."

Then I take Herbie by the hand and, as if I'm dragging a chain, I go up the trail, snaking past the entire line. Hand in hand, the rest of the troop follows. I pass Andy and keep walking.

And when I'm twice the distance of the line-up, I stop. What I've done is turn the entire troop around so that the boys have exactly the opposite order they had before.

"Now listen up!" I say. "This is the order you're going to stay in until we reach where we're going. Understood? Nobody passes anybody. Everybody just tries to keep up with the person in front of him. Herbie will lead."

Herbie looks shocked and amazed. "Me?"

Everyone else looks aghast too.

"You want *him* to lead?" asks Andy.

"But he's the slowest one!" says another kid.

And I say, "The idea of this hike is not to see who can get there the fastest. The idea is to get there together. We're not a bunch of individuals out here. We're a team. And the team does not arrive in camp until all of us arrive in camp."

So we start off again. And it works. No kidding. Everybody stays together behind Herbie. I've gone to the back of the line so I can keep tabs, and I keep waiting for the gaps to appear, but they don't. In the middle of the line I see someone pause to adjust his pack straps. But as soon as he starts again, we all walk just a little faster and we're caught up. Nobody's out of breath. What a difference!

Of course, it isn't long before the fast kids in the back of the line start their grumbling.

"Hey, Herpes!" yells one of them. "I'm going to sleep back here. Can't you speed it up a little?"

"He's doing the best he can," says the kid behind Herbie, "so lay off him!"

"Mr. Rogo, can't we put somebody faster up front?" asks a kid ahead of me.

"Listen, if you guys want to go faster, then you have to figure out a way to let Herbie go faster," I tell them.

It gets quiet for a few minutes.

Then one of the kids in the rear says, "Hey, Herbie, what have you got in your pack?"

"None of your business!" says Herbie.

But I say, "Okay, let's hold up for a minute."

Herbie stops and turns around. I tell him to come to the back of the line and take off his pack. As he does, I take the pack from him—and nearly drop it.

"Herbie, this thing weighs a ton," I say. "What have you got in here?"

"Nothing much," says Herbie.

I open it up and reach in. Out comes a six-pack of soda. Next are some cans of spaghetti. Then come a box of candy bars, a jar of pickles, and two cans of tuna fish. Beneath a rain coat and rubber boots and a bag of tent stakes, I pull out a large iron skillet. And off to the side is an army-surplus collapsible steel shovel.

"Herbie, why did you ever decide to bring all this along?" I ask.

He looks abashed. "We're supposed to be prepared, you know."

"Okay, let's divide this stuff up," I say.

"I can carry it!" Herbie insists.

"Herbie, look, you've done a great job of lugging this stuff so far. But we have to make you able to move faster," I say. "If we take some of the load off you, you'll be able to do a better job at the front of the line."

Herbie finally seems to understand. Andy takes the iron skillet, and a few of the others pick up a couple of the items I've pulled out of the pack. I take most of it and put it into my own pack, because I'm the biggest. Herbie goes back to the head of the line.

Again we start walking. But this time, Herbie can really move. Relieved of most of the weight in his pack, it's as if he's walking on air. We're flying now, doing twice the speed as a troop that we did before. And we still stay together. Inventory is down. Throughput is up.

Devil's Gulch is lovely in the late afternoon sun. Down in what appears to be the gulch, the Rampage River goes creaming past boulders and outcroppings of rock. Golden rays of sunlight shift through the trees. Birds are tweeting. And off in the distance is the unmistakable melody of high-speed automobile traffic.

"Look!" shouts Andy as he stands atop the promontory, "There's a shopping center out there!"

"Does it have a Burger King?" asks Herbie.

Dave complains, "Hey, this isn't The Wilderness."

"They just don't make wildernesses the way they used to,"

I tell him. "Look, we'll have to settle for what we've got. Let's make camp."

The time is now five o'clock. This means that after relieving Herbie of his pack, we covered about four miles in two hours. Herbie was the key to controlling the entire troop.

Tents are erected. A spaghetti dinner is prepared by Dave and Evan. Feeling somewhat guilty because I set up the rules that drove them into their servitude, I give them a hand with cleaning up afterwards.

Dave and I share the same tent that night. We're lying inside it, both of us tired. Dave is quiet for a while. Then he speaks up.

He says, "You know, Dad, I was really proud of you today."

"You were? How come?"

"The way you figured out what was going on and kept everyone together, and put Herbie in front—we'd probably have been on that trail forever if it hadn't been for you," he says. "None of the other guys' parents took any responsibility for anything. But you did."

"Thanks," I tell him. "Actually, I learned a lot of things today."

"You did?"

"Yeah, stuff that I think is going to help me straighten out the plant," I say.

"Really? Like what?"

"Are you sure you want to hear about it?"

"Sure I am," he claims.

We're awake for some time talking about everything. He hangs in there, even asks some questions. By the time we're finished, all we can hear is some snoring from the other tents, a few crickets . . . and the squealing tires of some idiot turning donuts out there on the highway.

# 16

Davey and I get home around 4:30 on Sunday afternoon. Both of us are tired, but we're feeling pretty good in spite of the miles. After I pull into the driveway, Dave hops out to open the garage door. I ease the Buick in and go around to open the trunk so we can get our packs.

"I wonder where Mom went," says Dave.

I look over and notice that her car is gone.

"She's probably out shopping or something," I tell Dave.

Inside, Dave stows the camping gear while I go into the bedroom to change clothes. A hot shower is going to feel absolutely terrific. After I wash off the great outdoors, I'm thinking, maybe I'll take everybody out to dinner, get us a good meal as kind of a celebration of the triumphant return of father and son.

A closet door is open in the bedroom. When I reach to shut it, I see that most of Julie's clothes are gone. I stand there for a minute looking at the empty space. Dave comes up behind me.

"Dad?"

I turn.

"This was on the kitchen table. I guess Mom left it."

He hands me a sealed envelope.

"Thanks Dave."

I wait until he's gone to open it. Inside is just a short handwritten note. It says:

Al,

I can't handle always being last in line for you. I need more of you and it's clear now that you won't change. I'm going away for a while. Need to think things over. Sorry to do this to you. I know you're busy.

Yours truly,
Julie

P.S.—I left Sharon with your mother.

When I'm able to move, I put the note in my pocket and go

find Davey. I tell him I have to go across town to pick up Sharon, and that he's to stay here. If his mother calls, he's to ask her where she's calling from and get a number where I can call her back. He wants to know if something is wrong. I tell him not to worry and promise to explain when I get back.

I go rocketing over to my mother's house. When she opens the door, she starts talking about Julie before I can even say hello.

"Alex, do you know your wife did the strangest thing," she says. "I was just making lunch yesterday when the doorbell rang, and when I opened the door Sharon was standing here on the step with her little suitcase. And your wife was in the car at the curb there, but she wouldn't get out and when I went down to talk to her, she drove away."

By now I'm in the door. Sharon runs to greet me from the living room where she is watching television. I pick her up and she gives me a long hug. My mother is still talking.

"What on earth could be wrong with her?" my mother asks me.

"We'll talk about it later," I tell her.

"I just don't understand what—"

"*Later,* okay?"

Then I look at Sharon. Her face is rigid. Her eyes are frozen big. She's terrified.

"So . . . did you have a nice visit with Grandma?" I ask her.

She nods but doesn't say anything.

"What do you say we go home now?"

She looks down at the floor.

"Don't you want to go home?" I ask.

She shrugs her shoulders.

"Do you like it here with Grandma?" my smiling mother asks her.

Sharon starts to cry.

I get Sharon and her suitcase into the car. We start home. After I've driven a couple of blocks, I look over at her. She's like a little statue sitting there staring straight ahead with her red eyes focused on the top of the dashboard. At the next stoplight, I reach over for her and pull her next to me.

She's very quiet for a while, but then she finally looks up at me and whispers, "Is Mommy still mad at me?"

"Mad at you? She isn't mad at you," I tell her.

"Yes she is. She wouldn't talk to me."

"No, no, no, Sharon," I say. "Your mother isn't upset with you. You didn't do anything wrong."

"Then why?" she asks.

I say, "Why don't we wait until we get home. I'll explain it to both you and your brother then."

I think that explaining the situation to both of the kids at the same time turns out to be easier on me than on them. I've always been reasonably adept at maintaining the outward illusion of control in the midst of chaos. I tell them Julie has simply gone away for a little while, maybe only a day or so. She'll be back. She just has to get over a few things that are upsetting and confusing her. I give them all the standard reassurances: your mom still loves you; I still love you; there was nothing that either of you could have done; everything will work out for the best. For the most part, both of them sit there like little rocks. Maybe they're reflecting back what I'm giving them.

We go out and get a pizza for dinner. That normally would be kind of a fun thing. Tonight, it's very quiet. Nobody has anything to say. We mechanically chew and then leave.

When we get back, I make both of the kids do homework for school. I don't know if they do it or not. I go to the phone, and after a long debate with myself, I try to make a couple of calls.

Julie doesn't have any friends in Bearington. None that I know of. So it would be useless to try to call the neighbors. They wouldn't know anything, and the story about us having problems would spread instantly.

Instead, I try calling Jane, the friend from the last place we lived, the one whom Julie claimed to have spent the night with last Thursday. There is no answer at Jane's.

So then I try Julie's parents. I get her father on the phone. After some small talk about the weather and the kids, it's clear he isn't going to make any declarations. I conclude that her parents don't know what's going on. But before I can think of a casual way to end the call and avoid the explanations, her old man asks me, "So is Julie going to talk to us?"

"Ah, well, that's actually why I was calling," I say.

"Oh? Nothing is wrong I hope," he says.

"I'm afraid there is," I say. "She left yesterday while I was on a camping trip with Dave. I was wondering if you had heard from her."

Immediately he's spreading the alarm to Julie's mother. She gets on the phone.

"Why did she leave?" she asks.

"I don't know."

"Well, I know the daughter we raised, and she wouldn't just leave without a very good reason," says Julie's mother.

"She just left me a note saying she had to get away for awhile."

"*What did you do to her?*" yells her mother.

"Nothing!" I plead, feeling like a liar in the onslaught.

Then her father gets back on the phone and asks if I've talked to the police. He suggests that maybe she was kidnapped. I tell him that's highly unlikely, because my mother saw her drive away and nobody had a gun to her head.

Finally I say, "If you hear from her, would you please have her give me a call? I'm very worried about her."

An hour later, I do call the police. But, as I expected, they won't help unless I have some evidence that something criminal has taken place. I go and put the kids to bed.

Sometime after midnight, I'm staring at the dark bedroom ceiling and I hear a car turning into the driveway. I leap out of bed and run to the window. By the time I get there, the headlights are arcing back toward the street. It's just a stranger turning around. The car drives away.

# 17

Monday morning is a disaster.

It starts with Davey trying to make breakfast for himself and Sharon and me. Which is a nice, responsible thing to do, but he totally screws it up. While I'm in the shower, he attempts pancakes. I'm midway through shaving when I hear the fight from the kitchen. I rush down to find Dave and Sharon pushing each other. There is a skillet on the floor with lumps of batter, black on one side and raw on the other, splattered.

"Hey! What's going on?" I shout.

"It's all her fault!" yells Dave pointing at his sister.

"You were burning them!" Sharon says.

"I was not!"

Smoke is fuming off the stove where something spilled. I step over to shut it off.

Sharon appeals to me. "I was just trying to help. But he wouldn't let me." Then she turns to Dave. "Even *I* know how to make pancakes."

"Okay, because both of you want to help, you can help clean up," I say.

When everything is back in some semblance of order, I feed them cold cereal. We eat another meal in silence.

With all the disruption and delay. Sharon misses her school bus. I get Davey out the door, and go looking for her so I can drive her to school. She's lying down on her bed.

"Ready whenever you are, Miz Rogo."

"I can't go to school," she says.

"Why not?"

"I'm sick."

"Sharon, you have to go to school," I say.

"But I'm sick!" she says.

I go sit down on the edge of the bed.

"I know you're upset. I am too," I tell her. "But these are facts: I have to go to work. I can't stay home with you, and I won't leave you here by yourself. You can go to your grandmother's house for the day. Or you can go to school."

She sits up. I put my arm around her.

After a minute, she says, "I guess I'll go to school."

I give her a squeeze and say, "Atta way, kid. I knew you'd do the right thing."

By the time I get both kids to school and myself to work, it's past nine o'clock. As I walk in, Fran waves a message slip at me. I grab it and read it. It's from Hilton Smyth, marked "urgent" and double underlined.

I call him.

"Well, it's about time," says Hilton. "I tried to reach you an hour ago."

I roll my eyes. "What's the problem, Hilton?"

"Your people are sitting on a hundred sub-assemblies I need," says Smyth.

"Hilton, we're not sitting on anything," I say.

He raises his voice. "Then why aren't they here? I've got a customer order we can't ship because your people dropped the ball!"

"Just give me the particulars, and I'll have somebody look into it," I tell him.

He gives some reference numbers and I write them down.

"Okay, I'll have somebody get back to you."

"You'd better do more than that, pal," says Hilton. "You'd better make sure we get those sub-assemblies by the end of the day—and I mean all 100 pieces, not 87, not 99, but *all* of them. Because I'm not going to have my people do two setups for final assembly on account of your lateness."

"Look, we'll do our best," I tell him, "but I'm not going to make any promises."

"Oh? Well, let's just put it this way," he says. "If we don't get 100 sub-assemblies from you today, I'm talking to Peach. And from what I hear you're in enough trouble with him already."

"Listen, *pal,* my status with Bill Peach is none of your damn business," I tell him. "What makes you think you can threaten me?"

The pause is so long I think he's going to hang up on me.

Then he says, "Maybe you ought to read your mail."

"What do you mean by that?"

I can hear him smiling.

"Just get me the sub-assemblies by the end of the day," he says sweetly. "Bye-bye."

I hang up.

"Weird," I mumble.

I talk to Fran. She calls Bob Donovan for me and then notifies the staff that there will be a meeting at ten o'clock. Donovan comes in and I ask him to have an expeditor see what's holding up the job for Smyth's plant. Almost gritting my teeth as I say it, I tell him to make sure the sub-assemblies go out today. After he's gone, I try to forget about the call, but I can't. Finally, I go ask Fran if anything has come in recently that mentions Hilton Smyth. She thinks for a minute, then reaches for a folder.

"This memo just came in on Friday," she says. "It looks like Mr. Smyth got a promotion."

I take the memo she hands me. It's from Bill Peach. It's an announcement that he's named Smyth to the newly-created position of division productivity manager. The appointment is effective at the end of this week. The job description says that all plant managers will now report on a dotted line to Smyth, who will "give special attention to manufacturing–productivity improvement with emphasis on cost reduction."

And I start to sing, "Oh, what a beautiful morning . . . !"

Whatever enthusiasm I expected from the staff with regard to my education over the weekend . . . well, I don't get it. Maybe I thought all I had to do was walk in and open my mouth to reveal my discoveries, and they'd all be instantly converted by the obvious rightness. But it doesn't work that way. We—Lou, Bob, Stacey, and Ralph Nakamura, who runs data processing for the plant—are in the conference room. I'm standing in front next to an easel which holds a big pad of paper, sheet after sheet of which is covered with little diagrams I've drawn during my explanations. I've invested a couple of hours in making those explanations. But now it's almost time for lunch, and they're all just sitting there unimpressed.

Looking down the table at the faces looking back at me, I can see they don't know what to make of what I've told them. Okay, I think I see a faint glimmer of understanding in Stacey's eyes. Bob Donovan is on the fence; he seems to have intuitively grasped some of it. Ralph is not sure what it is I'm really saying. And Lou is frowning at me. One sympathizer, one undecided, one bewildered, and one skeptic.

"Okay, what's the problem?" I ask.

They glance at each other.

"Come on," I say. "This is like I just proved two and two equals four and you don't believe me." I look straight at Lou. "What's the problem you're having?"

Lou sits back and shakes his head. "I don't know, Al. It's just that . . . well, you said how you figured this out by watching a bunch of kids on a hike in the woods."

"So what's wrong with that?"

"Nothing. But how do you know these things are really going on out there in the plant?"

I flip back a few sheets on the easel until I find the one with the names of Jonah's two phenomena written on it.

"Look at this: do we have statistical fluctuations in our operations?" I ask, pointing to the words.

"Yes, we do," he says.

"And do we have dependent events in our plant?" I ask.

"Yes," he says again.

"Then what I've told you has to be right," I say.

"Now hold on a minute," says Bob. "Robots don't have statistical fluctuations. They always work at the same pace. That's one of the reasons we bought the damn things—consistency. And I thought the main reason you went to see this Jonah guy was to find out what to do about the robots."

"It's okay to say that fluctuations in cycle time for a robot would be almost flat while it was working," I tell him. "But we're not dealing just with a robotic operation. Our other operations do have both phenomena. And, remember, the goal isn't to make the robots productive; it's to make the whole system productive. Isn't that right, Lou?"

"Well, Bob may have a point. We've got a lot of automated equipment out there, and the process times ought to be fairly consistent," says Lou.

Stacey turns to him. "But what he's saying—"

Just then the conference room door opens. Fred, one of our expeditors, puts his head into the room and looks at Bob Donovan.

"May I see you for a second?" he asks Bob. "It's about the job for Hilton Smyth."

Bob stands up to leave the room, but I tell Fred to come in. Like it or not, I have to be interested in what's happening on this "crisis" for Hilton Smyth. Fred explains that the job has to go through two more departments before the sub-assemblies are complete and ready for shipment.

"Can we get them out today?" I ask.

"It's going to be close, but we can try," says Fred. "The truck shuttle leaves at five o'clock."

The shuttle is a private trucking service that all the plants in the division use to move parts back and forth.

"Five o'clock is the last run of the day that we can use to reach Smyth's plant," says Bob. "If we don't make that trip, the next shuttle won't be until tomorrow afternoon."

"What has to be done?" I ask.

"Peter Schnell's department has to do some fabricating. Then the pieces have to be welded," says Fred. "We're going to set up one of the robots to do the welds."

"Ah, yes, the robots," I say. "You think we can do it?"

"According to the quotas, Pete's people are supposed to give us the parts for twenty-five units every hour," says Fred. "And I know the robot is capable of welding twenty-five units of this sub-assembly per hour."

Bob asks about moving the pieces to the robot. In a normal situation, the pieces finished by Pete's people probably would be moved to the robot only once a day, or maybe not until the entire batch was finished. We can't wait that long. The robot has to begin its work as soon as possible.

"I'll make arrangements to have a materials handler stop at Pete's department every hour on the hour," says Fred.

"Okay," says Bob. "How soon can Pete start?"

Fred says, "Pete can start on the job at noon, so we've got five hours."

"You know that Pete's people quit at four," says Bob.

"Yeah, I told you it's going to be close," says Fred. "But all we can do is try. That's what you want, isn't it?"

This gives me an idea. I talk to the staff. "You people don't really know what to make of what I told you this morning. But if what I've told you is correct, then we should be able to see the effects occurring out there on the floor. Am I right?"

The heads nod.

"And if we know that Jonah is correct, we'd be pretty stupid to continue running the plant the same way as before—right? So I'm going to let you see for yourselves what's happening. You say Pete's going to start on this at noon?"

"Right," says Fred. "Everyone in that department is at lunch now. They went at eleven-thirty. So they'll start at twelve.

And the robot will be set up by one o'clock, when the materials handler will make the first transfer.''

I take some paper and a pencil and start sketching a simple schedule.

"The output has to be one hundred pieces by five o'clock—no less than that. Hilton says he won't accept a partial shipment. So if we can't do the whole job, then I don't want us to ship anything," I say. "Now Pete's people are supposed to produce at the rate of twenty-five pieces per hour. But that doesn't mean they'll always have twenty-five at the end of every hour. Sometimes they'll be a few pieces short, sometimes they'll be a few ahead."

I look around; everyone is with me.

"So we've got statistical fluctuations going on," I say. "But we're planning that from noon until four o'clock, Pete's department should have averaged an output of one hundred pieces. The robot, on the other hand, is supposed to be more precise in its output. It will be set up to work at the rate of twenty-five pieces per hour—no more, no less. We also have dependent events, because the robot cannot begin its welding until the materials handler has delivered the pieces from Pete's department.

"The robot can't start until one o'clock," I say, "but by five o'clock when the truck is ready to leave, we want to be loading the last piece into the back. So, expressed in a diagram, this is what is supposed to happen . . .''

I show them the finished schedule, which looks like this:

```
Demand = 100 pcs.   Quota = 25 pcs. per hour
_____

            12 noon  1        2       3       4       5 p.m.
                     [25]
Pete's       --25--  |      [50]
People               |  --25--  |      [75]
                                |  --25--  |      [100]
                                           |  --25--  |

                              [25]
Robot                         --25--  |      [50]
                                      |  --25--  |      [75]
                                                 |  --25--  |      [100]
                                                            |  --25--  |
```

"Okay, I want Pete to keep a log of exactly how many parts are actually completed by his department hour by hour," I say. "And I want Fred to keep the same type of log for the robot. And remember: no cheating. We need the real numbers. Okay?"

"Sure, no problem," says Fred.

"By the way, do you actually think we'll be able to ship one hundred pieces today?" I ask.

"I guess it's up to Pete," says Bob. "If he says he can do it, I don't see why not."

"Tell you what," I say to Bob. "I'll bet you ten bucks we don't ship today."

"You serious?" asks Bob.

"Sure I am."

"Okay, you're on," says Bob. "Ten bucks."

While everyone else is at lunch, I call Hilton Smyth. Hilton is at lunch as well, but I leave a message for him. I tell his secretary the sub-assemblies will definitely arrive at his plant tomorrow, but that's the best we can do—unless Hilton wants to pay for a special shipment tonight. (Knowing his concern for holding down costs, I'm sure Hilton won't want to shell out anything extra.)

After that call, I sit back and try to think about my marriage and what to do. Obviously, there has been no news from Julie. I'm mad as hell that she took off—I'm also very worried about her. But what can I do? I can't cruise the streets looking for her. She could be anywhere; I just have to be patient. Eventually I should hear from her. Or her lawyer. Meanwhile, there are two kids who have to be taken care of. Well, for all practical purposes, we'd better make that three kids.

Fran comes into my office with another message slip. She says, "One of the other secretaries just gave me this as I got back from lunch. While you were on the phone, you got a call from David Rogo. Is that your son?"

"Yes, what's the problem?"

"It says here he's worried he won't be able to get into the house after school," she says. "Is your wife gone?"

"Yeah, she's out of town for a few days," I tell her. "Fran, you've got a couple of kids. How do you manage to hold a job and take care of them?"

She laughs. "Well, 'tain't easy. On the other hand, I don't work the long hours you do. If I were you, I'd get some help until she gets back."

When she leaves, I pick up the phone again.

"Hello, Mom? It's Alex."

"Have you heard from Julie yet?" she asks.

"No, I haven't," I say. "Listen, Mom, would you mind staying with me and the kids until Julie gets back?"

At two o'clock I slip out to pick up my mother and take her to the house before the kids get home from school. When I arrive at her house, she's at the door with two suitcases and four cardboard boxes filled with half of her kitchen.

"Mom, we've already got pots and pans at my house," I tell her.

"They're just not the same as mine," she says.

So we load the trunk. I take her and her pots and pans over to the house and unload. She waits for the kids to come home from school, and I race back to the plant.

Around four o'clock, at the end of first shift, I go down to Bob Donovan's office to find out what the story is on Smyth's shipment. He's waiting for me.

"Well, well, well. Good afternoon!" says Bob as I open the door and walk in. "How nice of you to drop by!"

"What are you so happy about?" I ask him.

"I'm always happy when people who owe me money drop by," says Bob.

"Oh, is that right?" I ask him. "What makes you think anybody owes you money?"

Bob holds out his hand and wiggles his fingers. "Come on! Don't tell me you forgot about the bet we made! Ten bucks, remember? I just talked to Pete and his people are indeed going to finish the hundred units of parts. So the robot should have no problem finishing that shipment for Smyth's plant."

"Yeah? Well, if that's true I won't mind losing," I tell him.

"So you concede defeat?"

"No way. Not until those sub-assemblies get on the five o'clock truck," I tell him.

"Suit yourself," says Bob.

"Let's go see what's really going on out there," I say.

We take a walk out on the floor to Pete's office. Before we get there, we pass the robot, who's brightening the area with its weld flashes. Coming the other way are two guys. Just as they pass the welding area, they stop and give a little cheer.

"We beat the robot! We beat the robot!" they say.

"Must be from Pete's department," says Bob.

We smile as we pass them. They didn't really beat anything, of course, but what the hell. They look happy. Bob and I continue on to Pete's office, which is a little steel-sided shack among the machines.

"Hello there," says Pete as we walk in. "We got that rush job done for you today."

"Good, Pete. But do you have that log sheet you were supposed to keep," I ask him.

"Yes, I do," says Pete. "Now where did I put it?"

He sorts through the papers on his desk, talking as he hunts for it.

"You should have seen my people this afternoon. I mean, they really moved. I went around and told them how important this shipment is, and they really put themselves into it. You know how things usually slow down a little at the end of a shift. But today they hustled. They were proud when they walked out of here today."

"Yeah, we noticed," says Bob.

He puts the log sheet down on top of a table in front of us.

"There you are," he says.

We read it.

Demand = 100 pcs.   Quota = 25 pcs. per hour

```
        12 noon  1        2        3        4        5 p.m.
                 19 [-6]
Pete's   --19--  |        40 [-10]
People           |  --21--  |        68 [-7]
                 |        |  --28--  |        100 [0]
                 |        |        |  --32--  |
```

Output = 100 pcs.

"Okay, so you only got nineteen pieces done in the first hour," I say.

"Well, it took us a little longer to get organized, and one guy was late coming back from lunch," says Pete. "But at one o'clock we had a materials handler take the nineteen over to the robot so it could get started."

"Then from one to two, you still missed the quota by four pieces," says Bob.

"Yeah, but so what?" says Pete. "Look what happened from two o'clock to three: we beat the quota by three pieces. Then when I saw we were still behind, I went around and told everyone how important it was for us to get those hundred pieces done by the end of the shift."

"So everyone went a little faster," I say.

"That's right," says Pete. "And we made up for the slow start."

"Yeah, thirty-two pieces in the last hour," says Bob. "So what do you say, Al?"

"Let's go see what's happening with the robot," I say.

At five minutes past five o'clock, the robot is still turning out welded sub-assemblies. Donovan is pacing. Fred walks up.

"Is that truck going to wait?" asks Bob.

"I asked the driver, and he says he can't. He's got other stops to make and if he waits for us, he'll be late all night," says Fred.

Bob turns to the machine. "Well, what the heck is wrong with this stupid robot? It's got all the parts it needs."

I tap him on the shoulder.

"Here," I say. "Look at this."

I show him the sheet of paper on which Fred has been recording the output of the robot. From my shirt pocket, I take out Pete's log and fold the bottom of it so we can put the two pieces of paper together.

Combined, the two of them look like this:

I tell him, "You see, the first hour Pete's people did nineteen pieces. The robot was capable of doing twenty-five, but Pete delivered less than that, so nineteen became the robot's true capacity for that hour."

"Same with the second hour," says Fred. "Pete delivered twenty-one, the robot could only do twenty-one."

Demand = 100 pcs.   Quota = 25 pcs. per hour

```
             12 noon 1        2        3        4        5 p.m.
                        19 [−6]
Pete's           --19--  |        40 [−10]
People                   |  --21--  |        68 [−7]
                         |    --28--  |        100 [0]
                         |        --32--  |

                        19 [−6]
Robot                  --19--  |        40 [−10]
                         |  --21--  |        65 [−10]
                         |    --25--  |        90 [−10]
                         |        --25--  |
```

Output = 90 pcs.

"Every time Pete's area got behind, it was passed on to the robot," I say. "But when Pete delivered 28 pieces, the robot could still only do twenty-five. That meant that when the final delivery of thirty-two pieces arrived at four o'clock, the robot still had three pieces to work on from the last batch. So it couldn't start on the final batch right away."

"Okay, I see now," says Bob.

Fred says, "You know, the most Pete was ever behind was ten pieces. Kind of funny how that's exactly the number of pieces we ended up short."

"That's the effect of the mathematical principle I was trying to explain this morning," I say. "The maximum deviation of a preceding operation will become the starting point of a subsequent operation."

Bob reaches for his wallet.

"Well, I guess I owe *you* ten bucks," he says to me.

"Tell you what," I say. "Instead of paying me, why don't you give the money to Pete so he can spring for a round of coffee or something for the people in his department—just a little way to say thanks for the extra effort this afternoon."

"Yeah, right, that's a good idea," says Bob. "Listen, sorry we couldn't ship today. Hope it doesn't get us in trouble."

"We can't worry about it now," I tell him. "The gain we made today is that we learned something. But I'll tell you one thing: we've got to take a close look at our incentives here."

"How come?" asks Bob.

"Don't you see? It didn't matter that Pete got his hundred pieces done, because we still couldn't ship," I say. "But Pete and his people thought they were heroes. Ordinarily, *we* might have thought the same thing. That isn't right."

# 18

When I get home that evening, both of the kids greet me at the door. My mother is in the background, with steam pouring out of the kitchen. I presume it has something to do with dinner and that she has everything under control. In front of me, Sharon's face is beaming up at me.

"Guess what!" she says.

"I give up," I say.

"Mommy called on the phone," Sharon says.

"She did!" I say.

I glance up at my mother. She shakes her head.

"Davey answered the phone," she says. "I didn't talk to her."

I look down at Sharon. "So what did Mommy say?"

"She said she loved Davey and me," says Sharon.

"And she said she would be away for a while," adds Davey. "But that we shouldn't worry about her."

"Did she say when she would be coming back?" I ask.

"I asked her that," says Davey. "But she said she couldn't say right now."

"Did you get a phone number so I can call her back?" I ask him.

He looks down at the floor.

"David! You were supposed to ask her for the number if she called!"

He mumbles, "I did, but . . . she didn't want to give it to me."

"Oh," I say.

"Sorry, Dad."

"It's okay, Dave. Thanks for trying."

"Why don't we all sit down to dinner," my mother says cheerily.

This time the meal is not silent. My mother talks, and she does her best to cheer us up. She tells us stories about the Depression and how lucky we are to have food to eat.

Tuesday morning is a little bit more normal. Joining efforts, my mother and I manage to get the kids to school and me to

135

work on time. By 8:30, Bob, Stacey, Lou, and Ralph are in my office, and we're talking about what happened yesterday. Today, I find them much more attentive. Maybe it's because they've seen the proof of the idea take place on their own turf, so to speak.

"This combination of dependency and fluctuations is what we're up against every day," I tell them. "I think it explains why we have so many late orders."

Lou and Ralph are examining the two charts we made yesterday.

"What would have happened if the second operation hadn't been a robot, if it had been some kind of job with people?" asks Lou.

"We would have had another set of statistical fluctuations to complicate things," I say. "Don't forget we only had two operations here. You can imagine what happens when we've got dependency running through ten or fifteen operations, each with its own set of fluctuations, just to make one part. And some of our products involve hundreds of parts."

Stacey is troubled. She asks, "Then how can we ever cotrol what's going on out there?"

I say, "That's the billion-dollar question: how can we control the fifty-thousand or—who knows?—maybe it's fifty-million variables which exist in this plant?"

"We'd have to buy a new main-frame computer just to keep track of all of them," says Ralph.

I say, "A new computer wouldn't save us. Data management alone isn't going to give us more control."

"What about longer lead times?" asks Bob.

"Oh, you really think longer lead time would have guaranteed our ability to ship that order to Hilton Smyth's plant?" I ask him. "How long had we already known about that order before yesterday, Bob?"

Bob wiggles back and forth. "Hey, all I'm saying is that we'd have some slop in there to make up for the delays."

Then Stacey says, "Longer lead times increase inventory, Bob. And that isn't the goal."

"Okay, I know that," Bob is saying. "I'm not fighting you. The only reason I mention the lead times is I want to know what we do about all this."

Everybody turns to me.

I say, "This much is clear to me. We have to change the way we think about production capacity. We cannot measure the capacity of a resource in isolation. Its true productive capacity depends upon where it is in the plant. And trying to level capacity with demand to minimize expense has really screwed us up. We shouldn't be trying to do that at all."

"But that's what everybody else does," says Bob.

"Yes, everybody does. Or claims to. As we now can see, it's a stupid thing to try," I say.

"So how do other manufacturers survive?" asks Lou.

I tell him I was wondering that myself. What I suspect is that as a plant comes close to being balanced through the efforts of engineers and managers doing the wrong things, events head toward a crisis and the plant is very quickly *un*balanced by shifting workers or by overtime or by calling back some people from layoff. The survival incentive overrides false beliefs.

"Okay, but again, what are we going to do?" asks Bob. "We can't hire without division approval. And we've even got a policy against overtime."

"Maybe it's time to call Jonah again," says Stacey.

And I say, "I think maybe you're right."

It takes Fran half an hour to locate the area of the world where Jonah happens to be today, and another hour passes before Jonah can get to the phone to talk to us. As soon as he's on the line, I have another secretary round up the staff again and corral them in my office so we can hear him on a speaker phone. While they're coming in, I tell Jonah about the hike with Herbie where I discovered the meaning of what he was telling me, and what we've learned about the effects of the two phenomena in the plant.

"What we know now," I tell him, "is that we shouldn't be looking at each local area and trying to trim it. We should be trying to optimize the whole system. Some resources have to have more capacity than others. The ones at the end of the line should have more than the ones at the beginning—sometimes a lot more. Am I right?"

"You're on the money," says Jonah.

"Good. Glad to hear we're getting somewhere," I say. "Only the reason I called is, we need to know where to go from here."

He says, "What you have to do next, Alex, is distinguish

between two types of resources in your plant. One type is what I call a bottleneck resource. The other is, very simply, a non-bottleneck resource.''

I whisper to everybody to start taking some notes on this.

"A bottleneck," Jonah continues, "is any resource whose capacity is equal to or *less than* the demand placed upon it. And a non-bottleneck is any resource whose capacity is greater than the demand placed on it. Got that?"

"Right," I tell him.

"Once you have recognized these two types of resources," says Jonah, "you will begin to see vast implications."

"But, Jonah, where does market demand come in?" Stacey asks. "There has to be some relationship between demand and capacity."

He says, "Yes, but as you already know, you should not balance *capacity* with demand. What you need to do instead is balance the *flow of product* through the plant with demand from the market. This, in fact, is the first of nine rules that express the relationships between bottlenecks and non-bottlenecks and how you should manage your plant. So let me repeat it for you: Balance flow, not capacity."

Stacey is still puzzled. She says, "I'm not sure I understand. Where do the bottlenecks and non-bottlenecks come into the picture?"

Jonah says, "Let me ask you: which of the two types of resources determines the effective capacity of the plant?"

"It would have to be the bottleneck," she says.

I say, "That's right. It's like the kid on that hike last weekend—Herbie. He had the least capacity and he was the one who actually determined how fast the troop as a whole could move."

"So where should you balance the flow?" asks Jonah.

"Oh, I see," says Stacey. "The idea is to make the flow through the bottleneck equal to demand from the market."

"Basically, yes, you've got it," says Jonah. "Actually, the flow should be a tiny bit less than the demand."

"How come?" asks Lou.

"Because if you keep it equal to demand and the market demand goes down, you'll lose money," says Jonah. "But that's a fine point. Speaking fundamentally, the bottleneck flow should be on a par with demand."

Bob Donovan is now making various noises, trying to get into the conversation.

"Excuse me, but I thought bottlenecks were bad," says Bob. "They ought to be eliminated where possible, right?"

"No, bottlenecks are not necessarily bad—or good," says Jonah, "they are simply a reality. What I am suggesting is that where they exist, you must then use them to control the flow through the system and into the market."

That makes sense to me as I'm listening, because I'm remembering how I used Herbie to control the troop during the hike.

"Now I have to run," says Jonah, "because you caught me during a ten-minute break in a presentation."

I jump in. "Jonah, before you go—!"

"Yes?"

"What's our next step?"

He says, "Well, first of all, does your plant have any bottlenecks?"

"We don't know," I tell him.

"Then that's your next step," he says. "You have to find this out, because it makes an enormous difference in how you manage your resources."

"How do we do find the bottlenecks?" says Stacey.

"It's very simple, but it would take a few minutes to explain. Look, try to figure that out for yourselves," says Jonah. "It's really easy to do if you think about it first."

I say, "Okay, but. . . ."

"Good-bye for now," he says. "Call me when you know if you have a bottleneck."

The speaker phone issues a click, followed by a fuzzy hum.

"Well . . . what now?" asks Lou.

"I guess we look at all our resources," I say, "and compare them against market demand. If we find one in which demand is greater than capacity, then we'll know we've got a bottleneck."

"What happens if we find one?" asks Stacey.

"I guess the best thing to do would be what I did to the scout troop," I say. "We adjust capacity so the bottleneck is at the front of production."

"My question," Lou says, "is what happens if our resource with the least capacity in fact has a capacity greater than what market demand calls for?"

"Then I guess we'd have something like a bottle without a neck," I say.

"But there would still be limits," says Stacey. "The bottle

would still have walls. But they'd be greater than the market demand."

"And if that's the case?" asks Lou.

"I don't know," I tell him. "I guess the first thing to do is find out if we've got a bottleneck first."

"So we go look for Herbie," says Ralph. "If he's out there."

"Yeah, quick, before we talk ourselves to death," says Bob.

I walk into the conference room a few days later and there's paper everywhere. The main table is covered with computer print-outs and binders. Over in the corner, a data terminal has been installed; next to it, a printer is churning out even more paper. The wastebaskets are full. So are all the ashtrays. The litter of white styrofoam coffee cups, empty sugar packets and creamer containers, napkins, candy bar and cracker wrappers, and so on is scattered about. What has happened is the place has been turned into our headquarters in the search for Herbie. We have not found him yet. And we're getting tired.

Sitting at the far end of the main table is Ralph Nakamura. He and his data processing people, and the system data base they manage, are essential to the search.

Ralph does not look happy as I come in. He's running his skinny fingers through his thinning black hair.

"This isn't the way it's supposed to be," he's saying to Stacey and Bob.

"Ahh, perfect timing," says Ralph when he sees me. "Do you know what we just did?"

"You found Herbie?" I say.

Ralph says, "No, we just spent two and a half hours calculating the demand for machines that don't exist."

"Why'd you do that?"

Ralph starts to sputter. Then Bob stops him.

"Wait, wait, wait a minute. Let me explain," says Bob. "What happened was they came across some routings which still listed some of the old milling machines as being part of the processing. We don't use them—"

"Not only don't we use them, I just found out we sold them a year ago," says Ralph.

"Everybody down in that department knows those machines aren't there anymore, so it's never been a problem," says Bob.

So it goes. We're trying to calculate demand for every resource, every piece of equipment, in the plant. Jonah had said a bottleneck is any resource which is equal to or less than the market demand placed on it. To find out if we've got one then, we concluded we first would have to know the total market demand for products coming out of this plant. And, second, we would have to find out how much time each resource has to contribute toward filling that demand. If the number of available hours for production (discounting maintenance time for machines, lunch and breaks for people, and so on) for the resource is equal to or less than the hours demanded, then we know we've found our Herbie.

Getting a fix on the total market demand is matter of pulling together data which we have on hand anyway—the existing backlog of customer orders, and the forecast for new product and spare parts. It's the complete product mix for the entire plant, including what we "sell" to other plants and divisions in the company.

Having done that, we're now in the process of calculating the hours each "work center" has to contribute. We're defining a work center as any group of the same resources. Ten welders with the same skills constitute a work center. Four identical machines constitute another. The four machinists who set up and run the machines are still another, and so on. Dividing the total of work center hours needed, by the number of resources in it, gives us the relative effort per resource, a standard we can use for comparison.

Yesterday, for instance, we found the demand for injection molding machines is about 260 hours a month for all the injection molded parts that they have to process. The available time for those machines is about 280 hours per month, per resource. So that means we still have reserve capacity on those machines.

But the more we get into this, the more we're finding that the accuracy of our data is less than perfect. We're coming up with bills of material that don't match the routings, routings that don't have the current run–times—or the correct machines, as we just found out—and so on.

"The problem is, we've been under the gun so much that a lot of the updating has just fallen by the wayside," says Stacey.

"Hell, with engineering changes, shifting labor around, and all that happening all the time, it's just plain tough to keep up with it no matter what," says Bob.

Ralph shakes his head. "To double-check and update every piece of data relevant to this plant could take months!"

"Or years," mumbles Bob.

I sit down and close my eyes for a second. When I open my eyes, they're all looking at me.

"Obviously, we're not going to have time for that," I say. "We've only got ten weeks now to make something happen before Peach blows the whistle. I know we're on the right track, but we're still just limping along here. We've got to accept the fact we're not going to have perfect data to work with."

Ralph says, "Then I have to remind you of the old data processing aphorism: Garbage in, garbage out."

"Wait a minute," I say. "Maybe we're being a little too methodical. Searching a data base isn't the only way to find answers. Can't we come up with some other faster way to isolate the bottleneck—or at least identify the candidates? When I think back to the model of the boys on the hike, it was obvious who the slower kids were on the trail. Doesn't anybody have any hunches where the Herbie might be in the plant?"

"But we don't even know if we've got one yet," says Stacey.

Bob has his hands on his hips. His mouth is half open as if he might say something. Finally, he does.

"Hell, I've been at this plant for more than twenty years. After that much time, I know where the problems usually seem to start," he says. "I think I could put together a list of areas where we might be short on capacity; at least that would narrow the focus for us. It might save some time."

Stacey turns to him. "You know, you just gave me an idea. If we talk to the expeditors, they could probably tell us which parts they're missing most of the time, and in which departments they usually go to look for them."

"What good is that going to do?" asks Ralph.

"The parts most frequently in short supply are probably the ones that would pass through a bottleneck," she says. "And the department where the expeditors go to look for them is probably where we'll find our Herbie."

I sit up in my seat. "Yeah, that makes a lot of sense."

I stand up and start to pace.

"And I'll tell you something *I* just thought of," I say. "Out on the trail, you could tell the slower kids by the gaps in the line. The slower the kid, the greater the distance betwen him and the kid in front of him. In terms of the analogy, those gaps were inventory."

Bob, Ralph and Stacey stare at me.

"Don't you see?" I ask them. "If we've got a Herbie, it's probably going to have a huge pile of work-in-process sitting in front of it."

"Yeah, but we got huge piles all over the place out there," says Bob.

"Then we find the biggest one," I say.

"Right! That's got to be another sure sign," says Stacey.

I turn and ask, "What do you think, Ralph?"

"Well, it all sounds worth a try," says Ralph. "Once you've narrowed the field to maybe three of four work centers, it won't take long for us to check your findings against the historical data just to be sure."

Bob looks at Ralph and says in a kidding voice, "Yeah, well, we've all seen how good that is."

But Ralph doesn't take it in a kidding way. He looks embarrassed.

"Hey, I can only work with what I've got," he says. "What do you want me to do?"

"Okay, the important thing is that we have new methods to try," I say. "Let's not waste time pinning the blame on bad data. Let's get to work."

Fueled by the energy of new ideas, we go to work, and the search goes quickly . . . so quickly, in fact, that what we discover makes me feel as though we've run ourselves straight into a wall.

"This is it. Hello, Herbie," says Bob.

In front of us is the NCX-10.

"Are you sure this is a bottleneck?" I ask.

"There's some of the proof," he says as he points to the stacks of work-in-process inventory nearby—weeks of backlog according to the report Ralph and Stacey put together and which we reviewed about an hour ago.

"We talked to the expeditors," says Bob. "They say we're always waiting for parts from this machine. Supervisors say the same. And the guy who runs this area got himself a set of earplugs to keep him from going deaf from all the bitching he gets from everyone."

"But this is supposed to be one of our most efficient pieces of equipment," I say.

"It is," says Bob. "It's the lowest-cost, highest-rate means we have of producing these particular parts."

"So why is this a bottleneck?"

"This is the only one like it we've got," he says.

"Yes, I know that," I say, and I stare at him until he explains.

"See, this machine here is only about two years old. Before we installed it, we used other machines to do what it does. But this machine can do all the operations that used to take three different machines," says Bob.

He tells me about how they used to process these parts using the three separate types of machines. In one typical instance, the process times per part were something like two minutes on the first machine, eight minutes on the second, and four minutes on the third—a grand total of fourteen minutes per part. But the new NCX-10 machine can do all three processes in ten minutes per part.

I say, "You're telling me we're saving four minutes per part. Doesn't that mean we're producing more parts per hour than we were? How come we've got so much inventory stacked up for this thing?"

"With the old way, we had more machines," he says. "We had two of the first type, five of the second type, and three of the third type."

I nod, understanding now. "So you could do more parts, even though it took you longer per part. Then why did we buy the NCX-10?"

"Each of the other machines had to have a machinist to run it," Bob says. "The NCX-10 only needs two guys on it for setups. Like I said, it's the lowest cost way for us to produce these parts."

I take a slow walk all the way around the machine.

"We do run this thing three shifts, don't we?" I ask Bob.

"Well, we just started to again. It took a while to find a replacement for Tony, the setup guy on third shift who quit."

"Oh, yeah . . ." I say. Man, Peach really did it to us that day. I ask, "Bob, how long does it take to train new people on this machine?"

"About six months," he says.

I shake my head.

"That's a big part of the problem, Al. We train somebody and after a couple of years they can go elsewhere and make a few dollars more with somebody else," says Bob. "And we can't seem to attract anybody good with the wages we offer."

"Well why don't we pay more for people on this equipment?"

"The union," says Bob. "We'd get complaints, and the union would want us to up the pay–grade for all the setup people."

I take a last look.

"Okay, so much for this," I say.

But that isn't all. The two of us walk to the other side of the plant where Bob gives me a second introduction.

"Meet Herbie Number Two: the heat-treat department," says Bob.

This one looks more like what you might think of in terms of an industrial Herbie. It's dirty. It's hot. It's ugly. It's dull. And it's indispensable.

Heat–treat basically is a pair of furnaces . . . a couple of grimy, dingy, steel boxes, the insides of which are lined with ceramic blocks. Gas burners raise the internal temperatures to the 1500-degree-Fahrenheit range.

Certain parts, after they've been machined or cold–worked or whatever at ordinary temperatures, can't be worked on anymore until they've been treated with heat for an extended period of time. Most often, we need to soften the metal, which becomes very hard and brittle during processing, so it can have more machining done to it.

So the furnace operators put in the parts, from a dozen or less to a couple of hundred, then they fire up the thing and cook the parts in there for a long time—anywhere from six hours to sixteen hours. And afterwards, the parts always have to go through a further cool-down to air temperature outside the furnace. We lose a lot of time on this process.

"What's the problem here—we need bigger furnaces?" I ask.

Bob says, "Well . . . yes and no. Most of the time these furnaces are running half empty."

"How come?"

"It's the expeditors who seem to cause the problem," he

says. "They're always running over here and having us run five of this part or a dozen of that part just so they can have enough to assemble a shipment. So we end up having fifty parts wait while we heat–treat a handful. I mean, this operation is run like a barbershop—take a number and stand in line."

"So we're not running full batches."

"Yeah, sometimes we are. But sometimes even if we do a full batch in number, it's not enough to fill the furnace."

"The batches are too small?"

"Or too big in size, and we have to run a second heat to handle the pieces that wouldn't fit in the first. It just nevere seems to work out," says Bob. "You know, a couple of years ago, there was a proposal to add a third furnace, on account of the problems."

"What happened to it?"

"It was killed at the division level. They wouldn't authorize the funds because of low efficiencies. They told us to use the capacity we've got. Then maybe they'd talk expansion. Besides, there was all kinds of noise about how we've got to save energy and how another furnace would burn twice as much fuel and all that."

"Okay, but if we filled the furnace every time, would we have enough capacity to meet demand?" I ask.

Bob laughs.

"I don't know. We've never done it that way before."

Once upon a time, I had an idea for doing to the plant essentially what I did with the boys on the hike. I thought the best thing to do would be to reorganize everything so the resource with the least capacity would be first in the routings. All other resources would have gradual increases in capacity to make up for the statistical fluctuations passed on through dependency.

Well, the staff and I meet right after Bob and I get back to the office, and it's pretty obvious, awfully damn quick, that my grand plan for the perfect *un*balanced plant with Herbie in front is just not going to fly.

"From a production standpoint, we can't do it," says Stacey.

"There is just no way we can move even one Herbie—let alone two—to the front of production," Bob says. "The sequence of operations has to stay the way it is. There's nothing we can do about it.''

"Okay, I already can see that," I say.

"We're stuck with a set of dependent events," says Lou.

As I listen to them, I get that old familiar feeling which comes whenever a lot of work and energy are about to go down the tubes. It's kind of like watching a tire go flat.

I say, "Okay, if we can't do anything to change their position in the sequence, then maybe we can increase their capacities. We'll make them into non-bottlenecks."

Stacey asks, "But what about the step-up in capacity from beginning to end?"

"We'll reorganize . . . we'll decrease capacity at the head of production and increase it each stage on through," I suggest.

"Al, we're not just talking about moving people around. How can we add capacity without adding equipment?" asks Bob. "And if we're talking about equipment, we're getting ourselves into some major capital. A second furnace on heat–treat, and possibly a second n/c machine . . . brother, you're talking megabucks."

"The bottom line," says Lou, "is that we don't have the money. If we think we can go to Peach and ask him for *excess* capacity for a plant that currently isn't making money in the middle of one of the worst years in the company's history . . . well, excuse my French, but we're out of our goddamned minds."

# 19

My mother and the kids and I are having dinner that evening when Mom says to me, "Aren't you going to eat your peas, Alex?"

I tell her, "Mom, I'm an adult now. It's my option whether or not to eat my peas."

She looks hurt.

I say, "Sorry. I'm a little depressed tonight."

"What's wrong, Dad?" asks Davey.

"Well . . . it's kind of complicated," I say. "Let's just finish dinner. I've got to leave for the airport in a few minutes."

"Are you going away?" asks Sharon.

"No, I'm just going to pick up somebody," I say.

"Is it Mommy?" asks Sharon.

"No, not Mommy. I wish it could be."

"Alex, tell your children what's bothering you," says my mother. "It affects them, too."

I look at the kids and realize my mother's right. I say, "We found out we've got some problems at the plant which we might not be able to solve."

"What about the man you called?" she asks. "Can't you talk to him?"

"You mean Jonah? That's who I'm picking up at the airport," I say. "But I'm not sure even Jonah's help will do any good."

Hearing this, Dave is shocked. He says, "You mean . . . all that stuff we learned about on the hike, about Herbie setting the speed for the whole troop and all that—none of that was true?"

"Of course it's still true, Dave," I tell him. "The problem is, we discovered we've got *two* Herbies at the plant, and they're right where we don't want them. It would be as if we couldn't rearrange the boys on the trail and Herbie had a twin brother—and now they're both stuck in the middle of the line. They're holding everything up. We can't move them. We've got piles and piles of inventory stacked up in front of them. I don't know what we can do."

Mom says, "Well, if they can't do the work, you'll just have to let them go."

*148*

"It's not people; it's equipment," I explain. "We can't fire machines. And, anyway, what they do is essential. We couldn't produce most of our products without these two operations."

"So why don't you make them go faster?" asks Sharon.

"Sure, Dad," says Davey. "Remember what happened on the hike when you took Herbie's pack from him? Maybe you could do something kind of like that in the plant."

"Yeah, but it's not quite that simple," I say.

Mom says, "Alex, I know you'll do the best you can. If you've got these two slow pokes holding everything up, you'll just have to keep after them and make sure they don't waste any more time."

I say, "Yeah, well, I've got to run. Don't wait up for me. I'll see you in the morning."

Waiting at the gate, I watch Jonah's plane taxi up to the terminal. I talked to him in Boston this afternoon just before he was leaving for Los Angeles. I told him I wanted to thank him for his advice, but that the situation at the plant was impossible so far as we could see.

"Alex, how do you know it's impossible?" he asked.

I told him, "We've only got two months left before my boss goes to the board of directors with his recommendation. If we had more time, maybe we could do something, but with only two months. . . ."

"Two months is still enough time to show an improvement," he said. "But you have to learn how to run your plant by its constraints."

"Jonah, we've analyzed the situation thoroughly—"

He said, "Alex, there are two ways that the ideas I'm giving you won't work. One is if there isn't any demand for the products your plant makes."

"No, we have a demand, although it's shrinking as our prices go up and service deteriorates," I said. "But we still have a sizeable backlog of orders."

"I also can't help you if you're determined not to change. Have you made up your mind to do nothing and let the plant close?"

"It's not that we want to give up," I told him. "It's that we don't see any other possibilities."

"Okay then. Have you tried to take some of the load off the bottlenecks by using other resources?" he asked.

"You mean offloading? We can't. These are the only two resources of their type in the plant."

He paused for a moment and finally he said, "All right, one more question: Does Bearington have an airport?"

And so here he is tonight, walking out of Gate Two. He changed his flight to Los Angeles to make a stop here for the evening. I walk up to him and shake his hand.

"How was your flight?" I ask him.

"Have you ever spent time in a sardine can?" he says, then adds, "I shouldn't complain. I'm still breathing."

"Well, thanks for coming," I tell him. "I appreciate you changing your plans, although I'm still not sure you can help us."

"Alex, having a bottleneck—"

"Two bottlenecks," I remind him.

"Having *two* bottlenecks doesn't mean you can't make money," he says. "Quite the contrary, in fact. Most manufacturing plants do not have bottlenecks. They have enormous excess capacity. But they should have them—one on every part they make."

He reads the puzzled look on my face.

"You don't understand, but you will," he says. "Now I want you to give me as much background on your plant as you can."

All the way from the airport, I talk non–stop about our predicament. When we reach the plant, I park the Buick in front of the offices. Waiting for us inside are Bob, Lou, Stacey and Ralph. They're standing around the vacant receptionist's desk. Everyone is cordial, but as I make the introductions I can tell the staff is waiting to see if this Jonah guy—who bears no resemblance to any consultant they've ever seen walk through the door—really knows what he's doing. Jonah stands in front of them and begins to pace as he talks.

"Alex called me today because you perceive a problem with the bottlenecks you've discovered in your plant," says Jonah. "Actually, you are experiencing a combination of several problems. But first things first. From what Alex has told me, your most immediate need is to increase throughput and improve your cash flow. Am I right?"

"That sure would be a big help," says Lou. "How do you think we might be able to do that?"

"Your bottlenecks are not maintaining a flow sufficient to meet demand and make money," he says. "So there is only one thing to do. We have to find more capacity."

"But we don't have the money for more capacity," says Lou.

"Or the time to install it," says Bob.

"I'm not talking about more capacity from one end of the plant to the other," says Jonah. "To increase the capacity of the plant is to increase the capacity of *only* the bottlenecks."

"You mean make them into non-bottlenecks," says Stacey.

"No," he says. "Absolutely not. The bottlenecks stay bottlenecks. What we must do is find enough capacity for the bottlenecks to become more equal to demand."

"Where're we going to find it?" asks Bob. "You mean it's just layin' around out there?"

"In effect, yes," says Jonah. "If you are like most manufacturers, you will have capacity that is *hidden* from you because some of your thinking is incorrect. And I suggest that first of all we go into your plant and see for ourselves exactly how you are managing your two bottlenecks."

"Why not," I say. "After all, no one visits this plant and escapes without a tour."

The six of us put on the safety glasses and hats and go into the plant. Jonah and I head the column as we walk through the double doors into the orange light. It's about halfway into second shift now and somewhat quieter than it is on day turn. That's good because it lets us hear each other better when we talk. I point out various stages of production to Jonah as we walk. I notice Jonah's eyes measuring the stacks of inventory piled everywhere. I try to hurry us along.

"This is our NCX-10 n/c machine," I tell Jonah as we arrive at the big machine.

"And this is your bottleneck, correct?" asks Jonah.

"One of them," I say.

"Can you tell me why isn't it working right now?" asks Jonah.

Indeed, the NCX-10 is stopped at the moment.

I say, "Well . . . ah, good question. Bob, why isn't the NCX-10 running?"

Bob glances at his watch.

"Probably because the set–up people went on break about ten minutes ago," says Bob. "They should be back in about twenty minutes."

"There is a clause in our union contract which stipulates there must be a half-hour break after every four hours of work," I explain to Jonah.

He asks, "But why should they take their break now instead of when the machine is running?"

Bob says, "Because it was eight o'clock and—"

Jonah holds up his hands and says, "Wait a minute. On any *non*-bottleneck machine in your plant, no problem. Because, after all, some percentage of a non-bottleneck's time *should* be idle. So who cares when those people take their breaks? It's no big deal. But on a bottleneck? It's exactly the opposite."

He points to the NCX-10 and says, "You have on this machine only so many hours available for production—what is it . . . 600, 700 hours?"

"It's around 585 hours a month," says Ralph.

"Whatever is available, the demand is even greater," says Jonah. "If you lose one of those hours, or even half of it, you have lost it forever. You cannot recover it someplace else in the system. Your throughput for the entire plant will be lower by whatever amount the bottleneck produces in that time. And that makes an enormously expensive lunch break."

"But we have a union to deal with," says Bob.

Jonah says, "So talk to them. They have a stake in this plant. They're not stupid. But you have to make them understand."

Yeah, I'm thinking; that's easier said than done. On the other hand . . .

Jonah is walking around the NCX-10 now, but he's not just looking at it alone. He's looking at other equipment in the plant. He comes back to us.

"You've told me this is the only machine of its type in the plant," says Jonah, "But this is a relatively new machine. Where are the older machines that this one replaced? Do you still have those?"

Bob says vaguely, "Well, some of them we do. Some of them we got rid of. They were practically antiques."

"Do you have at least one of each type of the older machines necessary to do what this X-what-ever-it-is machine does?" Jonah asks.

Lou edges in and and says, "Excuse me, but you're not actually suggesting we use that old equipment, are you?"

"If it's still operational, then yes, I might suggest it," says Jonah.

Lou's eyes blink.

He says, "Well, I'm not sure what that would do to our cost profile. But I have to tell you that those old machines are going to be much more expensive to operate."

Jonah says, "We'll deal with that directly. First, I just want to know if you have the machines or not."

For the answer, we turn to Bob—who chuckles.

"Sorry to disappoint you all," he says, "but we got rid of an entire class of machine that we'd need to supplement the NCX-10."

"Why did we go do a dumb thing like that?" I ask.

Bob says, "We needed the floor space for that new pen to hold inventory."

I say, "Oh."

"It seemed like a good idea at the time." says Stacey.

Moving right along to heat–treat, we gather in front of the furnaces.

The first thing Jonah does is look at the stacks of parts and ask, "Are you sure all this inventory requires heat-treat?"

"Oh, absolutely," says Bob.

"There are no alternatives in the processing ahead of this department that would prevent the need for heat–treat on at least some of these parts?" he asks.

We all look at each other.

"I guess we'd have to consult with engineering," I say.

Bob rolls his eyes.

"What's the matter?" I ask.

"Let's just say our friends in engineering aren't as responsive as they could be," says Bob. "They're not too happy about changing requirements. Their attitude is usually, 'Do it this way because we said so.' "

To Jonah, I say, "I'm afraid he does have a point. Even if we can get them to cooperate, it might take a month of Sundays for them to approve it."

Jonah says, "Okay, let me ask you this: are there vendors in the area who can heat–treat parts for you?"

"There are," says Stacey, "but going outside would increase our cost–per–part."

The expression on Jonah's face says he's getting a little bored with this stonewalling. He points at the mountains of parts.

"How much money is represented in that pile?" he asks.

Lou says, "I don't know . . . maybe ten or fifteen thousand dollars in parts."

"No, it isn't *thousands* of dollars, not if this is a bottleneck," says Jonah. "Think again. It's considerably more."

Stacey says, "I can go dig up the records if you like, but the cost won't be much more than what Lou said. At the most, I'd guess we've got about twenty thousands dollars in material—"

"No, no," says Jonah. "I'm not just talking about the cost of materials. How many products are you going to sell to customers as soon as you can process this entire pile?"

The staff and I talk among ourselves for a moment.

"It's kind of hard to say," says Bob.

"We're not sure all the parts in that pile would translate into immediate sales," says Stacey.

"Oh really? You are making your bottlenecks work on parts that will not contribute to throughput?" asks Jonah.

"Well . . . some of them become spare parts or they go into finished goods inventory. Eventually it becomes throughput," says Lou.

"*Eventually,*" says Jonah. "And, meanwhile, how big did you say your backlog of overdue orders is?"

I explain to him that sometimes we inflate the batch quantities to improve efficiency.

"Tell me again how this improves your efficiency," says Jonah.

I feel myself starting to turn red with the memory of earlier conversations.

"Okay, never mind that for now," says Jonah. "Let's concern ourselves strictly with throughput. I'll put my question differently: how many products are you *unable* to ship because you are missing the parts in that pile?"

That's easier to determine because we know what our backlog is. I tell him how many millions we've got in backlog and about what percent of that is held up on account of bottleneck parts.

"And if you could finish the parts in that pile, you could assemble and ship the product?" he asks.

"Sure, no problem," says Bob.

"And what is the selling price of each unit?"

"About a thousand dollars a unit on the average," says Lou, "although it varies, of course."

"Then we are not dealing with ten or fifteen or even twenty thousand dollars here," says Jonah. "Because we are dealing with how many parts in that pile?"

"Perhaps, a thousand," says Stacey.

"And each part means you can ship a product?"

"Generally, yes," she says.

"And each product shipped means a thousand dollars," says Jonah. "A thousand units times a thousand dollars is how much money?"

In unison, our faces turn toward the mountain.

"One million dollars," I say with awe.

"On one condition!" says Jonah. "That you get these parts in and out of heat–treat and shipped as a finished product before your customers get tired of waiting and go elsewhere!"

He looks at us, his eyes shifting from face to face.

"Can you afford to rule out any possibility," he asks, "especially one that is as easy to invoke as a change in policy?"

Everyone is quiet.

"By the way, I'll tell you more about how to look at the costs in a moment. But one more thing," says Jonah. "I want to know where you do quality inspection on bottleneck parts."

I explain to him that most inspection is done prior to final assembly.

"Show me," says Jonah.

So we go to an area where we do quality inspections. Jonah asks about bottleneck parts that we reject. Immediately, Bob points to a pallet stacked with shiny steel parts. On top of them is a pink sheet of paper, which indicates rejection by Quality Control, or Q.C. as it's known. Bob picks up the job jacket and reads the forms inside.

"I'm not sure what's wrong with these, but they must be defective for some reason," says Bob.

Jonah asks, "Did these parts come through a bottleneck?"

"Yeah, they did," says Bob.

"Do you realize what the rejection by Q.C. has done to you?" asks Jonah.

"It means we have to scrap about a hundred parts," says Bob.

"No, think again," says Jonah. "These are *bottleneck* parts."

It dawns on me what he's getting at.

"We lost the time on the bottleneck," I say.

Jonah whirls toward me.

"Exactly right!" he says. "And what does lost time on a bottleneck mean? It means you have lost throughput."

"But you're not saying we should ignore quality, are you?" asks Bob.

"Absolutely not. You can't make money for long without a quality product," says Jonah. "But I am suggesting you use quality control in a different way."

I ask, "You mean we should put Q.C. in front of the bottleneck?"

Jonah raises a finger and says, "Very perceptive of you. Make sure the bottleneck works only on good parts by weeding out the ones that are defective. If you scrap a part before it reaches the bottleneck, all you have lost is a scrapped part. But if you scrap the part after it's passed the bottleneck, you have lost time that cannot be recovered."

"Suppose we get sub-standard quality downstream from the bottleneck?" says Stacey.

"That's another aspect of the same idea," says Jonah. "Be sure the process controls on bottleneck parts are very good, so these parts don't become defective in later processing. Are you with me?"

Bob says, "Just one question: where do we get the inspectors?"

"What's wrong with shifting the ones you already have to the bottlenecks?" asks Jonah.

"That's something we can think about," I tell him.

"Good. Let's go back to the offices," says Jonah.

We go back to the office building and meet in the conference room.

"I want to be absolutely sure you understand the importance

of the bottlenecks," says Jonah. "Every time a bottleneck finishes a part, you are making it possible to ship a finished product. And how much does that mean to you in sales?"

"It averages around a thousand dollars a unit," says Lou.

"And you're worried about spending a dollar or two at the bottlenecks to make them more productive?" he asks. "First of all, what do you think the cost of, let's say, the X machine is for one hour?"

Lou says, "That's well established. It costs us $32.50 per hour."

"And heat–treat?"

"That's $21 per hour," says Lou.

"Both of those amounts are incorrect," says Jonah.

"But our cost data—"

"The numbers are wrong, not because you have made a calculating error, but because the costs were determined as if these work centers existed in isolation," says Jonah. "Let me explain: when I was a physicist, people would come to me from time to time with problems in mathematics they couldn't solve. They wanted me to check their numbers for them. But after a while I learned not to waste my time checking the numbers— because the numbers were almost always right. However, if I checked the *assumptions,* they were almost always wrong."

Jonah pulls a cigar out of his pocket and lights it with a match.

"That's what's going on here," he says between puffs. "You have calculated the cost of operating these two work centers according to standard accounting procedures . . . *without* considering the fact that both are bottlenecks."

"How does that change their costs?" asks Lou.

"What you have learned is that the capacity of the plant is equal to the capacity of its bottlenecks," says Jonah. "Whatever the bottlenecks produce in an hour is the equivalent of what the plant produces in an hour. So . . . an hour lost at a bottleneck is an hour lost for the entire system."

"Right, we're with you," says Lou.

"Then how much would it cost for this entire plant to be idle for one hour?" asks Jonah.

"I really can't say, but it would very expensive," admits Lou.

"Tell me something," says Jonah. "How much does it cost you to operate your plant each month?"

Lou says, "Our total operating expense is around $1.6 million per month."

"And let's just take the X machine as an example," he says. "How many hours a month did you say it's available for production?"

"About 585," says Ralph.

"The actual cost of a bottleneck is the total expense of the system divided by the number of hours the bottleneck produces," says Jonah. "What does this make it?"

Lou takes out his calculator from his coat pocket and punches in the numbers.

"That's $2,735," says Lou. "Now wait a minute. Is that right?"

"Yes, it's right," says Jonah. "If your bottlenecks are not working, you haven't just lost $32 or $21. The true cost is the cost of an hour of the entire system. And that's twenty seven *hundred* dollars."

Lou is flabbergasted.

"That puts a little different perspective on it," says Stacey.

"Of course it does," says Jonah. "And with that in mind, how do we optimize the use of the bottlenecks? There are two principal themes on which you need to concentrate . . .

"First, make sure the bottlenecks' time is not wasted," he says. "How is the time of a bottleneck wasted? One way is for it to be sitting idle during a lunch break. Another is for it to be processing parts which are already defective—or which will become defective through a careless worker or poor process control. A third way to waste a bottleneck's time is to make it work on parts you don't need."

"You mean spare parts?" asks Bob.

"I mean anything that isn't within the current demand," he says. "Because what happens when you build inventory now that you won't sell for months in the future? You are sacrificing present money for future money; the question is, can your cash flow sustain it? In your case, absolutely not."

"He's right," admits Lou.

"Then make the bottlenecks work only on what will contribute to throughput *today* . . . not nine months from now," says Jonah. "That's one way to increase the capacity of the bottlenecks. The other way you increase bottleneck capacity is to take some of the load off the bottlenecks and give it to non-bottle-necks.''

I ask, "Yeah, but how do we do that?"

"That's why I was asking those questions when we were out in the plant," he says. "Do all of the parts have to be processed by the bottleneck? If not, the ones which don't can be shifted to non-bottlenecks for processing. And the result is you gain capacity on your bottleneck. A second question: do you have other machines to do the same process? If you have the machines, or if you have a vendor with the right equipment, you can offload from the bottleneck. And, again, you gain capacity which enables you to increase throughput.''

I come into the kitchen for breakfast the next morning and sit down to a big steaming bowl of my mother's oat-meal . . . which I have hated ever since I was a kid. I'm staring at the oatmeal (and the oatmeal is staring back) when Mom/Grandma asks, "So how did everything go last night?"

I say, "Well, actually, you and the kids were on the right track at dinner."

"We were?" asks Dave.

"We need to make the Herbies go faster," I say. "And last night Jonah pointed out some ways to do that. So we learned a lot."

"Well, now, isn't that good news," says my mother.

She pours a cup of coffee for herself and sits down at the table. It's quiet for a moment. Then I notice that Mom and the kids are eyeing each other.

"Something wrong?" I ask.

"Their mother called again last night while you were gone," says my mother.

Julie has been calling the kids regularly since she left. But for whatever reason of her own, she still won't tell them where she is. I'm debating whether to hire a private detective to find out where she's hiding.

"Sharon says she heard something when she was on the phone talking," says my mother.

I look at Sharon.

"You know that music Grandpa always listens to?" she says.

I say, "You mean Grandpa Barnett?"

"Uh-huh, you know," she says, "the music that puts you to sleep, with the —what are they called?"

"Violins," says Dave.

"Right, the violins," says Sharon. "Well, when Mom wasn't talking, I heard that on the phone last night."

"I heard 'em too," says Dave.

"Really?" I say. "That's very interesting. Thank you both for noticing that. Maybe I'll give Grandma and Grandpa Barnett another call today."

I finish my coffee and stand up.

"Alex, you haven't even touched your oatmeal," says Mom.

I lean down and kiss her on the cheek. "Sorry, I'm late for school."

I wave to the kids and hurry to grab my briefcase.

"Well, I'll just have to save it so you can eat it tomorrow," says my mother.

# 20

Driving to the plant, I pass the motel where Jonah stayed last night. I know he's long gone—he had a 6:30 A.M. flight to catch. I offered to pick him up this morning and drive him to the airport, but (lucky for me) he refused and said he'd take a cab.

As soon as I get to the office, I tell Fran to set up a meeting with the staff. Meanwhile, I start to write down a list of the actions Jonah suggested last night. But Julie comes to mind and won't leave. I close my office door and sit down at my desk. I find the number for Julie's parents and dial it.

The first day after Julie left, her parents called to ask me if I had heard anything. They haven't called back since. A day or two ago, I tried getting in touch with them to find out if *they* had heard anything. I called in the afternoon and I talked to Julie's mother, Ada. She said she didn't know where Julie was. Even then, I didn't quite believe her.

Now Ada answers again.

"Hi, this is Alex," I tell her. "Let me talk to Julie."

Ada is flustered. "Well, um, ah . . . she isn't here."

"Yes, she is."

I hear Ada sigh.

"She *is* there, isn't she," I say.

Finally Ada says, "She does not want to talk to you."

"How long, Ada? How long has she been there? Were you lying to me even that Sunday night when I called?"

"No, we were not *lying* to you," she says indignantly. "We had no idea where she was. She was with her friend, Jane, for a few days."

"Sure, and what about the other day when I called?"

"Julie simply asked me not to say where she was," says Ada, "and I shouldn't even be telling you now. She wants to be by herself for a while."

"Ada, I need to speak with her," I say.

"She will not come to the phone," says Ada.

"How do you know until you've asked?"

The phone on Ada's end is put down on the table. Footsteps fade away and return a minute later.

"She says she'll call you when she's ready," says Ada.

"What does that mean?"

"If you hadn't neglected her all these years, you wouldn't be in this situation," she says.

"Ada—"

"Good-bye," she says.

She hangs up the phone. I try calling back right away, but there is no answer. After a few minutes, I force my mind back to getting ready to talk to the staff.

At ten o'clock, the meeting starts in my office.

"I'd like to know what you think about what you heard last night," I say. "Lou, what was your reaction?"

Lou says, "Well . . . I just couldn't believe what he was saying about an hour of a bottleneck. I went home last night and thought it over to see if it all made sense. And, actually, we were wrong about a lost hour of a bottleneck costing $2,700."

"We were?" I ask.

"Only eighty percent of our products flow through the bottlenecks," says Lou as he takes a piece of note paper from his shirt pocket. "So the truer cost ought to be eighty percent of our operating expense, and that comes to $2,188 an hour—not $2,735."

"Oh," I say. "I suppose you're right."

Then Lou smiles.

"Nevertheless," he says, "I have to admit it was quite an eye-opener to look at the situation from that perspective."

"I agree," I tell him. "What about the rest of you?"

I go from person to person around the office asking for reactions, and we're all pretty much in agreement. Even so, Bob seems hesitant about committing to some of the changes Jonah was talking about. And Ralph isn't sure yet where he fits in. But Stacey is a strong advocate.

She sums up, saying, "I think it makes enough sense to risk the changes."

"Although I'm nervous about anything that increases operating expense at this point in time," says Lou, "I agree with Stacey. As Jonah said, we may face a bigger risk just staying on the path we've been following."

Bob raises one of his meaty hands in preparation for a comment.

"Okay, but some of what Jonah talked about will be easier

and faster to make happen than the rest,'' he says. ''Why don't we go ahead with the easier things right away and see what kind of effect they have while we're developing the others.''

I tell him, ''That sounds reasonable. What would you do first?''

''I think I'd wanna move the Q.C. inspection points first, to check parts going into the bottlenecks,'' says Bob. ''The other Q.C. measures will take a little time, but we can have an inspector checking pre–bottleneck parts in no time—by the end of today if you want.''

I nod. ''Good. What about new rules for lunch breaks?''

''We might have a squawk or two from the union,'' he says.

I shake my head. ''I think they'll go along with it. Work out the details and I'll talk to O'Donnell.''

Bob makes a note on the paper pad on his lap. I stand up and step around the desk to emphasize what I'm about to say.

''One of the questions Jonah raised last night really struck home for me,'' I tell them. ''Why are we making the bottlenecks work on inventory that won't increase throughput?''

Bob looks at Stacey, and she looks back at him.

''That's a good question,'' she says.

Bob says, ''We made the decision—''

''I know the decision,'' I say. ''Build inventory to maintain efficiencies. ''But our problem is not efficiencies. Our problem is our backlog of overdue orders. And it's very visible to our customers and to division management. We positively must do something to improve our due-date performance, and Jonah has given us the insight on what that something has to be.

''Until now, we've expedited orders on the basis of who's screamed the loudest,'' I say. ''From now on, late orders should get first priority over the others. An order that's two weeks late gets priority over an order that's one week late, and so on.''

''We've tried that from time to time in the past,'' says Stacey.

''Yes, but the key this time is we make sure the *bottlenecks* are processing parts for those late orders according to the same priority,'' I say.

''That's the sane approach to the problem, Al,'' says Bob, ''Now how do we make it happen?''

''We have to find out which inventory en route to the bottlenecks is needed for late orders and which is simply going to end up in a warehouse. So here's what we need to do," I say. "Ralph, I want you to make us a list of all the overdue orders. Have them ranked in priority ranging from the most days overdue to the least days overdue. How soon can you have that for us?"

"Well, that in itself won't take very long," he says. "The problem is we've got the monthlies to run."

I shake my head. "Nothing is more important to us right now than making the bottlenecks more productive. We need that list as soon as possible, because once you've got it, I want you to work with Stacey and her people in inventory control—find out what parts still have to be processed by either of the bottlenecks to complete those orders."

I turn to Stacey.

"After you know which parts are missing, get together with Bob and schedule the bottlenecks to start working on the parts for the latest order first, the next latest, and so on."

"What about the parts that don't go through either one of the bottlenecks?" asks Bob.

"I'm not going to worry about those at the moment," I tell him. "Let's work on the assumption that anything not needing to go through a bottleneck is either waiting in front of assembly already, or will be by the time the bottleneck parts arrive."

Bob nods.

"Everybody got it?" I ask. "Nothing else takes priority over this. We don't have time to take a step back and do some kind of headquarters number where everyone takes six months to think about it. We know what we have to do. Let's get it done."

That evening, I'm driving along the Interstate. Around sunset, I'm looking around at the rooftops of suburban houses to either side of the highway. A sign goes by which says I'm two miles from the exit to Forest Grove. Julie's parents live in Forest Grove. I take that exit.

Neither the Barnetts nor Julie know I'm coming. I told my mother not to tell the kids. I simply hopped in the car after work and headed down here. I've had enough of this hide-and-seek game she's playing.

From a four-lane highway, I turn onto a smooth blacktop street which winds through a quiet neighborhood. It's a nice neighborhood. The homes are unquestionably expensive and the lawns without exception are immaculate. The streets are lined with trees just getting the new leaves of spring. They are brilliant green in the golden setting sun.

I see the house halfway down the street. It's the two-story brick colonial painted white. It has shutters. The shutters are made of aluminium and have no hinges; they are non-functional but traditional. This is where Julie grew up.

I park the Buick by the curb in front of the house. I look up the driveway, and sure enough, there is Julie's Accord in front of the garage.

Before I have reached the front door, it opens. Ada Barnett is standing behind the screen. I see her hand reach down and click the screen door lock as I approach.

"Hello," I say.

"I told you she doesn't want to talk to you," says Ada.

"Will you just ask her please?" I ask. "She *is* my wife."

"If you want to talk to Julie, you can do it through her lawyer," says Ada.

She starts to close the door.

I say, "Ada, I am not leaving until I talk to your daughter."

"If you don't leave, I will call the police to have you removed from our property," says Ada Barnett.

"Then I will wait in my car," I say. "You don't own the street."

The door closes. I walk across the lawn and over the sidewalk, and get in the Buick. I sit there and stare at the house. Every so often, I notice the curtains move behind the window glass of the Barnett house. After about forty five minutes, the sun has set and I'm seriously wondering how long I can sit here when the front door opens again.

Julie walks out. She's wearing jeans and sneakers and a sweater. The jeans and sneakers make her look young. She reminds me of a teenager meeting a boyfriend her parents disapprove of. She comes across the lawn and I get out of the car. When she's about ten feet away she stops, as if she's worried about getting too close, where I might grab her, pull her into the car, and drive like the wind to my tent in the desert or something. We look each other over. I slide my hands into my pockets.

For openers, I say, "So . . . how have you been?"

"If you want to know the truth," she says, "I've been rotten. How have you been?"

"Worried about you."

She glances away. I slap the roof of the Buick.

"Let's go for a ride," I say.

"No, I can't," she says.

"How about a walk then?" I ask.

"Alex, just tell me what you want, okay?" she says.

"I want to know why you're doing this!"

"Because I don't know if I want to be married to you any-more," she says. "Isn't that obvious?"

"Okay, can't we talk about it?"

She says nothing.

"Come on," I say. "Let's take that walk—just once around the block. Unless you want to give the neighbors lots to talk about."

Julie looks around at the houses and realizes we're a spec-tacle. Awkwardly, she steps toward me. I hold out my hand. She doesn't take it, but we turn together and begin a stroll down the sidewalk. I wave to the Barnett house and note the flurry of a curtain. Julie and I walk a hundred feet or so in the twilight before we say anything. At last I break the silence.

"Look, I'm sorry about what happened that weekend," I tell her. "But what else could I do? Davey expected me—"

"It wasn't because you went on the hike with Davey," she says. "That was just the last straw. All of a sudden, I just couldn't stand it anymore. I had to get away."

"Julie, why didn't you at least let me know where you were?"

"Listen," she says, "I went away from you so I could be alone."

Hesitantly, I ask, "So . . . do you want a divorce?"

"I don't know yet," she says.

"Well, when will you know?"

"Al, this has been a very mixed up time for me," she says. "I don't know what to do. I can't decide anything. My mother tells me one thing. My father tells me something else. My friends tell me something else. Everyone except me knows what I should do."

"You went off to be by yourself to make a decision that's going to affect both of us as well as our kids. And you're listening to everyone except the three other people whose lives are going to be screwed up if you don't come back," I say.

"This is something I need to figure out on my own, away from the pressures of you three."

"All I'm suggesting is that we talk about what's bothering you."

She sighs in exasperation and says, "Al, we've been over it a million times already!"

"Okay, look, just tell me this: are you having an affair?"

Julie stops. We have reached the corner.

She says coldly, "I think I've gone far enough with you."

I stand there for a moment as she turns and heads back toward her parents' house. I catch up with her.

I say, "Well? Are you or aren't you?"

"Of course I'm not having an affair!" she yells. "Do you think I'd be staying with my *parents* if I were having an affair?"

A man who is walking his dog turns and stares at us. Julie and I stride past him in stiff silence.

I whisper to Julie, "I just had to know . . . that's all."

"If you think I'd leave my children just to go have a fling with some stranger, you have no understanding of who I am," she says.

I feel as if she'd slapped my face.

"Julie, I'm sorry," I tell her. "That kind of thing sometimes happens, and I just needed to make sure of what's going on."

She slows her walk. I put my hand on her shoulder. She brushes it off.

"Al, I've been unhappy for a long time," she says. "And I'll tell you something: I feel guilty about it. I feel as though I don't have a right to be unhappy. I just know I am."

With irritation, I see we're back in front of her parents' house. The walk was too short. Ada is standing in plain view at the window. Julie and I stop. I lean against the rear fender of the Buick.

"Why don't you pack your things and come home with me," I suggest, but she's shaking her head before I've even finished the sentence.

"No, I'm not ready to do that," she says.

"Okay, look," I say. "The choice is this: You stay away and we get a divorce. Or we get back together and struggle to make the marriage work. The longer you stay away, the more we're going to drift apart from each other and toward a divorce.

And if we get a divorce, you know what's going to happen. We've seen it happen over and over to our friends. Do you really want that? Come on, come home. I promise we can make it better.''

She shakes her head. "I can't, Al. I've heard too many promises before."

I say, "Then you want a divorce?"

Julie says, "I told you, I don't know!"

"Okay," I say finally. "I can't make up your mind for you. Maybe it is your decision. All I can say is I want you back. I'm sure that's what the kids want too. Give me a call when you know what *you* want."

"That was exactly what I planned to do, Al."

I get into the Buick and start the engine. Rolling down the window, I look up at her as she stands on the sidewalk next to the car.

"You know, I do happen to love you," I tell her.

This finally melts her. She comes to the car and leans down. Reaching through the window, I take her hand for a moment. She kisses me. Then without a word she stands up and walks away; halfway across the lawn, she breaks into a run. I watch her until she's disappeared through the door. Then I shake my head, put the car into gear, and drive away.

# 21

I'm home by ten o'clock that night. Depressed, but home. Rummaging through the refrigerator, I attempt to find dinner, but have to settle for cold spaghetti and some leftover peas. Washing it down with some leftover vodka, I dine in dejection.

I'm wondering while I'm eating what I'm going to do if Julie doesn't come back. If I don't have a wife, do I start to date women again? Where would I meet them? I have a sudden vision of myself standing in the bar of the Bearington Holiday Inn, attempting to be sexy while asking strange females, "What's your sign?"

Is *that* my fate? My God. And anyway, do lines like that even work these days? Did they ever?

I must know *somebody* to go out with.

For a while, I sit there thinking of all the available women I know. Who would go out with me? Whom would I want to go out with? It doesn't take long to exhaust the list. Then one women comes to mind. Getting up from my chair, I go to the phone and spend about five minutes staring at it.

Should I?

Nervously, I dial the number. I hang up before it rings. I stare at the phone some more. Oh, what the hell! All she can do is say no, right? I dial the number again. It rings about ten times before anyone answers.

"Hello." It's her father.

"May I speak to Julie please."

Pause. "Just a minute."

The moments pass.

"Hello?" says Julie.

"Hi, it's me."

"Al?"

I say, "Yeah, listen, I know it's late, but I just want to ask you something."

"If it has to be with getting a divorce or coming home—"

"No, no, no," I tell her. "I was just wondering if while you're making up your mind, there would be any harm in us seeing each other once in a while."

She says, "Well . . . I guess not."

"Good. What are you doing Saturday night?" I ask.

There is a moment of silence as the smile forms on her face. Amused, she asks, "Are you asking me for a date?"

"Yes, I am."

Long pause.

I say, "So would you like to go out with me?"

"Yes, I'd like that a lot," she says finally.

"Great. How about I see you at 7:30?"

"I'll be ready," she says.

The next morning in the conference room, we've got the two supervisors of the bottlenecks with us. By "us," I mean Stacey, Bob, Ralph and me. Ted Spencer is the supervisor responsible for the heat–treat furnaces. He's an older guy with hair that looks like steel wool and a body like a steel file. We've got him and Mario DeMonte, supervisor of the machining center with the NCX-10. Mario is as old as Ted, but plumper.

Stacey and Ralph both have red eyes. Before we sat down, they told me about the work that went into this morning's meeting.

Getting the list of overdue orders was easy. The computer listed them and sorted them according to lateness. Nothing to it, didn't even take an hour. But then they had to go over the bills of material for each of the orders and find out which parts are done by the bottlenecks. And they had to establish whether there was inventory to make those parts. That took most of the night.

Stacey told me this morning this was the first time she really appreciated the existence of the computer.

We all have our own photocopies of a hand-written list Ralph has had prepared. Listed in the print-out is a grand total of sixty seven records, our total backlog of overdue orders. They have been sorted from most–days–past–due to least–days. The worst one, at the top of the list, is an order that is fifty eight days beyond the delivery date promised by marketing. The best are one day late; there are three of those orders.

"We did some checking," says Ralph. "And about ninety percent of the current overdues have parts that flow through one or both of the bottleneck operations. Of those, about eighty five percent are held up at assembly because we're waiting for those parts to arrive before we can build and ship."

"So it's obvious those parts get first priority," I explain to the two supervisors.

Then Ralph says, "We went ahead and made a list for both heat–treat and the NCX-10 as to which parts they each have to process and in what order—again, the same sequence of latest order to least late. In about a week we can generate the list by computer and stop burning the midnight oil."

"Fantastic, Ralph. I think both you and Stacey have done a super job," I tell him. Then I turn to Ted and Mario. "Now, all you gentlemen have to do is have your foremen start at the top of the list and work their way down."

"That sounds easy enough," says Ted. "I think we can handle that."

"You know, we may have to go track some of these down," says Mario.

"So you'll have to do some digging through the inventory," says Stacey. "What's the problem?"

Mario frowns and says, "No problem. You just want us to do what's on this list, right?"

"Yep, it's that simple," I say. "I don't want to see either of you working on something not on that list. If the expeditors give you any problems, tell them to come see me. And be sure you stick to the sequence we've given you."

Ted and Mario both nod.

I turn to Stacey and say, "You do understand how important it is for the expeditors not to interfere with this priority list, don't you?"

Stacey says, "Okay, but you have to promise me you won't change it because of pressure from marketing."

"My word of honor," I tell her. Then I say to Ted and Mario, "In all seriousness, I hope you two guys know that heat–treat and the NCX-10 are the most important processes in the whole plant. How well you manage those two could very well determine whether this plant has a future."

"We'll do our best," says Ted.

"I can assure you that they will," says Bob Donovan.

Right after that meeting, I go down the hall to the personnel relations for a meeting with Mike O'Donnell, the union local president. When I walk in, my personnel manager, Scott Dolin, is gripping the armrests of his chair with white knuckles, while O'Donnell is talking at the top of his voice.

"What's the problem here?" I ask.

"You know very well what the problem is: your new lunch rules in heat–treat and n/c machining," says O'Donnell. "They're in violation of the contract. I refer you to Section Seven, Paragraph Four . . . "

I say, "Okay, wait a minute, Mike. It's time we gave the union an update on the situation of the plant."

For the rest of the morning I describe for him the situation the plant is in. Then I tell him some of what we've discovered and explain why the changes are necessary.

Wrapping up, I say, "You understand, don't you, that it's probably only going to affect about twenty people at the most?"

He shakes his head.

"Look, I appreciate you trying to explain all this," he says. "But we got a contract. Now if we look the other way on one thing, what's to say you won't start changing whatever else you don't like?"

I say, "Mike, in all honesty, I can't tell you that down the road aways, we won't need to make other changes. But we're ultimately talking about jobs. I'm not asking for cuts in wages or concessions on benefits. But I am asking for flexibility. We have to have the leeway necessary to make changes that will allow the plant to make money. Or, very simply, there may not be a plant in a few months."

"Sounds like scare tactics to me," he says finally.

"Mike, all I can say is, if you want to wait a couple of months to see if I'm just trying to scare everyone, it'll be too late."

O'Donnell is quiet for a moment.

Finally he says, "I'll have to think about it, talk it over and all that. We'll get back to you."

By early afternoon, I can't stand it anymore. I'm anxious to find out how the new priority system is working. I try calling Bob Donovan, but he's out in the plant. So I decide to go have a look for myself.

The first place I check is the NCX-10. But when I get to the machine, there's nobody to ask. Being an automated machine, it runs a lot of the time with nobody tending it. The problem is that when I walk up, the damn thing is just sitting there. It isn't running and nobody is doing a set-up. I get mad.

I go find Mario.

"Why the hell isn't that machine working?" I ask him.

He checks with the foreman. Finally he walks back to me.

"We don't have the materials," he says.

"What do you mean, *you don't have materials*," I shout. "What do you call these stacks of steel everywhere?"

"But you told us to work according to what's on the list," says Mario.

"You mean you finished all the late parts?"

"No, they did the first two batches of parts," says Mario. "When they got to the third part on the list, they looked all around and couldn't find the materials for it in the queue. So we're shut down until they turn up."

I'm ready to strangle him.

"That's what you wanted us to do, right?" says Mario. "You wanted us to do only what was on the list and in the same order as listed, didn't you? Isn't that what you said?"

Finally I say, "Yes, that is what I said. But didn't it occur to you that if you couldn't do one item on the list you should go on to the next?"

Mario looks helpless.

"Well, where the hell are the materials you need?" I ask him.

"I have no idea," he says. "They could be any of half–a–dozen places. But I think Bob Donovan might have somebody looking for them already."

"Okay, look," I tell him. "You have the setup people get this machine ready for whatever is the *next* part on that list for which you do have the materials. And keep this hunk of junk running."

"Yes sir," says Mario.

Fuming mad, I start back to the office to have Donovan paged, so I can find out what went wrong. Halfway there, I pass some lathes and there he is, talking to Otto the foreman. I don't know how civil the tone is. Otto appears to be dismayed by Bob's presence. I stop and stand there waiting for Bob to finish and notice me. Which happens directly. Otto walks over and calls his machinists together. Bob comes over to me.

I say, "You know about what's going on—"

"Yes, I know," he says. "That's why I'm here."

"What's the problem?"

"Nothing, no problem," he says. "Just standard operating procedure."

It turns out, as Bob explains to me, that the parts they were waiting for at the NCX-10 have been sitting here for about a week. Otto has been running other batches of parts. He didn't know about the importance of the parts destined for the NCX-10. To him they looked like any other batch—and a rather unimportant one judging from the size. When Bob got here, they were in the middle of a big, long run. Otto didn't want to stop . . . until Donovan explained it to him, that is.

"Dammit, Al, it's just like before," Bob says. "They get set up and they start running one thing, and then they have to break in the middle so we can finish something else. It's the same damn thing!"

"Now hold on," I say. "Let's think about this for a second."

Bob shakes his head. "What is there to think about?"

"Let's just try to reason this through," I say. "What was the problem?"

"The parts didn't arrive at the NCX-10, which meant the operators couldn't run the batch they were supposed to be running," says Bob in kind of a sing-song way.

"And the cause was that the bottleneck parts were held up by this non-bottleneck machine running non-bottleneck parts," I say. "Now we've got to ask ourselves why that happened."

"The guy in charge here was just trying to stay busy, that's all," says Bob.

"Right. Because if he didn't stay busy, someone like you would come along and jump all over him," I say.

"Yeah, and if I didn't, then someone like you would jump all over me," says Bob.

"Okay, granted. But even though this guy was busy, he wasn't helping to move us toward the goal," I say.

"Well . . . "

"He wasn't, Bob! Look," I say. I point to the parts destined for the NCX-10. "We need those parts now, not tomorrow. The non-bottleneck parts we may not need for weeks, or even months—maybe never. So by continuing to run the non-bottleneck parts, this guy was actually interfering with our ability to get an order out the door and make money."

"But he didn't know any better," says Bob.

"Exactly. He couldn't distinguish between an important batch of parts and an unimportant one," I say. "Why not?"

"Nobody told him."

"Until you came along," I say. "But you can't be everywhere, and this same kind of thing is going to happen again. So how do we communicate to everybody in the plant which parts are important?"

"I guess we need some kind of system," says Bob.

"Fine. Let's go work on one right away so we don't have to keep putting up with this crap," I say. "And before we do anything else, let's make sure that people at both of the bottlenecks know to keep working on the order with the highest priority number on the list."

Bob has a final chat with Otto to make sure he knows what to do with the parts. Then the two of us head for the bottlenecks.

Finally we're walking back to the office. Glancing at Bob's face, I can tell he's still bothered by what happened.

"What's wrong? You look unconvinced about all this," I say.

"Al, what's going to happen if we repeatedly have people break up process runs to run parts for the bottlenecks?" he asks.

"We should be able to avoid idle time on the bottlenecks," I say.

"But what's going to happen to our costs on the other 98 percent of the work centers we got here?" he asks.

"Right now, don't worry about it. Let's just keep the bottlenecks busy," I say. "Look, I'm convinced you did the right thing back there. Aren't you?"

"Maybe I did the right thing," he says, "but I had to break all the rules to do it."

"Then the rules had to be broken," I say. "And maybe they weren't good rules to begin with. You know we've always had to break up process runs for expediency to get orders shipped. The difference between then and now is that now we know to do it ahead of time, before the external pressure comes. We've got to have faith in what we know."

Bob nods in agreement. But I know he'll only believe the proof. Maybe I'm the same, if I'm honest about it.

A few days pass while we develop a system to cure the problem. But at eight o'clock on Friday morning, at the beginning of first shift, I'm in the cafeteria watching the employees wander in. With me is Bob Donovan.

After our earlier misunderstanding, I decided that the more people who know about the bottlenecks and how important they are, the better off we'll be. We're holding fifteen-minute meetings with everyone working in the plant, both foremen and hourly people. This afternoon, we'll do the same thing with people working second shift, and I'll come in late tonight to talk to the third shift as well. When we've got everybody this morning, I get up in front of them and talk.

"All of you know that this plant has been in a downward slide for some time. What you don't know is that we're in the position to begin to change that," I tell them. "You're here in this meeting because we're introducing a new system today . . . a system which we think will make the plant more productive than it's been in the past. In the next few minutes, I'm going to explain briefly some of the background that made us develop this new system. And then Bob Donovan is going to tell you how it works."

Trying to keep meetings to fifteen minutes doesn't give us the time to tell them very much. But using the analogy of an hourglass, I do explain briefly about the bottlenecks and why we have to give priority to parts on the heat—treat and NCX-10 routings. For the things I can't take time to tell them, there is going to be a newsletter, which will replace the old plant employee paper, and which will report developments and progress in the plant.

Anyway, I turn over the microphone to Donovan and he tells them how we're going to prioritize all materials in the plant so everybody knows what to work on.

"By the end of today, all work-in-process on the floor will be marked by a tag with a number on it," he says and holds up some samples. "The tag will be one of two colors: red or green.

"A red marker means the work attached to it has first priority. The red tags go on any materials needing to be processed by a bottleneck. When a batch of parts with that color marker arrives at your work station, you are to work on them right away."

Bob explains what we mean by "right away." If the employee is working on a different job, it's okay to finish what he's doing, as long as it doesn't take more than half an hour. Before n hour has passed, certainly, the red–tagged parts should be getting attention.

"If you are in the middle of a setup, break the setup immediately and get ready for the red parts. When you've finished the bottleneck parts, you can go back to what you were doing before.

"The second color is green. When there is a choice between working on parts with a red marker and part with a green marker, you work on the parts with the red marker first. By far, most of the work-in-process out there will be marked by green. Even so, you work on green orders only if you don't have any red ones in queue.

"That explains the priority of the colors. But what happens when you've got two batches of the same color? Each tag will have a number marked on it. You should always work on the materials with the lowest number."

Donovan explains some of the details and answers a couple of questions, after which I wrap it up.

I tell them, "This meeting was my idea. I decided to take you away from your jobs, mostly because I wanted everyone to hear the same message at the same time, so that—I hope—you'll have a better understanding of what's going on. But another reason is that I know it's been a long time since most of you have heard any good news about the plant. What you've just heard about is a beginning. Even so, the future of this plant and the security of your jobs will only be assured when we start making money again. The most important thing you can do is to work with us . . . and, together, we'll all be working to keep this plant working."

Late that afternoon, my phone rings.

"Hi, this is O'Donnell. Go ahead with the new policy on lunch and coffee breaks. We won't challenge it."

I relay the news to Donovan. And with these small victories, the week ends.

At 7:29 on Saturday evening, I park the washed, waxed, buffed and vacuumed Buick in the Barnett driveway. I reach for the bouquet of flowers beside me on the seat, and step out onto the lawn wearing my new courting duds. At 7:30, I ring the doorbell.

Julie opens the door.

"Well, don't you look nice," she says.

"So do you," I tell her.

And she does.

There are a few stiff minutes spent talking with her parents. Mr. Barnett asks how everything is going at the plant. I tell him it looks like we may be on our way to a recovery, and mention the new priority system and what it will do for the NCX-10 and heat–treat. Both of her parents look at me blankly.

"Shall we go?" suggests Julie.

Joking, I tell Julie's mother, "I'll have her home by ten o'clock."

"Good," says Mrs. Barnett. "We'll be waiting."

# 22

"There you have it," says Ralph.

"Not bad," says Stacey.

"Not bad? It's a lot better than not bad," says Bob.

"We must be doing something right," says Stacey.

"Yeah, but it isn't enough," I mutter.

A week has passed. We're grouped around a computer terminal in the conference room. Ralph has extracted from the computer a list of overdue orders that we shipped last week.

"Isn't enough? At least it's progress," says Stacey. "We shipped twelve orders last week. For this plant, that's not bad. And they were our twelve most overdue orders."

"By the way, our worst overdue order is now only forty four days late," says Ralph. "As you may recall, the worst one used to be fifty eight days."

"All right!" says Donovan.

I step back to the table and sit down.

Their enthusiasm is somewhat justified. The new system of tagging all the batches according to priority and routing has been working fairly well. The bottlenecks are getting their parts promptly. In fact, the piles of inventory in front of them have grown. Following bottleneck processing, the red-tagged parts have been getting to final assembly faster. It's as if we've created an "express lane" through the plant for bottleneck parts.

After putting Q.C. in front of the bottlenecks, we discovered that about five percent of the parts going into the NCX-10 and about seven percent going into heat–treat did not conform to quality requirements. If those percentages hold true in the future, we'll effectively have gained that time for additional throughput.

The new policy of having people cover the bottlenecks on lunch breaks has also gone into effect. We're not sure how much we've gained from that, because we didn't know how much we were losing before. At least we're doing the right thing now. But I have heard reports that from time to time the NCX-10 is idle— and it happens when there is nobody on break. Donovan is supposed to be looking into the causes.

The combination of these has allowed us to ship our most critical orders and to ship a few more of them than normal. But

I know we're not going fast enough. A few weeks ago we were limping along; now we're walking, but we ought to be jogging.

Glancing back toward the data terminal, I see the eyes are upon me.

"Listen . . . I know we've taken a step in the right direction," I explain. "But we have to accelerate the progress. It's good that we got twelve shipments out last week. But we're still having some customer orders become past due. It's not as many, I'll grant you, but we still have to do better. We really shouldn't have *any* late orders."

Everyone walks away from the terminal and joins me around the table. Bob Donovan starts telling me how they're planning some refinements on what we've already done.

I say, "Bob, those are fine, but they're minor. How are we coming on the other suggestions Jonah made?"

Bob glances away.

"Well . . . we're looking into them," he says.

I say, "I want recommendations on offloading the bottlenecks ready for our Wednesday staff meeting."

Bob nods, but says nothing.

"You'll have them for us?" I ask.

"Whatever it takes," he says.

That afternoon in my office, I have a meeting with Elroy Langston, our Q.C. manager, and Barbara Penn, who handles employee communications. Barbara writes the newsletters, which are now explaining the background and reasons for the changes taking place in the plant. Last week, we distributed the first issue. I put her together with Langston to have her work on a new project.

After parts exit the bottlenecks, they often tend to look almost identical to the parts going *into* the bottlenecks. Only a close examination by a trained eye will detect the difference in some cases. The problem is how to make it easy for the employee to tell the two apart . . . and to make it possible for the employee to treat the post-bottleneck parts so more of them make it to assembly and are shipped as quality products. Langston and Penn are in my office to talk about what they've come up with.

"We already have the red tags," says Penn. "So that tells us the part is on a bottleneck routing. What we need is a simple way to show people the parts they need to treat with special attention—the ones they need to treat like gold."

"That's a suitable comparison," I tell her.

She says, "So what if we simply mark the tags with pieces of yellow tape after the parts are finished by the bottlenecks. The tape would tell people on sight that these are the parts you treat like gold. In conjunction with this, I'll do an internal promotion to spread the word about what the tape means. For media, we might use some sort of bulletin board poster, an announcement that the foremen would read to the hourly people, maybe a banner which would hang in the plant—those kinds of things."

"As long as the tape can be added without slowing down the bottlenecks, that sounds fine," I say.

"I'm sure we can find a way to do it so it doesn't interfere," says Langston.

"Good," I say. "One other concern of mine is that I don't want this to be just a lot of promotion."

"That's perfectly understood," says Langston with a smile. "Right now, we're systematically identifying the causes of quality problems on the bottlenecks and in subsequent processing. Once we know where to aim, we'll be having specific procedures developed for bottleneck–routed parts and processes. And once they're established, we'll set up training sessions so people can learn those procedures. But that's obviously going to take some time. For the short term, we're specifying that the existing procedures be double-checked for accuracy on the bottleneck routes."

We talk that over for a few minutes, but basically all of it seems sound to me. I tell them to proceed full speed and to keep me informed of what's happening.

"Nice job," I say to both of them as they stand up to leave. "By the way, Roy, I thought Bob Donovan was going to sit in on this meeting."

"That man is hard to catch these days," says Langston. "But I'll brief him on what we talked about."

Just then, the phone rings. Reaching with one had to answer it, I wave to Langston and Penn with the other as they walk out the door.

"Hi, this is Donovan."

"It's too late to call in sick," I tell him. "Don't you know you just missed a meeting?"

That doesn't faze him.

"Al, have I got something to show you!" says Bob. "Got time to take a little walk?"

"Yeah, I guess so. What's this all about?"

"Well . . . I'll tell you when you get here," says Bob. "Meet me on the receiving dock."

I walk down to the dock, where I see Bob; he's standing there waving to me as I if I might miss him. Which would be impossible. There is a flat-bed truck backed up to the dock, and in the middle of the bed is a large object on a skid. The object is covered by a gray canvas tarp which has ropes tying it down. A couple of guys are working with an overhead crane to move the thing off of the truck. They're raising it into the air as I walk up to Bob. He cups his hands around his mouth.

"Easy there," Bob calls as he watches the big gray thing sway back and forth.

Slowly, the crane maneuvers the cargo back from the truck and lowers it safely to the concrete floor. The workers release the hoist chains. Bob walks over and has them untie the ropes holding down the canvas.

"We'll have it off in a minute," Bob assures me.

I stand there patiently, but Bob can't refrain from helping. When all the ropes are untied, Donovan takes hold of the tarp and, with a flair of gusto, flings it off of what it's concealing.

"Ta-da!" he says as stands back and gestures to what has to be one of the oldest pieces of equipment I've ever seen.

"What the hell is it?" I ask.

"It's a Zmegma," he says.

He takes a rag and wipes off some of the grime.

"They don't build 'em like this anymore," he says.

"I'm very glad to hear that," I say.

"Al," he says, "the Zmegma is just the machine we need!"

"That thing looks like it might have been state-of-the-art for 1942. How's it going to help us?"

"Well . . . I admit it ain't no match for the NCX-10. But if you take this baby right here," he says patting the Zmegma, "and one of those Screwmeisters over there," he says pointing across the way, "and that other machine off in the corner, together they can do all the things the NCX-10 can do."

I glance around at the different machines. All of them are old and idle. I step closer to the Zmegma to look it over.

"So this must be one of the machines you told Jonah we sold to make way for the inventory holding pen," I say.

"You got it," he says.

"It's practically an antique. All of them are," I say, referring to the other machines. "Are you sure they can give us acceptable quality?"

"It isn't automated equipment, so with human error we might have a few more mistakes," says Bob. "But if you want capacity, this is a quick way to get it."

I smile. "It's looking better and better. Where did you find this thing?"

"I called a buddy of mine this morning up at our South End plant," he says. "He told me he still had a couple of these sitting around and he'd have no problem parting with one of them. So I grabbed a guy from maintenance and we took a ride up to have a look."

I ask him, "What did it cost us?"

"The rental fee on the truck to haul it down here," says Bob. "The guy at South End told us just to go ahead and take it. He'll write it off as scrap. With all the paperwork he'd have to do, it was too much trouble to sell it to us."

"Does it still work?"

"It did before we left," says Bob. "Let's find out."

The maintenance man connects the power cable to an outlet on a nearby steel column. Bob reaches for the power switch and hits the ON button. For a second, nothing happens. Then we hear the slow, gathering whirr from somewhere in the guts of the old machine. Poofs of dust blow out of the antique fan housing. Bob turns to be with a dumb grin on his big face.

"Guess we're in business," he says.

# 23

Rain is beating at the windows in my office. Outside, the world is gray and blurred. It's the middle of a middle-of-the-week morning. In front of me are some so-called "Productivity Bulletins" put out by Hilton Smyth which I've come across in my in-basket. I haven't been able to make myself read past the first paragraph of the one on top. Instead, I'm gazing at the rain and pondering the situation with my wife.

Julie and I went out on our "date" that Saturday night, and we actually had a good time. It was nothing exotic. We went to a movie, we got a bite to eat afterwards, and for the heck of it we took a drive through the park on the way home. Very tame. But it was exactly what we needed. It was good just to *relax* with her. I admit that at first I felt kind of like we were back in high school or something. But, after a while, I decided that wasn't such a bad feeling. I brought her back to her parents at two in the morning, and we made out in the driveway until her old man turned on the porch light.

Since that night, we've continued to see each other. A couple of times last week, I made the drive up to see her. Once, we met halfway at a restaurant. I've been dragging myself to work in the morning, but with no complaints. We've had fun together.

By some unspoken agreement, neither of us talk about divorce or marriage. The subject has only come up once, which happened when we talked about the kids and agreed they should stay with Julie and her folks as soon as school ends. I tried then to push us into some answers, but the old argument syndrome began to brew quickly, and I backed off to preserve the peace.

It's a strange state of limbo we're in. It almost feels the way it did before we got married and "settled down." Only now, we're both quite familiar to each other. And there is this storm which has gone south for a while, but which is sure to swing back someday.

A soft tap at the door interrupts this meditation. I see Fran's face peeking around the edge of the door.

"Ted Spencer is outside," she says. "He says he needs to talk to you about something."

"What about?"

Fran steps into the office and closes the door behind her. She quickly comes over to my desk and whispers to me.

"I don't know, but I heard on the grapevine that he had an argument with Ralph Nakamura about an hour ago," she says.

"Oh," I say. "Okay, thanks for the warning. Send him in."

A moment later Ted Spencer comes in. He looks mad. I ask him what's happening down in heat–treat.

He says, "Al, you've got to get that computer guy off my back."

"You mean Ralph? What have you got against him?"

"He's trying to turn me into some kind of clerk or something," says Ted. "He's been coming around and asking all kinds of dumb questions. Now he wants me to keep some kind of special records on what happens in heat–treat."

"What kind of records?" I ask.

"I don't know . . . he wants me to keep a detailed log of everything that goes in and out of the furnaces . . . the times we put 'em in, the times we take 'em out, how much time between heats, all that stuff," says Ted. "And I've got too much to do to be bothered with all that. In addition to heat–treat, I've got three other work centers I'm responsible for."

"Why does he want this time log?" I ask.

"How should I know? I mean, we've already got enough paperwork to satisfy anybody, as far as I'm concerned," says Ted. "I think Ralph just wants to play games with numbers. If he's got the time for it, then fine, let him do it in his own department. I've got the productivity of *my* department to worry about."

Wanting to end this, I nod to him. "Okay, I hear you. Let me look into it."

"Will you keep him out of my area?" asks Ted.

"I'll let you know, Ted."

After he's gone, I have Fran track down Ralph Nakamura for me. What's puzzling me is that Ralph is not what you'd call an abrasive person, and yet he sure seems to have made Ted very upset.

"You wanted to see me?" asks Ralph from the door.

"Yeah, come on in and sit down," I say to him.

He seats himself in front of my desk.

"So tell me what you did to light Ted Spencer's fuse," I say to him.

Ralph rolls his eyes and says, "All I wanted from him was to keep an accurate record of the actual times for each heat of parts in the furnace. I thought it was a simple enough request."

"What prompted you to ask him?"

"I had a couple of reasons," says Ralph. "One of them is that the data we have on heat–treat seems to be very inaccurate. And if what you say is true, that this operation is so vital to the plant, then it seems to me we ought to have valid statistics on it."

"What makes you think our data is so inaccurate?" I ask.

"Because after I saw the total on last week's shipments I was kind of bothered by something. A few days ago on my own, I did some projections of how many shipments we would actually be able to make last week based on the output of parts from the bottlenecks. According to those projections, we should have been able to do about eighteen to twenty shipments instead of twelve. The projections were so far off that I figured at first I must have made a big mistake. So I took a closer look, double-checked my math and couldn't find anything wrong. Then I saw that the estimates for the NCX-10 were within the ballpark. But for heat–treat, there was a big difference."

"And that's what made you think that the data base must be in error," I say.

"Right," he says. "So I went down to talk to Spencer. And, ah . . . ."

"And what?"

"Well, I noticed some funny things were happening," he says. "He was kind of tight-lipped when I started asking him questions. Finally, I just happened to ask him when the parts that were being treated in the furnace at the moment were going to be finished. I thought I'd get a time on an actual heat by myself, just to see if we were close to the standard. He said the parts could come out at around 3 P.M. So I went away, and came back at three. But nobody was around. I waited for about ten minutes, then went to look for Ted. When I found him, he said he had the furnace helpers working somewhere else and they'd get around to unloading the furnace in a little while. I didn't think much about it. Then around 5:30, as I was leaving for the day,

I decided I'd go by the furnace to ask what time the parts had actually come out. But the same parts were still in there.''

"Two-and-a-half hours after they *could* have come out, they hadn't been unloaded?'' I ask.

"That's right,'' says Ralph. "So I found Sammy, the second–shift foreman down there, and asked him what was going on. He told me he was short-handed that night, and they'd get to it later. He said it didn't hurt the parts to stay in the furnace. While I was there, he shut off the burners, but I found out later that the parts didn't come out until about eight o'clock. I didn't mean to start trouble, but I'd thought if we recorded the actual times per heat, we'd at least have some realistic figures to use for estimating. You see, I asked some of the hourly people down there and they told me those kinds of delays happen a lot in heat–treat.''

"No kidding,'' I say. "Ralph . . . I want you to take all the measurements down there that you need. Don't worry about Ted. And do the same thing on the NCX-10.''

"Well, I'd like to, but it's kind of a chore,'' he says. "That's why I wanted Ted and the others just to jot down the times and all.''

I say, "Okay, we'll take care of that. And, ah . . . thanks very much.''

"You're welcome,'' he says.

"By the way, what was the other reason?'' I ask him. "You mentioned you had more than one.''

"Oh, well, it's probably not that important.''

"No, tell me,'' I say.

"I don't really know if we can do it or not,'' says Ralph, "but it occurred to me we might find a way to use the bottlenecks to predict when we'll be able to ship an order.''

I contemplate that possibility.

"Sounds interesting,'' I tell him. "Let me know what you come up with.''

Bob Donovan's ears are on fire by the time I've finished telling him what Ralph discovered about heat–treat on his own. I'm very upset about this. He's sitting in a chair in my office while I walk in circles in front of him.

But when I'm done, Bob tells me, "Al, the trouble is there is nothing for the guys down there to do while heat–treat is cook-in' the parts. You load up one of the damn furnaces, shut the doors, and that's it for six or eight hours, or however long it takes. What are they supposed to do? Stand around and twiddle their thumbs?''

"I don't care what they do between times as long as they get the parts in and out of the furnace pronto," I say. "We could have done almost another batch of parts in the five hours of waiting for people to finish what they were doing elsewhere and change loads.''

"All right," says Bob. "How about this: we loan the people to other areas while the parts cook, but as soon as the time is up, we make sure we call them back immediately so—"

"No, because what's going to happen is everybody will be very conscientious about it for two days, and then it'll slip back to the way it is now," I say. "I want people at those furnaces standing by, ready to load and unload twenty four hours a day, seven days a week. The first ones I want assigned there are foremen who are responsible full-time for what happens down there. And tell Ted Spencer that the next time I see him, he'd better know what's going on in heat–treat or I'll kick his ass.''

"You bet," says Bob. "But you know you're talking about two, maybe three people per shift.''

"Is that all?" I ask. "Don't you remember what lost time on a bottleneck costs us?''

"Okay, I'm with you," he says. "Tell you the truth, what Ralph found out about heat–treat is a lot like what I found out on my own about those rumors of idle time on the NXC-10.''

"What's going on there?''

Bob tells me that, indeed, it's true the NCX-10 is sitting idle for as much as half an hour or more at a time. But the problem is not lunch breaks. If the NCX-10 is being set up and lunch time rolls around, the two guys stay until the setup is completed. Or, if the setup is a long one, they spell each other, so one goes and eats while the other continues with the setup. We're covered fine during breaks. But if the machine stops, say, in the middle of the afternoon, it may sit there for twenty, thirty, forty minutes or so before anyone gets around to starting a new setup. The reason is the setup people are busy with *other* machines, with non-bottlenecks.

"Then let's do the same thing on the NCX-10 as I want to do on heat–treat," I tell Bob. "Let's get a machinist and a helper and have them permanently stationed at the NCX-10. When it stops, they can get to work on it immediately.''

"That's just dandy with me," says Bob. "But you know how it's going to look on paper. It's going to seem like we increased the direct labor content of the parts coming out of heat treat and the NCX-10.''

I slump into the chair behind my desk.

"Let's fight one battle at a time," I say.

The next morning, Bob comes to the staff meeting with his recommendations. They basically consist of four actions. The first two concern what he and I talked about the day before—dedicating a machinist and helper to the NCX-10, and stationing a foreman and two workers at the heat–treat furnaces. The assignments would apply to all three shifts. The other two recommendations concern offloading the bottlenecks. Bob has determined if we could activate one each of those old machines—the Zmegma and the two others—just one shift a day, we could add eighteen percent to the output of parts of the type produced by the NCX-10. Last of all, is that we take some of the parts queued at heat–treat and send them out to the vendor across town.

As he's presenting these, I'm wondering what Lou is going to say. As it happens, Lou offers little resistance.

"Knowing what we know now," says Lou, "it's perfectly legitimate for us to assign people to the bottlenecks if it will increase our throughput. We can certainly justify the cost if it increases sales—and thereby increases cash flow. My question is, where are you going to get the people?''

Bob says we could call them back from layoff.

"No, you can't. See, the problem we have," says Lou, "is that the division has a recall freeze in effect. We can't recall without their approval.''

"Do we have people in the plant who can do these jobs?" asks Stacey.

"You mean steal people from other areas?" asks Bob.

"Sure," I say. "Take people from the non-bottlenecks. By definition, they have excess capacity anyway.''

Bob thinks about it for a minute. Then he explains that finding helpers for heat–treat is no big deal. And we do have some old machinists, who haven't been laid off because of seniority, who are qualified to run the Zmegma and the other two machines. Establishing a two-person set-up crew on the NCX-10, however, has him worried.

"Who's going to set up the other machines?" he asks.

"The helpers on the other machines know enough to set up their own equipment," I say.

"Well, I guess we can try it," says Bob. "But what happens if stealing people turns non-bottlenecks into bottlenecks?"

I tell him, "The important thing is to maintain the flow. If we take a worker away, and we can't maintain the flow, then we'll put the worker back and steal a body from someplace else. And if we still can't keep the flow going, then we'll have no choice but to go to division and insist that we either go to overtime or call a few people back from layoff."

"Okay," says Bob. "I'll go for it."

Lou gives us his blessing.

"Good. Let's do it," I say. "And, Bob, make sure the people you pick are good. From now on, we put only our best people to work on the bottlenecks."

And so it is done.

The NCX-10 gets a dedicated setup crew. The Zmegma and the other machines go to work. The outfit across town is only too glad to take our surplus parts for heat–treating. And in our own heat-treat department, two people per shift are assigned to stand by, ready to load and unload parts from the furnaces. Donovan juggles the work-center responsibilities so heat–treat has a foreman there at all times.

For a foreman, heat–treat seems like a very small kingdom, not much of a prize. There is nothing intrinsically attractive about running that operation, and having only two people to manage makes it seem like no big deal. To prevent it from seeming like a demotion to them, I make a point to go down there periodically on each of the shifts. In talking to the foreman, I drop some rather direct hints that the rewards will be great for anyone who can improve the output of heat–treated parts.

Shortly thereafter, some amazing things happen. Very early one morning, I'm down there at the end of third shift. A young guy named Mike Haley is the foreman. He's a big black man whose arms always look as though they're going to burst the sleeves on his shirts. We've noticed that over the past week he's pushed about ten percent more parts through heat–treat on his shift than the others have. Records are not usually set on third shift, and we're starting to wonder if it's Mike's biceps that are doing the trick. Anyway, I go down there to try to learn what he's doing.

As I walk up, I see the two helpers are not just standing around with nothing to do. They're moving parts. In front of the furnaces are two tightly organized stacks of work-in-process, which the helpers are building. I call Mike over and ask him what they're doing.

"They're getting ready," he says.

"What do you mean?"

"They're getting ready for when we have to load one of the furnaces again," he says. "The parts in each stack are all treated at the same temperature."

"So you're splitting and overlapping some batches," I say.

"Sure," he says. "I know we're not really supposed to do that, but you need the parts, right?"

"Sure, no problem. You're still doing the treating according to the priority system?" I ask.

"Oh, yeah," he says. "Come here. Let me show you."

Mike leads me past the control console for the furnaces to a worn old battleship of a desk. He finds the computer print-out for the week's most important overdue orders.

"See, look at number 22," he says pointing to it. "We need fifty of the high stress RB-dash-11's. They get treated at a 1200–degree temperature cycle. But fifty of them won't fill up the furnace. So we look down and what do we see here but item number 31, which calls for 300 fitted retaining rings. Those also take a 1200–degree cycle."

"So you'll fill up the furnace with as many of the retaining rings after you've loaded the fifty of the first item," I say.

"Yeah, that's it," says Mike. "Only we do the sorting and stacking in advance so we can load the furnace faster."

"That's good thinking," I tell him.

"Well, we could do even better if I could get someone to listen to an idea I got," he says.

"What do you have in mind?"

"Well, right now, it takes anywhere up to an hour or so to change a furnace load using the crane or doing it by hand. We could cut that down to a couple of minutes if we had a better system." He points to the furnaces. "Each one of those has a table which the parts sit on. They slide in and out on rollers. If we could get some steel plate and maybe a little help from engineering, we could make those tables interchangeable. That way we could stack a load of parts in advance and switch loads with the use of a forklift. If it saves us a couple of hours a day, that means we can do an extra heat of parts over the course of a week."

I look from the furnaces back to Mike. I say, "Mike, I want you take tomorrow night off. We'll get one of the other foremen to cover for you."

"Sounds good to me," he says with a grin. "How come?"

"Because the day after tomorrow, I want you on day turn. I'm going to have Bob Donovan put you together with an I.E. to write up these procedures formally, so we can start using them round the clock," I tell him. "You keep that mind of yours working. We need it."

Later that morning, Donovan happens by my office.

"Hi, there," he says.

"Well, hello," I tell him. "Did you get my note on Haley?"

"It's being taken care of," says Bob.

"Good. And let's make sure he gets some more money out of this whenever the wage freeze is lifted," I say.

"Okay," says Bob as a smile spreads across his face. Then he leans against the doorway.

"Something else?" I ask.

"Got good news for you," says Bob.

"How good?"

"Remember when Jonah asked us if all the parts going through heat–treat really needed it?"

I tell him I remember.

"I just found out that in three cases, it wasn't engineering that specified heat–treat. It was us," says Bob.

"What do you mean?"

He explains that about five years ago some group of hot-shots were trying to improve the efficiencies of several of the machining centers. To speed up the processing, the cutting tool "bite" was increased. So on each pass, instead of shaving a chip that was a millimeter thick, the tool took off three millimeters.

But increasing the amount of metal taken off on each pass made the metal brittle. And this necessitated heat–treating.

"The thing is, the machines we made more efficient happen to be non-bottlenecks," says Bob. "We have enough capacity on them to slow down and still meet demand. And if we go back to the slower processing, we don't need the heat–treat. Which means we can take about twenty percent of the current load off the furnaces."

"Sounds fantastic," I tell him. "What about getting it approved by engineering?"

"That's the beauty of it," says Bob. "*We* were the ones who initiated the change five years ago."

"So if it was our option to begin with," I say, "we can change it back any time we want."

"Right! We don't need to get an engineering change order, because we already have an approved procedure on the books," says Bob.

He leaves shortly with my blessing to implement the change as soon as possible. I sit there marveling that we're going to *reduce* the efficiency of some operations and make the entire plant more productive. They'd never believe it on the fifteenth floor.

# 24

It's a Friday afternoon. Out in the parking lot, the people on first shift are getting into their cars to go home. There is the usual congestion at the gate. I'm in my office—minding my own business—when suddenly, from through the half-open door . . . BAM!

Something ricochets off the ceiling tiles. I jump to my feet, check myself for wounds and, finding none, search the carpet for the offending missile. It's a champagne cork.

There is laughing outside my door. In the next instant, it seems as though everyone is in my office. There is Stacey, Bob Donovan (who holds the bottle from which the cork came), Ralph, Fran, a couple of the secretaries, and a swarm of other people—even Lou joins us. Fran hands me one of the styrofoam coffee cups she's dispensing to everyone. Bob fills it from the bottle.

"What's this all about?" I ask.

"I'll tell you in the toast I'm going to make as soon as everyone has something to swallow," says Bob.

More bottles are opened—there is a case of this stuff—and when all the cups are filled, Bob lifts his own.

"Here's to a new plant record in shipments of product," he says. "Lou went through the records for us and discovered that until now the best this place has ever done in a month was thirty-one orders shipped at value of about two million dollars. This month we topped that. We shipped fifty-seven customer orders with a value of . . . well, in round numbers, we'll call it a cool three million."

"Not only did we ship more product," says Stacey, "but, having just calculated our inventory levels, I am pleased to report that between last month and now, we've had a twelve percent net decline in work-in-process inventory."

"Well, then, let's drink to making money!" I say.

And we do.

"Mmmmm . . . industrial strength champagne," says Stacey.

"Very distinctive," says Ralph to Bob. "Did you pick this out yourself?"

"Keep drinking it. It gets better," says Donovan.

I'm just about to hazard a second cup when I notice Fran beside me.

"Mr. Rogo?"

"Yes."

"Bill Peach is on the line," says Fran.

I shake my head wondering what the hell it's going to be this time.

"I'll take it at your desk, Fran."

I go out there and punch the blinking button on my phone and pick it up.

"Yes, Bill, what can I do for you?"

"I was just talking to Johnny Jons," says Peach.

I automatically grab a pencil and pull over a pad of paper to take down the particulars on whatever order is causing us grief. I wait for Peach to continue, but he doesn't say anything for a second.

"What's the problem?" I ask him.

"No problem," says Peach. "Actually he was very happy."

"Really? What about?"

"He mentioned you've been coming through lately for him on a lot of late customer orders," says Peach. "Some kind of special effort I guess."

"Well, yes and no. We're doing a few things a little differently now," I say.

"Well, whatever. The reason I called is I know how I'm always on your case when things go wrong, Al, so I just wanted to tell you thanks from me and Jons for doing something right," says Peach.

"Thanks, Bill," I tell him. "Thanks for calling."

"Thankyouthankyouthankyouthankyouthankyou," I'm blithering to Stacey as she parks her car in my driveway. "You are truly a wonderful person for driving me home . . . and I truly meant that truly."

"Don't mention it," she says. "I'm glad we had something to celebrate."

She shuts off the engine. I look up at my house, which is dark except for one light. I had the good sense earlier to call my mother and tell her not to hold dinner for me. That was smart because the celebration continued onward and outward after

Peach's call. About half of the original group went to dinner together. Lou and Ralph threw in the towel early. But Donovan, Stacey and I—along with three or four die–hards—went to a bar after we ate and we had a good time. Now it is 1:30 and I am blissfully stinko.

The Buick, for safety's sake, is still parked behind the bar. Stacey, who switched to club soda a couple of hours ago, has generously played chauffeur to Bob and me. About ten minutes ago, we nudged Donovan through his kitchen door where he stood there bewildered for a moment before bidding us a good evening. If he remembers, Donovan is supposed to enlist his wife later today to drive us over to the bar and retrieve our vehicles.

Stacey gets out of the car and comes around and opens my door so I can spill myself onto the driveway. Standing up on uncertain legs, I steady myself against the car.

"I've never seen you smile so much," says Stacey.

"I've got a lot to smile about," I tell her.

"Wish you could be this happy in staff meetings," she says.

"Henceforth, I shall smile continuously through all staff meetings," I proclaim.

"Come on, I'll make sure you get to the door," she says.

With her hands around my arm to steady me, she guides me up the front walk to the door.

When we're at the door, I ask her, "How about some coffee?"

"No, thanks," she says. "It's late and I'd better get home."

"Sure?"

"Absolutely."

I fumble with the keys, find the lock, and the door swings open to a dark living room. I turn to Stacey and extend my hand.

"Thank you for a wonderful evening," I tell her. "I had a swell time."

Then as we're shaking hands, I for some reason step backwards, trip over the doorstep and lose all my balance.

"Woops!"

The next thing I know Stacey and I are sprawled on the floor together. Fortunately—or maybe not as it turns out—Stacey thinks this is colossally funny. She's laughing so hard, tears start to roll down her cheeks. And so I start laughing too. Both of us are rolling on the floor with laughter—when the lights come on.

"You bastard!"

I look up, my eyes adjusting to the sudden light, and there she is.

"Julie? What are you doing here?"

Without answering, she's now stomping through the kitchen. As I get to my feet and stagger after her, the door to the garage opens. The light switch in the garage clicks. I see her in silhouette for half a second.

"Julie! Wait a minute!"

I hear the garage door rumbling open as I attempt to follow her. As I go into the garage, she's already getting into her car. The door slams. I zig-zag closer, wildly waving my arms. The engine starts.

"I sit here waiting for you all night, putting up with your mother for six hours," she yells through the rolled–down window, "and you come home drunk with some floozy!"

"But Stacey isn't a floozy, she's—"

Accelerating to about thirty miles per hour in reverse, Julie backs out of the garage, down the driveway (narrowly missing Stacey's car) and into the street. I'm left standing there in the light of the garage. The tires of her car chirp upon the asphalt.

She's gone.

On Saturday morning, I wake up and groan a couple of times. The first groan is from the hangover. The second groan is from the memory of what happened.

When I'm able, I get dressed and venture into the kitchen in quest of coffee. My mother is there.

"You know your wife was here last night," says my mother as I pour my first cup.

So then I find out what happened. Julie showed up just after I called here last night. She had driven over on impulse, because she had missed me and she had wanted to see the kids. She apparently wanted to surprise me, which she did.

Later, I call the Barnett's number. Ada gives me the routine of "She doesn't want to talk to you anymore."

When I get to the plant on Monday, Fran tells me Stacey has been looking for me since she arrived this morning. I have just settled in behind my desk when Stacey appears at the door.

"Hi. Can we talk?" she asks.

"Sure. Come on in," I say.

She seems disturbed about something. She's avoiding my eyes as she sits down.

I say, "Listen, about Friday night, I'm sorry about what happened when you dropped me off."

Stacey says, "It's okay. Did your wife come back?"

"Uh, well, no, she didn't. She's staying with her parents for a little while," I say.

"Was it just because of me?" she asks.

"No, we've been having some problems lately."

"Al, I still feel kind of responsible," she says. "Look, why don't I talk to her."

"No, you don't have to do that," I say.

"Really, I think I ought to talk to her," says Stacey. "What's her number?"

I finally admit to myself it might be worth a try. So I give the Barnett's number to Stacey. She writes it down, and promises to call sometime today. Then she continues to sit there.

"Was there something else?" I ask.

"I'm afraid there is," she says.

She pauses.

"So what is it?"

"I don't think you're going to like this," she says. "But I'm pretty sure about it . . ."

"Stacey," I say. *"What?"*

"The bottlenecks have spread."

"What do you mean 'the bottlenecks have spread'?" I ask. "Is there a disease out there or something?"

"No, what I mean is we have a new bottleneck—or maybe even more than one; I'm not sure yet. Here, let me show you," she says as she comes around the side of the desk with some computer print-outs she's brought. "These are listings of parts that are queued up at final assembly."

She goes over the lists with me. As always, the bottleneck parts are still in short supply. But lately there have been shortages of some *non*-bottleneck parts as well.

She says, "Last week we had a case in which we had to build an order for 200 DBD-50's. Out of 172 different parts, we were missing 17. Only one of them was a red-tagged part. The rest were green tags. The red part came out of heat–treat on Thursday and was ready by Friday morning. But the others are still missing."

I lean back in my chair and pinch the bridge of my nose.

"Dammit, what the hell is going on out there? I had assumed the parts that have to go through a bottleneck would reach assembly last. Is there a materials shortage on those green–tagged parts? Some kind of vendor problem?" I ask her.

Stacey shakes her head. "No, I haven't had any problems with purchasing. And none of the parts have any processing by outside contractors. The problem definitely is internal. That's why I really think we have one or more new bottlenecks."

I get up from my desk, walk around the office.

"Maybe with the increase in throughput, we've loaded the plant to a level that we've run out of capacity on some other resources in addition to heat–treat and the NCX-10," Stacey suggests quietly.

I nod. Yes, that sounds like a possibility. With the bottlenecks more productive now, our throughput has gone up and our backlog is declining. But making the bottlenecks more productive has put more demand on the other work centers. If the demand on another work center has gone above one hundred percent, then we've created a *new* bottleneck.

Of the ceiling, I ask, "Does this mean we're going to have to go through the whole process of finding the bottlenecks all over again? Just when it seemed like we were on our way out of this mess. . . ."

Stacey folds the print-outs.

I tell her, "Okay, look, I want you to find out everything you can—exactly which parts, how many, what products are affected, which routings they're on, how often they're missing, all that stuff. Meanwhile, I'm going to try to get hold of Jonah to see what he has to say about all this."

After Stacey leaves, and Fran does the calling to locate Jonah, I stand by the window in my office and stare at the lawn while I think. I took it as a good sign that inventory levels had declined after we implemented the new measures to make the bottlenecks more productive. A month ago we were *wading* through parts on the non-bottleneck routings. There were piles and piles, and the piles kept growing. But some of the stocks have dwindled over the past couple of weeks of product assembly. Last week, for the first time since I've been at this plant, you could actually walk over to the assembly line without having to turn sideways to squeeze between the stacks and bins of inventory. I thought it was good. But now this happens.

"Mr. Rogo," says Fran through the intercom speaker. "I've got him on the line."

I pick up the phone. "Jonah? Hi. Listen, we've got trouble here."

"What's wrong?" he asks.

After I tell him the symptoms, Jonah asks what we've done since his visit. So I relate all the history to him—putting Q.C. in front of the bottlenecks, training people to give special care to bottleneck parts, activating the three machines to supplement the NCX-10, the new lunch rules, assigning certain people to work only at the bottlenecks, increasing the batch sizes going into heat–treat, implementing the new priority system in the plant. . . .

"New priority system?" asks Jonah.

"Right," I say, and then I explain about the red tags and green tags, and how the system works.

Jonah says, "Maybe I'd better come have another look."

I'm at home that night when the phone rings.

"Hi," says Julie's voice when I answer.

"Hi."

"I owe you an apology. I'm sorry about what happened on Friday night," she says. "Stacey called me here. Al, I'm really embarrassed. I completely misunderstood."

"Yeah, well . . . it seems to me there's a lot of misunderstanding between us lately," I say.

"All I can say is I'm sorry. I drove down thinking you'd be glad to see me."

"I would have been if you'd stayed," I say. "In fact, if I'd known you were coming, I would have come home after work."

"I know I should have called," she says, "but I was just in one of those moods."

"I guess you shouldn't have waited for me," I tell her.

She says, "I just kept thinking you'd be home any minute. And the whole time, your mother kept giving me the evil eye.

Finally she and the kids went to bed, and about an hour later I fell asleep on the sofa and slept until you came in.''

"Well . . . you want to be friends again?"

I can hear her relief.

"Yes, I would," she says. "When will I see you?"

I suggest we try Friday all over again. She says she can't wait that long. We compromise on Wednesday.

# 25

Déjà vu. At the airport the next morning, I again greet Jonah as he walks out of Gate Two.

By ten o'clock, we're in the conference room at the plant. Sitting around the table are Lou, Bob, Ralph and Stacey. Jonah paces in front of us.

"Let's start with some basic questions," he says. "First of all, have you determined exactly which parts are giving you the problem?"

Stacey, who is sitting at the table with a veritable fortress of paper around her and looking as if she's ready for a siege, holds up a list.

She says, "Yes, we've identified them. In fact, I spent last night tracking them down and double checking the data with what's on the floor out there. Turns out the problem covers about thirty parts."

Jonah asks, "Are you sure you released the materials for them?"

"Oh, yes," says Stacey. "No problem there. They've been released according to schedule. But they're not reaching final assembly. They're stuck in front of our new bottleneck."

"Wait a minute. How do you *know* it's really a bottleneck?" asks Jonah.

She says, "Well, since the parts are held up, I just figured it had to be . . ."

"Before we jump to conclusions, let's invest half an hour to go into the plant so we can all find out what's happening," Jonah says.

So we parade into the plant, and a few minutes later we're standing in front of a group of milling machines. Off to one side are big stacks of inventory marked with green tags. Stacey stands there and points out the parts that are needed in final assembly. Most of the missing parts are right here and all bear green tags. Bob calls over the foreman, a hefty guy by the name of Jake, and introduces him to Jonah.

"Yeah, all them parts been sittin' here for about two, three weeks or more," says Jake.

"But we need them now," I say. "How come they're not being worked on?"

Jake shrugs his shoulders. "You know which ones you want, we'll do 'em right now. But that goes against them rules you set up in that there priority system."

He points to some other skids of materials nearby.

"You see over there?" says Jake. "They all got red tags. We got to do all of 'em before we touch the stuff with green tags. That's what you told us, right?"

Uh-huh. It's becoming clear what's been happening.

"You mean," says Stacey, "that while the materials with green tags have been building up, you've been spending all your time on the parts bound for the bottlenecks."

"Yeah, well, most of it," says Jake. "Hey, like we only got so many hours in a day, you know what I mean?"

"How much of your work is on bottleneck parts?" asks Jonah.

"Maybe seventy-five or eighty percent," says Jake. "See, everything that goes to heat–treat or the NCX-10 has to pass through here first. As long as the red parts keep coming—and they haven't let up one bit since that new system started—we just don't have the time to work on very many of the green-tag parts."

There is a moment of silence. I look from the parts to the machines and back to Jake again.

"What the hell do we do now?" asks Donovan in echo to my own thoughts. "Do we switch tags? Make the missing parts red instead of green?"

I throw up my hands in frustration and say, "I guess the only solution is to expedite."

"No, actually, that is not the solution at all," Jonah says, "because if you resort to expediting now, you'll have to expedite all the time, and the situation will only get worse."

"But what else can we do?" asks Stacey.

Jonah says, "First, I want us to go look at the bottlenecks, because there is another aspect to the problem."

Before we can see the NCX-10, we see the inventory. It's stacked as high as the biggest forklift can reach. It's not just a mountain, but a mountain with many peaks. The piles here are even bigger now than before we identified the machine as a bottleneck. And tied to every bin, hanging from every pallet of parts is a red tag. Somewhere behind it all, its own hugeness obscured from our view, is the NCX-10.

"How do we get there from here?" asks Ralph, looking for a path through the inventory.

"Here, let me show you," says Bob.

And he leads us through the maze of materials until we reach the machine.

Gazing at all the work-in-process around us, Jonah says to us, "You know, I would guess, just from looking at it, that you have at least a month or more of work lined-up here for this machine. And I bet if we went to heat–treat we would find the same situation. Tell me, do you know why you have such a huge pile of inventory here?"

"Because everyone ahead of this machine is giving first priority to red parts," I suggest.

"Yes, that's part of the reason," says Jonah. "But why is so much inventory coming through the plant to get stuck here?"

Nobody answers.

"Okay, I see I'm going to have to explain some of the basic relationships between bottlenecks and non-bottlenecks," says Jonah. Then he looks at me and says, "By the way, do you remember when I told you that a plant in which everyone is working all the time is very *in*efficient? Now you'll see exactly what I was talking about."

Jonah walks over to the nearby Q.C. station and takes a piece of chalk the inspectors use to mark defects on the parts they reject. He kneels down to the concrete floor and points to the NCX-10.

"Here is your bottleneck," he says, "the X-what-ever-it-is machine. We'll simply call it 'X'."

He writes an X on the floor. Then he gestures to the other machines back down the aisle.

"And feeding parts to X are various non-bottleneck machines and workers," he says. "Because we designated the bottleneck as X, we'll refer to these non-bottlenecks as 'Y' resources. Now, for the sake of simplicity, let's just consider one non-bottleneck in combination with one bottleneck . . ."

With the chalk, he writes on the floor:

## Y ---> X

Product parts are what join the two in a relationship with each other, Jonah explains, and the arrow obviously indicates the flow of parts from one to the other. He adds that we can consider *any* non-bottleneck feeding parts to X, because no matter which one we choose, its inventory must be processed at some subsequent point in time by X.

"By the definition of a non-bottleneck, we know that Y has extra capacity. Because of its extra capacity, we also know that Y will be faster in filling the demand than X," says Jonah. "Let's say both X and Y have 600 hours a month available for production. Because it is a bottleneck, you will need all 600 hours of the X machine to meet demand. But let's say you need only 450 hours a month, or 75 percent, of Y to keep the flow equal to demand. What happens when Y has worked its 450 hours? Do you let it sit idle?"

Bob says, "No, we'll find something else for it to do."

"But Y has already satisfied market demand," says Jonah.

Bob says, "Well, then we let it get a head start on next month's work."

"And if there is nothing for it to work on?" asks Jonah.

Bob says, "Then we'll have to release more materials."

"And *that* is the problem," says Jonah. "Because what happens to those extra hours of production from Y? Well, that inventory has to go somewhere. Y is faster than X. And by keeping Y active, the flow of parts to X must be greater than the flow of parts leaving X. Which means. . . ."

He walks over to the work-in-process mountain and makes a sweeping gesture.

"You end up with all this in front of the X machine," he says. "And when you're pushing in more material than the system can convert into throughput, what are you getting?"

"Excess inventory," says Stacey.

"Exactly," says Jonah. "But what about another combination? What happens when X is feeding parts to Y?"

Jonah writes that on the floor with the chalk like this . . .

## X---> Y

"How much of Y's 600 hours can be used productively here?" asks Jonah.

"Only 450 hours again," says Stacey.

"That's right," says Jonah. "If Y is depending exclusively upon X to feed it inventory, the maximum number of hours it can work is determined by the output of X. And 600 hours from X equates to 450 hours for Y. After working those hours, Y will be starved for inventory to process. Which, by the way, is quite acceptable."

"Wait a minute," I say. "We have bottlenecks feeding non-bottlenecks here in the plant. For instance, whatever leaves the NCX-10 will be processed by a non-bottleneck. But I know we don't let non-bottleneck work centers downstream from the NCX-10 sit idle after they're processed the bottleneck parts."

Bob says, "Well, you're right. We feed them work from areas that aren't choked by the bottleneck."

"From other non-bottlenecks you mean. And do you know what happens when you keep Y active that way?" asks Jonah. "Look at this."

He draws a third diagram on the floor with the chalk.

$$
\begin{array}{c}
Y \rightarrow A \\
X \rightarrow S \\
S \\
E \\
M \\
B \\
L \\
Y
\end{array}
$$

In this case, Jonah explains, some parts do not flow through a bottleneck; their processing is done only by a non-bottleneck and the flow is directly from Y to assembly. The other parts *do* flow through a bottleneck, and they are on the X route to assembly where they are mated to the Y parts into a finished product.

In a real situation, the Y route probably would consist of one non-bottleneck feeding another non-bottleneck, feeding yet another non-bottleneck, and so on, to final assembly. The X route might have a series of non-bottlenecks feeding a bottleneck, which in turn feeds a chain of more non-bottlenecks. In our case, Jonah says, we've got a group of non-bottleneck machines downstream from X which can process parts from either the X or the Y route.

"But to keep it simple, I've diagrammed the combination with the fewest number of elements—one X and one Y. No matter how many non-bottlenecks are in the system, the result of activating Y just to keep it busy is the same. So let's say you keep both X and Y working continuously for every available hour. How efficient would the system be?"

"Super efficient," says Bob.

"No, you're wrong," says Jonah. "Because what happens when all this inventory from Y reaches final assembly?"

Bob shrugs and says, "We build the orders and ship them."

"How can you?" asks Jonah. "Eighty percent of your products require at least one part from a bottleneck. What are you going to substitute for the bottleneck part that hasn't shown up yet?"

Bob scratches his head and says, "Oh, yeah . . . I forgot."

"So if we can't assemble," says Stacey, "we get piles of inventory again. Only this time the excess inventory doesn't accumulate in front of a bottleneck; it stacks up in front of final assembly."

"Yeah," says Lou, "and another million bucks sits still just to keep the wheels turning."

And Jonah says, "You see? Once more, the non-bottleneck does not determine throughput, even if it works twenty-four hours a day."

Bob asks, "Okay, but what about that twenty percent of products *without* any bottleneck parts? We can still get high efficiencies with them."

"You think so?" asks Jonah.

On the floor he diagrams it like this . . .

Y → PRODUCT A
X → PRODUCT B

This time, he says, the X and Y operate independently of one another. They are each filling separate marketing demands.

"How much of Y's 600 hours can the system use here?" asks Jonah.

"All of 'em," says Bob.

"Absolutely not," says Jonah. "Sure, at first glance it looks as if we can use one hundred percent of Y, but think again."

"We can only use as much as the market demand can absorb," I say.

"Correct. By definition, Y has excess capacity," says Jonah. "So if you work Y to the maximum, you once again get excess inventory. And this time you end up, not with excess work-in-process, but with excess finished goods. The constraint here is not in production. The constraint is marketing's ability to sell."

As he says this, I'm thinking to myself about the finished goods we've got crammed into warehouses. At least two-thirds of those inventories are products made entirely with non-bottleneck parts. By running non-bottlenecks for "efficiency," we've built inventories far in excess of demand. And what about the remaining third of our finished goods? They have bottleneck parts, but most of those products have been sitting on the shelf now for a couple of years. They're obsolete. Out of 1,500 or so units in stock, we're lucky if we can sell ten a month. Just about all of the *competitive* products with bottleneck parts are sold virtually as soon as they come out of final assembly. A few of them sit in the warehouse a day or two before they go to the customer, but due to the backlog, not many.

I look at Jonah. To the four diagrams on the floor, he has now added numbers so that together they look like this . . .

```
1) Y → X      3) Y →A      4) Y → PRODUCT A
                 X →S          X → PRODUCT B
2) X → Y         S
                 E
                 M
                 B
                 L
                 Y
```

Jonah says, "We've examined four linear combinations involving X and Y. Now, of course, we can create endless combinations of X and Y. But the four in front of us are fundamental enough that we don't have to go any further. Because if we use these like building blocks, we can represent *any* manufacturing situation. We don't have to look at trillions of combinations of X and Y to find what is universally true in all of them; we can generalize the truth simply by identifying what happens in each of these four cases. Can you tell me what you have noticed to be similar in all of them?"

Stacey points out immediately that in no case does Y ever determine throughput for the system. Whenever it's possible to activate Y above the level of X, doing so results only in excess inventory, not in greater throughput.

"Yes, and if we follow that thought to a logical conclusion," says Jonah, "we can form a simple rule which will be true in every case: the level of utilization of a non-bottleneck is not determined by its own potential, but by some other constraint in the system."

He points to the NCX-10.

"A major constraint here in your system is this machine," says Jonah. "When you make a non-bottleneck do more work than this machine, you are not increasing productivity. On the contrary, you are doing exactly the opposite. You are creating excess inventory, which is against the goal."

"But what are we supposed to do?" asks Bob. "If we don't keep people working, we'll have idle time, and idle time will lower our efficiencies."

"*So what?*" asks Jonah.

Donovan is taken aback. "Beg pardon, but how the hell can you say that?"

"Just take a look behind you," says Jonah. "Take a look at the monster you've made. It did not create itself. You have created this mountain of inventory with your own decisions. And why? Because of the wrong assumption that you must make the workers produce one hundred percent of the time, or else get rid of them to 'save' money."

Lou says, "Well, granted that maybe one hundred percent is unrealistic. We just ask for some acceptable percentage, say, ninety percent."

"Why is ninety percent acceptable?" asks Jonah. "Why not

sixty percent, or twenty-five? The numbers are meaningless unless they are based upon the constraints of the system. With enough raw materials, you can keep one worker busy from now until retirement. But *should* you do it? Not if you want to make money."

Then Ralph suggests, "What you're saying is that making an employee work and profiting from that work are two different things."

"Yes, and that's a very close approximation of the second rule we can logically derive from the four combinations of X and Y we talked about," says Jonah. "Putting it precisely, activating a resource and utilizing a resource are not synonymous."

He explains that in both rules, "utilizing" a resource means making use of the resource in a way that moves the system toward the goal. "Activating" a resource is like pressing the ON switch of a machine; it runs whether or not there is any benefit to be derived from the work it's doing. So, really, activating a non-bottleneck to its maximum is an act of maximum stupidity.

"And the implication of these rules is that we must *not* seek to optimize every resource in the system," says Jonah. "A system of local optimums is not an optimum system at all; it is a very inefficient system."

"Okay," I say, "but how does knowing this help us get the missing parts unstuck at the milling machines and moved to final assembly?"

Jonah says, "Think about the build-up of inventory both here and at your milling machines in terms of these two rules we just talked about."

"I think I see the cause of the problem," Stacey says, "We're releasing material faster than the bottlenecks can process it."

"Yes," says Jonah. "You are sending work onto the floor whenever *non*-bottlenecks are running out of work to do."

I say, "Granted, but the milling machines are a bottleneck."

Jonah shakes his head and says, "No, they are not—as evidenced by all this excess inventory behind you. You see, the milling machines are not intrinsically a bottleneck. *You* have turned them into one."

He tells us that with an increase in throughput, it is possible to create new bottlenecks. But most plants have so much extra capacity that it takes an enormous increase in throughput before this happens. We've only had a twenty percent increase. When I had talked to him by phone, he thought it unlikely a new bottleneck would have occurred.

What happened was that even as throughput increased, we continued loading the plant with inventory as if we expected to keep all our workers fully activated. This increased the load dumped upon the milling machines and pushed them beyond their capacity. The first-priority, red-tagged parts were processed, but the green-tagged parts piled up. So not only did we get excess inventory at the NCX-10 and at heat–treat, but due to the volume of bottleneck parts, we clogged the flow at another work center and prevented non-bottleneck parts from reaching assembly.

When he's finished, I say, "All right, I see now the error of our ways. Can you tell us what we should do to correct the problem?"

"I want you all to think about it as we walk back to your conference room and then we'll talk about what you should do," says Jonah. "The solution is fairly simple."

# 26

Just how simple the solution is doesn't become apparent to me until I'm at home that night. I'm sitting at the kitchen table with a pad of paper and a pencil thinking about what was suggested today when Sharon comes in.

"Hi," she says as she sits down.

"Hi," I say back. "What's up?"

"Not much," she says. "Just wondered what you were doing."

"I'm working," I tell her.

"Can I help?" she asks.

"Well . . . I don't know," I say. "It's kind of technical. I think you'll probably be bored by it."

"Oh," she says. "Does that mean you want me to leave?"

Guilt strikes.

"No, not if you want to stay," I tell her. "Do you want to try to solve a problem?"

"Okay," she says, brightening.

I say, "All right. Let me think of how to put this to you. Do you know about the scout hike Dave and I were on?"

"She doesn't, but I do!" says Dave, racing into the kitchen. He skids to a stop on the smooth floor and says, "Sharon doesn't know anything about the hike. But I can help you."

I say, "Son, I think there is a career for you in sales."

Sharon indignantly says, "Yes, I *do* know about the hike."

"You weren't even there," says Dave.

"I've heard everybody talk about it," she says.

"Okay, *both* of you can work on this," I say. "Here's the problem: We've got a line of kids on a hike in the woods. In the middle of the line, we've got Herbie. We've already taken the pack off Herbie's back to help him go faster, but he's still the slowest. Everybody wants to go faster than Herbie. But if that happens, the line will spread out and some of the kids will get lost. For one reason or another, we can't move Herbie from the middle of the line. Now, how do we keep the line from spreading?"

They both become thoughtful.

I say, "All right, now both of you go into the other room. I'll give you ten minutes, and then we'll see which one of you comes up with the best idea to keep everyone together in the line."

"What does the winner get?" asks Dave.

"Well . . . anything within reason."

*"Anything?"* asks Sharon.

*"Within reason,"* I repeat.

So they leave and I get about ten minutes of peace and quiet. Then I see the two faces looking around the corner.

"Ready?" I ask.

They come in and sit down at the kitchen table with me.

"Want to hear my idea?" asks Sharon.

"My idea is better," says Dave.

"It is not!" she tells him.

"Okay, enough!" I say. "What's your idea, Sharon?"

Sharon says, "A drummer."

"Pardon me?"

"You know . . . like in a parade," she says.

"Oh, I know what you mean," I say, realizing what she has in mind. "There aren't any gaps in a parade. Everybody is marching in step."

Sharon beams. Dave gives her a dirty look.

"So everybody's marching in step . . . to a beat," I say, thinking out loud. "Sure. But how do you keep the people in front of Herbie from setting a faster pace?"

"You have Herbie beat the drum," says Sharon.

I think about it and say, "Yeah, that's not bad."

"But my idea is better," says Dave.

I turn to him. "Okay, wise guy, what's your idea?"

"Tie ropes to everyone," says Dave.

"Ropes?"

"You know, like mountain climbers," he says. "You tie everyone together at the waist with one long rope. So, that way, no one could get left behind, and nobody could speed up without everybody speeding up."

I say, "Hmmm . . . that's very good."

It would mean that the line—which would translate to the total inventory in the plant—could never be longer than the rope. And the rope, of course, could be of a pre-determined length, which means we could control it with precision. Everyone would have to walk at the same speed. I look at Dave, a little in awe of his creativity.

"Come to think of it, the rope makes it sound like having physical links between all the equipment," I tell him, "which is like an assembly line."

"Yeah, an assembly line," says Dave. "Didn't you tell me once that an assembly line is supposed to be the best way to make things?"

"Well, yes, it's the most efficient way to manufacture," I say. "In fact, we use that approach when we do the final assembly for most of our products. The problem is that an assembly line won't work throughout the whole plant."

"Oh," says Dave.

"But those are both good ideas you two thought up," I tell them. "In fact, if we changed each of your ideas just a little bit we'd almost have the solution suggested to us today."

"Like how?" asks Sharon.

"See, to keep the line from spreading, it actually wouldn't be necessary to keep everyone marching to exactly the same step or to keep everyone tied to the rope," I tell them. "What we really have to do is just keep the kid at the front of the line from walking faster than Herbie. If we can do that, then everybody will stay together."

"So we just tie the rope from Herbie to the kid at the front," says Dave.

"Or, maybe Herbie and the boy at the front of the line have signals," says Sharon. "When the boy in front goes too fast, Herbie tells him to wait or slow down."

"That's right," I say. "Both of you figured it out."

"So what do we *both* win?" asks Sharon.

"What do you want?" I ask. "A pizza with everything? A night at the movies?"

They're quiet for a moment.

"The movies sound good," says Sharon, "but what I'd really like is if you could get Mom to come home again."

Now it gets very quiet.

Dave says finally, "But if you can't, we'll understand."

"Well, I'm doing my best," I say. "Meanwhile, how about the movies?"

After the kids have gone to bed, I sit up wondering for the hundredth time whether Julie will come back. Compared with my marital difficulties, the inventory problem at the plant seems simple—or at least it seems simple now. I guess every problem is easy once you've figured it out.

We are, in effect, going to do what my two kids came up with. The Herbies (the bottlenecks) are going to tell us when to let more inventory into the system—except we're going to use the aid of computers instead of drums and ropes.

After we returned to the conference room in the office building today, we started talking, and we all agreed that we're obviously releasing too much material. We don't need five or six weeks of inventory in front of the bottleneck to keep it productive.

"If we can withhold materials for red parts, instead of pushing them out there as soon as the first non-bottleneck has nothing to do," said Stacey, "the milling machines will then have time to work on the green parts. And the parts we're missing will reach assembly with no problem."

Jonah nodded and said, "That's right. What you have to do is find a way to release the material for the red parts according to the rate at which the bottlenecks need material—and strictly at that rate."

Then I said, "Fine, but how do we time each release of material so it arrives at the bottleneck when it's needed?"

Stacey said, "I'm not sure, but I see what you're worried about. We don't want the opposite problem of no work in front of the bottleneck."

"Hell, we got at least a month before that happens, even if we released no more red tags from today on," said Bob. "But I know what you mean. If we idle the bottleneck, we lose throughput."

"What we need," I said, "is some kind of signal to link the bottlenecks with the release-of-materials schedule."

Then Ralph, to my surprise, spoke up and said, "Excuse me, this is just a thought. But maybe we can predict when to release material by some kind of system based on the data we've kept on both the bottlenecks."

I asked him what he was getting at.

He said, "Well, since we started keeping data on the bottlenecks, I've been noticing I'm able to predict several weeks in advance what each bottleneck will be working on at a particular time. See, as long as I know exactly what's in queue, I just take the average setup and process times for each type of part, and I'm able to calculate when each batch should clear the bottleneck. Because we're only dealing with one work center, with much less dependency, we can average the statistical fluctuations and get a better degree of accuracy."

Ralph went on to say that he knows from observation it takes about two weeks, plus or minus a day or two, for material to reach the bottlenecks from the first operations.

"So by adding two weeks to the setup and process times of what's in queue at the bottleneck," said Ralph, "I know how long it will take until the bottleneck is actually working on material we release. And as each batch leaves the bottleneck, we can update our information and calculate a date when Stacey should release more red-tag material."

Jonah looked at Ralph and said, "that's excellent!"

"Ralph," I said, "that's terrific. How accurate do you really think we can be with this?"

"I'd say we'd be accurate to within plus or minus a day," he said. "So if we keep, say, a three-day stock of work-in-process in front of each bottleneck, we should be safe."

Everyone was telling Ralph how impressed they were when Jonah said, "But, in fact, Ralph, you can do much more than that with the same information."

"Like what?" asked Ralph.

Jonah said, "You can also attack the inventory problems in front of assembly."

"You mean we not only can do something about excess inventory on the bottleneck parts, but on the non-bottleneck parts as well?" I asked.

"Exactly," said Jonah.

But Ralph said, "Sorry, folks, I'm not sure how I'd do that."

Then Jonah explained it to him—and all of us. If Ralph can determine a schedule for releasing red-tag materials based on the bottlenecks, he can also determine a schedule for final assembly. Once he knows when the bottleneck parts will reach final assembly, he can calculate backwards and determine the release of the non-bottleneck materials along each of their routes. In this way, the bottlenecks will be determining the release of all the materials in the plant.

I said, "You know, that's going to produce the same effect as moving the bottlenecks to the head of production, which is what I'd intended for us to do."

"Yeah, it sounds good," said Ralph. "But I have to warn you, I can't say how long it'll take before I can make the computer do all that. I mean, I can have a schedule for the red-tagged materials worked out in fairly short order. The rest of it will take awhile."

"Aw, come on, Ralphie," said Bob, "a computer wiz like you ought to be able to crank that out in no time."

"I can crank something out in no time," said Ralph, "but I'm not going to promise it'll work."

I told him, "Relax; as long as we ease the load on the milling machines, we'll be okay for the short haul. That'll give you the time to get something basic in place."

"You may feel you have the time now to relax," said Jonah, "but I have to catch a plane for Chicago in thirty-five minutes."

"Oh, shit," I muttered, automatically glancing at my watch. "I guess we'd better move."

It was not a graceful parting. Jonah and I ran out of the building, and I broke numerous speed limits—without incident—getting him to the airport.

"I have, shall we say, a special interest in plants like yours," said Jonah. "So I'd appreciate it if you'd keep me informed of what happens."

"Sure," I told him. "No problem. In fact, I'd planned on it."

"Good," said Jonah. "I'll be talking to you."

And with that he was out of the car and, with a wave, was sprinting through the terminal doors. I didn't get a call, so I suppose he made it.

When I go to work the next morning, we have a meeting about how to implement this approach. But before we can get down to talking about it, Bob Donovan starts waving a red flag at us.

"You know, we could be walking into a big problem," says Bob.

"What's that?" I ask.

"What happens if efficiencies all over the plant go down?" he asks.

I say, "Well, I think that's a risk we'll have to take."

"Yeah, but it sounds like we're going to have a lot of people idle around here if we do this," says Bob.

"Yeah, we might have some people idle from time to time," I admit.

"So are we just supposed to let everyone stand around out there?" asks Bob.

"Why not?" asks Stacey. "Once the somebody is already on the payroll, it doesn't cost us any more to have him be idle. Whether somebody produces parts or waits a few minutes doesn't increase our operating expense. But excess inventory . . . now *that* ties up a lot of money."

"Okay," says Bob, "but what about the reporting system? Seems to me that at the end of the month, when old Bill Peach is ready to decide if we stay open or if we close down, he's not going to be awfully positive about us if he sees our efficiencies have taken a dive. I hear they do tend to frown upon that at headquarters."

There is quiet in the room. Then Lou says, "He does have a point, Al."

I listen to the hum of the air conditioning for a moment.

"All right, look," I say finally. "If we *don't* go ahead with a system to withhold inventory and release it according to the bottlenecks, we'll be missing a major opportunity to improve performance and save the plant. And I'm not about to stand by and let that happen just to maintain a standard that obviously has more impact on middle management politics than it does on the bottom line. I say we go ahead with this. And if efficiencies drop, let them."

After those brave words, so reminiscent of Admiral Farragut and his Damn-the-Torpedoes speech, the others are a little misty-eyed.

"And, ah, Bob," I tell Donovan, "if there *is* a lot of idle time out there, don't hassle anybody—just make damn sure it doesn't show up in the efficiency reports next month, okay?"

"Gotcha, boss."

# 27

". . . Let me say in conclusion that had it not been for the increase in revenue generated last month by the Bearington plant and its products, the UniWare Division's losses would have continued for the seventh consecutive month. All of the other manufacturing operations in the division reported only marginal gains in performance or sustained losses. Despite the improvement at Bearington and the fact that as a result the division recorded its first operating profit of this year, we have a long way to go before we are back on solid financial footing."

Having said that, Ethan Frost gets the nod from Bill Peach and sits down. I'm sitting halfway down a long table where all the plant managers are gathered. On Peach's right is Hilton Smyth, who happens to be glowering at me in the aftermath of Frost's tribute to my plant. I relax in my chair and for a moment allow myself to contemplate the view through the broad plate-glass window, a sunny city on an early summer day.

May has ended. Aside from the problem with the shortages of non-bottleneck parts, which have now gone away, it's been an excellent month. We're now timing the release of all materials according to a new system Ralph Nakamura developed, which is keyed to the speed of the bottlenecks. He's got a data terminal now at both of the bottlenecks, so as inventory is processed, the latest information can be fed directly into the plant data base. With the new system, we're beginning to see excellent results.

Ralph did a little experimenting with the system and soon discovered we can predict within a day, more or less, when a shipment will leave the plant. Based on this, we've been able to put together a report to marketing listing all customer orders and dates when they will be shipped. (I don't know if anybody in marketing really believes that report, but so far it's been highly accurate.)

"Rogo," says Peach, "because you seem to be the only one among us who has improved to any degree, we'll let you start the round of reports."

I open up the cover of my report and launch into a presentation of the highlights. By almost every standard, we've had a good month. Inventory levels have fallen and are continuing to fall rapidly. Withholding some materials has meant we're no longer choking on work-in-process. Parts are reaching the bottlenecks when they're supposed to, and the flow through the plant is much smoother than before.

And what happened to efficiencies? Well, they did fall initially as we began to withhold raw material from the floor, but not as much as we had been afraid they would—it turns out we were consuming excess inventory. But with the rate of shipments up dramatically, that excess has melted quickly. And now that we're beginning to resume releases of materials to non-bottlenecks again, efficiencies are on their way back up. Donovan has even told me confidentially he thinks the real numbers in the future will be almost the same as before.

The best news is we've wiped out our backlog of overdue orders. Amazing as it seems, we're completely caught up. So customer service has improved. Throughput is up. We're on our way back. It's too bad the standard report we've prepared can't begin to tell the full story of what's really going on.

When I've finished, I look up the table and see Hilton Smyth whispering something to Bill Peach. There is quiet around the table for a moment. Then Bill nods to Hilton and talks to me.

"Good job, Al," Bill says stiffly.

Through with me, Bill asks another manager to deliver his report. I sit back, irritated slightly that Peach wasn't more positive, that he didn't put more praise on me the way Frost had indicated he should. I came in here feeling as though we'd really turned the plant around. And I guess I expected a little more than a "good job", a pat on the head.

But then I have to remind myself that Peach doesn't know the extent of the change. Should he know? Should we be telling him? Lou has asked me about this. And I've told him, no; let's hold off for a while.

We could go to Bill Peach and make a presentation to him, put all our cards on the table and let him decide. In fact, that's exactly what we will do eventually. But not yet. And I think I have a good reason.

I've worked with Bill Peach for a lot of years; I know him pretty well. He's a smart man—but he is not an innovator. A couple of years ago, he might have let us run with this for a while. Not today. I have a feeling if we go to him now, he'll put on his hard nose and tell me to run the plant by the cost accounting methods he believes in.

I have to bide my time until I can go to him with a solid case that my way (Jonah's way, really) is the one that truly works. It's too early for that. We've broken too many rules to tell him the full story now.

But will we have the time? That's what I keep asking myself. Peach hasn't voluntarily lifted the threat to close the plant. I thought he might say something (publicly or privately) after this report, but he hasn't. I look at him at the end of the table. He seems distracted, not like himself. The others talk and he seems only half interested. Hilton seems to cue him on what to say. What's with him?

The meeting breaks up about an hour after lunch, and by then I've decided to have a private talk with Peach if I can get it. I follow him out into the corridor from the conference room and ask him. He invites me into his office.

"So when are you going to let us off the hook?" I ask him after the door is closed.

Bill sits down in a big upholstered chair and I take the one opposite him. Without the desk between us, it's a nice little intimate chat.

Bill looks straight at me and says, "What makes you think I'm going to?"

"Bearington is on its way back," I tell him. "We can make that plant make money for the division."

"Can you?" he asks. "Look, Al, you've had a good month. That's a step in the right direction. But can you give us a second good month? And a third and fourth? That's what I'm waiting to see."

"We'll give them to you," I say to him.

"I'm going to be frank," says Peach. "I'm not yet convinced this hasn't been just a flash in the pan, so to speak. You had a huge overdue backlog. It was inevitable you'd ship it eventually. What have you done to reduce costs? Nothing that I can see. It's going to take a ten or fifteen percent reduction in operating expense to make the plant profitable for the long term."

I feel my heart sink. Finally, I say, "Bill, if next month we turn in another improvement, will you at least delay the recommendation to close the plant?"

He shakes his head. "It'll have to be a bigger improvement than what you gave us in this past period."

"How big?"

"Just give me fifteen percent more on the bottom line than you did this month," he says.

I nod. "I think we can do that," I say—and note the split second of shock blink onto Peach's face.

Then he says, "Fine. If you can deliver that, and keep delivering it, we'll keep Bearington open."

I smile. If I do this for you, I'm thinking, you'd be an idiot to close us.

Peach stands, our chat concluded.

I fly the Buick up the entrance ramp to the Interstate with the accelerator floored and the radio turned up loud. The adrenalin is pumping. The thoughts in my head are racing faster than the car.

Two months ago I figured I might be sending out my resume by now. But Peach just said if we turned in another good month he'd let the plant stay open. We're almost there. We just might be able to pull this off. Just one more month.

*But fifteen percent?*

We've been eating up our backlog of orders at a terrific rate. And by doing so we've been able to ship a tremendous volume of product—tremendous by any comparison: last month, last quarter, last year. It's given us a big surge of income, and it's looked fantastic on the books. But now that we've shipped all the overdues, and we're putting out new orders much faster than before. . . .

The thought creeps up on me that I'm in really big trouble. Where the hell am I going to get the orders that will give me an extra fifteen percent?

Peach isn't just asking for another good month; he's demanding an incredible month. He hasn't promised anything; he's have—and probably too much. I'm trying to remember the orders scheduled for the coming weeks and attempting to calculate in my head if we're going to have the volume of business necessary for the bottom-line increase Peach wants to see. I have a scary feeling it won't be enough.

Okay, I can ship ahead of schedule. I can take the orders scheduled for the first week or two of July and ship them in June instead.

But what am I going to do after that? I'm going to be putting us into a huge hole in which we have nothing else to do. *We need more business.*

# THE GOAL

I wonder where Jonah is these days.

Glancing down at the speedometer, I find to my surprise that I'm zipping along at eighty. I slow down. I loosen my tie. No sense killing myself trying to get back to the plant. It occurs to me, in fact, that by the time I get back to the plant it'll be time to go home.

Just about then, I pass a sign saying I'm two miles from the interchange that would put me on the highway to Forest Grove. Well, why not? I haven't seen Julie or the kids in a couple of days. Since the end of school, the kids have been staying with Julie and her parents.

I take the interchange and get off at the next exit. At a gas station on the corner, I find a pay phone and make a call to the office. Fran answers and I tell her two things: First, pass the word to Bob, Stacey, Ralph and Lou that the meeting went well for us. And, second, I tell her not to expect me to come in this afternoon.

When I get to the Barnett's house, I get a nice welcome. I spend quite a while just talking to Sharon and Dave. Then Julie suggests we go for a walk together. It's a fine summer afternoon outside.

As I'm hugging Sharon to say goodbye, she whispers in my ear, "Daddy, when are we all going to go home together?"

"Real soon, I hope," I tell her.

Despite the assurance I gave her, Sharon's question doesn't go away. I've been wondering the same thing myself.

Julie and I go to the park, and after walking for awhile, we sit down on a bench by the river. We sit without saying anything for awhile. She asks me if something is wrong. I tell her about Sharon's question.

"She asks me that all the time," says Julie.

"She does? What do you tell her?"

Julie says, "I tell her we'll be going home real soon."

I laugh. "That's what I said to her. Do you really mean that?"

She's quiet for a second. Finally, she smiles at me and says sincerely, "You've been a lot of fun to be around in the last few weeks."

"Thanks. The feeling is mutual," I say.

She takes my hand and says, "But . . . I'm sorry, Al. I'm still worried about coming home."

"Why? We're getting along a lot better now," I say. "What's the problem?"

"Look, we've had some good times for a change. And that's fine. I've really needed this time with you," she says. "But if we go back to living together, you know what's going to happen don't you? Everything will be fine for about two days. But a week from now we'll be having the same arguments. And a month later, or six months, or a year from now . . . well, you know what I mean."

I sigh. "Julie, was it that bad living with me?"

"Al, it wasn't *bad,*" she says. "It was just . . . I don't know. You weren't paying any attention to me."

"But I was having all kinds of problems in my job. I was really in over my head for awhile. What did you expect from me?"

"More than what I was getting," Julie says. "You know, when I was growing up, my father always came home from work at the same time. The whole family always ate together. He spent the evenings at home. With you, I never know what's going on."

"You can't compare me to your father," I say. "He's a dentist. After the last tooth of the day is filled, he can lock up and go home. My business isn't like that."

"Alex, the problem is *you* are not like that," she says. "Other people go to work and come home at regular times."

"Yes, you're partially right. I am not like other people," I admit. "When I get involved in something, I really get involved. And maybe that has to do with the way *I* was brought up. Look at my family—we hardly ever ate together. Somebody always had to be minding the store. It was my father's rule: the business was what fed us, so it came first. We all understood that and we all worked together."

"So what does that prove except our families were different?" she asks. "I'm telling you about something that bothered me so much and for so long that I wasn't even sure if I loved you anymore."

"So what makes you sure you love me now?"

"Do you want another fight?" she asks.

I look the other way.

"No, I don't want to fight," I tell her.

I hear her sigh. Then she says, "You see? Nothing has changed . . . has it."

# THE GOAL

Neither of us says a word for quite awhile. Julie gets up and walks over to the river. It looks for a second as if she might run away. She doesn't. She comes back again and sits down on the bench.

She says to me, "When I was eighteen, I had everything planned—college, a teaching degree, marriage, a house, children. In that order. All the decisions were made. I knew what china pattern I wanted. I knew the names I wanted for the kids. I knew what the house should look like and what color the rug should be. Everything was certain. And it was so important that I have it all. But now . . . I have it all, only it's different somehow. None of it seems to matter."

"Julie, why does your life have to conform to this . . . this perfect image you have in your head?" I ask her. "Do you even know *why* you want the things you do?"

"Because that's how I grew up," she says. "And what about you? Why do you have to have this big career? Why do you feel compelled to work twenty-four hours a day?"

Silence.

Then she says, "I'm sorry. I'm just very confused."

"No, that's okay," I say. "It was a good question. I have no idea why I wouldn't be satisfied being a grocer, or a nine-to-five office worker."

"Al, why don't we just try to forget all this," she suggests.

"No, I don't think so," I tell her. "I think we should do the opposite. We ought to start asking a few more questions."

Julie gives me a skeptical look and asks, "Like what?"

"Like what is our marriage supposed to do for us?" I ask her. "My idea of the goal of a marriage is not living in a perfect house where everything happens according to a clock. Is that the goal for you?"

"All I'm asking for is a little dependability from my husband," she says. "And what's all this about a *goal?* When you're married, you're just married. There is no goal."

"Then why be married?" I ask.

"You get married because of commitment . . . because of love . . . because of all the reasons everybody else does," she says. "Alex, you're asking a lot of dumb questions."

"Whether they're dumb or smart, I'm asking them because we've been living together for fifteen years and we have no clear understanding of what our marriage is supposed to do . . . or become . . . or anything!'' I sputter. ''We're just coasting along, doing 'what everyone else does.' And it turns out the two of us have some very different assumptions of what our lives are supposed to be like.''

''My parents have been married for thirty-seven years,'' she says, ''and they never asked any questions. Nobody ever asks 'What is the goal of a marriage?' People just get married because they're in love.''

''Oh. Well, that explains everything, doesn't it,'' I say.

''Al, please don't ask these questions,'' she says. ''They don't have any answers. And if we keep talking this way, we're going to ruin everything. If this is your way of saying you're having second thoughts about us—''

''Julie, I'm not having second thoughts about you. But you're the one who can't figure out what's wrong with us. Maybe if you tried to think about this logically instead of simply comparing us to the characters in a romance novel—''

''I do not read romance novels,'' she says.

''Then where did you get your ideas about how a marriage is supposed to be?'' I ask her.

She says nothing.

''All I'm saying is we ought to throw away for the moment all the pre-conceptions we have about our marriage, and just take a look at how we are right now,'' I tell her. ''Then we ought to figure out what we want to have happen and go in that direction.''

But Julie doesn't seem to be listening. She stands up.

''I think it's time we walked back,'' she says.

On the way back to the Barnett house, we're as silent as two icebergs in January, the two of us drifting together. I look at one side of the street; Julie looks at the opposite. When we walk through the door, Mrs. Barnett invites me to stay for dinner, but I say I've got to be going. I say goodbye to the kids, give Julie a wave and leave.

I'm getting into the Buick when I hear her come running after me.

''Will I see you again on Saturday?'' she asks.

I smile a little. ''Yeah, sure. Sounds good.''

She says, ''I'm sorry about what happened.''

''I guess we'll just have to keep trying until we get it right.''

We both start smiling. Then we do some of that nice stuff that makes an argument almost worth the agony.

# 28

I get home just as the sun is starting to set. The sky is rosy pink. As I'm unlocking the kitchen door, I hear the phone ringing inside. I rush in to grab it.

"Good morning," says Jonah.

"Morning?" Outside the window, the sun is almost below the horizon. I laugh. "I'm watching the sun set. Where are *you* calling from?"

"Singapore," he says.

"Oh."

"By the way, from my hotel I'm watching the sun *rise*," Jonah says. "Alex, I wouldn't have called you at home, but I'm not going to be able to talk to you again for a few weeks."

"Why not?"

"Well, it's a long story and I can't go into it now," he says. "But I'm sure we'll have a chance to discuss it some time."

"I see. . . ." I wonder what's going on, but say, "That's too bad. It puts me in a kind of a bind, because I was just about to ask for your help again."

"Has something gone wrong?" he asks.

"No," I tell him. "Everything is generally going very well from an operations standpoint. But I just had a meeting with my division vice president, and I was told the plant has to show an even bigger improvement."

"You're still not making money?" he asks.

I say, "Yes, we are making money again, but we need to accelerate the improvement to save the plant from being shut down."

I hear the trace of a chuckle on the other end of the line, and Jonah says, "If I were you, I wouldn't worry too much about being shut down."

"Well, from what the head of the division has told me, the possibility of a shut-down is real," I tell him. "And until he says otherwise, I can't afford to take this lightly."

"Alex, if you want to improve the plant even more, I'm with you all the way," Jonah says. "And since I won't have the opportunity to speak to you for awhile, let's talk about it now. Bring me up to date on what's happening."

So I do. Then, wondering if we've reached some theoretical limit by now, I ask him if there is anything else we can try.

"Anything else?" he says. "Believe me, we have only begun. Now, here's what I suggest . . . ."

Early the next morning, I'm in my office at the plant considering what Jonah told me. Outside is the dawn of the day he's already seen in Singapore. Stepping out to get a cup of coffee, I find Stacey at the coffee machine.

"Hello there," she says. "I hear everything went fairly well for us at headquarters yesterday."

"Well, not bad," I say. "I'm afraid we still have a way to go before we convince Peach we're good for the long term. But I talked to Jonah last night."

"Did you tell him about our progress?" she asks.

"Yes," I say. "And he suggested we try what he called 'the next logical step.' "

I see her face take on a nervous grin. "What's that?"

"Cut our batch sizes in half on non-bottlenecks," I say.

Stacy takes a step back as she thinks about this.

"But why?" she asks.

I say with a smile, "Because in the end we'll make more money."

"I don't understand," she says. "How is that going to help us?"

"Hey, Stacey, you're in charge of inventory control," I tell her. "You tell me what would happen if we cut our batch sizes in half."

Thinking, she sips her coffee for a moment. Her brow compresses in concentration. Then she says, "If we cut our batch sizes in half, then I guess that at any one time we'd have half the work-in-process on the floor. I guess that means we'd only need half the investment in work-in-process to keep the plant working. If we could work it out with our vendors, we could conceivably cut all our inventories in half, and by cutting our inventories in half, we reduce the amount of cash tied up at any one time, which eases the pressure on cash flow."

I'm nodding each time she says a sentence, and finally I say, "That's right. That's *one* set of benefits."

She says, "But to reap those benefits fully, we'd have to have our suppliers increase the frequency of deliveries to us and reduce the quantity of each delivery. That's going to take some negotiating through purchasing, and I'm not sure all the vendors will go for it."

I tell her, "That's something we can work on. Eventually they'll go for it because it's to their advantage as well as ours."

"But if we go to smaller batch sizes," she says, squinting at me in cynicism, "doesn't that mean we'll have to have more setups on equipment?"

"Sure," I say, "don't worry about it."

"Don't — ?"

"Yeah, don't worry about it."

"But Donovan — "

"Donovan will do just fine, even with more setups," I say. "And, meanwhile, there is *another* set of benefits, aside from what you said, that we can have almost immediately."

"What's that?" she asks.

"You really want to know?"

"Sure, I do."

"Good. You set up a meeting with the other functions and I'll tell everyone at the same time."

For dumping that little chore of the meeting arrangements on her, Stacey pays me back in kind by setting the meeting for noon at the most expensive restaurant in town — with lunch billable to *my* expense number, of course.

"What could I do?" she asks as we sit down at the table. "It was the only time everybody was available, right, Bob?"

"Right," says Bob.

I'm not mad. Given the quality and quantity of work these people have done recently, I can't complain about picking up the tab for lunch. I get right down to telling everybody what Stacey and I had talked about this morning, and lead up to the other set of benefits.

Part of what Jonah told me last night over the phone had to do with the time a piece of material spends inside a plant. If you consider the total time from the moment the material comes into the plant to the minute it goes out the door as part of a finished product, you can divide that time into four elements.

One of them is setup, the time the part spends waiting for a resource, while the resource is preparing itself to work on the part.

Another is process time, which is the amount of time the part spends being modified into a new, more valuable form.

A third element is queue time, which is the time the part spends in line for a resource while the resource is busy working on something else ahead of it.

The fourth element is wait time, which is the time the part waits, not for a resource, but for another part so they can be assembled together.

As Jonah pointed out last night, setup and process are a small portion of the total elapsed time for any part. But queue and wait often consume large amounts of time—in fact, the majority of the elapsed total that the part spends inside the plant.

For parts that are going through *bottlenecks*, queue is the dominant portion. The part is stuck in front of the bottleneck for a long time. For parts that are only going through *non-bottle-necks*, wait is dominant, because they are waiting in front of assembly for parts that are coming from the bottlenecks. Which means that in each case, the bottlenecks are what dictate this elapsed time. Which, in turn, means the bottlenecks dictate inventory as well as throughput.

We have been setting batch sizes according to an economical batch quantity (or EBQ) formula. Last night, Jonah told me that although he didn't have time over the phone to go into all the reasons, EBQ has a number of flawed assumptions underlying it. Instead, he asked me to consider what would happen if we cut batch sizes by half from their present quantities.

If we reduce batch sizes by half, we also reduce by half the time it will take to process a batch. That means we reduce queue and wait by half as well. Reduce those by half, and we reduce by about half the total time parts spend in the plant. Reduce the time parts spend in the plant, and. . . .

"Our total lead time condenses," I explain. "And with less time spent sitting in a pile, the speed of the flow of parts increases."

"And with faster turn-around on orders, customers get their orders faster," says Lou.

"Not only that," says Stacey, "but with shorter lead times we can respond faster."

"That's right!" I say. "If we can respond to the market faster, we get an advantage in the marketplace."

"That means more customers come to us because we can deliver faster," says Lou.

"Our sales increase!" I say.

"And so do our bonuses!" says Stacey.

"Whoa! Whoa now! Hold up here a minute!" says Bob.

"What's the matter?" I ask him.

"What about setup time?" he says. "You cut batch sizes in half, you double the number of setups. What about direct labor? We got to save on setups to keep down costs."

"Okay, I knew this would come up," I tell them. "Now look, it's time to think about this carefully. Jonah told me last night that there was a corresponding rule to the one about an hour lost at a bottleneck. You remember that? An hour lost at a bottleneck is an hour lost for the entire system."

"Yeah, I remember," Bob says.

I say, "The rule he gave me last night is that an hour saved at a non-bottleneck is a mirage."

"A *mirage!*" he says. "What do you mean, an hour saved at a non-bottleneck is a mirage? An hour saved is an hour saved!"

"No, it isn't," I tell him. "Since we began withholding materials from the floor until the bottlenecks are ready for them, the non-bottlenecks now have idle time. It's perfectly okay to have more setups on non-bottlenecks, because all we're doing is cutting into time the machines would spend being idle. Saving setups at a non-bottleneck doesn't make the system one bit more productive. The time and money saved is an illusion. Even if we double the number of setups, it won't consume all the idle time."

"Okay, okay," says Bob. "I guess I can see what you mean."

"Now Jonah said, first of all, to cut the batch sizes in half. Then he suggested I go immediately to marketing and convince them to conduct a new campaign which will promise customers earlier deliveries."

"Can we do it?" asks Lou.

I tell them, "Already, our lead times have condensed considerably over what they were before thanks to the priority system and making the bottlenecks more productive. We have reduced lead time of about three to four months down to two months or even less. If we cut our batch sizes in half, how fast do you think we can respond?"

There is an eternity of hemming and hawing while this is debated.

Finally, Bob admits, "Okay, if we cut batch sizes in half, then that means it ought to take half the time it does now. So instead of six to eight weeks, it should take about four weeks . . . maybe even three weeks in a lot of cases."

"Suppose I go to marketing and tell them to promise customers deliveries in three weeks?" I say.

"Whoa! Hold on!" says Bob.

"Yeah, give us a break!" says Stacey.

"All right, four weeks then," I say. "That's reasonable, isn't it?"

"Sounds reasonable to me," says Ralph.

"Well . . . okay," says Stacey.

"I think we should risk it," says Lou.

"So are you willing to commit to this with us?" I ask Bob.

Bob sits back and says, "Well . . . I'm all for bigger bonuses. What the hell. Let's try it."

Friday morning finds the Buick and me again hustling up the Interstate toward headquarters. I hit town just as the sun hits the glass of the UniCo building and reflects a blinding glare. Kind of pretty actually. For a moment, it takes my mind off my nerves. I've got a meeting scheduled with Johnny Jons in his office. When I called, he was quite willing to see me, but sounded less than enthusiastic about what I said I'd like to talk about. I feel there's a lot riding on my ability to convince him to go along with what we want to do. So I've found myself biting a fingernail or two during the trip.

Jons doesn't really have a desk in his office. He has a sheet of glass on chrome legs. I guess that's so that everyone can get a good look at his Gucci loafers and silk socks — which he exposes as he leans back in this chair, interweaves his fingers and puts them behind his head.

He says, "So . . . how is everything going?"

"Everything is going very well right now," I say. "In fact, that's why I wanted to talk to you."

Jons immediately dons an impassive face.

"All right, listen," I tell him, "I'm going to lay my cards out for you. I'm not exaggerating when I say everything is going well. It is. We've worked off our backlog of overdue orders, as you know. At the beginning of last week, the plant began producing strictly to meet projected due dates."

Jons nods and says, "Yes, I've noticed my phone hasn't been ringing lately with complaints from customers missing their orders."

"My point," I tell him, "is that we've really turned the plant around. Here, look at this."

From my briefcase, I take the latest computer-generated list of customer orders. Among other things, it shows the due dates promised, along with the dates when Ralph expected shipment, and the dates the products were actually shipped.

"You see," I tell Jons as he studies the list on the glass top of his table, "we can predict to within twenty-four hours one way or the other when an order will leave the plant."

"Yes, I've seen something like this floating around," says Jons. "These are the dates?"

"Of course."

"This is impressive," says Jons.

"As you can see by comparing a few recently shipped orders with ones of a month or so before, our production lead times have condensed dramatically. Four months' lead time is no longer a holy number with us. From the day you sign the contract with the customer to the day we ship, the current average is about two months. Now, tell me, do you think that could help us in the marketplace?"

"Sure it could," says Jons.

'Then how about *four weeks*?"

"*What*? Al, don't be ridiculous,"says Jons. "Four weeks!"

"We can do it."

"Come on!" he says. "Last winter, when demand for every damn thing we make was way down, we were promising delivery in four months, and it was taking six! Now you're telling me you can go from contract to finished product in four weeks?"

"I wouldn't be here talking to you if we couldn't," I tell him, hoping desperately that we're right.

Jons snorts, unconvinced.

"Johnny, the truth is I need more business," I tell him. "With our overdues gone, and our current backlog declining, I've got to get more work into my plant. Now we both know the business is out there; it's just that the competition is getting more of it than we are."

Jons looks at me through narrowed eyes. "You can really turn around an order of 200 Model 12's or 300 DBD-50's in four weeks?"

"Try me," I tell him. "Get me five orders — hell, get me *ten* orders — and I'll prove it to you."

"And what happens to our credibility if you can't come through?" he asks.

Flustered, I look down through the glass table.

"Johnny," I say, "I'll make a bet with you. If I don't deliver in four weeks, I'll buy you a brand new pair of Gucci's."

He laughs, shakes his head and finally says, "Okay, you're on. I'll pass the word to the salespeople that on all your products, we're offering terms of factory shipment in six weeks."

I start to protest. Jons holds up a hand.

"I know you're confident," he says. "And if you ship any new orders in less than five weeks, I'll buy *you* a new pair of shoes."

# 29

A full moon is shining through the bedroom window and into my eyes. The night is still. I look at the clock beside me, which says it's 4:20 A.M. Next to me in bed, Julie is sleeping.

Resting on my elbow, I look down at Julie. With her dark hair spilled out on the white pillow, she looks nice sleeping in the moonlight. I watch her for a while. I wonder what her dreams are like.

When I woke up, I was having a nightmare. It was about the plant. I was running up and down the aisles and Bill Peach was chasing me in his crimson Mercedes. Every time he was about to run me over, I'd duck between a couple of machines or hop on a passing forklift. He was yelling at me from the window about my bottom line not being good enough. Finally he trapped me in the shipping department. I had my back against stacks of cardboard cartons, and the Mercedes was racing toward me at a hundred miles an hour. I tried to shield my eyes from the blinding headlights. Just as Peach was about to get me, I woke up and discovered that the headlights were moonbeams on my face.

Now I'm too much awake, and too aware of the problem I was trying to forget this past evening with Julie for me to fall back to sleep. Not wanting to awaken Julie with my restlessness, I slip out of bed.

The house is all ours tonight. We started out this evening with nothing particular to do, when we remembered we had a whole house in Bearington with nobody in it to bother us. So we bought a bottle of wine, some cheese and a loaf of bread, came here and got comfortable.

From the living room window where I stand in the dark looking out, it seems as though the whole world is asleep except me. I'm angry with myself at not being able to sleep. But I can't let go of what's on my mind.

Yesterday we had a staff meeting. There was some good news—and some bad news. Actually, there was a lot of good news. High among the headlines were the new contracts marketing has been winning for us. We've picked up about half–a–dozen new orders since I talked to Johnny. More good news was the fact that efficiencies have gone up, not down, as a result of what we've been doing in the plant. After we began withholding the release of materials and timing the releases according to the completed processing of heat–treat and the NCX-10, efficiencies dipped somewhat. But that was because we were consuming excess inventories. When the excess inventories were exhausted— which happened quickly as a result of the increase in throughput—efficiencies came back up again.

Then, two weeks ago, we implemented the new smaller batch sizes. When we cut batch sizes in half for non-bottlenecks, efficiencies stayed solid, and now it seems as though we're keeping the work force even more occupied than before.

That's because a really terrific thing has happened. Before we reduced batch sizes, it wasn't uncommon for a work center to be forced idle because it didn't have anything to process— even though we were wading through excess inventory. It was usually because the idle work center had to wait for the one preceding it to finish a large batch of some item. Unless told otherwise by an expeditor, the materials handlers would wait until an entire batch was completed before moving it. In fact, that's still the case. But now that the batches are smaller, the parts are ready to be moved to the next work station *sooner* than they were before.

What we had been doing many times was turning a non-bottleneck into a temporary bottleneck. This was forcing other work centers downstream from it to be idle, which reflected poorly on efficiencies. Now, even though we've recognized that non-bottlenecks have to be idle periodically, there is actually *less* idle time than before. Since we cut batch sizes, work is flowing through the plant more smoothly than ever. And it's weird, but the idle time we do have is less noticeable. It's spread out in shorter segments. Instead of people hanging around with nothing to do for a couple of hours, now they'll have maybe a few ten- to twenty-minute waits through the day for the same volume of work. From everybody's standpoint, that's much better.

Still more good news is that inventories are at their lowest ever in the plant. It's almost shocking to walk out into the plant now. Those stacks and piles of parts and sub-assemblies have shrunk to half their former size. It's as if a fleet of trucks had come and hauled everything away. Which is, in fact, about what happened. We've shipped that excess inventory as finished product. Of course, the notable part of the story is that we haven't filled the plant back up again by dumping new work-in-process on the floor. The only work-in-process out there now is for current demand.

But then there's the bad news. Which is what I'm thinking about when I hear footsteps on the carpet behind me in the dark.

"Al?"

"Yeah."

"How come you're out here in the dark?"

"Can't sleep."

"What's wrong?"

"Nothing."

"Then why don't you come back to bed?"

"I'm just thinking about some things."

It's quiet for a second. For a moment, I think she's gone away. Then I feel her beside me.

"Is it the plant?" she asks.

"Yeah."

"But I thought everything was getting better," she says. "What's wrong?"

"It has to do with our cost measurement," I tell her.

She sits down beside me.

"Why don't you tell me about it," she says.

"Sure you want to hear about it?" I ask.

"Yes, I do."

So I tell her: the cost of parts looks as though it's gone up because of the additional setups necessitated by the smaller batch sizes.

"Oh," she says. "I guess that's bad, right?"

"Politically speaking, yes," I tell her. "Financially speaking, it doesn't make a damn bit of difference."

"How come?" she asks.

"Well . . . do you know why it looks like the cost has gone up?" I ask her.

"No, not at all," she says.

I get up to switch on a lamp and find a piece of paper and pencil.

I tell her, "Okay, I'll give you an example. Suppose we have a batch of 100 parts. The time to set up the machine is 2 hours, or 120 mintues. And the process time per part is 5 minutes. So we've invested per part 2 hours *plus* 2 hours of set-up divided by 100. It comes to 1.2 minutes of set-up per part. According to the accountants, the cost of the part is based upon direct labor of 6.2 minutes.

"Now if we cut the batch in half, we still have the same amount of set-up time. But it's spread over 50 parts instead of 100. So now we've got 5 minutes of process time, plus 2.4 minutes of set-up for a grand total of 7.4 minutes of direct labor. And the calculations are all based on the cost of direct labor."

Then I explain the way costs are calcualted. First, there is the raw material cost. Then there is the cost of direct labor. And finally there is "burden," which essentially works out to be cost of the direct labor multiplied by a factor, in our case, of about three. So on paper, if the direct labor goes up, the burden also goes up.

"So with more set-ups, the cost of making parts goes up," says Julie.

"It *looks* that way," I tell her, "but in fact it hasn't really done anything to our actual expenses. We haven't added more people to the payroll. We haven't added any additional cost by doing more set-ups. In fact, the cost of parts has gone down since we began the smaller batch sizes."

"Down? How come?"

"Because we've reduced inventory and increased the amount of money we're bringing in through sales," I explain. "So the same burden, the same direct labor cost is now spread over more *product*. By making and selling more product for the same cost, our operating expense has gone down, not up."

"How could the measurement be wrong?" she asks.

I say, "The measurement assumes that all of the workers in the plant are always going to be fully occupied, and therefore, in order to do more set-ups, you have to hire more people. That isn't true."

"What are you going to do?" she asks me.

I look up at the window. The sun is now over the roof of my neighbor's house. I reach over for her hand.

"What am I going to do? I'm going to take you out to break-fast."

When I get to the office, Lou walks in.

"More bad news for me?" I joke.

He says, "Look . . . I think I can help you out on this cost of products thing."

"Yeah? Like how?"

"I can change the base we're using for determining the cost of parts. Instead of using the cost factor of the past twelve months, which is what I'm supposed to be doing, we can use the past two months. That will help us, because for the past two months, we've had big increases in throughput."

"Yeah," I say, sensing the possibilities. "Yeah, that might work. And actually the past two months are a lot more representative of what's really going on here than what happened last year."

Lou leans from side to side. He says, "We-l-l-l, yes, that's true. But according to accounting policy, it's not valid."

"Okay, but we have a good excuse," I say. "The plant *is* different now. We're really a hell of a lot better than we were."

"Al, the problem is Ethan Frost will never buy it," says Lou.

"Then why did you suggest it?"

"Frost won't buy it *if* he knows about it," says Lou.

I nod slowly. "I see."

"I can give you something that will slide through on the first glance," says Lou. "But if Frost and his assistants at division do any checking, they'll see through it in no time."

"You're saying we could end up in very hot water," I say.

"Yeah, but if you want to take a chance. . . ." says Lou.

"It could give us a couple more months to really show what we can do," I say, finishing the thought for him.

I get up and walk around for a minute turning this over in my mind.

Finally I look at Lou and say, "There is no way I can show Peach an increase in the cost of parts and convince him the plant is better off this month than last. If he sees these numbers and gets the idea our costs are going up, we'll be in hot water anyway."

"So you want to try it?" Lou asks.

"Sure."

"All right," he says. "Remember, if we get caught — "

"Don't worry. I'll practice my tap dancing."

As Lou is on his way out, Fran buzzes me to say Johnny Jons is on my line. I pick up the phone.

"Hello there," I tell him. We're practically old pals by now; I've been on the phone with him just about every day — and sometimes three or four times a day — for the past few weeks. "What can I do for you today?"

"Remember our dear friend Bucky Burnside?" says Jons.

"How could I forget good ole Bucky," I say. "Is he still complaining about us?"

"No, not anymore," says Jons. "At the moment, in fact, we don't even have a single active contract with Burnside's people. That's the reason I'm calling. For the first time in months, they've expressed interest in buying something from us again."

"What are they interested in?"

"Model 12's," he says. "They need a thousand units."

"Terrific!"

"Maybe not," says Jons. "They need the whole order by the end of the month."

"That's only about two weeks away," I say.

"I know," says Jons. "The sales rep on this already checked with the warehouse. Turns out we've only got about fifty of the Model 12's in stock."

He's telling me, of course, we'll have to manufacture the other 950 by the end of the month if we want the business.

"Well . . . Johnny, look, I know I told you I wanted business, and you've pulled in some nice contracts since I talked to you," I say. "But a thousand Model 12's in two weeks is asking a lot."

He says, "Al, to tell you the truth, I didn't really think we could do anything with this one when I called. But I thought I'd let you know about it, just in case you knew something I didn't. After all, a thousand units means a little over a million dollars in sales to us."

"Yes, I realize that," I say. "Look, what's going on that they need these things so fast?"

He tells me he did some digging and found out that the order had originally gone to our number-one competitor, who makes a product similar to the Model 12. The competitor had had the order on its books for about five months. But they hadn't filled it yet, and this week it became clear they would not be able to meet the due date.

"My guess is that Burnside turned to us, because they've heard about us offering such fast turn-around to everyone else," he says. "Frankly, I think they're desperate. And, hell, if there is any way we can pull this off, it'd sure be a good way for us to save face with them."

"Well, I don't know. I'd like that business back again, too, but. . . ."

"The real kick in the head is if we had only had the foresight to build a finished goods inventory of Model 12's while we had those slow sales months, we could have made this sale," he says.

I have to smile to myself, because at the beginning of the year I might have agreed with that.

"It's too bad," Johnny is saying. "Aside from the initial business, it could have been a big opportunity for us."

"How big?"

"Strong hints have been dropped that if we can come through on this one, we could become their preferred supplier," says Jons.

I'm quiet for a moment.

"All right. You really want this, don't you?" I ask him.

"So bad I can taste it," he says. "But if it's impossible. . . ."

"When do you have to let them know?" I ask.

"Probably sometime today, or tomorrow at the latest," he says. "Why? Do you think we can really do it?"

"Maybe there's a way. Let me see how we stand and I'll give you a call back," I tell him.

As soon as I get off the phone with Jons, I round up Bob, Stacey, and Ralph for a meeting in my office, and when we're all together I tell them what Jons told me.

"Ordinarily, I would think this is out of the question," I say. "But before we say no, let's think about it."

Everybody looks at me with the certain knowledge this is going to be a waste of time.

I say, "Let's just see what we can do, okay?"

For the rest of the morning, we're busy with this. We go over the bill of material. Stacey checks on raw materials inventories. Ralph does a quick estimate of how long it will take to produce a thousand units after the materials are on hand. By eleven o'clock, he has calculated that the bottlenecks can turn out parts for the Model 12 at the rate of about one-hundred per day.

"So, yes, it would be technically feasible for us to do take the order," says Ralph. "But that's only if we work on nothing else for two weeks except the thousand units for Burnside."

"No, I don't want to do that," I tell him, thinking about us screwing up relations with a dozen customers just to please one. "Let's try something else."

"Like what?" asks Bob, who is sitting there with us, looking about as enthusiastic as a bump on a log.

I say, "A few weeks ago, we cut our batch sizes by half, and the result was we could condense the time inventory spends in the plant, which also gave us an increase in throughput. What if we cut the batch sizes by half *again*?"

Ralph says, "Gee, I hadn't thought of that."

Bob leans forward. "Cut them again? Sorry, Al, but I don't see how the heck that can help us, not with the volume we're already committed to."

"You know," says Ralph, "we have quite a few orders we'd planned to ship ahead of their due dates. We could re-schedule some of those in the priority system so they'd ship when promised instead of early. That could give us more time available on the bottlenecks, and it wouldn't hurt anybody."

"Good point, Ralph," I tell him.

"But, hell, we still can't get a thousand units done no-how," drawls Bob. "Not in two weeks."

I say, "Well, then, if we cut the batch sizes, how many units *can* we do in two weeks and still ship our current orders on time?"

Bob pulls on his chin and says, "I guess we could look into it."

"I'll see what I can find out," says Ralph, standing so he can leave and go back to his computer.

His interest finallly piqued, Bob says, "Maybe I'd better go with you so we can noodle this thing out together."

While Ralph and Bob are wrestling with this new possibility, Stacey enters with news about inventories. She's ascertained we can obtain all the materials we need either from our own stocks or from vendors within a few days, with one exception.

"The electronic control modules for the Model 12 are a problem," says Stacey. "We don't have enough of this type in stock. And we don't have the technology to build them in-house. *But* we've located a vendor in California who has them. Unfortunately, the vendor can't promise a shipment of that quantity in less than four to six weeks, including shipping. I'd say we might as well forget it.''

"Wait a minute, Stacey; we're thinking about a little change in strategy. How many modules could they give us per week?'' I ask her. "And how soon could they ship the first week's quantity to us?''

"I don't know, but doing it that way, we might not be able to get a volume discount,'' says Stacey.

"Why not?'' I ask. "We'd be committing to the same thousand units—it's just that we'd be staggering the shipments.''

"Well, then there's the added shipping cost,'' she says.

"Stacey, we're talking a million dollars in business here,'' I tell her.

"Okay, but they'll take at least three days to a week to get here by truck,'' she says.

"So why can't we have them shipped air freight?'' I ask. "They're not very big parts.''

"Well. . . . '' says Stacey.

"Look into it, but I doubt if the air freight bill is going to eat up the profit on a million-dollar sale,'' I tell her. "And if we can't get these parts, we can't get the sale.''

"All right. I'll see what they can do,'' she says.

At the end of the day, the details are still being sweated out, but we know enough for me to place a call to Jons.

"I've got a deal on those Model 12's for you to relay to Burnside,'' I say.

"Really?'' says Jons excitedly. "You want to take the business?''

"Under certain conditions,'' I tell him. "First of all, there is no way we can deliver the full thousand units in two weeks. But we can ship 250 per week to them for four weeks.''

"Well, okay, they might go for that,'' says Jons, "but when can you start shipping?''

"Two weeks from the day they give us the order,'' I say.

"Are you sure about this?'' asks Johnny.

"The units will ship when we say they will,'' I tell him.

"You're that confident?''

"Yes.''

"Okay, okay. I'll call them and see if they're interested. But, Al, I just hope what you're telling me is real, because I don't want to go through all the hassles we had before with these people.''

A couple of hours later, my phone rings at home.

''Al? We got it! We got the order!'' shouts Jons into my right ear.

And in my left ear, I hear a million bucks rung up on the cash register.

''You know what?'' Jons is saying. ''They even like the smaller shipments *better* than getting all thousand units at once!''

I tell him, ''Okay, great, I'll get the ball rolling right away. You can tell them that two weeks from today, we'll ship the first 250.''

# 30

At the beginning of the new month, we have a staff meeting. Everyone is present except Lou. Bob tells me he'll be in shortly. I sit down and fidget. To get the meeting rolling while we're waiting for Lou, I ask about shipments.

"How is Burnside's order coming along?" I ask.

"The first shipment went out as scheduled," says Donovan.

"How about the rest of it?" I ask.

"No problems to speak of," says Stacey. "The control boxes were a day late, but there was time enough for us to assemble without delaying the shipment. We got this week's batch from the vendor on time."

I say, "Good. What's the latest on the smaller batches?"

"The flow through the shop is even better now," says Bob.

"Excellent," I say.

Just then Lou comes into the meeting. He's late because he was finishing the figures for this month. He sits down and looks straight at me.

"Well?" I ask. "Did we get our fifteen percent?"

"No," he says, "we got seventeen percent, thanks in part to Burnside. And the coming month looks just fine."

Then he goes into a wrap-up of how we performed through the second quarter. We're now solidly in the black. Inventories are about forty percent of what they were three months ago. Throughput has doubled.

"Well, we've come a long way, haven't we?" I ask.

Sitting on my desk when I get back from lunch the next day are two crisp, white envelopes with the UniWare Division logo in the upper left corner. I open one and unfold the stiff stationery. The body of the letter is only two short paragraphs, with Bill Peach's signature on the bottom. It's congratulating us on the Burnside business. Tearing open the other, I find it too is from Peach. It too is short and to the point. It formally directs me to prepare for a performance review of the plant, which is to be held at headquarters.

The smile I had from reading the first letter broadens. Three months ago, that second letter would have dunked me into dread, because although it doesn't say so directly, I presume the review will be the occasion for determining the future of the plant. I was expecting some kind of formal evaluation. And now I am no longer dreading it—on the contrary, I welcome it. What do we have to worry about? Hell, this is an opportunity to show what we've done!

Throughput is going up as marketing spreads the word about us to other customers. Inventories are a fraction of what they were and still falling. With more business and more parts over which to spread the costs, operating expense is down. We're making money.

The following week, I'm away from the plant for two days with my personnel manager, Scott Dolin. We're at an off-site, very confidential meeting in St. Louis with the division's labor relations group and the other plant managers. Most of the discussion is about winning wage concessions from the various unions. It's a frustrating session for me—at Bearington, we don't particularly need to lower wages. So I'm less than enthusiastic about much of the strategy suggested, knowing it could lead to problems with the union, which could lead to a strike, which could kill the progress we've been making with customers. Aside from all that, the meeting is poorly run and ends with very little decided. I return to Bearington.

About four in the afternoon, I walk through the doors of the office building. The receptionist flags me down as I pass. She tells me Bob Donovan has asked to see me the moment I arrive. I have Bob paged and he comes hurrying into my office a few minutes later.

"What's up, Bob?" I ask.

"Hilton Symth, " he says. "He was here in the plant today."

"He was *here*?" I ask. "Why?"

Bob shakes his head and says, "Remember the videotape about robots that was in the works a couple of months ago?"

"That was killed," I say.

"Well, it was reincarnated," says Bob. "Only now it's Hilton, because he's productivity manager for the division, doing the speech instead of Granby. I was having a cup of coffee out of the machine over by C-aisle this morning when I see this T.V. crew come trooping along. By the time I found out what they were doing here, Hilton Smyth is standing at my elbow."

"Didn't anybody here know they were coming?" I ask.

He tells me Barbara Penn, our employee communicator, knew about it.

"And she didn't think to *tell anybody?*" I say.

"See, the whole thing was re-scheduled on short notice," says Bob. "Since you and Scott weren't around, she went ahead on her own, cleared it with the union, and made all the arrangements. She sent around a memo, but nobody got a copy until this morning."

"Nothing like initiative," I mutter.

He goes on to tell me about how Hilton's crew proceeded to set up in front of one of the robots — not the welding types, but another kind of robot which stacks materials. It soon became obvious there was a problem, however: the robot didn't have anything to do. There was no inventory for it, and no work on its way.

In a videotape about productivity, the robot, of course, could not simply sit there in the background and do nothing. It had to be *producing*. So for an hour, Donovan and a couple of assistants searched every corner of the plant for something the robot could manipulate. Meanwhile, Smyth became bored with the wait, so he started wandering around, and it wasn't long before he noticed a few things.

"When we got back with the materials, Hilton started asking all kinds of things about our batch sizes," says Bob. "I didn't know what to tell him, because I wasn't sure what you've said up at headquarters and, uh . . . well, I just thought you ought to know."

I feel my stomach twisting. Just then the phone rings. I pick it up at my desk. It's Ethan Frost at headquarters. He tells me he's just had a talk with Hilton Smyth. I excuse myself to Bob, and he leaves. When he's gone and the door is shut, I talk to Frost for a couple of minutes and afterwards go down to see Lou.

I walk though the door and start to tap dance.

Two days later, an audit team from headquarters arrives at the plant. The team is headed by the division's assistant controller, Neil Cravitz, a fiftyish man who has the most bone-crushing handshake and the most humorless stare of anyone I've ever met. They march in and take over the conference room. In hardly any time at all, they've found we changed the base for determining the cost of products.

"This is highly irregular," says Cravitz, peering at us over the tops of his glasses as he looks up from the spreadsheets.

Lou stammers that, okay, maybe it wasn't exactly according to policy, but we had valid reasons for basing costs on a current two-month period.

I add, "It's actually a more truthful representation this way."

"Sorry, Mr. Rogo," says Cravitz. "We have to observe standard policy."

"But the plant *is* different now!"

Around the table, all five accountants are frowning at Lou and me. I finally shake my head. There is no sense attempting to appeal to them. All they know are their accounting standards.

The audit team recalculates the numbers, and it now looks as if our costs have gone up. When they leave, I try to head them off by calling Peach before they can return, but Peach is unexpectedly out of town. I try Frost, but he's gone too. One of the secretaries offers to put me through to Smyth, who seems to be the only manager in the offices, but I ungracefully decline.

For a week, I wait for the blast from headquarters. But it never comes. Lou gets a rebuke from Frost in the form of a memo warning him to stick to approved policy, and a formal order to redo our quarterly report according to the old cost standards and to submit it before the review. From Peach, there is nothing.

I'm in the middle of a meeting with Lou over our *revised* monthly report early one afternoon. I'm crestfallen. With the numbers based on the old cost factor, we're not going to make our fifteen percent. We're only going to record a 12.8 percent increase on the bottom line, not the seventeen percent Lou originally calculated.

"Lou, can't we massage this a little more?" I'm pleading.

He shakes his head. "From now on, Frost is going to be scrutinizing everything we submit. I can't do any better than what you see now."

Just then I become aware of this sound outside the offices that's getting louder and louder.

Wuppa-wuppa-wuppa-wuppa-wuppa-wuppa-wuppa-wuppa.

I look at Lou and he looks at me.

"Is that a helicopter?" I ask.

Lou goes to the window and looks out.

"Sure is, and it's landing on our lawn!" he says.

I get to the window just as it touches down. Dust and brown grass clippings are whirling in the prop wash around this sleek red and white helicopter. With the blades still twirling down to a stop, the door opens and two men get out.

"That first one looks like Johnny Jons," says Lou.

"It *is* Johnny Jons," I say.

"Who's the other guy?" asks Lou.

I'm not sure. I watch them cross the lawn and start to walk through the parking lot. Something about the girth and the striding, arrogant swagger of the huge, white-haired second man triggers the recollection of a distant meeting. It dawns on me who he is.

"Oh, god," I say.

"I didn't think He needed a helicopter to get around," says Lou.

"It's worse than God," I say. "It's Bucky Burnside!"

Before Lou can utter another word, I'm running for the door. I dash around the corner and into Stacey's office. She, along with her secretary and some people she's meeting with, are all at the window. Everybody is watching the damn helicopter.

"Stacey, quick, I need to talk to you right now!"

She comes over to the door and I pull her into the hallway.

"What's the status on Burnside's Model 12's?" I ask her.

"The last shipment went out two days ago."

"It was on time?"

"Sure," she says. "It went out the door with no problems, just like the previous shipments."

I'm running again, mumbling "thanks" over my shoulder to her.

"Donovan!"

He's not in his office. I stop at his secretary's desk.

"Where's Bob?" I ask her.

"I think he went to the men's room," she says.

I go sprinting in that direction. Bursting through the door, I find Bob washing his hands.

"On Burnside's order," I ask him, "were there any quality problems?"

"No," says Bob, startled to see me. "Nothing I know about."

"Were there *any* problems on that order?" I ask him.

249

He reaches for a paper towel and dries his hands. "No, the whole thing came off like clockwork."

I fall back against the wall. "Then what the hell is he doing here?"

"Is *who* doing here?" asks Bob.

"Burnside," I tell him. "He just landed in a helicopter with Johnny Jons."

"*What?*"

"Come with me," I tell him.

We go to the receptionist, but nobody is in the waiting area.

"Did Mr. Jons come through here just now with a customer?" I ask her.

She says, "The two men in the helicopter? No, I watched them and they went past here and into the plant."

Bob and I hustle side by side down the corridor and through the double doors, into the orange light and production din of the plant. One of the supervisors sees us from across the aisle and, without being asked, points in the direction Jons and Burnside took. As we head down the aisle, I spot them ahead of us.

Burnside is walking up to every employee he sees and he's *shaking hands* with each of them. Honest! He's shaking hands, clapping them on the arm, saying things to them. And he's smiling.

Jons is walking with him. He's doing the same thing. As soon as Burnside lets go of a hand, Jons shakes it as well. They're pumping everybody in sight.

Finally, Jons sees us approaching, taps Burnside on the shoulder, and says something to him. Burnside dons this big grin and comes striding up to me with his hand extended.

"Here's the man I especially want to congratulate," says Burnside in a growling kind of voice. "I was saving the best for last, but you beat me to it. How are you?"

"Fine, just fine, Mr. Burnside," I tell him.

"Rogo, I came down here because I want to shake the hand of every employee in your whole plant," growls Burnside. "That was a hell of job this plant did on our order. A hell of a good job! Those other bastards had the order for five months and still couldn't get it done, and here your people finish the whole thing in five weeks. Must have been an incredible effort!"

Before I can say anything, Jons jumps into the conversation and says, "Bucky and I were having lunch today, and I was

telling him how you pulled out all the stops for him, how everybody down here really gave it everything they had.''

I say, ''Ah . . . yeah, we just did our best.''

''Mind if I go ahead?'' asks Burnside, intending to continue
down the aisle.

''No, not at all,'' I say.

''Won't hurt your efficiency, will it?'' asks Burnside.

''Not one bit,'' I tell him. ''You go right ahead.''

I turn to Donovan then and out of the corner of my mouth
say, ''Get Barbara Penn down here right away with the camera
she uses for the employee news. And tell her to bring lots of
film.''

Donovan goes trotting off to the offices, and Jons and I follow Bucky up and down the aisles, the three of us shaking hands
with one and all.

Johnny, I notice, is virtually atwitter with excitement. When
Burnside is far enough ahead that he can't hear us, he turns to
me and asks, ''What's your shoe size?''

''Ten and a half,'' I tell him. ''Why?''

''I owe you a pair of shoes,'' says Jons.

I say, ''That's okay, Johnny; don't worry about it.''

''Al, I'm telling you, we're on our way! You hit us a home
run on this one,'' he says. ''We're meeting with Burnside's people next week on a long-term contract for Model 12's — 10,000
units a year!''

The number just about sends me reeling backwards.

''And I'm calling in my whole department when I get back,''
Jons continues as we walk. ''We're going to do a new campaign
pushing everything you make down here, because this is the only
plant we've got in this damn division that can ship a quality
product on time. With your lead times, Al, we're going to blow
everybody out of the market! Thanks to you, we've finally got
a winner.''

I'm beaming. ''Thanks Johnny. But, as it turned out, Burnside's order didn't take any extra effort at all.''

''Shhhh! Don't let Burnside know,'' Johnny says.

Behind me, I hear two hourly guys talking.

''What was that all about?'' asks one.

''Beats me,'' says the other. ''Guess we musta done some-
thin' right.''

On the eve of the plant performance review, with presentation rehearsed and ten copies of our report in hand, and with nothing more to do except imagine what could go wrong, I call Julie.

"Hi," I tell her. "Listen, I have to be at headquarters for a meeting tomorrow morning. And because Forest Grove is more or less on the way, I'd like to come up and be with you tonight. What do you think?"

"Sure, it sounds great," she says.

So I leave work a little early and hit the highway.

As I head up the Interstate, Bearington is spread out to my left. The "Buy Me!" sign on top of the high-rise office buiding is still in place. Living and breathing within the range of my sight are 30,000 people who have no idea that one small but important part of the town's economic future will be decided tomorrow. Most of them haven't the slightest interest in the plant or what we've done here—except if UniWare closes us, they'll be mad and scared. And if we stay open? Nobody will care. Nobody will even know what we went through.

Well, win or lose, I know I did my best.

When I get to Julie's parents' house, Sharon and Dave run up to the car. After getting out of my suit and into some "off-duty" clothes, I spend about an hour throwing a frisbee to the two kids. When they've exhausted me, Julie has the idea the two of us should go out to dinner. I get the feeling she wants to talk to me. I clean up a little and off we go. As we're driving along, we pass the park.

"Al, why don't we stop for awhile," says Julie.

"How come?" I ask.

"The last time we were here we never finished our walk," she says.

So I pull over. We get out and walk. By and by, we come to the bench by the river, and the two of us sit down.

"What's your meeting about tomorrow?" she asks.

"It's a plant performance review," I say. "The division will decide the future of the plant."

"Oh. What do you think they'll say?"

"We didn't quite make what I promised Bill Peach," I say. "One set of numbers doesn't look as good as it truly is because of the cost-of-products standards. You remember me telling you about some of that, don't you?"

She nods. I shake my head momentarily, still angry at what happened as a result of the audit.

"But even with that, we still had a good month. It just doesn't show up as the fantastic month we really had," I tell her.

"You don't think they'd still close the plant, do you?" she asks.

"I don't think so," I say. "A person would have to be an idiot to condemn us just because of an increase in cost of products. Even with screwed-up measurements, we're making money."

She reaches over to take my hand and says, "It was nice of you to take me out to breakfast that morning."

I smile and say,"After listening to me ramble on at five o'-clock in the morning, you deserved it."

"When you talked to me then, it made me realize how little I know about what you do," she says. "I wish you had told me more over the years."

I shrug. "I don't know why I haven't. I guess I thought you wouldn't want to hear it. Or I didn't want to burden you with it."

"Well, I should have asked you more questions," she says.

"I'm sure I didn't give you many opportunities by working those long hours."

"When you weren't coming home those days before I left, I really took it personally," she says. "I couldn't believe it didn't have something to do with me. Deep down, I thought you must be using it as an excuse to stay away from me."

"No, absolutely not, Julie. When all those crises were occurring, I just kept thinking you *must* know how important they were," I tell her. "I'm sorry. I should have told you more."

She squeezes my hand.

"I've been thinking about some of the things you said about our marriage when we were sitting here last time," she says. "I have to say you're right. For a long time, we *have* just been coasting along. In fact, we were drifting apart. I've watched you get more and more wrapped up in your job as the years have gone by. And to compensate for losing you, I got wrapped up in things like decorating the house and spending my time with friends. We lost sight of what was important."

I look at her in the sunlight. The awful frosting in her hair which she had when I came home the day the NCX-10 went down is finally gone. It's grown out. Her hair is thick and straight again, and all the same dark brown.

She says, "Al, the one thing I definitely know now is that I want more of you, not less. That's always been the problem for me."

She turns to me with her blue eyes, and I get a long-lost feeling about her.

"I finally figured out why I haven't wanted to go back to Bearington with you," she says. "And it isn't just the town, although I don't like it very much there. It's that since we've been living apart, we've actually spent more time being together. I mean, when we were living in the same house, I felt as though you took me for granted. Now you bring me flowers. You go out of your way to be with me. You take time to do things with me and the kids. Al, it's been nice. I know it can't go on this way forever — I think my parents are getting a little tired of the arrangement — but I haven't wanted it to end."

I start to feel very good.

I say, "At least we're sure we don't want to say good-bye."

"Al, I don't know exactly what our goal is, or ought to be, but I think we know there must be some kind of need between us," she says. "I know I want Sharon and Dave to grow up to be good people. And I want us to give each other what we need."

I put my arm around her.

"For starters, that sounds worth shooting for," I tell her. "Look, it's probably easier said than done, but I can certainly try to keep from taking you for granted. I'd like you to come home, but unfortunately, the pressures that caused all the problems are still going to be there. They're just not going to go away. I can't ignore my job."

"I've never asked you to," she says. "Just don't ignore me or the kids. And I'll really try to understand your work."

I smile.

"You remember a long time ago, after we got married and we both had jobs, how we'd come home and just talk to each other for a couple of hours, and sympathize with each other about the trials and tribulations we'd suffered during the day?" I ask. "That was nice."

"But then there were babies," says Julie. "And, later, you started putting in extra hours at work."

"Yeah, we got out of the habit," I tell her. "What do you say we make a point to do that again?"

"That sounds terrific," she says. "Look, Al, I know that leaving you must have seemed selfish on my part. I just went crazy for a little while. I'm sorry —"

"No, you don't have to be sorry," I tell her. "I should have been paying attention."

"But I'll try to make it up to you," she says. Then she smiles briefly and adds, "Since we're walking down memory lane, maybe you remember the first fight we had, how we promised afterwards we'd always try to look at a situation from the other's point of view as well as our own. Well, I think for the past couple of years we haven't been doing that very often. I'm willing to try it again if you are."

"I am too," I say.

There is a long hug.

"So . . . you want to get married?" I ask her.

She leans back in my arms and says, "I'll try anything twice."

"You know, don't you, it's not going to be perfect," I tell her. "You know we're still going to have fights."

"And I'll probably be selfish about you from time to time," she says.

"What the hell," I tell her, "let's go to Vegas and find a justice of the peace."

She laughs, "Are you serious?"

"Well, I can't go tonight," I say. "I've got that meeting in the morning. How about tomorrow night?"

"You are serious!"

"All I've been doing since you left is putting my paycheck in the bank. After tommorow, it'll definitely be time to blow some of it."

Julie smiles. "Okay, big spender. Let's do it."

# 31

The next morning on the fifteenth floor of the UniCo building, I walk into the conference room at a few minutes before ten o'clock. Sitting at the far end of the long table is Hilton Smyth and sitting next to him is Neil Cravitz. Flanking them are various staff people.

I say, "Good morning."

Hilton looks up at me without a smile and says, "If you close the door, we can begin."

"Wait a minute. Bill Peach isn't here yet," I say. "We're going to wait for him, aren't we?"

"Bill's not coming. He's involved in some negotiations," says Smyth.

"Then I would like this review to be postponed until he's available," I tell him.

Smyth's eyes get steely.

"Bill specifically told me to conduct this and to pass along my recommendation to him," says Smyth. "So if you want to make a case for your plant, I suggest you get started. Otherwise, we'll have to draw our own conclusions from your report. And with that increase in cost of products Neil has told me about, it sounds to me as if you have a little explaining to do. I, for one, would particularly like to know why you are not observing proper procedures for determining economical batch quantities."

I pace in front of them a moment before answering. The fuse to my anger has started a slow burn. I try to put it out and think about what this means. I don't like the situation one bit. Peach damn well *ought* to be here. And I was expecting to be making my presentation to Frost, not his assistant. But from the sound of it, Hilton may have set himself up with Peach to be my judge, jury, and possibly, executioner. I decide the safest bet is to talk.

"Fine," I say finally. "But before I go into my presentation of what has been happening at my plant, let me ask you a question. Is it the goal of the UniWare Division to reduce costs?"

"Of course it is," says Hilton impatiently.

"No, actually, that is not the goal," I tell them. "The goal of UniWare is to make money. Agreed?"

Cravitz sits up in his chair and says, "That's true."

Hilton gives me a tentative nod.

I say, "I'm going to demonstrate to you that regardless of what our costs look like according to standard measurements, my plant has never been in a better position to make money."

And so it begins.

An hour and a half later, I'm midway through an explanation of the effects of the bottlenecks upon inventory and throughput when Hilton stops me.

"Okay, you've taken a lot of time to tell us all this, and I personally can't see the significance," says Hilton. "Maybe at your plant you did have a couple of bottlenecks and you discovered what they were. Well, I mean *bravo* and all that, but when I was a plant manager we dealt with bottlenecks wandering everywhere."

"Hilton, we're dealing with fundamental assumptions that are wrong," I tell him.

"I can't see that you're dealing with anything fundamental," says Hilton. "It's at best simple common sense, and I'm being charitable at that."

"No, it's more than just common sense. Because we're doing things every day that are in direct contradiction to the established rules most people use in manufacturing," I tell him.

"Such as?" asks Cravitz.

"According to the cost-accounting rules that everybody has used in the past, we're supposed to balance capacity with demand first, then try to maintain the flow," I say. "But instead we shouldn't be trying to balance capacity at all; we need excess capacity. The rule we should be following is to balance the *flow* with demand, not the capacity.

"*Two*, the incentives we usually offer are based on the assumption that the level of utilization of any worker is determined by his own potential," I tell them. "That's totally false because of dependency. For any resource that is not a bottleneck, the level of activity from which the system is able to profit is not determined by its individual potential but by some other constraint within the system."

Hilton says impatiently, "What's the difference? When somebody is working, we're getting use out of him."

"No, and that's a *third* assumption that's wrong," I say. "We've assumed that utilization and activation are the same.

257

Activating a resource and utilizing a resource are not synony-mous.''

And the argument goes on.

*I* say an hour lost at a bottleneck is an hour out of the entire system. *Hilton* says an hour lost at a bottleneck is just an hour lost of that resource.

I say an hour saved at a non-bottleneck is worthless. *Hilton* says an hour saved at a non-bottleneck is an hour saved at that resource.

"All this talk about bottlenecks," says Hilton. "Bottlenecks temporarily limit throughput. Maybe your plant is proof of that. But they have little impact upon inventory."

"It's completely the opposite, Hilton," I say. "Bottlenecks govern both throughput and inventory. And I'll tell you what my plant really has shown: it's proved our performance measure-ments are wrong."

Cravitz drops the pen he's holding and it rolls noisily on the table.

"Then how are we to evaluate the performance of our op-erations?" asks Cravitz.

"By the bottom line," I tell him. "And based upon that evaluation, my plant has now become the best in the UniWare Division, and possibly the best in its industry. We're making money when none of the others are."

"*Temporarily* you may be making money. But if you're really running your plant this way, I can't possibly see how your plant can be profitable for very long," says Hilton.

I start to speak, but Hilton raises his voice and talks over me.

"The fact of the matter is that your cost-of-products mea-surement increased," says Hilton. "And when costs go up, prof-its have to go down. It's that simple. And that's the basis of what I'll be putting into my report to Bill Peach."

Afterwards, I find myself alone in the room. Messrs. Smyth and Cravitz have gone. I'm staring into my open briefcase—then with a fist, I slam it shut.

I'm muttering to myself something about their pigheadedness as I exit the conference room and go to the elevators. I press the "down" button. But when the elevator arrives, I'm not there. I'm walking back up the corridor again, and I'm heading for the corner office.

Bill's secretary, Meg, watches me approach. I stride up to her desk, where she's sorting paper clips.

"I need to see Bill," I tell her.

"He's going to be in meetings all day," she says.

"This is urgent," I tell her.

She gazes at me coolly. "He left instructions that he is not to be disturbed."

"Meg, I need to talk to him as soon as possible."

No sooner have I said that than Bill Peach comes walking around the corner. He's moving fast, but before he can disappear into his office, I rush up to him.

"Bill —"

"Hello, Al!" he says cheerily, but not stopping. "How's it going?"

"Not very well, Bill," I say. "I need a few minutes of your time."

He's already into his office, but I've followed him through the door before he has a chance to shut it. He turns to me.

"Can it wait until Monday?" he asks.

I say, "Hilton Smyth is going to submit a negative report about my plant, and I feel that you, as my manager, should at least hear me out before you come to any conclusions."

Peach pauses and turns to me. He points to a chair and says, "Have a seat."

We sit down on opposite sides of his desk. I start to talk, but Bill holds up his hand and leans forward. He puts his elbows on the desk top and his finger tips together in front of his face.

"First of all," he says, "I'm sorry about not being at your review, but I had to go into a meeting with Granby this morning. Second, there some things I want to tell you."

I wait.

He says, "I expect you to keep your mouth shut about this until the announcement is made, but we're well enough along that I can tell you about some changes that are coming. First of all, I won't be your boss after the end of this week."

"You're leaving?"

"I'll be taking a new position at corporate level," he says.

"Oh. Congratulations," I tell him. "May I ask who will be your replacement?"

He says, "Well, I haven't got the approval yet, but it looks like Hilton Smyth."

I feel as though the floor has dropped out from under me.

"Then I guess I've done a lot of work for nothing," I say, "because all Hilton can see is that my costs have gone up, which isn't even true."

Peach holds up his hands and says, "Now wait a minute, Al. It isn't what you think."

"But Hilton —"

"Hilton does not know everything that's going on," says Peach.

"That's for damn sure," I mutter.

"And neither do you," says Peach.

"What do you mean?"

He says, "Al, UniCo is forming a new division consisting of your plant and two others. The final arrangements will be completed within the next 30 days."

Now I'm really stunned.

"Hilton will head the current division until then. After the changeover, a new division head will be named and will report directly to me, as will Hilton for his division."

Voices filter in from just outside the office. Bill looks towards the door.

"Can you tell me who will head up the new division?" I ask quickly, sensing that the conversation will have to end.

"Well, I think someone else should do that" says Bill as he pushes back his chair and stands. I see him wave to someone outside.

I turn in my seat. Standing in the door is J. Bart Granby III, chairman of UniCo.

Looking at me over his half-frame glasses, Granby says "You know, Rogo, you surprised the hell out of me. We had you pretty well written off at the beginning of the year. But after a late start you really turned things around down there."

He's clapping me on the back as he's saying this.

"That's true," adds Peach. "With the exception of the increase in cost of products. . . ."

"Hell, Peach," growls Granby, "the man did more for the bottom line than anybody else you've got out there. That's what matters. In fact, if we do have to sell or close down any division, I'll bet it won't be yours."

There is a big grin on my face as I begin to get the picture.

Granby, also smiling now, says, "Well, since the cat's out of the bag, would you like to run the new division?"

I say, "Yes, I would."

"You can discuss new salaries with Peach later, but for now we were just on our way to have some lunch. If you don't have plans, Rogo, maybe you'd like to join us."

During the next month, although the memos from Hilton Smyth keep getting more and more threatening, I continue the plant on its new path with more and more orders coming in from Sales.

At last I am able to reach Jonah in New York and fill him in on the events of the last month. Although pleased for me, he does not seem surprised.

"And all this time I was just worried about saving my one plant," I tell him. "Now I have three."

"You did what you were supposed to do, Alex. You made your plant make money. Of course, the system is more than one plant," he says. "The outcome might have been different if the same ideas applied at your plant could have been applied to all the others. But three plants are better than one. And in time. . . ."

I say, "I guess I'm very lucky that everything turned out as it did."

"Alex, when you do it right, there is no such thing as luck."

"Well. . . ."

"Was it luck that you called me in London? Was it luck that you found your bottlenecks or cut your batch sizes? Luck had practically nothing to do with it."

I say, "Yeah, but if I hadn't been lucky enough to meet you that day in Chicago I never would have learned it all."

"Alex, given the momentum of events, I can say we probably would have found each other eventually. And let me tell you, in no way have you *learned it all*. Take, for instance, the rules I've been giving you. They express common truth about manufacturing. A company that observes the rules can make money. A company that does not, will not. So far there are nine rules; you have only learned about six of them. You have barely even begun to learn. So have I, and in the process," he says, "you are going to turn UniWare from a loser into a winner in a relatively short time and make lots of money for lots of people."

"Well, that's what it's all about," I say.

"What's that?"

I say, "That's what it's all about: making money. That's the goal."

"If you recall our original coversation in Chicago," he says, "you might just realize that I was concerned about something else besides making money. To me, it's something much more important."

"But I thought that making money is the goal. It is, isn't it?"

"Making money is the goal for a *manufacturing organization*," he says. "But it isn't mine, and I don't think it's yours."

"Then what is our goal?" I ask.

"What do you think should be the goal?" he asks.

And I say, "Well . . . ah, I don't know."

"This is good-bye for now, Alex," Jonah says. "We'll be in touch. Meanwhile, I have a suggestion for you."

"What's that?"

"Think about what the goal should be."

# THE GOAL – EPILOGUE

*The following Epilogue, by Dr. Eliyahu M. Goldratt and Dr. Alexander Klarman, has been added to this edition of "The Goal" in response to requests from readers who asked what they can do to institute within their own environments the improvements Alex Rogo effected within his.*

## OPT: A PROCESS OF ONGOING IMPROVEMENT

THE MARKETPLACE is today more crowded, faster-changing and fiercely competitive than at any time in history.

Industrial manufacturing is witnessing an intensification of the race for market-dominance: the life-cycles of products are becoming shorter; zero-defects are becoming the goal of quality within industry; new machine technology is being introduced each year and systems to control production replace each other at an unprecedented rate.

What was once relatively gradual change has in recent years turned into a race the intensity of which is increasing exponentially. Those unable to learn how to improve are falling behind, for success in such an environment requires more than a one-time improvement, however big that may be.

Each improvement does of course buy some precious time, but the race in the market continues relentlessly; the slope of the curve grows ever steeper and the time bought by any one improvement becomes ever shorter.

Clearly, something far greater than a few sporadic improvements is now needed. Indeed, the only way to secure and improve one's competitive position today is by instituting a process of ongoing improvement in one's organisation.

In the absence of such a process, the many improvements needed are certain to be sporadic and fragmented and a great deal of energy, time and resources are bound to be wasted.

What is required is a process which will, at any moment, identify clearly the area in which an improvement will yield the maximum global impact.

This process must also enable an organisation to achieve the maximum gain from such improvements, while simultaneously helping it to identify the area in which the next improvement is needed and to quantify the impact.

Such a process of ongoing improvement already exists. Available through Creative Output, it is called OPT – optimised production technology.


NOBODY would disagree that a process capable of generating an evolving, ongoing improvement would be beneficial, but anyone who has tried to introduce any new process to an organisation knows all too well the multitude of obstacles encountered.

Experience shows that, when these obstacles are closely examined, most will be found rooted in resistance to the process itself, on the part of the people affected.

Although such resistance may take different forms in various environments, the fact remains that, in order to achieve the goal of introducing the process of ongoing improvement, one has to accept and deal with the root cause of such a reaction.

There is in fact nothing more difficult for any organisation than change – any change. Each improvement is by definition such a change, although in the right direction, and each will predictably be met with resistance, despite its beneficial potential.

As for a *process* of improvement, it is by its very nature a process of continual change. The degree of resistance facing it may therefore be quite significant, although of course not all of it conscious, and it may come from any tier of the corporate structure, for a change is usually as unwelcome in the boardroom as on the production floor.

If, however, one accepts the existence of a race to survive and flourish in the market, and that one must have a competitive edge within that market, then there is no alternative to instituting such a process of continuing improvement.

Yet our deeply rooted, almost instinctive tendency to reject change makes the introduction of such a process extremely difficult, if not impossible.

Change is opposed, from wherever it may come, not because the change itself was ill-conceived, but simply because it is a change.

While one can try to crush opposition to change, this proves a trying and time-consuming effort, even when successful. To yield to resistance means, however, to give up the only effective, long-lasting remedy to the problem; hence the initial task is to change people's attitude towards change, to neutralise opposition.

How can that be achieved?

## Understanding Attitudes Towards Change

WE NEED first of all to try to understand the very different attitudes people have towards improvements, as contrasted with their response to change.

Although both are by definition changes, "improvement", unlike change, carries a positive connotation. Do we, therefore, simply need to get others to understand the beneficial nature of the change which we propose?

Let us refer back to personal experience. How many times have we tried to explain an innovation to others, whether they are our superiors, subordinates or peers, and felt that somehow the message simply did not get through? We may even have provided flawlessly logical arguments, crystal-clear explanations and eye-opening examples, but still our listeners have remained unconvinced, stubbornly sceptical about the value of what we proposed.

We may often have been left with the feeling that, although they heard us, they didn't really listen. Their energy seemed directed not at evaluating our proposal, but at finding out why it would not work. If we succeeded at all in conveying our message and, perhaps, in having it embraced by all, then we managed to do so only thanks to great effort and perseverance.

Clearly, such a method of introducing an improvement is utterly inappropriate, when applied to the need for acceptance of a process of ongoing improvement.

If we analyse our experience of introducing improvements, we are led inexorably to the conclusion that the resistance we encounter derives more from emotion than logic – that our proposal was perceived less as an improvement than as only a change and, as discussed before, change invariably raises emotional resistance at every level.

In fact, emotions are rarely involved only at the receiving end; our own emotions, not just our logic, probably helped us to persist and, finally perhaps, even succeed in implementing the improvement.

If we are the champions of an idea, we tend to identify strongly with it, often so much so that others regard it as our "baby". The process of introducing improvements can therefore partly become an emotional struggle, with the emotions involved in resisting change being finally overcome only by the stronger emotions derived from the conviction of the champion of change.

Our subject, however, is less the emotional nature of human beings than how to come to terms with, and even possibly use, this tendency so deeply ingrained in us all.

If it were possible for all the employees of an organisation to convince themselves of the need to adopt a process of ongoing improvement, then each individual would personally acquire a feeling of "ownership" of that idea. Then each person's emotional energy would be directed towards embracing this process, rather than rejecting it.

But how can one hope to achieve such a sense of universal, yet individual ownership – and have it occur simultaneously throughout an organisation?

## Attaining Universal Individual Ownership

INDIVIDUAL, yet universal, ownership – it sounds impossible, a contradiction in terms, but that is precisely what we need to achieve.

If we wish to create a climate in which a process of ongoing change will be welcome throughout an organisation, then we need to elicit the commitment of the individual together with a universal acceptance of the process.

If one were to build a tool to perform this miracle, what should characterise it?

It should be inexpensive enough to permit mass distribution, be readily available, require no set-ups or supporting resources, be convenient to use and be capable of being adapted by an individual to his pace or preferences.

Knowledge can, of course, be transmitted in a group environment but, except in cases where an extraordinary teacher is involved, what is lacking is emotional attachment and a sense of personal discovery.

Since the individual element is what we are seeking, the tool is narrowed down to something like a book.

However, not every kind of book can become a tool for acquiring personal ownership of an idea. Textbooks, though they convey information, usually fail to excite the imagination. Their readers may absorb the words, but do not identify with them. For that to happen, a reader needs to find that the text mirrors his own experience.

Because the ancients appreciated this, analogy has throughout the ages been used as a tool for teaching and communicating ideas.

We conceived the idea of writing *The Goal* by taking this didactic tool – analogy – and embodying it within the form of a novel, a popular medium which makes the acquisition of information enjoyable, so as to encourage readers to identify with the situation and characters employed.

We knew that *The Goal* had to portray the industrial environment vividly and realistically. It needed faithfully to reflect the pressures, problems and daily decisions confronting an individual in that environment. Moreover, it ought ideally to draw the reader into identifying with the conflicts faced by the protagonist, Alex Rogo, allowing the reader to share Rogo's anxiety to find solutions and save his plant.

We knew that *The Goal* would not be effective unless it drew the reader into the story and led him to an understanding of the causal relationships between the problems and the solutions in the analogy.

We hoped the reader would be struck by parallels to his own environment and see a spectrum of problems, many of them personally experienced. We wished him to experience vicariously the struggle to develop a commonsense approach to a class of problems leading to the first glimmer of light – a general solution.

As more specific implementable solutions are derived from the general solution, the reader would, we hoped, begin to perceive the pattern of how the specific solutions are generated. Sooner or later, we believed, that reader would make the intuitive leap from the thought process described in the analogy to applying this process to the problems encountered in his own environment.

He would then have had what psychologists call an "Aha! experience" – and the solutions he would then invent would be his own.

We came to appreciate that the elements the novel would need for it to be the tool we sought, rather than an academic exercise, were simple yet profound: a problem that is realistic and relevant and an easily understood, common-sense solution from which specific implementable solutions are derived.

Moreover, we needed also to address the aspect of an ongoing process by demonstrating the complex and changing character of the environment.

We believed that, no matter how many discrete solutions are implemented, they will not add up to a process of ongoing improvement.

What we have described so far has been a means of motivating a reader to take ownership of a specific improvement, but our goal was in fact far more ambitious.

We wanted the reader to develop a sense of ownership, not of a specific "invention", but of something much more nebulous. We wished him to take ownership of the idea of instituting a process of ongoing improvement in his own organisation.

What is meant by such a process of ongoing improvement? We need to understand that a very small number of constraints govern the overall level of performance in any organisation. If such constraints can be relieved, that will significantly raise the performance of the entire organisation.

Our experience has shown that, while other improvements which do not involve relieving such primary constraints may well have a positive impact, their effect will be of a lower order of magnitude.

The first step, then, is to identify precisely those primary constraints and to focus all our efforts on alleviating them. Once this has been achieved, the entire organisation will be raised to a new level of performance which, however, will itself be limited by the existence of still further constraints within the organisation.

It is the very essence of a process of ongoing improvement that we cannot allow ourselves to be satisfied with any one higher performance level, but that each must motivate us to focus, as rapidly as possible, on those emerging constraints which limit our attainment of even higher performance for the entire organisation.

This is a never-ending process. Constraints may shift from one sector of an organisation to another and may even shift to the market outside the organisation itself.

Nevertheless, regardless of where they originated, it is always possible to take actions within the organisation to alleviate the major constraints.

This, we knew, is the process the book needed to portray to the reader, to the extent that the reader could develop the feeling of personal ownership of the idea that such a process could be and, moreover, must be, possible within his own organisation.

We also believed that the book must be able to portray this process vividly and that it must describe several cycles in the process, satisfying the parameters we already established. But even that was not enough. Each of the cycles had to describe a situation where the constraints were of so common a nature that the reader would, in all probability, have encountered a similar constraint in his own experience.

If the book succeeded in choosing cycles from more than one of which the reader could draw specific solutions to his own environment, then the chances would be quite good that the reader would identify with the entire process of ongoing improvement.

The book's requirements, we knew, were extremely demanding. But we also knew that, if we did not succeed in meeting all of them, then we would probably fail to overcome resistance as we tried to encourage a process of ongoing improvement.

NOW that you have read *The Goal*, how do you feel about that process?

If you are like readers who have contacted us, you may well feel a strong urge to do at your plant what Alex Rogo did at his.

You may well have become convinced that it was only by instituting a process of ongoing improvement that Rogo's plant was able to survive and flourish.

You may right now be trying to address some of the most persistent problems of your organisation, using the same direction of solution as that described in the book.

We say this because it is a process undergone by most of the readers of *The Goal*. Of course, the closer a reader is to the particular environment depicted in the book, the stronger his sense of identification with it; those coming from production and assembly plants tend to identify with Rogo's situation more than those from process plants.

Although the principles of the solution may suit many fields, in the services as well as within industry, it is easier for people from manufacturing to find similarities to their environment and to identify with the people depicted in *The Goal*.

Those readers who have communicated with us tell us that the scenario of the book is true to life, that anxiety felt by Al Rogo, whether caused by his boss, his people or even his family, is one with which they are all too familiar.

They have found *The Goal* appealing not only because it realistically describes the events accompanying the introduction of the OPT process of ongoing improvement to a plant, but also because of the ways these pinpoint the main issues and concerns of contemporary manufacturing.

They have come to see how such a process works, by being exposed to the experience a particular plant had in introducing a particular process of ongoing improvement.

They have seen how the performance of an entire plant is influenced by the identification and eventual opening up of a bottleneck. Moreover, they have seen how further improvement is blocked by yet another problem – inventory management.

Their reading has shown them that the solution of this problem and, as a matter of fact, of any problem, creates a new reality in the plant which gives rise to still more problems. And that new, external, obstacles emerged as these internal problems were resolved.

Rogo discovered that, once his plant's manufacturing problems were settled and performances were markedly improved, marketing became his biggest problem.

Nevertheless, Rogo was able to deal with this external problem through internal actions.

What readers come to appreciate is that the reality of the plant is always shifting – that every improvement, as it produces its benefits, also creates a new reality which must be addressed, resolved and changed again. It is this process which is never-ending.


AS STATED, hundreds of letters we have received from readers of *The Goal* show that most of them feel a compelling urge to start changing things at their plants.

But a word of caution is required at this point. Whether an improvement deals with the tooling of a single machine or with the marketing policy of an entire plant, it remains an isolated, local action resulting from the initiative of only certain individuals. However beneficial, these improvements are not enough.

What is needed goes beyond the isolated, uncoordinated efforts of individuals trying to do their best. It calls for the coordinated efforts of an organised group. Only that can give the institution of a process of ongoing improvement a fighting chance.

We are therefore faced with the problem of how to bring an entire group to view the process of ongoing improvement in the same light and to embrace it together.

Even after people have reached general agreement, they tend to spend incredible amounts of time and effort arguing about differences in nuance, rather than focusing on underlying similarities.

How, then, does one bring a group of people to agree on the fundamental issues of a complex problem without them getting caught up in comparatively insignificant detail?

# THE GOAL – EPILOGUE
## Reaching a group consensus

EARLIER, we dealt with the problem of finding the means whereby an individual could acquire ownership of the idea that a process of ongoing improvement needs to be implemented in his organisation.

To achieve it, we used a book containing very detailed and explicit examples. Now we are confronted with the opposite problem: not how to motivate an individual, but how to turn the ownership of many individuals into a group consensus.

The means to achieve this need to be totally different. Instead of being directed at an individual, they must be aimed at a group. This already precludes a book.

Moreover, addressing a group with arguments based on a specific, detailed example is actually the best way of ensuring that consensus will *not* be attained. Everyone in the group will tend to draw differing parallels to his real-life situation and the only likely result is a fruitless and heated debate.

We need instead to base a process of ongoing improvement upon a very precise and logically flawless derivation of general rules and procedures.

One tends, however, to regard such general rules as vague, as fitting more than one interpretation. Trying, therefore, to encourage ownership through a group process of formulating such general rules would most probably also result in something vague to the point of meaninglessness.

Indeed, can general yet powerful rules applying to most industrial organisations be formulated?

*The Goal* contains some such rules but, though they are useful in focusing on and relieving major constraints, they do not address the process of ongoing improvement itself.

The example in the book merely suggested such a process. If, however, we don't succeed in formulating the general rules and procedures of such a process, the probability of achieving consensus is extremely low.

Without such consensus the seeds of resistance will reappear. As the organisation strives to develop and institute its own process of ongoing improvement, these seeds will grow into pockets of fierce resistance.

Merely presenting the appropriate rules and procedures to a group will not ensure their acceptance. Such a presentation needs to include the entire step-by-step derivation of those rules.

Consensus will be reached only if this derivation starts from a generally agreed-upon picture of the situation in industry today and proceeds using very precise, well-defined arguments, making sure that no gaps or flaws – even perceived flaws – leave an opening for misunderstanding. The logic must be so strong that it is perceived as common sense.

A very important ingredient in constructing the presentation is to include natural pauses throughout, allowing verbal consensus to be reached.

A presentation which meets these criteria is the "Competitive Edge" presentation developed by Creative Output.

WE HAVE learned that, when this "Competitive Edge" (CE) presentation is given by an experienced lecturer, it invariably achieves the desired result.

Since it is not feasible, nor even desirable, for an entire organisation to hear one presentation – as the important element of interaction with the lecturer would then be lacking – we have found it best for an experienced lecturer to be used only for the top group of a unit (plant management, division management, etc.) and for internal presenters to be used for other groups.

An "internal presenter" is usually a manager who has heard the CE presentation. In preparing his own presentation, he is assisted by the use of *The Race*, a manual developed by Creative Output which contains the necessary text and graphics.

But reaching consensus will not by itself yield a positive result. Another step needs to be undertaken.

It is a far from trivial task to make the transition from general rules and procedures into a workable process of improvement. This difficulty will immediately raise the question of applicability.

As is evident from reading *The Goal*, OPT has three different avenues of applicability, the first being applicability in the managerial sphere.

# THE GOAL – EPILOGUE

Management today tends to perceive problems and effects as independent events. One of the most appealing aspects of OPT stems from coming to a realisation that many seemingly unrelated events in a plant arise from a very few common sources.

The perception of these cause-and-effect relationships is to a large extent new and certainly provides a much more powerful way to run a business.

The second area of applicability is the logistical one. The drum/buffer/rope method used in *The Goal* and precisely analysed and defined in the CE presentation is a very attractive logistical system.

Its appeal comes from the fact that it eliminates both the confusion and the expediting mode in which most plants find themselves.

Buffer-management, which is formulated in the CE presentation, brings the local improvement activities under the same umbrella. In other words, the logistical applicability reduces confusion and brings order to daily activities.

The third area of applicability is the behavioural one. As can be deduced from *The Goal* and as is further highlighted in the CE presentation, a process of ongoing improvement has significant behavioural ramifications on the shopfloor, as well as within top management.

Applicability in these three areas has a significant impact on the bottom line.

In evaluating this impact, we should not ignore the strong connections and interrelationships among the three. Difficult as it might be, we must evaluate the degree of applicability in order that the consensus does not turn rapidly into frustration.

Before turning to the question of how to do so, we must remember that many organisations are not composed of a single plant.

Certainly the first two steps, accomplished by a reading of *The Goal* and attendance at a "Competitive Edge" presentation, should be undertaken by all levels within such organisations – division and corporate as well as plants.

Moreover, it is important to bear in mind that an evaluation of applicability should not be done for just a single plant, but for the entire division.

Let us now examine how it can first be done at the plant level.

## The Plant Level

A NUMBER of approaches could be appropriate in trying to assess the applicability of the OPT process at a particular plant.

One is to implement the OPT process in a part of the plant and extrapolate the applicability of OPT to the entire plant.

But this approach, by its very nature, provides only a very partial picture.

Instead of dealing with the tangled web of managerial, logistical and behavioural aspects, it can at best address the logistical aspect.

Dealing with only part of the plant provides a narrow focus which sidetracks one from the required global outlook. It may generate some benefit due to improved logistics, but not the desired process of ongoing improvement.

Another way to evaluate the applicability of OPT for a plant is through references. Here one looks for a plant similar to one's own which has already introduced the OPT process and then judges the results accordingly.

But what constitutes a "similar" plant? Is it the similarity of the end-product, of the technologies applied, or of size?

Is a plant only an assemblage of machines, a pile of materials and a stack of products? Does its equipment or its people characterises a plant more?

Are the problems of a plant inherent in its manufacturing systems or is it the interaction of people with their specific environment that creates a particular plant?

Just as people are themselves unique creations, so too do they create plants with individuality. It is not that one gains nothing from examining other plants which employ the OPT process; there will come a stage when one is well advised to do just that, but it will not initially help one to evaluate the applicability of OPT at one's own plant.

Given sufficient knowledge of OPT, the reader should be

able to analyse its applicability to his plant by himself. It *can* be done and the knowledge required will be his at some stage of the process. (*See below, under Corporate Level*).

However, exposure to *The Goal* and the "CE" alone are still insufficient to address this need.

What is still required is an analysis of one's *entire* plant – not just a segment of it – and the ability to distinguish results from their causes, whether they are the constraints of the plant's reality or constraints imposed by managerial policy.

A process of ongoing improvement should address those problems whose resolution will result in maximal gain in performance.

To achieve that, one must have the ability to pinpoint the root cause of one's most severe problems and to quantify the outcome on the bottom line measurements.

If we wish to assess the impact of the OPT process on the various aspects of a plant's reality and evaluate its applicability, we must first be able to construct for ourselves the effect-cause-effect linkages between the real constraints and the observed results.

How can this be achieved? How can one make the problems to which one was for so long apparently blind stand out sharply and clearly? Is this at all possible? Does one need a miracle to do it?

Not really; it is perfectly possible, provided one is equipped with some general principles and procedures to guide one in this task.

Exactly as in *The Goal* Jonah was able to pinpoint problems at Rogo's plant without seeing it, by means of a set of guiding principles, others may use them as well.

Although at times some data is required, making a visit through the plant necessary, a person experienced at this kind of analysis knows exactly which tree to look for within the forest of facts, policies and results.

A person trained in constructing these cause-effect linkages can use this methodology to analyse a plant quickly and thoroughly.

Indeed, this entire task is completed during a two-day Strategic Benefits Analysis (SBA) visit.

To be sure, the trained person performing that task requires free access to a plant's top people, as well as others if needed. Also, any information he requires needs to be be made readily available.

Assuming these preconditions are met, such an SBA visit takes the following form.

Plant management first of all presents its perception of the key business issues; then the analyst visits the production floor to check some of the current practices regarding the use being made of the plant's resources – people, machines, materials, tools, space and money. Also, the analyst obtains from the plant's staff whatever information he requires about such practices and their underlying managerial policies.

The object of this analysis is to reveal the causes behind the plant's problems, the cause-effect structures, and their bottom-line impact.

At the conclusion of such an SBA visit, the analyst or analysts present their findings and suggestions for change – first for verification to top management and then to the plant's entire management team.

These findings are presented in a form which reveal both the explicit and implicit results of the interaction of the plant's physical reality with management policy – together with their bottom-line impact.

They focus on the possible immediate and future contribution the OPT process can make in improving that plant's performance.

The picture these findings reveal may assist plant management in deciding whether the OPT process of ongoing improvement seems an applicable and beneficial solution to this particular plant's problems.

Is this, then, all that is needed to initiate the OPT process of ongoing improvement? Perhaps not.

We must remember that our most persistent problems are not usually rooted in the physical constraints of reality, but in managerial policies.

In most cases, such policies have been unquestioningly accepted for such a long time that they are viewed almost as facts of life, rather than as policies human beings have set and which can in be fact changed by them, if change is needed. While such a change may not be easy, it *can* be undertaken.

Let us now investigate the problems the corporate level faces, for they have a bearing on this issue.

## The Corporate Level

IF a plant (or plants) belongs to a bigger organisational structure, what the upper level primarily needs is the ability to assess independently the applicability of the proposed process of ongoing improvement at many sites.

The bigger this structure, the more justified is the effort to acquire the expertise needed to make a sound evaluation.

The prospect of having available someone with an unbiased analytical capability and a thorough knowledge of OPT typically creates a desire to have one's own in-house OPT analysts.

Management may consider hiring such a person from outside, but it should take into account that a knowledge of OPT is not all that is required.

One necessary requirement is an intimate knowledge of the company's real – as opposed to merely formal – power structure. Another is the ability to see its plants from the perspective of the upper corporate level. What therefore often proves quite fruitful is to select and educate existing corporate staff. An outsider, however, is usually much more free to express his findings and also has the advantage of being able to communicate with all levels and functions within an organisation without encountering barriers caused by his being identified with a particular branch of that organisation.

In fact, experience shows that what a corporation benefits most from is a blend of both internal and external.

The external experts may come from many sources, such as independent "Certified Implementors" trained by Creative Output.

As for internal expertise, corporate staff gains this by attending Creative Output's Business Analysis Courses (BAC).

These teach them methods of analysing manufacturing plants which have been developed by Creative Output, expose the characteristic problems of each of the three general types of plants and present the OPT approach of their analysis.

The knowledge acquired by those attending the BAC course enables them to analyse the symptoms of a plant systematically, thoroughly and quickly.

The underlying causes of problems are derived from these symptoms. A sound knowledge of OPT, acquired during the course, helps participants judge whether or not the OPT process is applicable at a particular plant and what its estimated beneficial potential is likely to be.

The people chosen to attend this course will serve as the "eyes and ears" of top level management; hence we term them "scouts" to describe their function.

Belonging to the upper levels of the organisational structure, having easy access to the top decisionmaker(s), these "scouts" will be instrumental in presenting an un-biased internal recommendation regarding the applicability and the beneficial potential of the introduction of the OPT process to the company's plants.

In both cases, whether the plant is a stand-alone unit and the SBA was performed by an OPT analyst from outside, or the plant belongs to a bigger structure and the SBA was performed by "scouts", the benefits emerge clearly.

The key business issues are sharply outlined, the potential for improvement is estimated and the criteria are established for evaluating the results of the OPT process of ongoing improvement.

Does this now mean that the plant is ready to embrace OPT? To assume so is to be naive; the fact that something is applicable and beneficial does not mean that it will automatically be introduced.

As already stated, it is necessary first to deal with the question of whether future benefits sufficiently offset the extent of adjustment required to accommodate the OPT process.

Before management decides whether to introduce OPT, it needs a very clear idea of the nature, the extent and the impact of the many changes needed to have it working at a plant.

One usually finds policies at the root of the limitations of a plant's performance. The need to change time-honoured policies is, perhaps, the most difficult to accept, as one is here dealing with a change influencing all aspects of the plant's activity.

Moreover, even acceptance by all is not enough – it must be achieved as an organised group, to enable the group to develop a coherent view of its impact.

But how does a group discuss changes in the policies responsible for most of its problems without involving clashes of individual egos and without entering into arguments about who is responsible?

Because it is clear that implementing a process of ongoing improvement requires changing some of a company's most fundamental policies, the question arises: can we live with such a change?

Since policies are often regarded as unquestionable facts of life, challenges to them easily trigger resistance much more profound than just that resistance encountered in change-rejection.

Recognising that fact seems to make the scope of the required changes more daunting than ever. In the face of it, how can we ensure cooperation?

We certainly need to get new agreement from the participants, but can we achieve that by oral presentation?

While members of the group may recognise the undesirability of certain policies, the significance of the changes required may convince them that others will oppose such changes and that agreement is therefore not possible.

To meet this dilemma, Creative Output developed a guided, open discussion – a three-day Synchronised Manufacturing Seminar (SMS) – which seeks to establish that there is overall conviction in favour of the proposed change.

The effect-cause-effect structure presented at the very end of each two-day SBA serves to demonstrate the inner connection between the "innocent" policy and the major problems indicated by the plant's people.

This structure is then reviewed again, and is thrown open to debate and discussion.

Once a consensus is reached that policies must be changed and suggested alternative policies are agreed, a new effect-cause-effect structure is derived.

This time it demonstrates the new set of policies, measures and rules, as well as their connection to future anticipated and improved results. Again, those effect-cause-effect connections are opened up to discussion.

The demerits of the old policies, the benefits gained from adopting new ones and the meaning of switching, are now laid on the table.

Participants find that they are making the decision together, using both new knowledge and the understanding of those – formerly unseen – interconnections between policies and business results.

The results of the SMS are crucial to the success of the OPT process of ongoing improvement.

These Synchronised Manufacturing Seminars have proved to be turning points in the lives of many organisations, making clear to them that a decision regarding OPT must take into account not only the consequences of going ahead towards implementing the process, but also the consequences of rejecting it.

Once understanding of the process has led to agreement being reached, what remains to be considered is the actual implementation phase. The OPT process is complex enough for management to pay particular attention to this process.

## How do we do it: the OPT implementation procedure

IMPLEMENTATION should take into account the three avenues: the managerial, the logistical and the behavioural. The success of an implementation depends on whether they have been properly synchronised.

Thus the next task is to draw up a detailed implementation plan.

Two factors govern the successful implementation of the OPT process: the ability to address the various aspects of a plant's reality and careful timing of the implementation procedures, so as to ensure their synchronised introduction at all plant levels.

This is not an easy task.

It requires, first of all, that top management has the

appropriate tools available to enable it to manage the plant in a quickly shifting environment. Next, tools are needed which make the execution of this policy possible.

The dynamic environment makes the logistics of the manufacturing process something of a nightmare. And the behavioural change needed to accommodate a process of ongoing improvement is likely to be unparalleled by anything the plant's people have ever undergone.

To address those needs, to introduce those tools in a coherent and coordinated way is a most demanding task. However, the single crucial factor for a successful implementation of OPT seems to be the ability of the people involved to know what to expect at each stage of the process.

As the reader will probably have surmised, there is no blueprint for the implementation procedure. Because each environment is unique, each requires a procedure specifically devised for it.

Finding this is the goal of Creative Output's four-day Productivity Management Workshop (PMW).

In this, plant management, OPT analysts and (where appropriate) top management "scouts" all bring their expertise together to devise a viable scheme of implementation.

Among the aids made available by the OPT analysts is the OPT software – a powerful tool which takes into account the finite nature of production resources.

It is a tool of simulation, providing a very fast "what-if" analysis, as well as being an actual planning device which generates viable, optimised work schedules.

The experience of the trained implementors, combined with the plant management's expertise of their own business, results in a clear perception of what should be done, when, where and by whom.

It should be realised that even the very first stage of the implementation procedure has to include quite a significant portion of the plant, and should be undertaken on a comprehensive scale.

Only if done in this manner, can the results of any particular stage be evaluated and proper, relevant conclusions be drawn.

The "scouts", if present, will estimate the impact made on the corporate scale by the changes the OPT implementation process calls for.

If the plant does not need to seek the approval of any external factor, then its management is now well-equipped with the required pertinent information to decide whether to embrace the OPT process of ongoing improvement.

A plant which is part of a bigger structure will still need the prior approval of the topmost level of management, before taking on a long-term commitment to introduce OPT.

What has proved effective in enabling corporate decision makers to understand clearly what is proposed is a joint session at which the plant management, the "scouts" and the OPT analysts all present their suggestions.

The plant's managers outline what they plan to change, why it is important and what will be the impact of such proposed changes.

The "scouts" present those changes in corporate terms, stressing the impact they will have on plant performance.

Creative Output personnel focus on the changes the corporate level needs to introduce if they are to give the plant a fighting chance to implement the OPT process.

These – to name just a few – may include an agreement not to use traditional efficiency measurements or other cost-accounting procedures if they are found counter-productive, as well as a re-evaluation of an existing make/buy policy.

Whether in a stand-alone plant or a part of a corporation, the entire process of implementing OPT is undertaken by the people of the plant themselves.

Although Creative Output or another OPT-introducing company will provide the means to make this process as smooth as possible, it is the plant's own management which carries out this task.

It needs to be understood that, apart from service and support, the entire implementation process is borne by the people who will be using OPT.

Even the training provided is meant to make the plant's own people able to perform the enormous task of internal education – or perhaps re-education.

What is now needed are the tools and procedures to make this exciting if traumatic transition period as brief and efficient as possible.

## The tools of change

IF THE implementation is to be as effective as possible, then a sizeable percentage of the plant's people need to undergo an educational process, aimed at the plant's various levels and departments.

Such people need to be trained to lead, teach and execute the agreed procedure. To meet this need, Creative Output has devised a number of courses and workshops which have proved effective.

### Project Manager Course

The person leading the effort to implement OPT needs a solid knowledge of OPT theory and practice. A six-week course at Creative Output's Education Centres, the first two parallel in content to the BAC, will enable the person attending it to become the key factor in the implementation of OPT in the plant.

Here, emphasis is put on gaining an understanding of the OPT process, for it will be this person's principal task to teach OPT to all others in the plant. The course enables him both to use OPT efficiently and to teach it, making use of the educational devices developed for this purpose, such as video courses and computer games.

### OPT Analyst Course

Simultaneously with the above PMC, line manufacturing personnel selected to be OPT analysts learn the OPT software at a six-week OPT Analyst Course, also given at Creative Output's Education Centres.

This trains them in using the OPT software as a tool

facilitating the execution of the logistical solutions characteristic of the OPT process.

Knowledge of existing information resources, together with an understanding of the logistical requirements of the OPT process, make the introduction of OPT software fast and not too complicated.

### Enhancement Course

Experience proves that both the project manager or managers, as well as OPT analysts, benefit from attending one of the week-long Enhancement Courses given at CO Education Centres.

These dedicated courses, which are given four to six weeks after a plant has begun to implement OPT, are designed to upgrade the participants' understanding in particular areas of greatest importance or concern, as encountered during the OPT implementation.

The course analyses and evaluates progress made so far and, where necessary, updates the plan for completion of implementation.

### OPT Simulator Workshop

As frequently stated, the behavioural change required by the OPT process seems to be the biggest stumbling-block to its adoption.

It takes a great deal of internal conviction to get rid of work routines which have become "second nature" to many.

To achieve this level of internal conviction, which greatly facilitates the introduction of OPT, a two-day PC-based workshop has been created.

This allows each worker to play a simulation game which will confront him – often for the first time – with the global results of his limited, local actions.

This unique tool considerably eases the pain of introducing a process of ongoing change to the production floor and, instead of resistance, helps to create an atmosphere of anticipation, as the beneficial potentials of OPT are more clearly understood.

## Introducing a New Beginning

JUST AS birth is the end of one process (pregnancy) while also the start of a new life, so the successful implementation of OPT marks a new beginning within an industrial environment.

Although assisted by external OPT experts, it is the plant management itself which will – once the process of ongoing improvement has started – be introducing improvements, refinements and changes to achieve and maintain its competitive edge in the market.

Those who have embraced OPT as their process of ongoing improvement will have available to them, as part of the service provided by Creative Output, any new theoretical as well as practical developments relating to the running of a manufacturing plant.

It is not an easy feat to live in an environment characterised by constant change – certainly not at the onset of this process. But once it is adopted as a way of life, the effort will be rewarded by the one thing that really counts: a chance to survive and flourish in the global marketplace.